Anne Douglas, after a varied life spent elsewhere, has made her home in Edinburgh, a city she has known for many years. She very much enjoys life in the modern capital, and finds its ever-present history fascinating.

She has written a number of novels, including *Catherine's Land*, *As The Years Go By*, *Bridge of Hope*, *The Butterfly Girls*, *Ginger Street*, *A Highland Engagement* and *The Road to the Sands*, all published by Piatkus.

Also by Anne Douglas

Catherine's Land
As The Years Go By
Bridge of Hope
The Butterfly Girls
Ginger Street
The Road to the Sands
The Edinburgh Bride

A Highland Engagement

Anne Douglas

PIATKUS

PIATKUS

First published in Great Britain in 2004 by Piatkus Books Ltd
This paperback edition published in 2009 by Piatkus

Copyright © 2004 by Anne Douglas

The moral right of the author has been asserted.

A CIP catalogue record for this book
is available from the British Library

ISBN 978-0-7499-3501-6

Typeset in Times by Action Publishing Technology Ltd, Gloucester
Printed and bound in Great Britain by
CPI Mackays, Chatham, ME5 8TD

Papers used by Piatkus are natural, renewable and recyclable
products sourced from well-managed forests and certified
in accordance with the rules of the Forest Stewardship Council.

Mixed Sources
Product group from well-managed
forests and other controlled sources
www.fsc.org Cert no. SGS-COC-004081
© 1996 Forest Stewardship Council

FSC

Piatkus
An imprint of
Little, Brown Book Group
100 Victoria Embankment
London EC4Y 0DY

An Hachette UK Company
www.hachette.co.uk

www.piatkus.co.uk

For Minnie

Author's Note:

Although the Highland section of this novel was inspired by the setting of the beautiful spa of Strathpeffer, the story, characters and the Hotel Grand Forest are all completely fictional. Real events from World War One and the Leith dock strike of 1913 are touched on and certain real names quotes, but again the characters and the action of the story are all imaginary.

In writing the novel, I found the following works particularly helpful:

Denbigh, Kathleen, *A Hundred British Spas*, Spa Publications, 1981.

Finlayson, Clarence, *The Strath*, Saint Andrew Press, 1979.

Marshall, James Scott, *The Life and Times of Leith*, John Donald, 1986.

Mowat, Sue, *The Port of Leith*, Forth Ports PLC in association with John Donald, 1994.

Part One

Part One

Chapter One

Lesley MacKenzie was putting on her hat, securing it to the knot of bright hair at her neck with a large strong pin. Listening to the March wind moaning round the Kirkgate, she thought she'd be lucky to keep her hat on when she went out, pin or no pin, but she wouldn't be put off by that. She and her sister, Carrie, always went walking in Leith on Sunday afternoons, dragging their brother Ned with them, if he could be persuaded to leave his fiddle; it was their one chance in the week for fresh air. Besides, today, Auntie Peg had Mr MacNab coming for his tea and wanted them out of the way while she 'got on', as she put it.

'Lesley, are you no' coming?' asked Carrie, from the door of the tiny room they shared. 'Auntie Peg's wanting to sweep the floor.'

'Well, I'm no' stopping her!'

Lesley, tall and slim in a tweed coat that almost covered her ankle-length skirt, laughed a little. She was nineteen years old, two years older than Carrie, three years younger than Ned, and where they were pale, with brown hair and great brown eyes like Auntie Peg's, Lesley had their mother's looks, all colour and vitality, blue eyes and strawberry-blonde hair. But their mother had been dead for many years, their father, too. Auntie Peg was all they had.

'You ken what she's like when there's company coming,' said Carrie, squeezing in to take a look at herself in the

3

mirror on their chest of drawers. 'Canna settle.'

'When Mr MacNab's coming, you mean.'

'He is her boss.'

'Aye, and she carries the place on for him.'

Sam MacNab owned a ship's chandler's business near the Shore, the waterfront of Leith, which was Edinburgh's port, though quite independent, of the city. Margaret Darroch, variously called Peg, or Peggie, and now forty-eight, had worked for him since she was a young woman, and very efficiently, too, but it was Aggie, his wife, who'd been her friend. It was only since Aggie's death two years before that Mr MacNab had begun coming over occasionally for his Sunday tea. Now, on that blustery March afternoon in 1913, Peg was as usual driving herself hard to have everything just right for him.

'Have you girls gone to sleep in there?' came Ned's voice. 'How long's it take to put a hat on?'

'Coming!' called Lesley.

Their aunt's tenement flat was in the bustling Kirkgate, where tall buildings, little houses and every kind of shop crowded together in pleasant harmony. Peg's parents had been tenants before her, bringing up their girls there, always considering themselves lucky because they'd had two bedrooms and their own lavatory. No bathroom, of course, but who had bathrooms? Now the furniture they'd saved to buy was in Peg's flat still.

'Aye, they were lucky, and I'm lucky,' Peg would say, and the MacKenzies would agree, even if the sisters' room was little more than a cupboard and Ned had to sleep on the pull-down bed in the living room. So were the tenants of Number Fifteen lucky, for they had jobs, sheets on their beds and boots on their feet.

'If you could just see the way some folk have to live!' Peg would sigh.

But the MacKenzies had seen and they knew, how some folk had to live. Out there, beyond their home, the cold

4

wind of poverty always blew. A different wind and worse, from the wind that was rattling the window frames on that Sunday afternoon when Lesley and Carrie joined Ned.

A french polisher by trade, Ned really thought of himself as a violinist. The only thing he minded about not having a room of his own, was that he had to keep his precious fiddle in his aunt's room along with his clothes. He had to practise there as well, because the girls said otherwise they'd have gone mad.

'It's no' the tunes we mind,' Carrie told him kindly. 'They're lovely. It's thae exercises and scales, you ken, seem to set our ears ringing.'

'And it's no' so bad, you see, with Auntie Peg's door shut,' put in Lesley.

The Jamesons, who shared their landing, never complained about Ned's playing, but whenever he got to what they called the scrapy bits, the Crawfords above would bang on the floor with shoes, and then he'd want to go out and shout up the stair and Auntie Peg would have to intervene.

'Och, what a life, eh!' he'd cry. 'Being a musician here!'

But he was good-natured enough on the whole and grinned now at his sisters, while Auntie Peg stooped over her baking, counting lardy cakes.

'Now, if Mr MacNab has two and Ned has two, I have one and the girls have one, that'll only leave one over ...' She raised her long sweet face and shook her head. 'Should've made more, eh? Trouble is, four got caught on, wi' that dratted oven. You can never tell what it's going to do.'

'I don't mind having the burnt ones,' Ned said cheerfully.

'They're no' burnt, just caught on.'

'Well, who says Mr MacNab'll want more than two?' asked Lesley. 'There's plenty, Auntie Peg, stop worrying.'

It always surprised her that her efficient aunt should appear so nervous when her boss visited. Today, she seemed to be particularly on edge, even though everything looked ready for the 'knife and fork' tea that they only had on Sundays when Sam came. If they'd had a good Sunday dinner, they usually just had sandwiches for their tea, but see, there was the ham shank laid out in the scullery today, hard-boiled eggs in a pan, the beetroot in a glass dish.

'And there's cake,' Carrie was saying comfortingly. 'Ginger cake – ma favourite!'

'You don't think it's sunk a wee bit?' asked Peg.

'It looks grand,' Ned told her. 'Come on, girls, let's away and leave Auntie Peg to get on.'

'Aye, I've the floor to sweep yet. Will you look at all that flour? There's more on the mat than on the board!' Peg sighed and covered her baking with a tea towel. 'Then I've to get maself ready.'

'Should've let us do the floor,' said Lesley. 'And we could've done the baking as well. You did the Sunday dinner.'

'Och, no, you work hard all the week.'

'So do you.'

'Aye, well, I want you to go for a bit blow and get some fresh air now. You're always indoors.'

Well, that was true. Lesley worked as a waitress in an Edinburgh hotel restaurant where she complained she scarcely saw the light of day, while Carrie served in a Leith draper's where it was so dark they had to light the gas in the morning. Ned did get out and about with his french polishing, but every evening he spent playing his fiddle in the pubs, making the odd bob he called it, and drinking far too much, his aunt and sisters told him.

Well, what was he to do, he protested? The pints came up for him, he couldn't turn them down! And he was never drunk. Now how often did they ever see him drunk? Ah, well, they'd let it go. But if they didn't see him drunk, they saw plenty who were in the streets of Leith. Fact of life, said Ned.

*

Out on the landing, they decided to give Adam up the stair a shout. If he hadn't a meeting on, he'd probably like to come with them.

'He'll be sure to have a meeting,' said Lesley. 'But ask him, Ned.'

Adam Kay, who lived in the top flat with his widower-father, a docker, had been at school with Ned and was now an official for the dockers' trade union. His life was almost completely absorbed by his work, yet he seemed willing to spare time for the MacKenzies when he could.

'I think he might be sweet on Lesley,' Carrie had once remarked.

'He was always sweet on Janie Scott at school,' Ned told her. 'Just up his street, is Janie.'

'I don't want anybody to be sweet on me,' declared Lesley. 'I don't want to get wed. At least, no' for years.'

'You'd change your mind if you met Mr Right,' said Carrie.

'Mr Right!' Lesley gave her sister an indulgent smile. 'I hope I don't meet him then. No' yet!'

Adam Kay, bounding down the stair at Ned's call, should have been Mr Right for somebody, thought Carrie. He was so handsome, so full of vitality – like Lesley, in a way. He had fair hair, too, but his eyes, as far-sighted as a sailor's, were grey, and he had the most determined chin surely anyone had ever seen. Needed it too, for his job. Imagine what it must be like, arguing all the time between the employers and the men!

'We're away to the Links,' Lesley told him. 'Want to come, if you haven't got a meeting?'

'I've time to come before the meeting, it's no' till six. But there's a bit of a wind today, mind. Brace yourselves.'

A bit of a wind? They were glad he'd told them to brace themselves. As soon as they opened the street door, they were caught in the blast and had to leave it to Adam's strong hands to get the door closed again behind them.

'Och, we'll lose our hats!' cried Carrie. 'Hold on, Lesley!'

'There's a fellow already lost his,' said Ned, watching a Leither in his Sunday suit chasing his bowler down the Kirkgate. 'And will you look at thae bottles rolling everywhere? Saturday night drinking, eh? You can always tell it's Sunday by what's in the gutters.'

'Shocking,' said his sisters, giving him meaningful looks, at which he waved his arms in protest.

'Don't look at me. I drink in the pub.'

'As we say!'

'Come on,' said Adam with diplomatic calm. 'Give us your hands, girls.'

And away they went, blown before the wind down the Kirkgate, dodging the bottles and flying papers, holding on to their hats and laughing, not a care in the world, it seemed, amongst them.

Chapter Two

It was no distance at all from the Kirkgate to the Links. Over the foot of Leith Walk, past the Central Station on the right of Duke Street, and there they were, at one of the largest open spaces in town. Long ago, it had been just a place of dunes and rough grass, with Leith Sands and the Forth in the distance. By 1913, the view of the Sands and the water had been obscured by buildings and docks, and the Links had acquired trees and paths, cricket pitches and seats, a bandstand for concerts on Saturdays and a long colourful history for folk to remember.

You could still see the old artillery mounds left on the Links by the English army back in 1560, for the early history of Leith had been stormy. It had been under siege; it had been burned on the orders of Henry VIII, and destroyed a second time by his son's Protector; there had always been the military around and usually on the Links. But more peaceful days succeeded the turmoil. The Links became a place for leisure.

For years folk played golf, said actually to have been invented on the Links, but then some said it caused trouble and the course wasn't good anyway, so it was moved away to Craigentinny. But that still left football to play, and cricket, bowls, or quoits, or anything else you fancied, as well as dancing and listening to the music from the bandstand. And what the Leithers really liked was to escape to the Links from the busy streets for a while, pretend they were in the country, walk the open spaces, get a 'bit blow'. Even if sometimes the blow was rather too much.

'Och, it's so cold!' cried Carrie, when the MacKenzies arrived with Adam on that wild Sunday afternoon. 'I'm away home.'

'Wait. Wait!' Ned was putting an imaginary telescope to his eye. 'What do I spy with my little eye? Something beginning with – J!'

'J?' Carrie was instantly alert. She dropped the hands she had put to her chilled face and screwed up her own eyes at two figures in the distance. 'It's Joe! It's our postie.'

'Aye,' said Ned. 'But J can stand for Janie as well as Joe.'

'That's Janie Scott with Joe?' asked Carrie. She shrugged. 'Oh, well, they're friends, you ken. Stay on the same stair.'

Janie's folks and Joe's lived round the corner from the Kirkgate in a tenement off Great Junction Street. Joe had only one brother, who was away in the merchant navy, but Janie was the eldest of four whose father was dead. It was she who kept the family together on her wages as a council office clerk.

Bright girl, Janie, thought Lesley. As bright as Adam. Yes, she was just up his street. But Carrie's eyes were still on Joe. Why go home yet? She didn't really mind the cold.

'Fancy meeting you folk!' cried Janie, as she and Joe reached the group of four. 'We thought sure we'd be the only ones out here today.'

'Why, what's a bit o' wind?' asked Adam, looking down at her, and she grinned.

'Doesn't bother me, I like it.'

'So do I,' said Lesley, but she knew she had very little else in common with Janie, so small and fierce, her hazel eyes always snapping, her dark hair always slipping from its pins and being pushed back with impatient hands. Janie didn't worry over her hair, or her looks, she cared about other things. How to improve the world, mainly, and you had to admire her for that. But, heavens, thought Lesley, there were easier folk, eh? Folk like Joe, for instance.

Joe Halliday was rather short and rather broad. He had curly brown hair and bright eyes with long lashes, a cleft in his chin and a ready smile. He was the most popular postie in the area, and though folk in the tenements didn't get many letters, they always looked out for Joe, just to see his cheerful face and have a bit crack. Carrie looked out for him, too. She was always first down in the morning, waiting for the post. Waiting for Joe.

The six of them began to walk, still blown by the wind, as more Leithers began to appear on the Links, some with small children, running and shrieking, some with dogs, fetching and carrying sticks, barking with joy. Sunday afternoon. A lovely break from the grind of the week. Soon be over, that was the trouble. All too soon for the MacKenzies in fact, for after they'd walked as far as the edge of the Links, Ned was saying they should be going home. Carrie, walking now only with Joe, was unwilling.

'Needn't go back yet!' she cried, as Ned pointed to the time on his grandfather's watch Auntie Peg had given him on his twenty-first birthday.

'Thought you were cold, thought you wanted to go home?'

'We're talking about the old Sands,' she answered loftily. 'We're saying we wished we could've gone to the races.'

'But no' the executions?' asked Adam with a grin. 'Used to hang folk on the Sands, you ken. Pirates and such.'

Carrie shuddered. 'No executions,' she said firmly.

'Aren't any now, thank the Lord. And it must be a hundred years since there were races on the Sands. Come to that, since we got the docks, there's no' much of the Sands left, anyway.'

'I'd like to have gone to the races too,' Ned remarked, carefully returning his watch to an inside pocket. 'There's nothing much to do in Leith these days, eh?'

'Don't say you're like Lesley, wanting away?' asked Carrie.

'Never said that.'

'Do you say that, Lesley?' asked Adam, looking at her. 'Do you want away?'

'Och, I talk sometimes,' she answered, smiling. 'But I don't know where I'd go.'

'Anywhere away from Leith?' asked Ned.

'Why, I canna understand you, Lesley!' cried Janie, suddenly halting. 'How can you talk of leaving Leith? There's so much to do! You're needed, we're all needed! And it's your home.'

'I never said I'd go for ever,' Lesley retorted, rather stung. 'All I'd want would be a change.'

'And why not?' asked Ned, as Janie impatiently tossed her head. He took Lesley's arm. 'Come on, old MacNab'll be waiting and Auntie Peg'll be sending out search parties.'

'Sam MacNab's coming to your place?' asked Joe.

'Aye, Auntie Peg invites him sometimes for his tea,' Carrie told him. 'Only now and again, mind.'

'Bet she's his right hand at the shop, eh? I like your Auntie Peg.'

'Everybody likes Auntie Peg.'

'Why'd she never marry, nice-looking woman like her?'

'Trust a man to ask that,' cried Janie. 'As though every woman has to marry.'

'Well, most do,' Joe answered easily. 'I was just wondering.'

'She did have a sweetheart, but he was in the army,' Lesley told him. 'Got killed abroad somewhere.'

'And she never met anyone else?'

'Took us on,' said Ned. 'We were lucky. It'd have been the orphanage for us, without Auntie Peg.'

Joe, of course, knew that. All the folk in the area knew

about Peg Darroch's taking on her sister's bairns, and the orphans themselves had learned to accept the interest that had come their way.

For it was a sad story, right enough. First, their dad had gone down in Ben Wallace's fishing trawler. Two years later, their mother had died of scarlet fever, caught from her own children. That was what sometimes happened with childish diseases – the young ones survived, the adults died, as Janie's father had died from diphtheria at the time his family recovered.

'Aye, you were lucky,' Janie herself now commented. 'Having Miss Darroch.'

'Well, you had your ma,' said Lesley, but Janie looked away across the Links. She said nothing of her mother and Lesley bit her lip, remembering that Mrs Scott had not been one to cope with widowhood and four fatherless bairns. There'd been talk of 'the bottle' and still was, and Janie, who'd had to bring up her brother and sisters, had added the temperance movement to her causes when she grew up.

'Are you walking back with us, Joe?' Carrie asked shyly, as the others turned for home.

'Aye, might as well,' he answered, his cheerful eyes on her face. 'Could do with a cup of tea. Wish there was somewhere you could buy one, eh?'

'What, on a Sunday?' Carrie smiled at the idea. Nothing was open on a Sunday except churches. 'But maybe you'd like to come back and have a cup with us, Joe? Auntie Peg'd be pleased to see you.'

'No, no, thanks, you've got company. Anyway, I have to get back maself. Ma'll be waiting.' He gave a rueful smile. 'Since Kenny's left, she's for ever on the look-out for me. Canna call ma soul ma own, but, och, she means well, eh?'

'Aye, means well,' said Janie with a grin. 'Mothers always mean well.'

'Come on, then, we'll away,' said Adam. 'Be walking into the wind going back, remember.'

'No need to remind us,' said Lesley, catching her breath.

Janie and Joe left them at the corner of the Kirkgate, with Lesley heaving a small sigh of relief at Janie's departure, while Carrie's gaze was tender on Joe's retreating back. At the door to Auntie Peg's flat, Ned asked Adam if he wouldn't care to come in for a bit, have a cup of tea with old MacNab?

'Thanks, all the same, but I've things to do before the meeting,' Adam answered. 'Good walk, though, eh? I'm glad I went, I feel the better for it.'

'Me, too,' said Lesley, as his gaze moved between the sisters.

'It's a fact, you both look grand. Bonnie Lesley, bonnie Carrie!'

'Och, there's no Burns poem for me,' said Carrie, blushing.

'And I wish there wasn't for me!' cried Lesley. 'If you knew how I'd been teased over that poem. "Bonnie Lesley" indeed! I wish Rabbie Burns had never written it.'

'"O saw ye bonnie Lesley, as she gaed o'er the Border?"' Adam quoted. 'Are you going over the Border, Lesley?'

'Who knows? I might.'

'I might, too,' said Ned.

'You're too idle,' said Lesley. 'You'd never get round to it.'

Ned laughed. 'I'll just stay at home and play ma fiddle, then.'

They were joining in his laughter as they parted, Adam to run up the stair, the MacKenzies to go into their aunt's flat. How cold they were, but so flushed, so exhilarated!

'Is that you back?' cried Peg, hurrying forward. 'Now here's Mr MacNab waiting for you. Tea's all ready.'

Chapter Three

If Sam MacNab had had a beard, he might have looked like Father Christmas. So the MacKenzies used to think when they were younger, for his hair was quite white – prematurely, they'd been told, though he looked old enough to them – and his face round and rosy. He smiled a lot, too, and was always very affable, but his eyes were shrewd. He was said to be a very good businessman. Not really like Father Christmas.

That afternoon, he was already sitting at the table Aunt Peg had laid so carefully, and greeted the MacKenzies with a beaming smile. He wore his Sunday suit of dark tweed, with a watch chain across his waistcoat and a silver pin in his tie, and looked very pleasant and prosperous. No different from usual, which could not be said of Auntie Peg, who was definitely not herself. She had changed into her best dress of green wool, with a cape at the shoulders, and would have looked very nice, the girls thought, if it hadn't been for her air of anxiety.

What was up with her? the sisters wondered and looked at Ned, but he was shaking hands with Mr MacNab and appeared to have noticed nothing.

'Och, you're cold!' cried Sam. 'Where've you been, then?'

'The Links,' Ned answered. 'And you're right, it was cold.'

'Get a good blow there. But you might've gone to the Shore. Always interesting on the Shore.'

'What, with all thae pubs and such?' asked Peg. 'It's no' what it was, anyway.'

'Heart of everything, one time,' Sam agreed. 'Our first harbour, eh? Where the Water o' Leith flowed in to the Forth. Should've seen the ships there in the old days! Now, of course, we've got the docks.'

'Plenty of docks, all right,' Peg commented. 'Never could see why they wanted so many.'

'The Edinburgh and the Imperial, the Victoria, the Albert, not to mention the old docks. All do their job, Peggie, all needed with increased trade.' Sam nodded his white head. 'Did I ever tell you I saw the Albert Dock opened back in 1869? I was a wee laddie at the time.' He gave a reminiscent smile. 'I can still remember the band playing "Rule Britannia".'

'Yes, well now the young folk are here, I think I'll make the tea,' said Peg. 'Take your coats off, girls – Ned – and wash your hands.'

'Thinks we're six years old,' murmured Lesley, but they obediently washed their hands at the cold tap in the scullery, and sat down at the table.

'Very nice,' said Sam genially. 'Always made a lovely spread, Peggie.'

Peggie? The MacKenzies, exchanging glances, noted the use of the name. It was not their own name for their aunt and not one Mr MacNab had used before. What had happened to 'Miss Darroch', then? And would their aunt be calling her employer 'Sam'? A strange feeling of unease hung over the table, so real they felt they could touch it.

Tea was over. There had been more than enough lardy cakes to follow the cold ham, and the ginger cake had not sunk in the least. The kettle had been boiled and reboiled and everyone had had several cups of tea and said at last they didn't want any more. Plates had been removed, chairs

16

pushed back, and Sam MacNab was taking out cigars and offering one to Ned.

'Cigars, eh?' Ned whistled.

'Aye, I'm partial to a good cigar. And this is a special occasion.' As the smoke rose and Ned's eyes watered a little as he drew on the cigar, Sam looked round for Peg.

'Peggie, what are you doing? Never mind thae pots, now. Come and sit down.' He patted the chair next to his. 'I think it's time we told 'em, eh?'

Peg sat down, fixing her eyes on the crumbs on the cloth. She said nothing.

'Tell us what?' asked Ned, while Lesley and Carrie fixed their eyes on their aunt.

Sam sat back in his chair and put his hand over Peg's that was by now fiddling with the same crumbs she had been studying. He said genially, 'Your aunt and me – we're getting wed.'

There was a silence. The MacKenzies couldn't speak. Sam, his eyes now very serious, watched them. Auntie Peg didn't raise her head.

'You're surprised?' asked Sam at last. He puffed strong smoke from his cigar. 'Now, I wonder why?'

'We – never thought of it,' said Ned.

'Never,' agreed Carrie.

Lesley, conscious of a great weight around her heart, still remained silent. What could you say, after all, when your world had changed with one small word? Wed. That was it. Wed. 'Your aunt and me are getting wed.' Had Sam MacNab really said that? The words echoed around them like a tolling bell, yet still seemed unreal.

'I canna believe it,' she said suddenly, in a voice she didn't recognise as her own. Her eyes went to her aunt, who slowly raised her head.

'I know it's a shock, pet.'

'Why'd you never say anything?'

'We've only just decided.'

'Today?'

'Well, a few days ago.' Peg's fingers were now kneading the crumbs hard. 'Mr MacNab – Sam – asked me if I'd consider him. I said I'd think it over.'

'And you never said a word to us!'

'It was your aunt's decision,' Sam said smoothly. 'She'd to make up her own mind, eh?'

'We're her family!' cried Lesley. 'What Auntie Peg decides concerns us.'

'Aye, that's right,' said Ned. 'If you go to stay at Mr MacNab's, Auntie Peg, what's going to happen to us, then?'

Another silence fell. Sam looked at Peg, whose great dark eyes went from Ned to Carrie to Lesley.

'You'll be all right,' she said breathlessly. 'I can get the tenancy put in Ned's name, you can stay on here.'

'Without you?' asked Carrie.

'Well, you're no' exactly children.' Sam laid his cigar in the ashtray Peg had provided. 'If you'd been bairns, of course, you'd have come with your aunt. But you're all fully grown, you've got jobs, you're independent. In no time, you'll be getting wed yourselves. Till then, you've got this good flat, as well as your aunt's furniture.'

'You'll be leaving Granddad's furniture?' asked Lesley, turning on Peg. 'You'll be having all Mrs MacNab's things?'

'I'm taking ma books and ma mother's chair,' Peg replied, bright spots of colour burning in her cheeks. 'And maybe a few other pieces, but you'll be needing the furniture yourselves, anyway. Och, it's for the best, Lesley, you'll see.'

'Of course it is,' Sam said softly. He pressed Peg's hand and stood up. 'Now, I'd better be going. You'll have plenty to talk over, eh? Ned, how did you like that cigar?'

It seemed an age before Auntie Peg came back from seeing Sam MacNab off at the front door. Maybe they'd kissed on the doorstep, like a couple of young lovers? Lesley, crashing cups and saucers into an enamel bowl at the sink, wondered how Ned could keep so calm, finishing that damned cigar, while Carrie seemed quite apart, as though nothing that had happened had anything to do with her. Did they not feel, as she felt, that their world had collapsed?

'I suppose all that matters to you, Ned, is that Carrie and me'll be here to look after you,' she said bitterly. 'We're losing Auntie Peg, but you'll still get your meals made, eh?'

'She's only going to Sam MacNab's,' he said, a little uneasily. 'We'll still be seeing her.'

'Oh, I wouldn't bank on that. Mr MacNab won't want her coming round here, will he? Aren't you upset she's going to marry him?'

'Yes, I am. I'm no' keen on the change. But if it's what she wants, what can we do?'

'Nothing,' said Carrie. 'I mean, you have to think of her. She's got no one of her own.'

'She's got us!' cried Lesley.

'It's no' the same.'

'So, you mean she's got no man and that's all that matters?' Lesley's eyes were flashing. 'And if she takes on Sam MacNab, you won't mind us being without her and looking after Ned?'

Carrie shrugged. She had a dreamy look in her eye that Lesley couldn't remember seeing before, and it made her feel irritated and apprehensive. In one short afternoon, everything she knew seemed to be changing and shifting, as though in an earthquake. And she was the only one standing up.

'Oh, you're doing the tea things?' came Auntie Peg's voice, and there she was, the one who had always been their rock and was now only part of the crumbling world. 'I'll just get ma pinny—'

'Auntie Peg!' cried Lesley, bursting into tears. 'Just tell us – why?'

Chapter Four

Ned had discreetly removed himself to Peg's room, where the women in the living room could hear him playing popular tunes on his fiddle – thank heavens, not exercises – but of course they weren't listening. Auntie Peg had opened up the range to give more heat and was sitting in her mother's chair, her hands folded over the apron she had put on to cover her best dress, while Lesley, her eyes stormy, waited for her to speak. Not saying a word, intent on keeping out of things, Carrie perched between them on a stool, darning one of her black stockings for tomorrow.

'Why?' Auntie Peg repeated at last. 'Why should I marry Sam? Well, I'm fond of him and he's fond of me. Nobody's saying we're in love.'

'But Auntie Peg, if you're getting married, you should be in love!' cried Lesley. 'You were once.'

At that, Carrie raised her eyes and drew in her breath sharply, as though shocked at Lesley's bringing up Auntie Peg's old engagement. They all knew their aunt didn't like talking about poor Gordon Forgan. She certainly wouldn't want to talk about him now.

But Peg only shook her head. 'Older folk get married for different reasons from young folk,' she said quietly. 'Companionship, for one. Sam's lonely.'

'But why should you be lonely, Auntie Peg?' Lesley protested. 'You've got us.'

'I won't always have you, I will be lonely.'

'Why, where are we going, then?'

'It's like Sam said today – you'll all be married. Maybe quite soon.'

'I won't! Ned won't!' Lesley turned her gaze on Carrie, who resolutely kept on darning a ladder, her head bent, but her cheeks scarlet. As Lesley frowned a little, her aunt smiled.

'I notice Carrie's very quiet.'

'What's that supposed to mean? She's engaged?'

'Of course I'm no' engaged!' cried Carrie. 'But I'd like to be married one day, yes, I would! Why shouldn't I?'

'All I'm saying is that Auntie Peg has no reason to feel lonely. No reason to marry Sam MacNab.' Lesley sat back in her chair, breathing hard. 'You were his wife's friend, anyway, Auntie Peg, no' his. You never even called him Sam that I remember – until today.'

Peg shifted uncomfortably in her chair. 'Aye, I was poor Aggie's friend,' she said softly and sighed deeply. 'I miss her still, you ken.'

'You were wonderful, nursing her, when she was so ill,' Carrie murmured. 'We all said that.'

'It was the least I could do, we'd always been that close.' Peg pleated a fold of her apron. 'One day she says to me – I've never told you this before – she says, when I go, I want you to promise me, Peggie, you'll take care of Sam.'

'Take care of Sam?' Lesley repeated stonily.

'Aye, he'll never manage on his own, she says, and I'm no' keen on thae housekeepers in ma home. I was that taken aback, I just said I would. And then she was easy, poor soul, in her mind.'

Lesley's cheeks were as red as Carrie's. 'Auntie Peg, are you saying you're marrying Sam MacNab because his wife asked you to! I don't believe it!'

'Just as well, because it's no' true. I could look after him without marrying him, Lesley, and he did get a house-keeper, anyway. But I am fond of him, I think I could be happy with him. And he'd be somebody of ma own.' Peg sat up straight and set her gentle mouth in a way her nieces recognised. Arguments were over. Their aunt had made up her mind. 'It's what everybody wants,' she added softly. 'Somebody of their own.'

Outside the tenement, the wind had died, as the sky had darkened and stars had appeared, but no one was looking at the stars. Ned had finished playing and was lying on the sofa reading yesterday's evening paper, while Carrie was putting away her mending and Peg, now changed from her good dress, was beckoning Lesley to the door of her room and drawing her into its cold depths.

'I just want to say, Lesley, pet, that I wish you'd no' take this so hard,' she said quickly, shivering a little. 'It's a change, all right, but life's like that, eh? Full of change.'

'We're happy as we are, is the way I see it,' Lesley answered after a pause, gazing at her aunt's neatly made bed, her best dress on its hanger, her well-worn shoes placed together. 'I thought you were happy, too.'

'You ken fine I'm happy.'

'Well, then.'

'Look, I've tried to explain.' Peg's dark eyes were pleading on Lesley's face. 'When you're all gone and I'm alone, will I still be happy then? Can you no' understand, why I want someone of ma own?'

'I suppose so,' Lesley said reluctantly.

'After all, even if you're no' thinking of getting married, you could soon be away, you ken. You're like your ma, wanting to be on the move, seeing something new.'

Lesley's pretty face relaxed into a smile. She knew her mother, Julie, had been a waitress, too, and a good one, always in demand, and fond of flitting from job to job when the fancy took her.

'I haven't moved around much so far, Auntie Peg.'

'Aye, but I can see you packing your box and taking yourself off somewhere, just like her.' Peg's voice faltered.

'I remember the time she met your dad, though. She was all set for a place in Harrogate – or, was it Scarborough – I canna recall – when along came your dad, bonnie Don MacKenzie, and she never moved again.'

Except to the churchyard, were the unspoken words hanging between Julie's sister and Julie's daughter. Neither spoke for a moment, until Lesley asked quietly,

'When are you thinking of getting wed, then?'

'Well, there's no point waiting. June, we're thinking, would be nice.'

'That's pretty soon.'

'Plenty of time to fix up a quiet wedding. We'll no' be wanting any fuss.' As a thought seemed to strike her, Peg stiffened a little. 'Lesley, you'll come, eh? You'll see me wed?'

'Of course I will! Fancy asking.'

'Well, the way you've been talking, I suddenly thought – och, never mind what I thought. But you'll be there, that's all that matters. We'll find some nice material and make ourselves something smart, eh? And talk to Carrie about it, too. Though she'll be away in the clouds, I expect, dreaming of Joe Halliday, as usual.'

'She'll be what?' asked Lesley.

'Well, you ken what's she's like over that postie. Nice laddie he is, and all. I hope it comes to something. Listen, shall we make some more tea? And put out the ginger cake again for Ned? You ken he's always ready for something else to eat.'

Lesley, filling the kettle, was asking herself was she blind, or what? Why had she never guessed what Carrie was feeling? Every morning, running down the stair just the time the postie came, when they hardly ever got any letters, anyway. Watching Janie Scott on the Links as though she were a rival. Staring up into Joe Halliday's face with eyes as big as saucers. No wonder Carrie was not concerned over Auntie Peg's departure. She was in a world of her own.

*

23

'Why'd you never tell me about Joe?' Lesley asked her sister when they were getting ready for bed. It was very cold, as it usually was at night, the canvas on the floor icy under their feet, the air they breathed quite wintry. Carrie, struggling into a flannel nightgown, was blushing again.

'What's to tell?'

'You're keen on him, eh?'

'It's none of your business, Lesley.'

'Look, I'm your sister. I'm interested.'

Carrie, now brushing her hair that had been released from its pins, said softly,

'Well, I do like him. But plenty of girls like Joe.'

'Has he asked you out?'

'No. But I think he will. Just the way he was looking at me today, I think he will.'

As Carrie smiled fondly at the memory, Lesley watched, rubbing her arms against the chill.

'You're awful young to get serious, Carrie.'

'Och, I'm a long way off that!'

Are you? wondered Lesley. She didn't know about Joe, but it seemed to her that her sister already had wedding bells ringing in her ears and they weren't for Auntie Peg.

'I'll go and get the hot bottle,' she said flatly. 'The kettle should be ready by now.'

Chapter Five

The Leith that was the MacKenzies' home was not just a port, it was a centre of industry, the proverbial hive of activity. Everything that could be made or built seemed to be made or built there, from soap to ships, from rope to glass, from engineering parts to whisky. Yet trade had been bad in recent years, with Leith up against fierce world competition. There was unemployment, poverty, folk on the breadline, falling off. Life in Leith could be a hazard.

On the other hand, it had its merchants and ship-owners, solid, well-to-do folk, who lived as well as any in Edinburgh. Wasn't it strange, Lesley sometimes thought, travelling to the capital, that folk always forgot that side of Leith?

Say Edinburgh, and they thought of lawyers and doctors, fine houses in the New Town, middle-class respectability. Say Leith, and it was sailors and brawls that came to mind, dirt and sweat, struggling workers, hungry children. But you'd only to take the tram up to Edinburgh's Old Town, to see slums as bad as any in Leith.

It was so unfair, in Lesley's view, that Edinburgh should look down on Leith. But then it always had. There'd always been friction, right down the centuries, because Leith long ago had been acquired by the capital and the capital called the tune. Och, how Leith had twisted under the yoke, longed for its independence! And in 1833, it had come.

They were free at last to run things their own way, have their own police, their own electric trams, even their own licensing laws. They would never be part of Edinburgh again.

Or, would they? There were those who said economic reasons would drive them back. Aye, one day they'd all be under control of the capital again, they'd be just another district, eh? No, cried others, they'd die first! Sometimes Lesley felt sick of all the strife, all the pressures, sick of all the Edinburgh folk saying, 'Oh, you come from Leith, fancy!' As though all Leithers lived on the waterfront and mixed with foreign sailors and loose women! When she went away, she'd go somewhere quite different, live a different life for a while. Find an identity all her own.

Yes. Rattling along the following morning in the Edinburgh train they called the 'penny jump', Lesley had already decided that if her life was to be changed, she'd do the changing. Her ticket in her glove, her bag on her knee, she stared out at the views she knew so well, taking no part in the chitchat of the clerks and other working girls around her. She'd been lucky to get a seat, but the journey only took seven minutes; very soon, she'd be at the restaurant, and then there'd be no time to think at all. But she didn't really need to think any more. As soon as Auntie Peg's wedding was over, she'd be away. Where? Somewhere.

'Hey, what's happened to you today?' a cheerful young man she knew by sight asked her. 'Not a word out of you. I'd give you a penny for your thoughts, only I bought my ticket with it.'

'I'm sure ma thoughts are no' worth a penny,' Lesley told him, laughing. She picked up her bag and adjusted her hat for they were coming into Edinburgh. 'Just got a lot on ma mind today.'

'Shame. Care to forget it all with a cup of tea at the station buffet?'

'Sorry, I've got to get to work.'

'One of these days, then.'

'Aye, one of these days.'

'See you this evening, maybe?'

'No, I'll be late going home. I'm working split shifts at the restaurant today.'

'Hard work, eh? Whyn't you try for an office job, something easier?'

'I like what I do. I like meeting new people.'

And that was true. As she hurried from the station through the crowds of people on their way to work, Lesley knew she would still try for a restaurant job when she made her breakaway. So, not such a new identity, after all, then? All would depend on what she found and where she went. Harrogate, maybe, like her ma? Or, Scarborough? Of course, her ma had never got to Harrogate, or Scarborough, she'd married Don MacKenzie instead. But marriage was not on Lesley's mind. On that chill Monday morning, she didn't even want to think about it for others, never mind herself.

The Princess Louise was not one of Edinburgh's grandest hotels, but it was large and well maintained and had a smart clientele. Lesley had worked there since she was sixteen and knew she'd done well. Folk liked the way she looked in her black dress and white apron, with her trim waist, her strawberry-blonde hair under its cap, her delicate white hands that were like her mother's and as deft.

The year before she had progressed to serving luncheons and dinners, something she considered a feather in her cap, for waitresses were not always considered acceptable for more formal work. When she came to apply for her new post, such experience would count for her.

As she put on her small apron and tidied her hair in a room off the hotel kitchens, other staff were coming in after serving breakfasts, but others, like her, were bemoaning the fact that it was Monday and would be, for those on the split shifts, a punishingly long day. But then they got a couple of hours off in the afternoon – that was something to be grateful for, eh?

'Where shall we go?' asked Sally Abbott, blonde and bouncy and a friend of Lesley's. 'Window shopping in Logie's?'

'Have to be window shopping, if it's Logie's,' Lesley replied, summoning up a smile. 'I've no' got much in ma purse.'

'We've enough for a cup of tea somewhere. Unless Alex treats us, eh? Alex, want to take us out for tea this afternoon?'

Alex Mitchie, a red-headed waiter who was one of Sally's admirers, grinned. 'We can get tea here for nothing, why go anywhere else?'

'Och, we need a break from this place, and we've got that Monday morning feeling and all. I say we all go up the Bridges and have tea at John Johnson's. They've a lovely orchestra there now, you ken. What do you say?'

'I say yes, if it's what you want, sweetheart.' Alex put his finger to his lips. 'Watch out, here's old Hawkeye.'

Mr Hawkins, the head waiter, had put his head round the door and was looking down his long nose at them.

'May I remind you that the restaurant is opening for coffee in five minutes? Places please.'

It was several hours later, when they'd finished serving luncheons and were getting ready for their break, that Sally asked Lesley if she was all right.

'You look that pale, you ken, and you're never pale. Have you got a headache?'

'No, I'm fine, thanks. Just a bit low in spirits.'

'Nothing wrong at home?'

'Och, no.' Not for the world would Lesley talk about Auntie Peg's marriage to folk at the hotel, even to Sally. 'I'm only thinking I might make a move.'

'From the Louise?'

'From Edinburgh.' Lesley buttoned up her coat. 'I want to see something new.'

Sally was winding a scarf round her plump neck in readiness for facing the wind crossing Princes Street and 'going up the Bridges'. 'Where'd you like to go, then?'

'England, maybe. I've never been over the border.'

'England? I'm no' sure I'd want to work down south. Too far away. I'd be homesick.'

'Well, I don't honestly know where I want to go. Could be anywhere.'

'Alex worked in London once, so did George. Alex, come here a minute! Tell Lesley how you liked London.'

'We liked it fine,' said Alex. 'Still came back to Edinburgh, didn't we, George?'

'Got homesick,' said George, who was Alex's brother and another redhead. He and Lesley had been out together twice and George would have liked to make it more than that, only Lesley had told him very kindly that she wasn't really interested. Now his soft brown eyes rested sadly on her pretty face, making her feel guilty, but what could she do?

'Why does everyone get homesick?' she asked lightly. 'You needn't stay away for ever.'

'Needn't stay away at all,' said George with meaning. 'You don't really want to go to London, do you, Lesley?'

'Depends what turns up.' To cheer his downcast face, she asked him if he was coming up the Bridges, and he said he certainly was.

'This place'll no' be the same without you,' he told her, on the way across town.

'Well, I might never go. Let's no' talk about it.'

But when they were enjoying their break at the big department store of John Johnson's, listening to the tearoom orchestra and being served by other poor devils instead of serving folk themselves, Sally returned to Lesley's plans.

'What you ought to do, if you really want another job, Lesley, is to go to one of the domestic agencies. They can tell you what jobs are going in hotel work.'

29

'I could do that. Or, just look at the vacancy columns in the papers.' Lesley drank her tea. 'I needn't go before the summer, anyway.'

'That's a relief,' said George. 'It's only March, now.'

'I'd no' mind making a move maself,' said Sally. 'Only I could never leave Ma. She depends on me, you ken.'

'Nobody depends on me,' Lesley said quietly. 'I'm free as the breeze.'

And there were George's big eyes on her still, saying as plain as plain, that he wished she weren't free, that he wished she were tied to him. Lesley made a point of looking away.

Chapter Six

Other eyes were on her in the train that evening, and because she wasn't expecting to see them, she didn't at first recognise whose they were. Then she smiled.

'Why, it's you, Adam! Whatever have you been doing in Edinburgh?'

Adam Kay took off his cap and moved to sit next to her on the dusty seat. 'Had to visit a fellow in the infirmary, got crushed by a bale at Albert Dock yesterday.'

'Oh, no! Is he very bad?'

'Pretty bad. He'll no' be working for a long time, even if he pulls through.' Adam set his cap back on his fair hair. 'Got a wife and a couple of bairns, as well.'

'What'll they do? Can the union help?'

'Aye, a bit. We've some funds.' He shook his head. 'Need more. Need a proper health service. Never get it, of course. Pie in the sky.'

'Adam, I'm sorry.'

'Let's talk about you. Had a long day?'

'Am I looking tired?'

'No. You're looking very nice. You always do.'

'I know I'm looking tired. Feel it, anyway. This was one of our split shift days.'

'Split shifts – murder, eh? Whyn't you try for something easier?'

'Someone else asked me that today. Crazy thing is, I

like ma work. It's just ma feet that don't.'

He laughed. 'So you'll stay with it?'

'Oh, I think so.' Lesley hesitated. She had not felt like talking about Auntie Peg to anyone at the Louise, but Adam was different. He was from Number Fifteen, he would soon know anyway. 'Adam, had you heard our Auntie Peg is getting married?'

'Married?' His grey eyes were wide. 'Your Auntie Peg? Why, who's she marrying, then?'

'Sam MacNab.'

'Fellow she works for? Well, he's a lucky devil, eh? Your aunt's a good-looking woman, and nice with it.' Adam drew his brows together. 'I'm no' so sure about her luck, mind.'

'You don't like him?'

'He's all right, I daresay. Great temperance man, you ken, and a bit of a Tory. A lot of a Tory, in fact. Got no time for dockers, that's for sure. When we were on strike in 1911, he'd plenty to say.'

'I think he's fond of Auntie Peg. I think he'll make her happy.' Lesley looked down at her hands in her lap. 'Hope so.'

'Och, he will! Look, I shouldn't have said anything. I'm sorry.' Adam was shaking his head at himself. 'But how about you, Lesley? This marriage'll make changes for you, I should think?'

'Yes, big changes.'

'You're no' really going over the Border, are you?'

'I think I might go somewhere.'

Adam was about to speak, but the train was pulling into Leith Central and he was looking out at the platform, where it was hard to recognise waiting faces in the dusk, even though the lamps were lit. But he had spotted the one he thought might be there.

'There's Janie,' he told Lesley. 'She said she might meet this train.'

'Oh, yes, I see her. Are you going to a meeting, or something?'

'No!' He laughed down at her. 'We don't always go to meetings, you ken. Tonight we're going to get some penny fillets at the chip shop, with peas and vinegar if we feel like splashing out. Listen, do you want to come?'

'I just want to put ma feet up, thanks all the same.'

'Hello, Lesley,' said Janie Scott, when they'd joined her on the platform. In the poor light, her face looked yellowish, but her eyes were bright on Adam and she did not wait for Lesley to answer. 'How is he, Adam? How's Barty Lang?'

When Adam had told her, she clicked her tongue and shook her head. 'I'll have to go round to see his wife soon as I can, she'll be in a state, eh?'

'I think I'll get home,' said Lesley. 'Hope Mr Lang'll be all right. Goodnight, then, enjoy your supper.'

When she reached the station exit, Lesley looked back and saw them still in conversation, Adam's head bent towards Janie, her small figure even from a distance seeming like a coiled spring ready for action.

'Is that you, Lesley?' called Auntie Peg, as Lesley climbed the stair and let herself into the flat. 'What an age you've been, poor girl! But the kettle's singing, and Carrie's got something to tell you.'

'Aye, Lesley, guess what?' Carrie was standing at the door, flushed and wreathed in smiles. 'Joe and me's going out tomorrow! We're going to the pictures.'

'Oh, that's lovely, Carrie,' Lesley said quickly. 'Did he ask you this morning, then?'

'No.' For a moment Carrie's smiles dimmed. 'I thought he would, when I went down for the post, you ken, but he didn't. I was that disappointed.'

She lived again the moment when Joe came to the door, his eyes seeming to light up at the sight of her. She saw him lay out the letters he had on the scuffed and scratched old table where he always put the tenants' post. One for the Crawfords she recalled, and several for Adam – he was the one who usually got letters – but nothing for the MacKenzies, and that was no surprise. She saw Joe looking at her and remembered how, for a long breathless moment, she'd looked back at him and been so sure he was going to speak. But he'd only gone away, whistling.

'Och, what a shame,' Auntie Peg said now. 'But then he came to the shop, didn't he? Came seeking you out of the blue?'

'Aye, but I didn't know he was going to do that.' Carrie shook her head, remembering again. 'I went back up the stair and I felt like crying, I thought, why shouldn't I ask Joe out maself? Why should women have to wait for men?'

'Because husbands keep wives, and wives don't keep husbands,' said Lesley. 'It all comes down to money.'

'Maybe one day it'll all change, then!'

'Maybe. Tell us about Joe coming into the shop.'

Carrie's smiles returned in full force. 'Och, Lesley, it was such a surprise! I was just measuring out curtain material for Mrs Doune, when I looked up and there he was. His face was bright red and he kept looking round at the piles of stuff, as though he didn't dare say a word.'

'And did you ask him if he wanted curtains?' asked Lesley, laughing.

'I just said, cool as a cucumber, I'd be with him in a moment. "If you wouldn't mind waiting, sir?"'

'He said he didn't mind and he sat on a chair at the counter, as if he was a customer. And as soon as I'd parcelled up Mrs Doune's material and she'd taken it to the cash desk, he just looked at me, and said, "Fancy going to the Palace tomorrow, see what's on?" I could've danced all over the shop, and if old Mr Simpson had no' been watching us, I might have done, too!'

Looking at her sister, so pretty in her happiness, Lesley's heart bounded in sympathy, and she went to her and kissed and hugged her, while her aunt looked fondly on. Maybe Carrie was risking a lot, letting herself be so obviously fond of Joe, but then Joe – good-hearted, cheerful Joe –

34

was not the kind to let her down. If Lesley would never want to risk herself in that way, she really didn't feel she need fear for her sister.

'Remember I went to the pictures with one of the fellows from the Louise?' she asked Carrie, gratefully taking off her boots and massaging her feet. 'Saw the Keystone Cops. What a laugh, eh?'

'Was that the ginger-haired waiter?' Peg asked with interest.

'George Mitchie, yes. His brother's a redhead, too. Sweet on ma friend, Sally.'

'You ought to go out with George more often, Lesley. It's time you had a young man, lovely girl like you.'

'Yes, Lesley, you should,' Carrie told her earnestly. 'Why are you always so choosy?'

'I thought you told me to find Mr Right?' Lesley lay back on the sofa, laughing. 'Well, George is NOT Mr Right.'

'Better wait, then,' said Peg, setting out cups and saucers. 'It's always better to wait and be sure.'

And you've waited long enough, thought Lesley, glancing at her sister who might have been thinking the same thing. Let's hope you're sure now, Auntie Peg.

Chapter Seven

It was strange, but as soon as the date was set for the wedding, the days went by on wings. Back in March, June had seemed to Peg to be quite some way off but, as the wedding day came nearer and nearer, she felt herself less and less prepared.

There'd been no problem about booking the parish church so close to them in the Kirkgate, or the little café where they were to hold the wedding breakfast, but then Sam said that being temperance, he didn't want any drink at the reception, and Ned said they'd all be laughing stocks if they didn't have drink at a wedding. So, there'd been arguments there, and delays and such, until a compromise was reached and Sam said other folk could have alcohol, but he would not.

'"My drink is water bright",' sang Ned, behind Sam's back, and Peg was sharp with him and said you had to respect a man's principles, eh?

'Funny, how anybody with principles always makes life difficult for other people,' Ned retorted, and his sisters knocked each other's ribs and thought it was just as well that Ned and Sam MacNab would not be sharing a home.

Then there were the difficulties for Peg of finding the right material for her outfit at a price she could afford, and when she'd found the material, she couldn't find a pattern. It was the same with Lesley and Carrie. They turned everything over in John Johnson's and still weren't satisfied, until Sally Abbott told them of a cut-price shop in Stockbridge where they chose both material and patterns, and then, thank the Lord, there were only the hats to find.

'What a performance!' cried Peg distractedly, but when she tried on a pretty hat with a feather and the girls said she looked so nice, she relaxed a little and said, well, maybe all the trouble was worth it in the end.

'And you girls are going to look so pretty,' she told her nieces. 'If I'd been a bit younger, you could've been ma bridesmaids, but I'm sure I'd look very foolish pretending to be a bride at the age of forty-eight.'

'Auntie Peg, of course you're a bride!' they cried. 'And you're going to look bonnie, too!'

'Ah, but wait till it's you getting wed, Carrie,' Peg sighed. 'What a picture you'll be, eh? And it's ma guess, it'll no' be long before you're following me.'

'Oh, well, I couldn't say about that,' said Carrie, lowering her eyes, but as she and Joe were continually going out together and so obviously in love, no one took the slightest notice of her caution.

'Joe'll be popping the question any day now,' Ned told Lesley. 'Mark ma words, Carrie'll be Mrs Halliday before the year's out.'

Lesley studied him. His tone, his gaze, were morose; it appeared his usual lightness of spirit had deserted him.

'Well, I'm happy for her – aren't you?'

'Sure, I am, and for Joe. But if Carrie gets wed and sets up somewhere with Joe, that's going to mean just you and me left to pay the rent here.' Ned looked hard at Lesley. 'You're no' still talking of going away, are you?'

'Didn't you say *you* might?' she countered.

'Och, you ken fine it's no' likely I will. But are you?'

'I haven't decided anything,' she answered cautiously, unwilling to upset him. 'And remember, Carrie and Joe might have a long engagement. There's no need to worry yet.'

'Maybe.'

'You could always marry one of your girl friends.'

'Me, get married?' Ned's look was hunted. 'Hey, you're teasing, eh?'

'Young men do get married, Ned.'

'No' me. I want to see a bit of life first.'

'Me too,' said Lesley.

Early in May, Sam MacNab asked Peg and her family round to his flat over the shop for Sunday dinner, which Peg was to cook, Sam's part-time housekeeper being so hopeless she couldn't even make gravy. Peg was in a state of nerves, of course, but managed very well with the girls' help in poor Aggie's kitchen, and on the gas cooker, too, which was a novelty. But when the meal was over and the washing-up done, Sam said he thought they ought to do a bit of decorating.

'Decorating?' repeated Peg.

'Aye, wallpapering and painting.'

They all looked round at Sam's living room that looked very pleasant to them. It was larger than Peg's and had a proper fireplace with a marble mantel, and two good windows from which you could just catch a glimpse of the Shore and the old harbour. The mahogany furniture had been a wedding present from Aggie's parents, who were said to have been better off, and was solid and well polished.

'This room looks very nice,' Peg said. 'I don't think we need to change it.'

'It's the bedroom, I'm talking about. Our bedroom.'

There was a silence. The MacKenzies could see that their aunt was thinking, Oh, but that's Aggie's bedroom, and then a flush rose to her cheek when she realised that it would be hers.

'I'm no' considering change for change's sake,' said Sam, 'but Aggie was ill a long time, you ken. You might want to brighten things up a bit.'

38

'Oh, yes, yes, maybe we should.'

Sam, drawing on his cigar, looked at Ned, doing the same.

'I thought you might give us a hand, Ned. No point paying a painter when a strong young chap like you could oblige.'

'Me?' Ned took the cigar from his mouth and stared, round-eyed, at Sam. 'I'm no painter!'

'You're a french polisher, eh? It's all the same.'

'I'm a violinist,' Ned said coldly. 'I have to take care of ma hands.'

'So, what about the french polishing, then?'

'I wear gloves.'

'Well, you can wear gloves to paint, if you like.' Sam smiled cheerily. 'Go and have a look at the room, see what you think.'

'I am not going to have a look at it, Mr MacNab.'

'We'll go, eh, girls?' cried Peg, jumping to her feet. 'We'll see what it needs, Sam.'

The girls leaped up with alacrity, glad to get away from simmering Ned, and followed their aunt into the main bedroom that had the same view as the living room and the same style of furniture, too. A heavy wardrobe and a dressing table with an oval mirror, Aggie's hairbrush still on a glass tray, her trinkets in a glass bowl. And in the centre of the room, facing the windows, was the great double bed. It had an eiderdown with a coverlet and on the hump of the pillows was what looked like Sam MacNab's folded nightshirt.

As the three of them looked at this, no one said a word, but another flood of colour raced from Auntie Peg's neck to her brow, and she quickly turned away.

'Yes, it could do with a bit of paint,' she said huskily. 'If Ned doesn't want to do it, I'm no' bad with a paint brush maself.'

'We'll give you a hand,' said Lesley. 'Don't worry about it, Auntie Peg.'

39

'Oh, I'm no' worrying!'

But she spent no more time in the bedroom.

In the end, Ned agreed to do the decorating, if with an ill grace, and Peg chose the wallpaper and made new curtains so that the room did, in fact, look quite different and the girls said it would soon seem truly hers. Especially as she had put away Aggie's things. Whether she was happy about Aggie's bed being hers, too, they didn't of course know, but just the thought of her in connection with it brought a blush to their own cheeks. They lived in a tenement, they knew about marriage, knew about beds, but it was knowledge they kept to themselves and never included their Auntie Peg.

The decorating finished and the preparations complete, they'd all thought they could relax, but without warning, almost as though it had crept up on them unawares, it was the night before the wedding. Sam, who'd said he was too old to be having a bachelor's night out, spent the evening with his two elderly cousins who were to be his only relatives at the ceremony next day, and Peg, of course, spent it with her nieces and nephew.

They'd all had their baths, Ned down at the public baths where he could be out of the way, Peg and the girls taking it in turn to boil kettles and fill the zinc bath before the range. Afterwards, the sisters made much play of pressing their frocks and studying themselves in their new hats, while Peg went quietly about packing her case and Ned, his hair still damp, playing wedding marches on his fiddle until Peg finally called to him to stop.

'Nice, Ned, but I canna think.'

'Well, what do you want to think about? You're all ready for the big day, eh?'

'Och, yes.' Peg lowered her eyes. 'It's a bit of a step, though, you ken, that's all that's in ma mind.'

The girls turned to look at her and Ned raised his eyebrows.

'You're no' wanting to change your mind?' he asked.

'No. Oh, no! As if I would!'

'I've heard o' folk doing that, though.' Carrie's voice was hushed. 'Can you imagine it? I'd die if it happened to me.'

Ned grinned and began to warble, '"There was I, waiting at the church ... he left me in the lurch ... Lor', how it did upset me!"'

'Ned!' cried Lesley. 'Be quiet!'

'Sorry. Just a joke. Fred Leigh's music hall song, you ken.'

'No' very funny just now.'

'I've said I'm sorry.' Ned suddenly whirled his aunt round and kissed her on the cheek. 'Nothing like that's going to happen tomorrow, Auntie Peg. You'll see, it'll all go like clockwork and you'll be very happy.'

She smiled and kissed him back. 'You're a good lad, Ned, I've always said that. Good-hearted.'

'We're good, too,' said Carrie.

'You are, you're all very good.' Peg blew her nose. 'I think I'll put the kettle on for some cocoa.'

'No,' said Ned solemnly. 'I will. You sit down.'

And to think he hasn't had a drink all evening, thought Lesley. Auntie Peg's right. Ned is good-hearted. Or, can be, when he likes.

Chapter Eight

Peg's wedding to Sam was, of course, a quiet affair. Peg had said all along that she didn't want any fuss. This wasn't intended to be a big splash, for the more you had, the more had to be paid for, and money was tight. Still, some friends and neighbours had to be invited, they had to have a bit of a do, and Peg had willingly withdrawn savings from the post office to pay for it, while Sam had made a contribution.

Though neither Peg nor Sam were regular church-goers, a civil marriage wouldn't have seemed right to them, and the ceremony was held in the parish church in the Kirkgate. It was here that Peg's own parents had been married, and Sam's, and if it had also seen the funeral services for their loved ones, that only made it more their special church.

Everyone agreed that the bride, in blue with a white hat and white flowers in her bouquet, looked the best they'd ever seen her and that Sam looked very proud of himself, as well he might, eh, persuading sweet and clever Peg to marry him? Lesley and Carrie, both in rose-pink dresses with large, deep-crowned hats, looked grand, and Ned very serious, as though conscious he were the head of the family now. But Joe Halliday couldn't seem to stop smiling, probably because he was thinking of taking Carrie down the aisle in the near future.

'Och, it wis a lovely wedding, hen,' Mrs Scott, Janie's

mother, told Peg at the reception, breathing strong fumes over her and working hard to straighten her tilting hat. 'If I'd the cash, I'd ha' one just like it for ma Janie, and get you to make the outfits, eh? What a – what a – needle-woman you are, then, Peg, and me that hopeless—'

'Come on, Ma,' said Janie patiently. 'Folk are sitting down now.'

'I'm on ma way, and verra grateful, too. And when you get yourself wed to Adam Kay, Janie, I'll be inviting Peg and that's a promise, eh?'

'Oh, Ma!' Janie exclaimed. 'Never mind about Adam, now, just come and sit down!'

'First time I've seen Janie embarrassed,' Ned murmured to his sisters. 'But I wouldn't be surprised if her mother was right. I told you Adam was sweet on Janie.'

They all looked at Adam, talking now to Janie's sisters, Margie and Shona, like her in looks but not in character, and their great lazy-bones of a brother, Hughie, who could never be persuaded to keep a job. Aye, it was a fact, none of those Scotts ever did a hand's turn to help their mother, except Janie.

'I always used to hope Auntie Peg'd marry Adam's dad,' said Carrie. 'But Adam said his dad never wanted to marry anyone else after his ma passed on.'

Their gaze passed to Adam's father, an older, shorter version of Adam himself, who was at that moment greeting Peg and kissing her cheek.

'Might have been a good idea,' Ned murmured, his gaze resting on Sam, his new uncle.

Adam would have been a sort of cousin to us, thought Lesley. Would we have liked that? Yes, but what about Janie Scott? She might have ended up our cousin, too, and noble though she was, a little of Janie went a long way.

Och, Lesley felt she was wandering – it wasn't going to happen now. Auntie Peg was Mrs Samuel MacNab, and as soon as they'd finished the cold ham and tongue, listened to the speeches, and sampled the cake, they'd all be drinking a

43

toast to the happy couple. Lucky that Sam had changed his mind about permitting alcohol, eh? He might be satisfied with 'water bright' himself, but Lesley couldn't see it satisfying anyone else.

'Long life and happiness to Auntie Peg and ma new Uncle Sam!' said Ned, who had lost his seriousness now that he'd had a drink or two in him. 'Raise your glasses, everyone!'

'Long life and happiness to Peg and Sam!' cried everybody, and drank.

'Oh, dear,' said Peg, bursting into tears. 'Oh, don't mind me, now!'

'Oh, Auntie Peg!' sobbed Carrie. 'Don't leave us!'

'I'm only going for a couple o' days, Carrie, pet, I'll be back before you know it.'

No, thought Lesley. No, you'll never be coming back to us, Auntie Peg, not like in the old days. And now Carrie and Ned are realising that, too. Things are never going to be the same for us again.

After Auntie Peg and Sam had driven off to the station to catch their train for Dunbar, everything fell rather flat. The guests made their thanks and took their leave, Adam going off with his father, Janie and her brother and sisters helping their mother home – just in time, it seemed, for Mrs Scott was tearful and saying she wanted her bed. With the staff at the café standing around giving meaningful glances, it was clearly time for the MacKenzies and Joe to go home too.

'Should've had a dance,' muttered Ned. 'I could've played.'

'Auntie Peg said dancing was for the young ones,' said Carrie.

'Well, we're young ones, eh?'

'I think she meant a young wedded couple,' Carrie murmured, glancing at Joe.

'She worries too much about her age,' said Lesley.

'What's it matter how old you are?'

The others looked at her with wry amusement. There was Lesley being different again. Everybody knew youth was all that counted anywhere. That was why you had to try to hang on to it.

'I don't want to go home,' said Carrie. 'It'll be horrible. First time without Auntie Peg!'

'Let's go out, then,' suggested Joe. 'Let's away home and change and all go out. It's a nice evening. We can walk on the Shore, or something.'

'I'm playing at one o' the pubs,' said Ned. 'Booked some time ago.'

'You come with us, then,' Carrie told Lesley. 'You'll no' want to be on your own.'

'No, no, I'll be all right. Don't worry about me. I'll go home and change and put ma feet up. It'll be a treat just not to be at work.'

Chapter Nine

It was not horrible, returning to Number Fifteen without Auntie Peg, just desolate. While Joe went on to his own home, promising to call back in half an hour, the MacKenzies let themselves in at their door and stood silently looking round at the empty living room. Everything neat and tidy. Floor swept, mats shaken, range black-leaded. But no kettle singing, no books on Auntie Peg's shelves, no chair with its creased old cushion that always took the shape of its owner.

'Oh, look!' cried Carrie hoarsely. 'The chair's gone!'

'And the books,' said Lesley.

'They've been gone for two days.' Ned was tearing off his jacket and new tie, running his finger round his collar, for the evening was warm. 'She's no' dead, you know. Just on the train to Dunbar.'

The girls shook their heads and wandered slowly into their own room, where they began to change from their wedding clothes.

'Ned misses Auntie Peg just as much as we do, you ken,' Carrie murmured. 'He just doesn't want to show it.'

Lesley put on a light cotton blouse and fastened the belt of her skirt at her slim waist. 'Things'll no' be so different for him, though. He'll have us to run around after him.'

'Aye, like Auntie Peg ran around after us. Do you think we let her do too much, Lesley?'

'Yes, she spoiled us. Folk here always thought that.'

'Well, she won't be doing that any more.'

'No, she won't.' Lesley moved away. 'Are you ready, Carrie? Your Joe'll be here any minute.'

'I wish you'd come with us, Lesley.'

'And play gooseberry?' Lesley smiled faintly. 'No, honestly, I'd just as soon be on ma own.'

But when the door had banged behind Ned, away to the pub with his fiddle, and Joe and Carrie had strolled out into the summer evening sunshine, Lesley suddenly no longer wanted to be on her own. For some moments, she walked up and down the flat, thinking of Auntie Peg arriving in seaside lodgings in Dunbar and worrying probably about that first night ahead with Sam MacNab. A new life was beginning for her, and a new one, which was the same as the old one, only worse, was beginning for Lesley.

'I'll no' put up with it!' she cried aloud. 'I'll go somewhere, so I will, and that's a promise.'

Snatching up her hat, she ran out of the flat, down the stair and into the street where she stood uncertainly for a minute or two before hurrying off towards Junction Bridge over the Water of Leith.

She spent some time looking down into the unpleasant depths of the river, ignoring Leithers hurrying by who had in any case no wish to join her. The waters were always full of filth from ships and various industries and always smelled bad, but worse in summer. She was in fact thinking of moving on herself, when she felt a touch on her arm, and found Adam Kay looking down on her. He jerked his head towards the water.

'Terrible, eh? The river?'

'Disgusting. Why isn't something done?'

'It'll have to be cleaned up one day. How come you're here?'

'Oh, I just walked out, after I'd got changed.'

'You all looked grand at the wedding – you and Carrie and your aunt.'

'You look pretty smart yourself,' Lesley commented, glancing at Adam's dark suit, his 'negotiating' suit, as he called it. 'You're no' changing?'

'Got to see the bosses.'

Lesley stared. 'What, now?'

'We've something to discuss.'

'Can't it wait? I thought you'd taken today off.'

'Part of it.' He hesitated. 'There's trouble ahead, that's the thing. Maybe a strike.'

'A dock strike? No! Oh, Adam, that'd be trouble, all right!'

Lesley knew, as all Leithers knew, that a dock strike would cause conflict and bad feeling in the town, as well as hardship for the families of the men concerned. At least the last strike in 1911 had been soon settled, but she could tell from the grimness of Adam's expression that he was already fearing they might not be so lucky this time.

'It's no' definite, though? Might you still settle it?'

He shook his head. 'Canna say. Look, I should never have mentioned it. Forget I said anything, eh?'

'I promise.' Her blue eyes on him were troubled. 'I'm sorry, Adam, this'll be hard on you.'

'On everybody.' He touched his cap. 'I'd better be going, Lesley. Nice to meet you.'

'And you.'

His face relaxing for a moment, he found a smile for her. 'Now that your aunt's truly married, are you really going, then? Over the Border?'

'I haven't decided anything yet.'

'I hope you find what you want, anyway.'

'Thanks, Adam, I hope I do.'

She watched him stride away through the crowds still enjoying the evening, then slowly walked on as far as the Shore where she stood for some time watching the activity of the old harbour.

This was, as Sam MacNab had said, less than in the old days, before the docks, built in the nineteenth century, had taken most of the trade. The harbour then would have been the hub of the port, filled with sailing ships and passenger smacks, and had once famously seen the arrival of George the Fourth in Scotland. What a day that would have been, Lesley reflected, with the red carpet rolled out, all the grand folk bowing and the crowds cheering the king!

Fame indeed for the harbour, but things had quietened since. Even if the docks had not been built, there would have been no more tall ships or smacks, for they'd been killed off by steam, but there were still a few ships around and boats of various kinds – rowing craft, pleasure craft, private fishing boats. Newhaven, a mile down the coast, was the real centre for fishing, however, as Lesley well knew. Her father, though a Leither, had fished from there, and it was from there that he had sailed after herring and never returned. In common with Ned and Carrie, she didn't care to think of Newhaven.

She was about to turn for home, hoping she would be better able to face it, when she was surprised and secretly pleased to hear her sister's voice calling her name.

'Lesley, Lesley – so you came out, after all?' Carrie, running up with Joe in tow, grasped Lesley's arm and hugged her. 'Och, I'm glad you didn't stay in by yourself, then. Come with us, we're away to the chippie for haddies!'

'What, after all you ate at the wedding?' asked Lesley, laughing.

'That was a long time ago,' said Joe, taking her other arm. 'Come on, eh? We've something to celebrate, and all.'

'Oh, what's that, then?' As if I didn't know, thought Lesley, feeling their joy surrounding her, drawing her in.

'We're engaged!' cried Carrie. 'Aye, Joe's asked me just now and I said yes. Well, he knew I would!'

'And you knew I'd ask you,' said Joe affectionately.

49

'Help, another wedding!' cried Lesley, kissing her sister and Joe, much to the interest of the onlookers on the Shore. 'Can I wear ma same dress? When's it to be?'

Not for a long time, they told her. Why, they'd have to save up, eh? But they could still afford fish and chips for three at the chippie.

'Let's away!' said Joe.

Chapter Ten

The dock strike began on Thursday, 16 June. No one had really expected it. Suddenly, it happened. Three thousand men stopped work, and the news ran through Leith like a fever.

Sam MacNab, just back from honeymoon, was furious. He and Peg had taken a morning train back from Dunbar and Sam had gone at once to check how his new assistant, Roddie Pringle, had been managing in his absence. 'A long drink o' water,' was how Sam privately described Roddie, who was very tall and skeleton thin, with a sharp profile, but had the promise, Sam believed, of a good business head on his shoulders. It was he who'd told Sam of the strike.

'I canna believe it!' Sam cried, thundering up the stair to find Peg, who was unpacking. 'Another dock strike's been called, Peggie! There'll be gangs o' thae layabouts all over Leith, getting in the way o' proper customers, putting everybody off decent trade.'

Peg looked stricken. 'Another strike? Oh, that's bad news, Sam.'

'Aye, I'm telling you! It's thae union fellas responsible, stirring the men up for no reason at all. Och, I'll have to sit down and rest maself. Make us some tea, Peggie, and put a few biscuits out, eh?'

'But what's the strike for?' asked Peg, filling the whistling kettle and setting it on the gas cooker. 'I'm sure

51

there'll be a good reason for it, Sam, the men don't like to be on strike, they lose money.'

'They get strike money, eh?' Sam mopped his brow. 'Och, they want another penny an hour, says young Roddie. Seemingly, the fellas in Glasgow get eightpence and ours get sevenpence. So they're going on strike, all thae thousands o' men, to get one penny more. Would you credit it?'

'Yes!' declared Peg. 'It's no' fair, that they should do the same work as Glasgow men and get paid less.'

'Aye, but the employers say our men get good wages if they do a full week and it's no' long since they had an increase.'

'Sam, you ken fine what dock work's like, it's no' regular, eh? And the men have to jostle around and wait to get picked, and if the foreman doesn't pick them, that's no' work for the day. How can they all do a full week?'

Peg made the tea and poured it out with a slightly trembling hand. She had no wish to argue with Sam, but she knew, if he didn't, how much difference that extra penny on the hour would make to the dockers' families.

'You're no sticking up for these fellas, Peggie?' asked Sam, drinking his tea.

'I'm just trying to put their point of view. Adam Kay, who was ma neighbour, you ken, is one o' the union men. I'm sure he'd never be getting the dockers out on strike for no reason. In fact, I might ask him about it, when I go over tonight.'

'Go over where?' asked Sam. 'To the Kirkgate? You're never going over there our first night back?'

Peg opened her large dark eyes at him. 'Why, I'll have to see them, Sam! See how they're getting on. And I've got ma little presents for them, and all.'

'Little presents!' groaned Sam. 'You were only away three or four days, and you'd to go buying presents! Och, I'll never understand women.'

She went to him and kissed him. 'Come on, then, it was

52

just the once. I'm no' likely to be away again in the near future, am I?'

'But you liked being away, eh?' He pulled her to his knee. 'You liked your honeymoon, then?'

'Yes, I did,' she told him truthfully. For while she had not been pleasantly surprised by her first night, which was just as embarrassing as she'd expected, succeeding nights had been – well, no' so bad, as she put it herself. And when they'd gone to bed one afternoon, sneaking up the stairs at the guest house when no one was about, she'd had to admit she'd actually enjoyed her bit of lovemaking.

Not that she was going to tell the girls that, of course. Not a word about it would ever pass her lips, but very likely they'd be able to see that she was happy. Had been happy, anyway, till she'd heard about the dock strike. Oh, dear Lord, it'd be the bairns that would suffer, eh? Always was the bairns. Sam talked about strike pay. It wasn't enough, was never enough. We'll all have to help somehow, thought Peg.

The reunion at Number Fifteen was as tearful as though Peg had been away for years, and Sam was groaning with exasperation until Carrie announced her own exciting news, when he had to join in the congratulations and kisses and conceal his objections to Ned's opening one or two bottles of beer by way of celebration.

'Och, I'm that pleased for you, pet,' Peg sighed over Carrie. 'What a shame Joe's no' here, then, so's we could've welcomed him into the family.'

'We didn't think you'd be round on your first night back, Auntie Peg.'

'What, when I've got ma presents for you? Now just let me get ma bag.'

'Auntie Peg, you shouldn't have gone buying us presents,' Lesley scolded. 'Why, you were only away five minutes!'

But it had seemed much more than that.

'Just little things, eh?' Peg was murmuring. 'A shell purse for Carrie, now. And a brooch for you, Lesley. Ned, I couldn't think what to get you, but you might like these hankies?'

'Why, they've got A Present From Dunbar stitched on the corners!' Ned cried, as his sisters hugged their aunt in thanks. 'They're grand, Auntie Peg.'

Peg, looking a little strange on the sofa instead of her mother's chair, sat back with a sigh. 'Tell us about the dock strike,' she said quietly.

There was a silence. Sam, next to Peg, shifted uneasily, while Ned shook his head and his sisters studied their new presents.

'I think it might be a long one,' Ned said, after a moment or two. 'Adam was too busy to say much when I saw him on the stair, but he said Mr Kessack thinks the employers are all set to dig in this time.'

'Kessack's the main union negotiator?' asked Sam.

'That's right. Adam works with him. They think they've a good case for this penny on the hour, but it's going to be a tough fight.'

'And we'll all suffer,' said Sam. As their faces turned to him, he added, 'What I mean is, the town'll suffer. The folk of Leith.'

'It'll no' just be folk in Leith,' said Ned. 'Adam says there'll be men laid off at the collieries, because they'll no' get their coal loaded, and the fruit trade'll stop, unless the companies can get their ships diverted. There'll be consequences all over Scotland.'

'It'll be the bairns,' Peg said mournfully. 'It's always the bairns that suffer.'

'And for why?' asked Sam. 'Because of their fathers. It's wicked, so it is, for men to withdraw their labour and cause all this misery.'

'I'd say so, too, if I didn't know the dockers live in misery anyway,' retorted Ned. 'You canna blame them for trying to make a few extra bob.'

'I do blame them!' cried Sam. 'I do! Specially when they riot, and cause violence!'

'Sam, don't let yourself get worked up,' said Peg. 'Nobody's saying violence is right. I just wish I could've had a word with Adam, asked him what might be happening.'

'Oh, you won't see Adam tonight,' Ned told her. 'There's meetings going on all over the place, he'll be up to his neck in talk.'

'Talk, talk, talk, that's all that ever happens,' Sam muttered, getting up from the sofa. 'Peggie, I think we'll away home, we've had a long day.'

On the stair, Peg embraced all the MacKenzies again, with a special hug for Carrie and a whispered hope to Lesley that she wasn't leaving home just yet.

'Nothing's happening, Auntie Peg,' Lesley murmured. 'I'll wait to see how the strike goes.'

'Aye, that's right. Wait to see if you're needed.'

There were waves and shouted goodbyes, as Sam and Peg went out, then Lesley looked at Carrie and Ned.

'She seems happy, eh? Auntie Peg?'

'God knows why, married to that old devil,' said Ned, slamming back into the flat. 'Let him try living on a docker's wage and then see if he's so holy about striking.'

'Aye, but she does seem more at ease,' Carrie was murmuring, scarcely listening. She giggled a little. 'Maybe marriage suits her more than she thought.'

'Maybe more than you thought,' said Ned.

'Well, I couldn't imagine being married to Sam MacNab!' cried Lesley.

'But then you're no' Auntie Peg!' Ned was looking in the tins where his aunt had always kept something interesting to eat and finding them empty. 'Have you girls no' made any cake, then?'

'There'll be Auntie Peg's wedding cake, when she slices it up.'

'But what's for now? There's no' even any biscuits!'

'Och, cut yourself some bread and butter,' said Lesley carelessly. 'You had a good tea.'

'And you complain about running after me,' Ned muttered. 'Things were different when Auntie Peg was here.'

'I wonder what she meant about saying I might be needed?' Lesley asked Carrie.

'Helping with strikers' children's meals, I expect. But how can we do that, when we're at work?'

'We'll have to do what we can,' said Lesley. 'What d'you bet Janie Scott'll find us something to do?'

'Wait and see how long the strike lasts,' called Ned, spreading bread and butter with jam. 'I could be wrong, it might soon be over.'

'I don't think you're wrong,' said Lesley.

Chapter Eleven

The dock strike hung over Leith's summer days like a dark winter fog, for what was Leith without its port activity? It was as though the town had temporarily lost its identity, as though folk couldn't settle to ordinary life, with those unhappy men wandering the streets, waiting for the next meeting, watching like hawks for the arrival of the first strike-breakers.

In those early days, no one at Number Fifteen set eyes on Adam, who was working closely with Mr O'Connor Kessack, the chief negotiator, and Councillor Kibble, the union secretary, but his father told Ned that he only came home at night to get a bite to eat and to snatch a few hours' sleep.

'And then he's off again, Ned, here, there, everywhere, wearing hisself to skin and bone, eh?' Jock Kay shook his head. 'The worst of it is, he'll get nowhere. Aye, folk like me've seen it all before. We'll be out, we'll talk, and we'll be back, without a thing being different. You wait and see.'

'I don't know how you can be so sure, Mr Kay,' Ned said uneasily. 'You've got a bit of power, you know, you can withdraw your labour.'

Jock smiled wryly. 'How long for, without gettin' paid?'

'Well, you'll have your strike pay.'

'Ten shillin' after we've been out seven days? Canna manage on that, Ned, no' for long. And if the employers

57

bring in strike-breakers, they'll no' miss us.'

'You fellows could stop the strike-breakers, eh?'

'Ever heard o' the polis?' asked Jock. 'There's an extra three hundred here already. Soon as the strike-breakers arrive, the polis'll close the dock gates, and then what do we do? Och, I tellt Adam when I seen him this forenoon, stay in your bed, laddie, you'll do just as much good.'

And I bet he was pleased about that, thought Ned. Yet he had the feeling that Adam's father might well be right; the men could suffer for weeks and get nothing. As he played his fiddle in one of the Shore pubs that evening, he felt a hard knot of guilt in his chest that he was not out on strike but doing something he liked and getting paid for it, as well as having a weekly wage he could count on. But what could he do? Put a few coppers in a collection, if one were set up for the striking dockers, and hope somebody was doing something about feeding the bairns?

'Want another, Ned?' asked a fellow bringing over a pint, and as he paused in his playing, Ned laughed.

'Aye, I'll drown ma sorrows,' he answered.

Only the sorrows weren't his.

Seemed somebody was doing something about feeding the families of the strikers, as news came early in July that the School Board was providing the children with hot meals under its school holidays feeding scheme.

'Aye, but I'm no' happy about it!' cried Janie Scott, calling in at Number Fifteen one evening, after seeking Adam and of course not finding him.

'Whyever not?' asked Lesley, who had just arrived home from work and was helping Carrie to get their tea together. Oh Lord, now was the time they missed Auntie Peg, who had always managed to produce excellent food as though out of a conjuror's hat, for she too had already done a full day's work before she began cooking. 'I'd have thought it was grand, that the bairns were sure o' getting something to eat. Carrie, have we any carrots left?'

'They're in the stew,' Carrie answered, looking dubiously into a pan she was stirring on the range. 'Can you do a few tatties?'

'Where's Ned? You'd think he could do a bit, eh? He gets in before me.'

'Bringing up the coal.' Carrie glanced across at Janie, who seemed oblivious of the fact that they were wondering why she was there and wishing she would go. 'Why aren't you happy, Janie?'

'Because I'm sure the Board'll no' keep it up, I'm sure they're already regretting it, because it'll look as though they're helping the strikers. And I've friends in the know, they say the same.'

'The Board'd never be so mean!' cried Lesley.

'Mean?' Janie gave a contemptuous laugh. 'Didn't you hear that a hundred and fifty men arrived yesterday to break the strike? Talk about mean! The Shipping Federation arranged it all and promised 'em thirty-five shilling a week. Thirty-five bob a week! Would you credit it?'

'What happened?' asked Carrie, her eyes large and apprehensive.

'Och, the polis took 'em along to the Imperial Dock. Then another lot came in by ship and the polis locked the dock gates.'

'Who locked the gates?' asked Ned, coming in with a hod of coal for the range. 'Hello, Janie, what brings you here?'

'I wanted to catch Adam, but he's out, of course. Just thought I'd look in on you folk.'

'Was it the polis locked the gates?'

'Who else?'

'Just what Adam's dad said they'd do when the strike-breakers came.' Ned wiped a dusty finger across his brow, leaving a large smudge. 'Was there no trouble, then?'

'Well, some of the lads persuaded the blacklegs to go home. Gave 'em a couple of bob each, and they had the decency to leave. The rest, och, no, they're at work.'

59

'There will be trouble,' Ned murmured. 'I think we can be sure of that.'

'There's more bad news,' said Janie. 'Really bad news, this is. Mr Kessack's had an accident on his motor bike, hurt his head and been taken to the Royal. Now where does that leave poor Adam? He'll have everything to do!'

'No wonder you wanted to see him,' remarked Lesley.

'Aye, but I was pretty certain I wouldn't find him. Listen, I wanted to ask you – if the school meals are stopped, would you girls be willing to help with another feeding scheme for the children?'

Lesley and Carrie hesitated. 'What sort of scheme?'

'Well, some of us are trying to work it out. There's a lady who says she could do it, if the worst comes to the worst, but we'd need cash and helpers. What do you say?'

'I'd like to help, but I'm at work in Edinburgh,' said Lesley. 'I canna get away.'

Janie swung round on Carrie. 'What about you, Carrie? You could do a bit in your dinner hour, couldn't you?'

'I suppose I could,' Carrie answered doubtfully. 'But old Simpson'd never give me time off, I'd have to be back on the dot.'

'I could try to raise a few bob at the Louise,' Lesley volunteered. 'And, Ned, you could take your hat round in the pubs.'

'Sure, I could. But why should the school meals stop?'

'They might not,' Janie answered. 'But there's a possibility and we have to be prepared. Well, I'll be going. Better no' hold you folks up from your tea.' She put on the straw hat she had been swinging in her hand, and smiled briefly. 'How are you getting on without your auntie, then?'

'Fine,' said Lesley promptly.

'We're managing,' said Carrie.

'Whyn't you ask Auntie Peg for help if you need it?' asked Ned. 'She'd cook for the bairns like a shot.'

Janie's eyes lit up. 'That's a grand idea, Ned. I'll ask her tomorrow. If you see Adam, tell him I was round, eh? Bye, then, bye!'

And she was gone, feet lightly taking her down the stair, and then they heard the street door bang behind her.

'Phew!' sighed Ned. 'What a live wire, eh?'

'Tiring live wire,' commented Lesley. 'Carrie, is that water boiling? These tatties can go in.'

'Bad news about Mr Kessack,' Ned murmured, rubbing his hankie over the smudge on his brow. 'Poor old Adam, he'll be up to his eyes.'

'As long as there's no trouble,' Carrie whispered.

'Oh, there will be,' Ned told her. 'Like I said. Just depends when.'

Chapter Twelve

Early on the morning of 9 July, Ned was wakened in his pull-down bed, though what had roused him, he didn't know. It was still dark, but not worth lighting the gas, and he struck a match instead to look at his watch. Half past three. Oh, God, that was a fine time to be pulled out of a fella's sleep, eh? But then he heard the voices and the steps on the stair.

Pulling on his trousers over his vest and underpants, he opened the door of the flat and looked out, in time to see Adam, fully dressed, hurrying past, accompanied by his father and a couple of men.

'Adam!' Ned hissed. 'What's going on? Where the hell are you going?'

'Sorry, Ned, canna stop. There's a train due at the Citadel carrying strike-breakers.' Adam gave a harassed grin. 'Sorry we woke you.'

As he turned to continue on downstairs, Ned ran after him. 'There's going to be trouble?'

'Aye, the men are gathering. We'll have to control them. The last thing we want is violence.'

'Do you want me to come?'

Adam hesitated, as his father waited and the other men stood, sighing and shifting from foot to foot, chafing at the delay.

'Why should you, Ned? I don't want you to get hurt.'

'You go on, I'll follow,' said Ned, already turning back to get dressed.

He was writing a note for his sisters by the light of a candle when they both appeared, hair in plaits, faces white, shawls over their nightgowns, for the summer morning was chill.

'Ned, what's up?' asked Lesley. 'Whatever are you doing, dressed and all?'

'We heard the voices on the stair,' said Carrie. 'Is there trouble?'

'Aye, Adam's gone to the Citadel Station, there's a whole gang of strike-breakers coming in and the men are looking for a fight.'

The girls' eyes grew large. 'Poor Adam,' whispered Lesley. 'What a job, eh? But why should you go, Ned? You might get hurt.'

'I might be able to help Adam, he's going to have to try to hold the men back.'

'The polis'll do that,' said Carrie. 'Have a cup of tea first, anyway.'

'You have tea,' Ned said. 'I'm away.'

The first streaks of the dawn were colouring the sky as Ned raced through the quiet streets towards the Citadel Station, passing on his way other men, also running, all dockers.

'What time's the train due in?' he asked one, who knew without asking which train he meant.

'We're no' sure, laddie, but there's folk along the line checking.' He took a deep breath and grinned. 'Soon as it comes, it'll get a welcome, eh? Too bloody right, it will! See what I've got?'

Oh, God, whatever can Adam do? thought Ned, looking at the large brick in the man's hand. Looks like he'll be dependent on the police to stop fellas like this.

At least, the police were already at the station, lined up, batons at the ready, facing a crowd of jeering dockers. These had been blocked from entering the station platform, but as Ned came up, panting, his heart sank, for it was plain that from where they were the dockers could still hit the train. And even if the strike-breakers tried to hide, they would eventually have to cross over Commercial Street to get to the dock gates, where the waiting men, a few women, too, would find them easy targets, police, or no police.

Oh, where's Adam? groaned Ned, searching the crowd with his eyes, and suddenly saw him, standing with Councillor Kibble and his father. Though his pallor was revealed by the light that was clearing with every moment, he looked as strong and resolute as Ned had ever seen him, his determined chin jutting out, his cap pushed to the back of his head, his great hands waving at the crowd.

'For God's sake, drop your stones!' he was shouting. 'Where's violence going to get you? If you all end up in gaol, how will we get an agreement?'

'Adam Kay, shut your mouth!' a heavily built man close to Adam shouted.

'Billy MacSween, shut yours!' retorted Jock Kay.

'No, no, Jock, we ken fine your boy's workin' for us, but we're no' listenin' to him today, eh, lads?'

'We're no' listenin'!' roared the crowd.

''Cause thae scabs are comin' here, takin' oor jobs, starvin' oor bairns—'

'Aye, starvin' oor bairns!' screamed a woman, holding a piece of concrete to her chest. 'D'ye want us tae stand by and see them dae it?'

'No, no!' the people round her cried, but Adam and Councillor Kibble were undaunted.

'No violence!' they shouted. 'The Union'll no' back up violence! Negotiation's the only way!'

But the crowd was hearing something more to their liking. It was the sound of an approaching train.

'Here they come!' the new cry went up. 'Let 'em have it, lads!'

As the train pulled up at the platform, stones, bricks

and bottles flew through the air, smashing windows and causing the men inside to cower in terror. They had expected hostility, but nothing like this, and at the looks on their faces, the crowd laughed and continued their bombardment.

'For God's sake, stop!' Adam shouted, but his voice was lost and he was forced to stand back as the police rushed to get the strike-breakers out of the train. Some had flung themselves to the floors of the carriages, others had leaped out and hidden beneath the train itself, but their efforts were pointless, they had to face the crowd to get to the dock gates and the crowd was waiting.

'Run!' the police shouted at their shaking charges, forming double lines across Commercial Street and, as the men hared towards the gates, the police drew batons and charged the crowd, now hurling bricks and stones again, and even concrete sets from the road which they had previously levered up.

'Adam,' Ned whispered, getting close to him at last. 'This is hell, eh? Nobody can do anything.'

Adam groaned and glanced at his father, who was shaking his head in despair. 'It's like it always is,' Adam muttered. 'A few trouble-makers egging on the rest. Most of 'em don't want this, Ned, they don't!'

'I know,' Ned was beginning to answer, when a sudden surge of the crowd carried him away. He felt a violently sharp pain to his head, then something flowed down the side of his face and he knew it was blood.

'Ned, Ned!' he could hear Adam's voice, but it was very faint. Now why was Adam's voice so faint? Soon, he couldn't hear it at all.

Back in the Kirkgate, Lesley and Carrie were ready to leave for work. They'd had their breakfast and washed up, they'd tidied everything in sight, they'd put on their summer straw hats with trembling fingers, all the time hardly daring to speak. For Ned had not come back and they knew in their hearts, as people do, that something bad had happened, either to him, or Adam, or someone.

'I've to leave for ma train,' Lesley said tightly. 'What'll we do? Ned's had no breakfast.'

'Where is he?' whispered Carrie. 'Oh, I wish Joe would come! Have you heard the post?'

'I'd have said if I had.' Lesley stood in thought. 'D'you think we should have gone to the Citadel? I kept thinking Ned'd be back, didn't you?'

'There's no time to go now.' Carrie grabbed her bag. 'I'm away down the stair to wait for Joe. He might've heard something.'

'I'll come, too.'

But Adam was already leaping up the stair towards them, his expression so grim, what colour they had left their faces.

'What is it?' cried Lesley. 'Is it Ned?'

'Aye, but don't worry, he's going to be all right.'

'He's hurt?' shrieked Carrie.

'He was accidentally hit by a piece of brick.' Adam put his arm round Carrie, who had instantly burst into tears, and looked with sombre eyes over her head at Lesley. 'He's been taken to Leith Hospital with a couple of other fellows, but he's no' badly hurt, I promise you.'

'Can we see him?' Lesley asked hoarsely.

'Aye, but he'll be waiting for stitches, I should think. A nurse did say he might be kept in overnight, just for observation, you ken.' Adam released Carrie, who stood wiping her eyes. 'Look, there were some ugly scenes at the station and I've got to go, I've to speak to the press and God knows what, but I wanted to tell you maself what had happened to Ned.'

'Thank you,' said Lesley, as Carrie continued to sob.

'We knew something had happened, didn't we, Lesley? Oh, I wish Joe'd come!'

'Anybody up there?' came Joe's voice from below and Carrie, as if pulled by wires, leaped down to greet him and fell into his arms.

'I shouldn't have let Ned come this morning,' Adam murmured to Lesley. 'It wasn't his war, but he wanted to help me.'

'You knew there'd be violence?'

'Aye, the men were spoiling for it.' Adam sighed and ran his hands through his hair. 'I suppose you canna blame them, in a way. It's their livelihood that's threatened, it's their families they have to think about.' He put forward his chin. 'But I won't have violence, Lesley. It's bad, it's wrong, and it does no good. The Councillor told 'em that, but they'd no' listen to anyone, once they'd worked themselves up for trouble.'

'And I suppose the strike-breakers got into the docks anyway?'

'Aye, they did.' Adam put on his cap and turned to go. 'Feel that bad about Ned, I canna tell you. But I'll try to get to the hospital to see him later on.'

'That's good of you,' Lesley murmured, then her eyes widened and she put a hand to her lips. 'Carrie, Carrie!' she called, running down the stair after Adam. 'We've forgotten Auntie Peg! We'll have to tell her about Ned, she'll want to go to the hospital.'

'We'll all want to go,' said Carrie, holding hands with sympathetic Joe, as Adam left them. 'But what'll we do about work?'

'Ask old Simpson to give you half an hour off, and I'll just go in late,' said Lesley. 'I'll get Sam to make a telephone call from his shop. Oh, and one of us'd better tell Ned's boss as well.'

'Want me to do that?' asked Joe. 'I pass Boyd's on ma route.'

'Would you, Joe? Oh, that'd be a help.' Lesley put her hand to her brow. 'So many things to think of, eh? But I'll run round now to see Auntie Peg, then we'll come to the shop for you, Carrie. We can all go to the hospital together.'

And holding her narrow skirt above her ankles, Lesley raced from the house.

Chapter Thirteen

It was evening before his family was allowed to see Ned, who had been put to bed in a ward and was only just conscious. As a doctor explained to Peg and his sisters when they arrived in the morning, it wasn't the blow from the brick that had caused the real damage, it was the fact that he when he collapsed, he had hit his head on a concrete block left by a striker. That might have caused concussion.

'He's feeling a bit sick, but we think he's going to be all right, we just want to see how he goes,' the doctor added. 'And we'd like you to leave visiting for a few hours, if you wouldn't mind. Could you come back this evening?'

'And only two at a time, please,' a nurse said briskly. 'For fifteen minutes at the most.'

'Oh, poor Ned,' sighed Peg, as they left the hospital. 'He should never have been at the station, anyway. He wasn't involved with the strikers.'

She'd said much the same at Sam's shop when Lesley had given her the news of Ned's accident, and Sam had snorted and cried, 'I hope not!'

'Did I no' tell you there'd be trouble?' he asked Peg. 'Did I no' say there'd be violence, just like we've had before?'

'I must get to see Ned,' was Peg's only reply. 'Where's ma hat, then?'

'You're going now? I thought you said you'd be helping young Roddie this forenoon?'

'Well I can't help him now, can I?' Peg found her hat and put it on. 'Ned comes first, Sam.'

'Of course, of course. But come back soon as you can, Peggie, you can always go round to the hospital this evening, eh? We can go together.'

'I'm seeing Ned this morning,' Peg said firmly.

And then of course they weren't allowed in, and had to return later, hearts in mouths, but without Sam, who had been persuaded to stay at home because of hospital rules.

'Only two visitors at a time,' Peg told him, and Sam had said, oh, well, then, he'd see Ned later, but they could tell him there'd be a cigar waiting for him, as soon as he was well enough.

A cigar, thought Peg. Who on earth could think of cigars at a time like this? But Sam meant well, that was the thing, his bark was worse than his bite, so it was.

'I'm so sorry I complained about you, Ned,' Lesley whispered, when she and Peg sat beside his bed in the long hospital ward, trying not to show concern over his white face and bandaged head. His eyes set against the pallor seemed almost black; they held none of their usual sparkle, they weren't Ned's eyes. Nor were the hands, lying so still on the coverlet, Ned's hands. Had he ever played his fiddle with those quiet hands?

'What wouldn't I give to hear him playing his tuneless exercises now?' Lesley asked herself, moving aside to let Auntie Peg get closer to him. And if he wanted Auntie Peg's room, he could have it, she wouldn't argue. (For, of course, there had been arguments about who would have their aunt's room now that she'd moved out, with Lesley and Carrie saying they should have it, there were two of them, they needed the extra space, and Ned saying it was obvious he should have it, wasn't it where he practised anyway?)

'Ned, we're thinking of you,' Auntie Peg was saying in

a low voice. 'The doctor says you'll soon be well, but could you just say a word or two? To let us know you're all right?'

There was a pause. Ned's lips parted. He said, slowly, 'I'm – all right, Auntie Peg.'

'Oh, thank God!' cried Peg, and burst into tears, at which the sister in charge, who was keeping an eye on them, frowned and said perhaps they should leave now, they might be tiring the patient.

'But my niece is still wanting in!' Peg protested, and the sister said if they would wait outside, one other relative could see him for a very short time.

'It's for his own good,' she told them kindly. 'Mr MacKenzie's doing well, but he has a little sickness and must be kept quiet, you understand.'

'We understand,' said Peg, and whispered to Lesley as they obediently left the ward, 'These people know what they're doing.'

'Oh, they do,' Lesley answered, her heart sinking at the idea that the irrepressible Ned should need to be kept quiet. 'But look who's here!'

It was Adam, with Janie Scott, in the waiting room.

'Seemingly we canna see Ned tonight, it's just the family,' Janie told them, as Carrie jumped up to take her turn. 'Poor laddie, eh? Getting hurt and him no' involved.'

'It's what comes of violence, the innocent do get hurt,' Adam grunted. 'But I'll have to take the blame, I should never have let him come to the Citadel.'

Janie's eyes flashed. 'No, you don't have to take the blame!' she cried passionately. 'Thae crazy hotheads who fancy a fight are the ones to blame, as well as thae black-legs for taking folk's jobs. What are you thinking of, Adam, to talk like that!'

'I'm weary,' he said frankly. 'And I'm no' done yet. I've to see the Councillor before I get to ma bed, we have to fix up more talks.'

'You go, then. I'll maybe see you tomorrow.'

'Aye.' Adam, touching his cap, said goodnight to Peg and Lesley. 'I'm that sorry, Mrs MacNab, but try no' to worry, eh? Ned's going to be all right.'

'Everybody says so,' Peg answered, with a confidence she didn't entirely feel. 'But don't you go blaming yourself, Adam, you've enough on your plate, eh?'

'I've never seen him so low,' Janie murmured, as Adam left the waiting room, head bent, shoulders hunched. 'He'll be back to himself tomorrow, though, you'll see. He's very strong.'

'Needs to be,' sighed Peg.

Janie was about to leave herself, when she suddenly turned from the door and fixed her eyes on Peg.

'Mrs MacNab, I've just remembered! I wanted to ask you – will you help to do meals for the strikers' bairns? It's just like I told Lesley they might, the School Board's backing out, we're going to have to do something ourselves.'

'The Board's no' going to give the children their dinners?' cried Peg. 'Och, that's shameful! That's mean!'

'Well, they don't want to seem to be taking sides, you ken. I said it would happen, and it has. But will you help?'

'Oh, I will, I will! Oh, thae poor bairns! Going to school with nothing to eat and fainting, I've seen it so often.'

'Me, too,' said Lesley. 'Carrie and me used to share our piece as far as we could, but it didn't go very far.'

'At least now they should get their dinners. I'll help whenever you want, Janie.'

Lesley looked at her aunt. 'But will it be all right with Sam, Auntie Peg?'

'All right with Sam? Of course it'll be all right!' Peg stared. 'Why shouldn't it be?'

'Well, you'll be going out over his dinner time.'

'Och, he'll no' mind, if it's for the bairns. Janie, when do you want me to start?'

'Well, there's a lady got it all planned, says we can do it ourselves if we can get the funds. She's worked out

71

menus and everything, all we need is the cash.'

'We'll do what we can about that,' Lesley promised, as Carrie joined them, looking tearful again.

'Are they sure Ned's going to be all right?' she whispered.

'Sure as sure,' said Peg. 'He's young and fit, he'll throw this off in no time.'

I hope she's right, thought Lesley, as she walked home, with Carrie. How dark the world seemed on that summer evening, in spite of the clear skies! No Auntie Peg to lean on, no Ned to tease and joke, no sound of his fiddle in the quiet flat.

'There's no ray of light, is there?' she murmured to Carrie, as they made their cocoa.

'Ray of light?'

'In the clouds. No silver lining.'

But Carrie was thinking of her own personal silver lining, and his name was Joe.

Chapter Fourteen

The doctors and Peg were right about Ned; he very quickly threw off the results of his injuries. After a two-day stay in hospital, during which he was treated for very slight concussion, he was allowed home, where he responded so quickly to being spoiled by his sisters and his aunt, he declared himself well again.

'I think I might be able to go to the pub,' he told Peg, who had come in to see to him while Lesley and Carrie were at work. 'No' to drink, just play a bit, you ken. And then tomorrow, I could go back to work.'

'Oh, no, Ned, that's out o' the question!' Peg cried. 'Why, you've still to get your stitches out, and the doctors said you must have the rest of this week off.'

'Mr Boyd'll kill me!'

'He quite understands, he said so. He's been very sympathetic.'

'That's a mystery, then, because he's another one who hates strikers.'

'Why, who else hates strikers?'

Ned, lying back on the bed in his aunt's old room, fingered the bandage over the stitched cut on his brow. 'Well, Sam's no' keen, is he?'

'Sam?' Peg's eyes flickered. 'He doesn't like violence, that's all.' She looked down at Ned's watch on the dressing table. 'Now, I'll just get your dinner for you, Ned, then I'll go home to get Sam's.'

'Aren't you going to be doing meals for the strikers' bairns pretty soon?'

'Day after tomorrow. Seeing as the talks have failed.'

'What talks?'

'Why, the union's talks with the employers. Adam said they got nowhere, and there's a big march planned for tomorrow. Don't look so excited, Ned, you canna go on it.'

'Who says I'm excited? I'm thinking there might be more trouble.'

'Well, thank God you'll be out of it, if there is. We don't want any more trips to the hospital, do we?'

The following evening several thousand strikers and sympathisers marched through Leith carrying placards with various slogans in support of their pay claim. Joe came round to Number Fifteen and said he'd be joining in, the people were only heading for the Links.

'I'm going with you!' cried Carrie, immediately putting on her straw hat. 'I'm no' letting you go without me, Joe, I'm no' sitting here worrying!'

'Carrie, you canna do that.' Joe flung his arms around her. 'If you got hurt, I'd never forgive maself.'

'But you do want to go on the march?' asked Lesley.

'Aye, I thought I'd just go along to give support, you ken, but if there was any stone throwing, I'd come home.' Joe looked pleadingly at Carrie. 'I promise you, pet, I'll be sensible, I'll keep out of trouble. It'll only be speeches at the Links, anyway. There's no need for you to come.'

'We're both coming,' Lesley said with decision. 'Ned, if Auntie Peg comes round, don't you dare tell her where we are!'

'It's sickening, me having to stay here,' Ned muttered. 'I feel quite well.'

'You don't look well, you're still very pale. You stay where you are and we'll bring you back something nice to eat.'

74

'What sort of thing?' he asked, brightening.

'Fritters, maybe.'

'Don't forget, then!'

It was strange, marching with so many people, and not a little frightening. For the first time, Lesley, Carrie and Joe realised how a crowd could take on a character of its own, quite distinct from the characters of its individual members. They realised, too, that it was the new character that could cause trouble, could make folk act with others in a way they would never act alone, and even though the crowd moving towards the Links was still peaceful, a thrill of apprehension ran through the young people and they moved closer together, holding hands.

'There's Adam,' Joe whispered, finding in that tall figure striding ahead a certain confidence. Yet Adam had not been able to prevent injury happening to Ned. Joe began to think – maybe they should turn back? He looked at the sisters, saw in their eyes that they were feeling the same, yet somehow, it wasn't possible, was it? Just to turn back?

'Once we reach the Links, I think we might go home,' he said in Carrie's ear, and she nodded eagerly.

'We'll go home, once we reach the Links,' she told Lesley.

'Yes, we'll have done our bit by then,' agreed Lesley, mouthing her words over the noise coming from a shrill fife band and tins being banged as accompaniment by a few young men. But at the Links, the crowd began to speak with one voice, and the voice was alien.

'Rush the docks!' it roared. 'Rush the docks!'

'Oh, God, they're making for Constitution Street,' cried Joe. 'They're going for the dock gates!'

They could see Adam waving his arms and shouting, but the crowd was streaming past him, and he and other union men were running to keep up.

'There'll be police at the gates,' Joe told the girls. 'There'll be more violence, we have to get away.'

They turned and tried to run out of the crowd's way, but there were too many people hurrying towards the docks and they were only whirled onwards. A woman carrying stones shouted to them.

'Are you no' coming with us? Are you no' going to help? We're going to throw thae blacklegs in the water, so we are!'

'That's where they belong!' yelled a man helping another to carry a long plank of wood. 'Come on, ye's folk, gi' us a hond, then!'

Joe's face was white as chalk, his usual cheerfulness stripped from him by fear and regret that he had brought this situation on Carrie and her sister, as well as himself. If only they could find Adam! But he was lost to them in the crowd.

'We'd better just go along with 'em,' Joe muttered. 'Say nothing, just keep going, and when we get the chance, run for it. We'll no' be the only ones wanting out o' this.'

That was true. They could see other faces registering the same sort of dread that was written on their own; folk going along with the mob, because they didn't know what else to do.

'Adam says it's always just a few who set the rest ablaze,' Lesley gasped, as they came in sight of the dock gates. 'But they're enough to do the damage.'

'Aye, because once folk are fired up, it's no' easy to stop 'em,' said Joe. 'Oh, God, will you look at that? There's people on the ground already!'

Stones were flying through the air again, the men with the plank were trying to use it against the gates as a battering ram, while police were already involved in baton charges and on the ground lay casualties, as Joe had seen.

'What'll we do?' cried Carrie. 'Oh, Joe, what'll we do?'

'Move,' said Lesley. 'It's all we can do. Look, the police are clearing the crowd, they're pushing them back from the gates.'

'You folk!' cried a young policeman running towards them. 'Watch yourselves!'

76

'Aren't we trying to do that?' cried Lesley. 'Where'd you want us to go?'

'Away from here, away from the dock gates. Get towards Bernard Street, there's more police there, you'll be safer.'

'We'll never be safe,' moaned Carrie, clinging on to Joe's arm, but Lesley was leading the way out, running fast towards the wide square that was Bernard Street, where there were so many solid lines of police in place, the crowd seemed to have given up throwing stones. As they began instead to boo and chant, the statue of Robert Burns looked down, as though alarmed at the sights around him.

'Mebbe he'd like to write a poem about the strike, eh?' gasped Joe, trying to manage a laugh, as it seemed they were out of the worst of danger, but Carrie was too shaken to smile, and Lesley only wanted to get the three of them back to the Kirkgate.

In fact, they were not completely out of danger, for as they made their way home, pots and pans and dishes were being showered down from houses on the heads of policemen trying to disperse mobs of strikers from the streets. It was clear that rioting would continue into the small hours and the only safe place to be was inside their own flat.

Yet Lesley was still thinking about fritters for Ned.

'Och, I did promise him,' she muttered, diving into a Kirkgate chip shop which had remained open. 'Thank heavens he wasn't with us!'

'I feel so terrible,' Joe groaned. 'I risked us all, eh? I was bloody stupid, that's all there is to say.' He held Carrie close, as they arrived back at Number Fifteen. 'For God's sake, girls, don't tell your Auntie Peg what happened to us tonight, will you?'

'Nothing happened to us,' said Lesley, running up to the flat with her bags of crispy fritters. 'We were lucky.'

'That's what I mean, that's what I mean!'

'Where've you been?' cried Ned, starting up from the sofa. 'I've been up and down the stair, looking out for you.

Gordie Jameson said there'd been riots at the docks again. You weren't there, were you?'

'Let's get the plates and eat these fritters,' said Lesley. 'Joe, find a chair.'

'You were there,' said Ned slowly, looking from face to face. 'I can tell by the way you look, you're frightened to death, you're white as sheets.'

'Do you want some o' these fritters, or not?' asked Lesley, buttering bread.

'My God, what'll Auntie Peg say?'

'We won't be telling her, Ned, and neither will you.'

'She'll be reading about the trouble in the papers tomorrow.'

'I think she'll have troubles of her own tomorrow,' said Lesley. 'She's doing meals for the bairns and she's no' told Sam MacNab.'

Chapter Fifteen

Sam was reading his morning newspaper over his breakfast porridge and spluttering with rage.

'Look at this, Peggie!' he cried. 'Thirty men taken to hospital with cuts and bruises after last night's rioting in Leith! Just see what they got up to! Windows smashed and shop goods all over the road and stones and bottles thrown at the polis again. Why, we even heard some o' the noise ourselves, didn't we?'

Peg put on her reading glasses and read the account in the paper over Sam's shoulder. 'That's terrible,' she murmured. 'I'm glad Ned was out of it this time.'

'But think of it, Peggie! A battering ram used on the dock gates! Is that no' shocking?'

'Shocking,' Peg agreed. 'But I see it says there were some folk arrested and they weren't strikers.' She took off her glasses and removed Sam's plate. 'You always get hooligans mixed up in this kind o' thing, Sam. D'you want your bacon now?'

'Aye, and some fried bread, please.' Sam shook his head. 'Well, whoever they were, they'd have been the worse for drink, of course, that'd be half the trouble.'

'The strikers have no money for drink, Sam.'

'They find it, Peggie, they find it. But this'll have done the negotiations no good, eh? Adam Kay'll have his work cut out to get them anything now.'

'It's a shame,' Peg called from her gas stove where she was frying the bacon. 'Most of the dockers don't want trouble, they know it'll harm their cause. And they've their families to consider.'

'Says here women were involved as well. Some carrying stones in their aprons. Can you credit it?'

'I suppose they're that depressed about the way things are going, Sam. I mean, there's no sign of a breakthrough.' Peg set down Sam's bacon and fried bread, poured his tea, and drank some tea herself. 'Meantime, there's so little money, the bairns are going hungry.'

'Well, their fathers should go back to work, that would solve that.'

'They don't get much when they do go back to work. That's what the strike's about, Sam.'

He laid down his knife and fork and looked up at Peg, who was not looking at him. 'What's up? You seem on edge. Is there anything wrong?'

'No, no. It's just – well, I should've told you before, but I promised Janie Scott I'd help out with dinners for the bairns.'

'The strikers' bairns?'

'Yes. There's a lady organising meals for them, but she'll need help, of course.'

'And it'll be yours, of course.' Sam's tone was acid. 'When are you doing these dinners, then?'

'Well, I said I'd start this morning.'

'And what about my dinner?'

'I'll leave it all ready, Sam. I'm going to do you a shepherd's pie. You've only to put it in the oven. And then there's jam tart to follow.'

'I'm no' putting anything in the oven, Peggie.' Sam continued his breakfast. 'That's your job.'

'It's just while the strike lasts, Sam.'

'And how long will that be?' He shook his head. 'I'm sorry, Peggie, you'll have to make your apologies.'

'I canna do that, I've promised I'd help.'

'Should've discussed it with me first.'

'I never thought you'd say no to helping bairns!' cried Peg hotly. 'Whatever you think o' their dads, it's no' their fault they're hungry.'

'Look, I don't want bairns to go hungry any more than you do, but you have to be sensible. There are things you can do and things you canna do, and leaving me without ma dinner is one of them.'

Peg sat without speaking. An image of herself as unwed Peg Darroch went through her mind. She would have been at work for Sam, but free in her dinner hour to offer her services. She saw the dockers' children as clear as clear, some without boots, most dressed in hand-me-downs, she saw their large eyes on the food being ladled out, potatoes and stew, rice puddings and jam roly-poly. Aye, she could have been there, as free as the breeze, feeling her heart sing as the children tucked in, but instead she was here, not single but married, she was Mrs Sam MacNab, and going nowhere. This was marriage, eh?

'I'm sorry,' Sam said, pushing his plate away. 'But you do see how things should be, Peggie?'

'Oh, yes.'

'I mean, if you'd discussed it with me—'

'I should've done that. My mistake.'

'If you want to go and help in the afternoon, maybe you could do that.'

'They'll all be finished by the afternoon.'

'Well, there'll be washing up and that, won't there? You could do that.'

Peg brightened a little. 'I suppose I could.'

Sam looked at his watch. 'Time for me to open up.' He stood at the door, hesitating. 'Don't like to see you upset, Peggie.'

'I don't like to upset you, Sam.' Peg went to him and took his hand. 'Maybe if I just went today, Sam, and then said I'd come to clear up in the afternoons? You could manage one day, eh?'

He sighed. 'I suppose I could get Roddie to light the oven, just for once.'

'Sam, you'd never ask Roddie to do that!'

'Well, he's a handy sort o' fella, he'd no' mind. I could give him a bit o' the shepherd's pie, he'd like that.'

'Honestly, Sam!' Peg didn't know whether to laugh or cry at Sam's handling of the situation, but as she cleared away the breakfast things, she knew she'd had a lesson she felt she should not have needed to learn. Young Lesley had had clearer eyes than her own. She had realised what marriage in its entirety would mean for Peg, while Peg herself had seen only the good side. But there was a good side, she knew it and must hang on to it, and next time try to be a little cleverer about managing Sam.

She'd make him put something into the strike funds, she promised herself, and if there were to be benefit football matches arranged, as Janie had said, she'd make Sam go. He liked football. Oh, yes, there were all sorts of things she'd get Sam to do, once she'd learned how, for marriage was like everything else – you needed to learn the tricks of the trade.

'All right, Peggie?' came Sam's voice from the shop.

'All right, Sam. I'm just starting on your shepherd's pie.'

Chapter Sixteen

While Carrie served children's dinners when she could and Peg did the washing up, Lesley went collecting for strike funds. There were those amongst her colleagues who were inclined to disapprove. After all, there'd been that riot, eh? Couldn't support lawlessness.

'I don't support lawlessness,' Lesley told them. 'Oh, no! I was there, I saw the mob. But a lot of the trouble was caused by folk who weren't strikers at all.'

'If you say so,' Alex Mitchie said doubtfully.

'And then the union's issued a statement saying they dissociate themselves from that kind of behaviour. Canna do more than that, eh?'

'Here's a shilling,' said George, giving Lesley a melting look. 'It's in a good cause.'

'That's really generous of you, George!' cried Lesley, wondering if the cause was the strikers' or his own, and sure enough he did ask her out again.

'I'm sorry, it just wouldn't be a good idea,' she told him gently. 'I'll soon be away, you see.'

'You're still thinking of that? Och, what's the point? Other girls are happy to settle down, eh? Look at your sister, she's engaged.'

'I know, but it's no' what I want.'

'What DO you want, Lesley?'

'I wish I knew, George. Just something different, I

suppose. And just at the moment, I feel – I don't know – all mixed up.'

And even afraid. Her experiences on the night of the riot had in fact affected Lesley quite deeply. She'd been shaken to the core to see the way quite ordinary people could behave, for though it was accepted now that hooligans and trouble-makers had caused the violence, it couldn't be denied that others had gone along with it.

Take that women carrying the stones who had urged the three young people to help in finding blacklegs to throw into the sea. Probably, she'd been just a pleasant little woman, who'd clean her stair and gossip at the steamie. But on the night of the riot she'd been transformed into a stranger, one so consumed by passion and hatred, she would have done anything to see men hurt.

Could such terrible feelings lie buried in everyone? Perhaps, even herself? Lesley wouldn't believe it. Yet the face of the little woman haunted her nights and sometimes her days, and she began to long for the strike to end so that she could get away. Put all her fears behind her. Yes, that was what she wanted, now she was sure. But would the strike ever end?

At the end of July, serious talks took place between government representatives and the two sides in the dispute, while another march was organised with the support of other industries.

'To think they're marching again!' Carrie wailed to Lesley. 'Oh, I canna bear it!'

'Don't worry, we won't be involved,' Lesley told her. 'We've learned our lesson.'

'And so has Joe. Poor lad, he's that ashamed he took us along, put us in danger, you ken.'

'He didn't take us along, we took ourselves,' Lesley said irritably. 'He's got nothing to be ashamed about.'

'But if we'd got hurt, like Ned, Lesley!'

'Well, we didn't. Look, let's put it out of our minds.'

'But they're marching again!'

'This time, there probably won't be any trouble.'

Lesley was right about that. The march passed off peacefully but served no purpose, just as the long negotiations ended only in deadlock. The employers had offered discussion on a matter to do with the handling of cargoes, but had once again turned down the claim for the extra penny on the dockers' hours. No one was surprised when the strikers voted to stay out, or that Adam Kay's face should grow paler and his eyes more strained, but he was completely at one with the men in their decision. They hadn't come as far as they had to give in now.

With everything seeming to point towards a long battle ahead, efforts to help the strikers continued. The promised benefit football matches took place, and though he grumbled about buying tickets, Sam was persuaded to attend. Carrie still served dinners, Peg still washed up, Janie Scott spent all her spare time flying about helping families, and Ned, now quite recovered, took his hat round in the pubs.

No one complained about what they did. No one asked how long would their efforts have to go on. 'As long as it takes' might have been the answer, and in the event they were stunned to find that that wasn't too long. Almost without warning, at a meeting in the Gaiety Theatre on 14 August, the strike collapsed. The men had gained almost nothing.

'I don't believe you!' Janie Scott cried to Adam Kay some time later, when he gave her the news. 'No, it canna be true! After all these weeks, all our work, you've given in! You've surrendered!'

Her eyes were filled with angry tears, her dark hair had slipped from its pins and was sliding over her shoulders as she stared into his desolate face and fiercely gripped his shoulders.

'Adam, how could you? How could you let it happen?'

'Janie, we'd no choice. Mr Kessack told the men—'

'Mr Kessack? I though he was injured?'

'He's recovered. He came to the meeting and he told the men they'd no hope of holding out against the Shipping Federation. They were just giving too much support to the employers.'

'You always knew that. They promised the strike-breakers thirty-five shillings a week right at the beginning.'

'Aye.' Adam shook his head tiredly. 'Maybe we should've realised then, we couldn't win. But we wanted to fight, we had to try.'

Janie, relaxing her hold on him, turned away. 'So the men voted to go back?'

'Most of 'em. They're weary, you ken. We're all weary. And they have to start earning again, for the families.'

'When's the return?'

'Monday.'

'On the same terms?' Janie gave a grim laugh. 'What a farce it's all been, eh? All that struggle and hardship – for nothing.'

'We'll be making modified offers. We'll fight on, Janie, as best we can. We'll fight on for better conditions.' Adam's eyes were hard, his head high. 'You can blame us for going back, if you like, but the struggle's no' over, I can tell you that. Just now, we need a rest. But soon, we'll start again.'

She gave a long shuddering sigh. 'I'll be with you when you do.'

He kissed her cheek. 'I know that, Janie.'

'The strike's over?' asked Ned blankly. He had just come in from work and was standing staring at his sisters, who were frying sausages. 'I canna believe it. When? When did they say it was over?'

'They had a meeting at the Gaiety,' Lesley told him. 'Mr Kessack was there and he told them it was pointless to go on. So they voted to go back.'

'They didn't get the extra penny?'

'Don't think so. Adam said they'd be making modified offers.'

Ned sat down heavily and put his fingers to the fresh, throbbing scar on his brow. 'So, what the hell was it all about, then?'

Carrie, mashing potatoes, shook her head. 'They had to try, Ned. You canna blame them for trying.'

'It's just like Adam's dad said,' Ned muttered. 'He told me it'd all be a waste of time. He said they'd come out, they'd talk, and then they'd go back, without a thing being different. And that's just what's happened.'

'We'll be dishing up in a minute,' said Lesley. 'Whyn't you wash your hands?'

'A waste of time, eh?' Carrie whispered, as Ned went off. 'He's thinking of his injury. And I'm thinking of us on that awful march. All for no' very much.'

'It's like you said, they had to try.'

'But all that effort, Lesley! Running along in ma dinner hour to help serve and Auntie Peg washing up, and you collecting and everything—'

'It was worse for the strikers' wives, trying to manage on ten bob a week.' Lesley began to serve up the sausages and mash. 'And think of poor Adam! Look how hard he worked!'

'And Janie Scott, rushing about like a paper kite! She'll be furious!'

'Think thae two'll get wed?' asked Ned, taking his place at the table.

'You're the one who always says they will,' said Carrie.

'Sometimes think they've both got too much to do.' Ned grinned. 'How about you, Carrie? Have you and Joe set a date?'

'You're always asking that. Are you thinking about losing ma share o' the rent?'

'No!' cried Ned, who was. 'Just interested, that's all. And then I'll need time to save up for your wedding present.'

'Well, you'll be the first to know, when we book the church.'

Lesley, her eyes on her plate, wasn't listening. With the strike over and Leith about to return to normal, she had suddenly realised she was free. Free to do what she wanted. To start looking for a new job. Why didn't she feel like doing that? I do, I do, she told herself. Just needed her energy to return, after these long weeks of involvement in the strike, that was all.

'Want these last sausages, Ned?' she asked, jumping up to take the pan off the range.

'As if you need to ask!'

As she put them on his plate, he glanced at her and wondered at her lack of sparkle. Not like Lesley, eh? She'd usually as much sparkle would make your eyes hurt. But she was probably as weary just then as everyone else, let down by the return of the strikers with so little achieved. They weren't dockers, but by God, they'd been through it all with them, and for what? Nothing.

He finished the sausages, sure in his mind that however Lesley was looking, she'd soon be off. Aye, to some grand hotel where she'd meet a fellow and come back engaged. And Carrie there was already fixed up. But that was girls, eh? They wanted marriage. Had to have it, seeing as they'd nothing else. Thank God, men weren't dependent like that. On the other hand – he mopped up his plate and drank some tea – he had his worries, too. How he was going to find the rent for this flat, for instance, if the girls weren't around to help. Could always take in lodgers, he supposed, as long as they could cook ...

'What are you thinking about, Ned?' asked Carrie, rising to clear away.

'Wedding bells, of course,' he told her with a grin.

'Forget wedding bells,' said Lesley. 'For the time being, anyway.'

Chapter Seventeen

As the warm days of August progressed, life for Leithers after the dock strike appeared to have returned to normal. But it was only surface normality. Under it lay a bitterness that would not be sweetened for many a long day, as those with experience of these matters said.

Adam and the other union officials did their best to keep hopes going that things might still improve, but there was no hope. Everybody knew that. Conditions would remain the same, or would perhaps seem worse, because earlier hopes had been taken away. The employers had in the end won so easily, the men knew where they were, and it was at the bottom of the pile.

One evening towards the end of the month when Ned had vanished to one of the pubs as usual, his sisters went out to sit on the stairs for coolness. Carrie was waiting for Joe to look in, while Lesley was yawning and stretching and wondering what she might do. There was a pile of ironing waiting for someone's attention, but she'd decided it wasn't going to be hers. The idea of heating flat irons on a summer evening did not appeal.

'Were you no' going to find yourself a new job?' Carrie asked, fanning herself with a handkerchief.

'Aye, I was,' Lesley answered. 'Well, I mean I am. When I get round to it.'

'Thought you were dying to leave us?'

'No' exactly dying. I want a change, yes. Just feel – och, I don't know – a bit low at the moment. Maybe most folk do.'

'I do.' Carrie winced as one of the babies up the stair began to howl. 'That's the Molloys' wean off again, eh?'

'You're feeling low?' asked Lesley. 'And you've got Joe? I thought he was all you wanted.'

'He is.' Carrie hesitated. She began to roll her handkerchief between her fingers. 'But the thing is, Lesley, we want to be wed.'

'Well, you will be.'

'What I mean is, we want to be wed now.'

Lesley turned to look at her sister. Carrie's face was turned away, her eyes cast down. Lesley's own gaze softened. She said gently, 'You're going to ruin that hankie, you know.'

'You don't know what it's like,' Carrie said in a low voice. 'Always saying goodnight.'

'I can imagine.'

'And if you don't say goodnight, there you are, in the family way.' Colour flooded Carrie's averted face. 'Happens all the time.'

'Well, you are engaged.'

'We're no' taking any chances, Lesley.' Carrie raised her eyes. 'But when we think how long we've to wait – och, it's a lifetime! And Joe's mother keeps going on, saying how much she'll miss him, and all of that, and he just wants to be with me.'

'Why don't you just get wed, then?'

'It's what we want to do. In fact, we'll have to, and that's all there is to it. But if we don't wait, we can't save up.' Carrie's voice trembled. 'How'll we manage without money?'

'I thought Auntie Peg was going to help you with the wedding?'

'The wedding, aye, she said she would. And I told her

we just wanted something nice and quiet, so it's no' the wedding I'm worrying about.'

'What, then?'

As the Molloys' baby continued to wail, Carrie shook her head and stood up.

'Let's go inside, Lesley. We canna talk here.'

Inside the flat, they found a bottle of fizzy lemonade and gratefully opened it.

'I'm desperate for a drink,' said Lesley, filling two glasses. 'Who'd have thought it'd be so warm, eh?'

'We do get summer now and again.' Carrie drank her lemonade, keeping her eyes fixed on her sister.

'So, what are you worrying about?' Lesley asked. 'Money for rent? Joe's got wages, he can afford something.'

'Aye, something, but we've no furniture. No chairs, no bed, no pots and pans.'

Carrie's gaze was so intent on her face, Lesley shifted uneasily and set down her glass.

'What's this leading up to, Carrie? I can tell you've got something in mind.'

The dark eyes left Lesley's face to look slowly round the living room.

'Everything we want is here,' Carrie said softly. 'Joe and me want to move in.'

There was a silence. Lesley swallowed, tried to smile. 'Well that's a surprise, Carrie, I never thought you'd want to stay on here.'

'Why not? It's the obvious thing to do. It's what families do, eh?' Carrie's eyes were shining. 'And oh Lesley, it'd be the answer to a prayer!'

Whose prayer, though, thought Lesley. What would Ned think?

'There's plenty of room, you ken,' Carrie was continuing, talking fast as though to prevent her sister from finding flaws in her proposal. 'I mean, think of the numbers that

91

live in these flats! There's seven Crawfords up the stair, all the bairns sleeping nose to tail. And then there's six Robsons and five Molloys—'

'Wait, wait,' said Lesley, succeeding in stemming the flow. 'You have to think o' Ned and me. You and Joe'd be newly weds, we'd be in the way.'

Carrie blushed. 'We wouldn't always be newly weds.'

'And then there'd be the bairns – you'd be sure to want children—'

Carrie's blush deepened. 'You and Ned might be gone by then.'

'I see. You want us away.'

'No! Oh, Lesley, just try to understand! What it'd mean to Joe and me to come here.'

Lesley stretched out and touched her sister's hand. 'I do understand, Carrie, and I think it's a good idea. As you say, it's the obvious thing. We should've thought of it all along.'

'Oh, Lesley, d'you mean that?'

'I do, but I'm no' the only one involved, remember. Ned's the official tenant. You'll have to speak to him.'

'We will, we will.' Carrie's face was lit by smiles. 'I'm sure he'll no' turn us down, though, he's a good lad, he'll understand. Oh, I canna wait to tell Joe!'

'Won't have to wait long,' said Lesley. 'I hear him now. That's his step on the stair.'

After all the kisses and hugs and sunshine looks from her sister and future brother-in-law, Lesley sent them on their way, to make their plans as they walked together, arms entwined, while she, after a little while, went out for an evening paper. But there was nothing for hotel staff in the Wanted ads. At least, nothing in any place she fancied.

Chapter Eighteen

'What it boils down to, is we're going to be Joe Halliday's lodgers,' said Ned, loping along beside Lesley on the way to the station. He had a french polishing job in the New Town – a huge mahogany directors' table that would take him a month of Sundays – but at least it meant he could go into town with Lesley and tell her what he thought of Carrie's plans.

'We are NOT going to be Joe's lodgers,' Lesley retorted. 'What a way to put it!'

'He wants to take on the tenancy, Carrie told me that last night. So, what else would we be?'

'Family. We'd just be a family living together.'

'Aye, I can imagine,' Ned muttered, as he and Lesley jostled with other commuters on the platform at the Central Station. 'Me back in the alcove bed, with the two newly weds in Auntie Peg's room that was going to be mine. And me with nowhere to practise any more, unless you let me play in your room, and I can guess what you think of that idea. Oh, yes, it'll be grand family living, so it will!'

'You did agree to let them move in, Ned.'

'What else could I do? With Carrie's great eyes staring at me?'

'And it's true, they've nowhere else to go. Could never live with Joe's mother, the way she goes on.'

'Aye, so they live with us and before you know it,

there'll be bairns all over the place.' Ned gave a groan. 'Heard that Molloy wean lately?'

'Don't remind me!'

'Soon won't need reminding. Look, the truth of the matter is, that once Carrie and Joe move in, everything will change.'

'The train's here,' said Lesley, thinking things had changed anyway, once Peg had gone.

'You ken fine I'm right,' said Ned, picking up his tool bag from the platform as the train steamed to a halt. 'Canna do much about it, though. It's right enough, Carrie and Joe have to have somewhere to live.'

'That's the thing.'

But when they'd managed to find seats and were squashed in together, Ned lit a Woodbine and gave Lesley a considering look.

'You've thought of something to do,' he said quietly.

'Move away?'

'Aye.'

'Haven't been very successful so far, doing that.'

'Och, you'll get something. Damn' good waitress like you.'

'You're a good violinist, why don't you look for a musician's job somewhere away from Leith?'

'It's what I'd like.'

'Why not, then?'

'Where's ma experience?' Ned blew smoke. 'Playing in pubs?'

'You do all that practising, I think you could play anything.'

'All right, you find me something.'

Lesley laughed. 'Have to find maself something first!'

That was easier said than done. Every morning, Lesley borrowed Alex's *Scotsman* and scanned the advertisements; every evening she bought the *News* and did the same. Nothing to suit. Plenty of jobs going in places she didn't want, but in the places she might consider, nothing. If she didn't find something soon, she'd have to try the agencies, but that meant taking time off, and they'd probably only have local posts anyway.

Meanwhile, Carrie was going about with starry eyes. Running round in her dinner hour to discuss wedding plans with Auntie Peg, buying dress patterns, visiting the minister with Joe, singing her heart out over peeling potatoes, or washing up. 'Westering home with a song in the air! Tumte-Tum, Tum-te-Tum, and it's goodbye to care!'

'Oh, God,' muttered Ned, shutting himself into Auntie Peg's room that was still his for a few weeks more, and playing his most difficult exercises and scales, until the Crawfords threw their shoes again and Ned was back on the landing, shouting.

Home, Sweet Home, thought Lesley, and was seriously thinking of paying a rare visit to the kirk and offering up a prayer, when the breakthrough came.

It was Sally who saw it first. She'd brought a *Scotsman* in from home before Lesley had had a chance to see Alex's, and before they began work, grabbed Lesley's arm.

'Found it for you!' she cried triumphantly. 'Just what you're looking for!'

'Where? Where?' Lesley was already turning the pages.

'Under Hotel Vacancies. Is that no' where you always look?'

'Yes, and so far there's been nothing.'

'Well, see that then!' Sally pointed a finger to an advertisement headed The Hotel Grand Forest, Glenmar, Ross-shire. 'Permanent hotel staff required: One assistant chef, two waiters, two waitresses, three chambermaids. Please write with copies of references to the assistant manager, the Hotel Grand Forest, by 7 September.'

Sally's eyes were dancing. 'Is that no' what you're looking for, Lesley?'

'But where's Glenmar?' asked Lesley, reading the advertisement again.

'It says, in Ross-shire. That's in the Highlands.'

'The Highlands?'

'Well, you said you wanted something different, eh? That'd be different.'

'But what sort of a place would it be? I mean, Glenmar?'

'Let's ask Alex, he knows everything. Alex, have you heard of a place called Glenmar?'

'I have,' said George, before Alex could speak. He took the newspaper from Lesley's hands and ran his eyes down the column. 'It's a spa. Pretty posh. Knew a fella worked there once. Said it was beautiful.'

'There you are, then!' cried Sally. 'A beautiful spa, Lesley! What could be nicer? It'll be full of rich folk taking the waters, like in Bath.'

'Or Harrogate, or Scarborough,' Lesley murmured. 'Sort of place my mother might've wanted to work.'

She raised her eyes to find George's brown gaze fixed on her.

'You're going to apply?' he asked softly.

'Well, it's the first thing I've seen that's of any interest.'

'How d'you fancy being in the Highlands in the winter?' asked Alex. 'I bet that's why they're advertising, can't even get enough locals to fill the posts, eh?'

'And all the seasonal staff'll be leaving,' added Sally.

'This fellow I knew, he said the weather in Glenmar wasn't too bad,' said George, then struck his brow. 'What am I saying? Lesley, it'll be horrible.'

'She's going anyway,' Alex said, grinning. 'I can see her thinking out what to write now.'

'We'd better get to work,' Lesley murmured. 'If Mr Hawkins sees me talking, he'll no' give me a good reference.'

'George, what happened to this fellow you knew?' asked Sally. 'Did he stay in Glenmar?'

'No, he came back to Edinburgh, as a matter of fact.'

'Don't tell me,' said Lesley. 'He got homesick?'

'Got promotion.'

'Good experience up there, then,' remarked Alex.

'Lesley won't be worrying about promotion,' George muttered, turning away. 'She'll probably get married to some rich patient at the spa.'

'If they're all taking the waters, they'll no' be very young,' Sally said, laughing. 'Hey, but if you end up lucky, Lesley, remember me, eh? I could do with meeting one or two rich patients!'

'How about a poor waiter?' asked Alex, and as he and Sally went off together, Sally still laughing, Lesley followed with her tray.

End up lucky? That would be if she got the job. It was all she wanted.

Chapter Nineteen

Now it was Lesley's turn to wait for the postie, hovering on the stair with Carrie, looking out for Joe. She always knew as soon as he came in that there was nothing for her, because his eyes went straight to her, even while Carrie was hanging on his arm, and those eyes of his were so kind.

'Nothing today, Lesley,' he'd call. 'Sorry, eh?'

Of course, he knew what she was waiting for. The whole of the Kirkgate seemed to know that Lesley MacKenzie had applied for a job in the Highlands and hadn't heard if they wanted her or not. Och, it was so embarrassing!

'Perhaps tomorrow?' Joe would say, and Lesley would smile and turn away, leaving him and Carrie to have their few precious moments together.

'Perhaps tomorrow,' Sally would say, her voice full of sympathy, and George would not say anything, because everybody knew what George wanted.

'Perhaps tomorrow,' Auntie Peg said, when she came round to Number Fifteen one evening to see if there was any news. 'They canna keep you hanging on for ever, Lesley.'

'I expect they've got hundreds of applications to answer, Auntie Peg.'

'Never! For a place way up there?' Peg shook her head. 'I bet they've a job to get staff when the summer's over. Think what the winter'll be like, eh?'

'Seemingly Glenmar is quite sheltered,' Lesley told her. 'I've been reading about it in the public library. It's in a wooded valley and very pretty.'

'Fancy. What else did they say about it?'

'Full o' nobs,' said Ned, coming in from Peg's old room with his violin under his arm. 'Big hotels, big houses, rich folk coming up by train from London and such, to take the waters. I've been reading about it, too.'

'I never know what these waters are,' Peg said. 'I mean, do they do any good?'

'They're mineral springs,' Lesley explained. 'Sulphur and that kind of thing. Somebody discovered some wells in Glenmar years ago, and then a doctor found the water helped folk with rheumatism and so on. Snowballed from there.'

'And now the place is fashionable? Seems funny, eh, up there in the Highlands?'

'Don't see why,' said Ned. 'What's wrong with the Highlands?'

'Well, you just think of the clans and fighting and that. Always wild, the Highlanders.'

'In Glenmar?' asked Lesley with a smile.

'Won't be any Highlanders there!' laughed Ned. 'I don't see the clansmen working in hotels.'

Just wish I could be, thought Lesley. How long till morning, when she could look again for a letter?

That night, when she and Carrie were drinking cocoa before they went to bed, Carrie suddenly said she felt bad.

'Awful bad, Lesley, about you.'

'Why?' Lesley started. 'What've you got to feel bad about?'

'Well, you leaving. I feel I've pushed you out.'

'That's a piece of nonsense, Carrie. You know I've been seeking to leave for a long time.'

'Aye, but that was just talk, eh? And now, wi' me and Joe, taking on the flat, you're really going.'

'Am I? I wish I knew.'

'I think you'll be going, all right. Because you think that you and Ned'll be in the way. That's what you said.'

'Look, don't worry about it, Carrie. It's best for you and Joe to be here. Ned and me both know that.' Lesley drained her cup. 'Now, I'm going to bed.'

'And then there's Ned,' Carrie went on, not listening. 'What's got into him? He's practising like a mad man. Is he leaving, too?'

'He's fancying a musician's job, I think.'

'He's already got one, hasn't he? He's playing at the pub now.'

'Wants something better than playing at the pubs.'

'And wants to be gone. You see, we've pushed him out, too.' Carrie sniffed. 'I knew he wasn't happy about me and Joe living here, I could see by the look on his face when we told him. And we'll be taking Auntie Peg's room off him, eh? He'll have nowhere to play his fiddle.'

'Come on, Carrie, cheer up! It's no' like you to be so low. Everything'll sort itself out, you'll see.'

'I'm just too happy,' groaned Carrie. 'I think I've turned selfish. And then there's Auntie Peg's furniture that she's left here – Joe and me don't expect to have it all. You and Ned should ask her about it. Take what you want, for when you get married.'

'For when we get married?' Lesley gave a burst of laughter. 'Don't worry about that, Carrie. You know how I feel about finding Mr Right. As for Ned, if you even mention getting wed, he turns pale!'

'I just want you to know how Joe and me feel,' Carrie told her. 'We're so happy, we want you and Ned to be happy, too.'

'I'll be happy if I get a letter in the morning, Carrie.' Lesley put their cocoa cups in the sink. 'With good news, of course. That goes without saying.'

And in the morning, there was such a letter. The assistant

manager of the Hotel Grand Forest, Glenmar, was happy to inform Miss MacKenzie that he was satisfied with her excellent references and wished to offer her the post of waitress in the main restaurant, duties to commence on 1 October. There would be a six months' period of probation and details of wages and all further information concerning the post would be found on the enclosed sheet. The assistant manager would be grateful if Miss MacKenzie would make her answer to his offer as soon as possible. The letter was signed Paul Armitage.

When she had read it through twice, Lesley slowly raised her eyes to meet Carrie's and Joe's. She cleared her throat.

'Well?' squeaked Carrie. 'What does it say?'

'I've got the job. One of 'em. I start in October.'

'Oh, Lesley!' Carrie flung her arms around her sister, and Joe leaned forward and planted a kiss on Lesley's cheek.

'That's grand, Lesley, that's really grand!'

'You've got what you wanted,' said Carrie. 'Haven't you?' She looked back up the stair and as Ned came leaping down, called to him. 'Lesley's got the job, Ned!'

'We're saying, she's got what she wanted,' said Joe, beaming, as Ned went to Lesley and gave her a quick hard hug.

'Wish I had,' he said lightly.

Chapter Twenty

George, of course, said it was his darkest day when Lesley told him she was leaving, and Sally sighed and said the Louise would be an empty shell without her. Even Mr Hawkins shook his head and said he wished he hadn't given her such a good reference, but he was an honest man, eh? He had to do what was right. So the Hotel Grand Forest's gain would be the Princess Louise's loss, and if the guests asked where that nice girl with the white hands had gone, he'd just have to tell them, 'Her heart's in the Highlands, her heart is not here.' At which Lesley blushed and said she didn't know about that, didn't know where her heart was.

'Och, you'll find out then, one day,' said Mr Hawkins, and Sally said, fancy old Hawkins talking like that! Proved he was human, after all.

'Are head waiters human?' asked Alex.

'Only when you're leaving,' said Sally. 'Wonder what the head waiter'll be like at the Grand Forest, Lesley?'

'Soon find out,' said Lesley gallantly.

Auntie Peg, rather red-eyed, said Lesley must have her mother's trunk that was still under the window in Peg's old room, and came round to Number Fifteen to sort it out for her.

'Still got all ma dress-making stuff in here, you ken,' she gasped, pulling the heavy, metal-bound trunk towards her and opening it up. 'What a collection, eh? Now I'll have to find room for it over at Sam's.'

'Where did Ma take this trunk, then?' asked Lesley, as she and Carrie helped to lift out the top tray that smelled of mothballs. 'She never did get down south, did she?'

'Well, she went to Berwick, and then to Moffat.' Peg sat back on her heels, thinking. 'And Peebles for a bit – she was in a lovely hotel there. Och, she was all over the place, your ma. Had this trunk packed and sent on, unpacked, sent back, I dinna ken how many times. Finally ended up here.'

After she'd died, the girls knew, and their parents' few pieces of furniture had been sold. But Auntie Peg had kept the trunk, and now it would be Lesley's.

'We'd better make arrangements to get this sent up to Glenmar a couple of days before you go,' Peg told Lesley. 'Then you'll just need your one case for the train.'

'Don't know that I'll have all that much to put in the trunk,' said Lesley. 'Haven't got that many clothes.'

'I'm going to help you buy one or two new things,' Peg promised. 'After all, I've a bit put by and I'll be helping Carrie, I should help you, too, Lesley.'

'Oh, yes,' said Carrie. 'I feel bad enough already, taking so much.'

'And I'll run you up a couple o' flannel nightgowns,' Peg went on. 'And don't tell me it's no' cold up there, because I know it's cold everywhere in Scotland in the winter.'

'Thank you, Auntie Peg.' Lesley and Carrie exchanged glances. Why did they always have to have flannel nightgowns? But it was true she'd probably need their warmth, Lesley thought.

'And we'd better get on with all of this,' Peg was saying. 'Time's running out. Still your bridesmaid's dress to think about and all, Lesley. Unless you wear the pink you had for mine.'

'Bridesmaid's dress?'

'You've no forgotten I'm getting wed?' asked Carrie.

'Oh, Lesley, it's November! You're just going to have to come back for it.'

'I will, I will!' she cried. 'I hadn't really forgotten, Carrie.'

But she had. Everything except her own new life had gone out of her mind. Now all she wanted was for the time to go by and her new life to begin. And the long goodbyes to be over.

One last goodbye was to Adam. She hadn't seen him for a while, though she had met Janie Scott in the street and Janie, though she had wished Lesley all the best, had been cool. She didn't approve of Lesley's leaving Leith, as she had already made plain. There was work to be done in Leith, by those Leithers who were more fortunate than others. Janie was willing to do it and Lesley should be willing too.

'We all have our own lives to live,' Lesley told Janie, answering the look in Janie's eyes, rather than her actual words.

'Och, it's no' for me to tell you what to do,' said Janie. 'Though how you'll like it up in the Highlands with rich folk pampering themselves, I couldn't say.'

'They're not pampering themselves, Janie! They're taking the waters to try to get better. Canna blame them for that.'

'And they need to be dressed up to the nines to drink a glass of sulphur water? If they ate a bit less and gave to the poor a bit more, they'd have no need to dose themselves.'

'Poor people do use the spa, Janie. I've read that they have their own pump room.'

Janie's lip curled. 'Oh, well, that's all right, then. Mustn't embarrass the well-to-do by using the same pump room, eh? Goodbye, Lesley, and the best of luck.'

Lesley, scarlet-faced, had walked smartly away, feeling furious that Janie always seemed to have the ability to make her feel small. She's no' the only one with a good heart, she told herself. But the way Janie talked, no one would think so.

It was a relief to be with Adam, who never made her feel on the defensive, though no one could say that Adam himself was as easy-going as, say, Joe. Heavens, look at that chin of his! The men in his union might have finished their fight, but Adam himself had not. No doubt he and the other union officials were already planning some new move, but whatever it was, Lesley wouldn't see it.

He'd knocked on the flat door on her last night, but when she'd asked him in, he couldn't of course stay, and they'd talked on the landing.

'You're really off, then, Lesley? But not over the Border?'

'No, the opposite.' She smiled. 'Up to the Highlands.'

'And a very grand hotel, Ned tells me. I hope you'll be happy, then. It'll be a new life for you, eh?'

'That's what I'm wanting.'

'You don't think you'll be homesick?'

'It's no' all that far. I mean, I'm no' going abroad.'

'Some Lowland Scots think the Highlands are abroad.' Adam laughed and Lesley laughed, too.

'I have the feeling Auntie Peg thinks that.'

'Me, too. Seems to me you'll be far away from Leith, anyway.'

'I'm hoping to be back for Carrie's wedding. So I'm no' really saying goodbye.'

He put out his hand. 'No goodbyes, then. But take care, bonnie Lesley. And good luck.'

'And to you, Adam.'

His eyes were grave. 'Thanks. I think I'll need it. Don't we all?'

She watched him run down the stair, waved when he looked back and smiled, and turned into the flat.

'Was that Adam out there?' asked Peg, who had come round with Sam for a special tea on Lesley's last night. 'Why didn't you ask him in?'

'He'd a meeting.'

'Always in meetings, that fella,' Sam muttered. 'Grand life, eh?'

'Wouldn't say that,' said Ned.

After the meal that had been cooked by Peg and was, Lesley and Carrie had to admit, better than anything they could manage, Ned, who had made the grand gesture of not going to the pub, brought out his fiddle and played for them. No exercises that night, of course, no awful 'studies', only the old Scottish tunes sounding so sweet and true, it was enough to bring a tear to the eye, Joe said, and certainly Peg's eyes were full of tears, and so were Carrie's.

'Honestly, anybody'd think I was going to India, or somewhere!' Lesley whispered. 'I'm only going to the Highlands.'

'You're still leaving us,' Carrie whispered back. 'And didn't you say Auntie Peg had left us when she only moved to Sam's?'

'It's true, she left us.'

'And so will you have left us, Lesley. I have the feeling, once you're away, you'll no' come back.'

'Why, I'm coming back for your wedding!'

'Aye, but things'll never be the same, will they?'

'Because now you've got Joe, Carrie. There's the real change, eh?'

Carrie's gaze softened as she looked across the room at Joe, listening patiently to Sam's account of the good old days in Leith.

'I've got Joe,' she agreed. 'But, oh Lesley, I'm going to miss you!'

Chapter Twenty-One

Tomorrow had turned into today. Time had run out, which was what Lesley had said she wanted, and there she was on the stair, ready to leave for her train, looking so radiant in the new blue outfit Auntie Peg had made, she quite dazzled her family.

I've made a good job o' that coat and skirt, Peg herself was thinking. Lesley looks lovely. But she's that excited, eh? Oh, I do hope she's no' disappointed! She's so far up, she can only come down.

But Ned was thinking, Aye, she's bonnie Lesley, all right, she'll come back from that hotel with a ring on her finger, what's the betting? And Carrie's thoughts were rather the same. Who wouldn't want her sparkling sister?

'Wish I could've come to the station,' she whispered, holding Lesley close. 'But send us a postcard soon as you get there, eh? Promise, now.'

'Promise.' Lesley picked up her small case, which Ned took from her. 'I'll write soon as I get there, then you'll really have some post for Joe to bring.'

'Here is Joe!' cried Carrie. 'Oh, Joe, you're just in time to see Lesley off.'

'Come away,' said Peg, as Lesley hugged Joe and kissed Carrie goodbye. 'Let's get to the Central, eh? You've to make your connection for Aviemore, Lesley.'

'I know,' said Lesley, swallowing hard. 'It's funny, you

ken, but I do feel I'm going to India, after all.'

She'd said she didn't want anyone to see her off from Waverley, yet it was comforting to have Auntie Peg and Ned travelling with her on the 'penny jumper' she had so often taken on her own. From the corner of her eye, she saw the cheerful young man she liked to talk to, and while Auntie Peg and Ned stared gloomily out of the window, she turned her head and smiled. The young man smiled back. Then his eyes went to her suitcase on the rack and his eyebrows lifted.

'Leaving?' he whispered, bending over her.

'Going to the Highlands.'

'For a holiday?'

'To work.'

His face fell. 'Och, that's a blow! Shall I no' see you again?'

'I'll come back one day.'

'I hope we meet again, then.'

'Edinburgh!' the guard was calling. Out scrambled the commuters, and Ned, setting Lesley's case and his tool bag on the platform, turned to give Peg a hand down. Lesley, with a last smile at the cheerful young man, followed.

'Who's that?' whispered Peg, taking her mind for a moment from her woes.

'Just a fellow I see on the train sometimes.'

'He's an admirer, I'd say.'

'I don't even know his name, Auntie Peg,' said Lesley, and thought how strange that was. It seemed to mark the end of a chapter, that she should be smiling goodbye to a man she had never got to know and now never would.

'Aviemore train,' said Ned, leading the way from a platform indicator. 'This way. Looks like it's already in.'

The three of them stood staring at the long train waiting at the platform, its great engine hissing, as passengers climbed aboard to take their seats and porters stowed luggage into the guard's van.

'Now, have you got your ticket?' asked Peg, determined to be calm and business-like. 'And your face flannel in your bag? Because you'll be sure to want to wash your face before you arrive. You know what these trains are like.'

'Got everything,' Lesley told her, the flame of her radiance wavering a little. 'Think I should find a seat?'

'Might as well,' said Ned. 'You'll be off soon. Change at Aviemore for the local train, eh?'

'Yes, it's a special express for the spa.'

They found her a third-class carriage in which the only other passengers were a middle-aged couple.

'This'll do fine,' Peg whispered. 'Have to watch out for fellows on trains, Lesley. Never know if they'll try to get into conversation.'

'Don't worry, I can take care of maself.' Lesley was smiling as she looked from her aunt to her brother, but her smile quickly faded. It was time to go.

Peg pressed a packet into her hands. 'Some lardy cakes, and a piece o' ma Dundee,' she whispered. 'Who knows when you'll get your tea?'

'Oh, Auntie Peg!' cried Lesley, throwing her arms around her aunt. 'I'll miss you, I'll miss you!'

'How about me?' asked Ned.

In the morning light, he looked weary and a little despondent, his cap hiding the scar on his brow, but not the knowledge that it was there. They had been through so much together, thought Lesley, and now she was leaving him behind. Leaving Auntie Peg, Carrie, Joe and all in Leith, and after Carrie's wedding it would be a long time before she saw any of them again.

'You know I'll miss you, Ned!' she told him, kissing his cheek, and he laughed.

'Miss making ma porridge, eh?'

'You devil, you'll still have Carrie making it for you now I'm away!'

The guard was holding his flag and looking at the doors of the train.

'Better get in, pet,' said Peg, as a porter advanced on the still-open door to Lesley's compartment. 'Write as soon as you can, eh? Keep in touch!'

'Oh, Auntie Peg!'

Last kisses, last embraces, then Lesley was in her seat and the porter had slammed the door.

'Stand back, please,' he ordered, and Peg and Ned obediently drew away. The guard's flag came down, the great train began to move, but Lesley, flinging up her window, was leaning out, crying 'Goodbye! Goodbye!'

Peg and Ned waved and waved until the train had disappeared, when they stood in silence. While other people seeing the train away were beginning to leave, they made no move.

'She's gone,' said Peg, after a moment. 'That's Lesley gone.'

'She'll be back for Carrie's wedding,' said Ned, putting his arm around his aunt.

'No, Ned, she's gone. She'll never truly be back. Never in the same way.'

'She says that about you, Aunt.'

Peg hesitated. 'I suppose I did make the break,' she murmured, as they began at last to walk slowly from the platform. 'But I'll never really leave you folk, Ned. I couldn't do that, whatever happened.'

'Well, it'll be the same for Lesley. Families are families, eh?' Ned pressed Peg's hand. 'How about a cup o' tea at the buffet?'

'Aye, I'd no' mind. But aren't you supposed to be at work?'

'I've some time yet.'

'I feel the better for that,' Peg sighed, when they'd drunk their tea in the station buffet. 'Thanks, Ned.'

'That's all right.' He was glancing through a copy of the *Scotsman* somebody had left. Only at the adverts, for nothing much seemed to be happening in the news.

Trouble in the Balkans, as usual. Always trouble in the Balkans, eh?

'Anything interesting?' asked Peg tiredly.

'Usual stuff.' Ned stuffed the paper in his pocket. 'Might as well read this later. Shall I see you to the train, Auntie Peg?'

'I think I'll just look round the shops a bit, now I'm here.' Peg smiled briefly. 'Take ma mind off saying goodbye to Lesley, eh?'

Lesley, in the train that was carrying her farther and farther away from all that she knew, was sitting quietly with folded hands. After all the excitement of getting ready and making her farewells she felt suddenly drained. Exhausted. Yet to the older couple, glancing at her from their magazines, she still seemed as bright as a shaft of sunlight in the dusty compartment. Where was she going? they couldn't help wondering. And where am I going? Lesley asked herself, too.

As the hours passed and the train ate up the miles, her fellow passengers went to the buffet car and Lesley looked in her bag for Auntie Peg's package. Oh, no! Her eyes pricked. There it was, Auntie Peg's lardy cake. Wasn't she a fool for crying over a buttered scone?

But she felt better when she'd eaten it and stood up, brushing crumbs away. When the others came back, she was looking out of the window, watching the flying landscape and working out in her mind how soon she would be in Aviemore.

'Going along for a cup of tea?' asked the woman kindly. 'It's good, we can recommend it.'

'Think I'll have one, then,' said Lesley, rising with a smile. 'It'll be a long time before I arrive.'

Part Two

Chapter Twenty-Two

It was a November morning, and early. Lesley MacKenzie and Ellaline Bailey were dressing in the room they shared at the Hotel Grand Forest. Ellaline, always called Ella, had just found a hole in the toe of one of her black stockings and was frantically scrabbling for a needle and thread in her workbag.

'Should've checked me stockings last night,' she sighed, pushing back the rich brown hair she hadn't yet pinned up. 'But that's me, eh? Always doing things at the last minute.'

'You get there in the end,' said Lesley, smiling, as she fastened the cuffs of her black dress, at which Ella grinned.

She was twenty-three years old, attractive and freckled, and a Londoner. Born and bred in Hackney, as she'd told Lesley on their first evening at the Grand Forest, though Hackney meant as little to Lesley as Leith meant to Ella.

'Well, it's not Mayfair!' Ella had said with a laugh and the way her warm brown eyes had danced had cheered Lesley just a little. And she seemed to need cheering, for she was already feeling something strange, something she'd never expected to feel and had wondered why others should. Couldn't be homesickness, could it? Never! Lesley was mortified. Homesickness was for other people.

Anyway, the minute she'd arrived at the splendid white hotel, with its turrets and gardens and views over the village, she'd known at once that it was the place for her.

It was what she'd come away to see. Grandness and beauty and guests who matched – everything was there, just as she'd pictured. Now why should she feel homesick?

Oh, Lord, because the Hotel Grand Forest wasn't the Kirkgate, and Glenmar village wasn't Leith.

Thank goodness, she had got over all that, thought Lesley four weeks later, as she waited for Ella, now pulling her stockings over her plump but shapely legs. And thank goodness for Ella!

It had been a wonderful bit of luck that they'd been allocated a room together, though Ella had said that their luck lay in having a room at the front of the hotel. Top floor of course, and half the size of the guests' rooms, but just look at the view! You could see right across the main square with its pump rooms and pavilion, past the silver birches and the massed rhododendrons, past the tall dark pines, to the blue hills beyond.

'See the pump rooms?' Ella had asked on their first morning. 'That'll be where the poor devils have to go for their early morning tipple. Wouldn't be them for the world, would you?'

The new staff at the Grand Forest had already been given details of the guests' regime. First glass of spa water to be taken at 7.30 am in the pump rooms. Then a stroll, or breakfast, followed by exercises, or baths, peat or mud, at a cost of ten shillings. More water to be taken before lunch, then more exercises, or walks or golf, then tea, and perhaps a talk in the pavilion before dinner.

After dinner, guests could amuse themselves. There might be dancing in the pavilion, there might be cards, but late nights were not encouraged. Early to bed, early to rise, was the motto, so that the whole cycle could begin again.

'Ten bob!' Ella had cried, talking of the baths. 'Can you imagine paying ten bob to be covered in mud?'

'I suppose they think it'll do them some good,' said Lesley. 'I mean, that's why they're here.'

116

And Ella, Lesley had wondered, why was she here? So far from home?

Seemed she'd fancied a change, just like Lesley. Seemed the Hotel Grand Forest liked to spread its net wide. There'd been an advertisement in a London paper and Ella had liked the idea of working in the Highlands. Liked to get around, you see, and was always willing to give everything a try, though not usually more than once!

Like Ma, Lesley had thought. And Auntie Peg might have said like Lesley, too. But who'd have thought the first time she came away, she'd just long to be back in the old places, when she was supposed to want something new? Here she was in the beautiful Highlands, and all she could think of were the boys on their bogey carts made out of old pram wheels racing up and down the Kirkgate! The folk buying broken biscuits and bacon pieces in the shops late at night; the Shore with its pubs and boats in the harbour; herself coming home from work to dear Auntie Peg. 'Is that you, Lesley? Kettle's on!'

'Let it go, dear,' Ella had called to her one night when she was lying staring into the darkness, her throat aching with tears she wouldn't shed. 'Go on, cry. It's the only way!'

'I'm no' crying.'

'That's the point. You should be. Well, you're crying inside, ain't you?'

Ella had come over to sit on Lesley's bed. 'Look, I know what you're feeling. I left home at fifteen. Went to work in Brighton. Lor', I was miserable! But I just gave in to it, cried meself to sleep every night for a week, then I felt better.' Ella patted Lesley's shoulder. 'You will, too. And it's no disgrace, is it? To miss home?'

'I feel such a fool,' Lesley muttered. 'I always thought I'd be happy, the minute I came away. Homesickness was no' for me. Showed how much I knew.'

'Well, you learn by experience. Doesn't matter how nice the new place is, if it's not home, you're sick at heart. But

117

then you get better. It's like the measles, you get over it.'

And Lesley had got over it. Gradually, as the days passed, the sharp pain of memory had become less acute and though she still thought of home, she had begun to enjoy her new life and to get to know the people who were a part of it.

Mr Wilcox, the manager, of course, she scarcely ever saw, but then managers were always grand and remote. He was considered to be nervy, anyway, and left much of the running of the hotel to the assistant manager, Paul Armitage, an austerely handsome man of twenty-nine who was said never to lose his temper.

'Unlike some!' Veronica Fyfe, the copper-haired senior receptionist, had told the new arrivals on the staff, and her bright young assistant, Alison Gow, nodded agreement. Vincent Chater, the head chef, for instance, you had to be careful not to cross him, he'd been known to throw plates. Then there was Colum MacNee, the head porter, always a crusty old devil, best watch your step with him, and Sadie Newall, the head housekeeper, oh, try to steer clear of her!

Ella said she'd already met Miss Newall's type before. Short, fair and narrow-eyed, she hadn't put herself out to make any of the new staff feel at home – and besides Lesley and Ella, there were three chambermaids, two waiters, a chef and Miss Newall's own assistant, Moyra Gillan.

'Thing is, she's just one of them women with a very good opinion of herself and a low one of everyone else,' Ella told Lesley. 'Always somebody like her around, dear, wherever you go. Just ignore her.'

'Well, I don't envy Moyra Gillan, working for her,' said Lesley who had already felt a certain hostility on the part of Miss Newall.

'She'll be all right. Nice-looking, but not pretty. It's the pretty ones Miss Newall doesn't like.' Ella had smiled. 'That's why she doesn't like you, Lesley. Isn't it bonnie Lesley those fellas call you?'

*

'Those fellas' were the waiters, old and new, whose eyes had lit up when Lesley first appeared on the scene. Big Bill Souter, from Glasgow, and Nick Lithgow, newly arrived from Edinburgh, others whose names were mixed in her mind and whose faces were a blur till she got them sorted out. And then, of course, there was the head waiter, Henry Vass, who was dapper and most superior, but who held a permanent grudge against the world, folk said, because he wasn't French.

'Aye, his name should've been Henri,' Bill said, grinning. 'Carries more weight in a place like this, if you can call yourself a Frenchie, eh? Like the head chef. He should be French, and all, but he's a Londoner. Mr Vass comes from Glasgow, you ken, though you'd never know it.'

'Talk about posh,' put in Nick, who was dark-haired and slender, with lively dark eyes. 'Canna blame him, though, for putting on the style. You'd expect a head waiter to do that here. Seemingly, they even get royalty staying now and again, so one o' the chefs told me.'

'Royalty!' Ella raised her eyebrows. 'Well, they'd be no trouble at all to Mr Vass, he's just the one for bowing and scraping.'

'Is he nice, do you think?' asked Lesley. 'I've got to ask him a favour.'

A favour? All eyes had rested on her with amused surprise. Only five minutes at the Grand Forest and bonnie Lesley was asking favours?

'It's ma sister's wedding at the end of the month, I'm her bridesmaid, I canna let her down.' Lesley's eyes had gone from face to face. 'I've no' dared to ask for the weekend off yet. What d'you think he'll say?'

'A weekend?' Nick shook his head. 'We don't get weekends off here, Lesley. A Saturday, or a Sunday, they said. No' both.'

'I know, but I thought, for a special occasion, they'd let me have it.'

'You look at him with your big blue eyes, Lesley, and

119

he'll no' have the heart to turn you down,' declared Bill. 'He's a bit of a ladies' man.'

'On the other hand, he might say you've to speak to Mr Armitage,' said Nick. 'And I'm no' sure your big blue eyes'll get you very far with him.'

'Hasn't even got a lady friend, they say, never mind a wife,' said Ella. 'But I'll tell you who'd take on the job tomorrow. Yes, little Miss Sadie Newall! Don't tell me you haven't seen the way she looks at him? That's why she hates all the pretty girls on the staff. They're rivals.'

'I think you're right,' agreed Nick, whose busy eyes missed nothing. 'I saw her yesterday, watching him cross the vestibule. No' the way she watches anybody else, I can tell you.'

'I know I'm right!' cried Ella. 'I tell you, I've seen her sort before. Always ready to set their caps at the bosses.'

'Ever have any luck?' asked Bill.

'Sure they do! Some fellas just take the line of least resistance. These women wear 'em down, like water dropping on a stone.'

'Can't see Mr Armitage giving in,' said Nick. 'He's a tough one, he is.'

All I need is to get to Carrie's wedding, Lesley had thought, letting the talk flow over her. Somehow she was going to have to find the courage to speak to Mr Vass.

But as she stood at the window on that November morning, it nagged at her like an aching tooth that she still hadn't done it.

Chapter Twenty-Three

'You ready, Ella?' Lesley called. 'We don't want to miss breakfast.'

'Ready!' Ella answered, putting a last pin in her hair. 'You're right, I don't want to miss breakfast. One thing about this hotel, the food's good.'

'Everything is good about this hotel,' said Lesley.

They left their room and made the long descent by the back stairs to the staff dining room in the basement. Here everyone was taking breakfast, the waiters and waitresses as quickly as possible, in order to be ready to serve the guests when they returned from the pump rooms. Some guests took early walks after downing their first glass of spa water, some strolled around, chatting, but most came hurrying back for breakfast just to get the taste of the sulphur out of their mouths. Who wouldn't?

'Ever tasted that stuff?' asked Ivor Greig, a wine waiter. 'Rotten eggs'd be an improvement!'

'The smell's enough for me,' said Ella.

'It's not really so bad,' declared Moyra Gillan, the assistant housekeeper. She was a Highlander from a neighbouring village, a pale, dark-haired girl with large luminous grey eyes. Lesley thought her very pretty, and not just nice-looking as Ella had said, and she certainly had one quality that nobody else seemed to share – she could get on with Miss Newall.

'You've tried it then?' asked Nick.

'Oh, yes, often enough.'

'Do you any good?'

Moyra smiled. 'As to that, I could not be saying.'

'Very diplomatic,' commented Bill Souter. 'Mustn't let on that the waters are no good, or where would we all be?'

'I'm sure they do some good, if people think they do,' said Ishbel Ord, a lanky young waitress with flaxen hair. 'And there are some bad cases here, you ken, they have to have some hope. Help, that reminds me – I'm on room service, got to fly.'

'Room service, what a chore,' Ella muttered, as she and Lesley also left the table.

'I don't mind it,' said Lesley, but her expression was preoccupied. 'Know what, Ella, today's the day. I've decided. I'm going to speak to Mr Vass.'

'About that weekend off?' Ella shook her head. 'Should've done that long ago, dear, seeing as you're going to need special permission.'

'Aye, but it wouldn't have looked good, would it? Asking for it when I'd just arrived?'

'Well, do what Bill said, open your blue eyes and flutter your eyelashes. That should do the trick.'

Even without Lesley's fluttering her eyelashes at him, Mr Vass had been very kind. He had said of course she must go to her sister's wedding, even if she wasn't entitled to the whole weekend. Especially as she was to be bridesmaid! He would be very surprised if she didn't outshine the bride. Had he not heard the young men calling her bonnie Lesley?

'Everything all right, Mr Vass?' asked Mr Armitage, suddenly appearing in Mr Vass's office by the kitchens, with Miss Newall in tow.

Oh, no! thought Lesley, her heart sinking, as Miss Newall's pale eyes ran over her. How her little mouth tightened, as she looked from Lesley to Mr Vass and back again. But Mr Armitage's dark eyes were quite expressionless. He dominated Mr Vass's office, as he dominated whichever place he happened to be in, but you could never tell what he was thinking.

'Everything is quite all right, Mr Armitage,' Mr Vass answered. 'Miss MacKenzie here was just telling me she would like to attend her sister's wedding at the end of the month. I have given her permission.'

As Miss Newall caught her breath in theatrical outrage, Mr Armitage's gaze moved to Lesley.

'Why didn't you ask us about this before, Miss MacKenzie?'

'I know I should've done—'

'Certainly you should!' cried Miss Newall. 'The very idea! Asking for a weekend off when you've just arrived!'

'We do make occasional concessions,' Mr Armitage said coolly. 'But if this wedding had been arranged before you were appointed, it was up to you to let us know you'd want time off.'

'It was arranged.' Lesley looked bravely into the assistant manager's sombre eyes. 'I just didn't like to ask when I first came.'

'Tell Mr Armitage you are to be bridesmaid,' put in Mr Vass, at which Miss Newall gave another cry of disapproval.

'Bridesmaid! Really, Miss MacKenzie, when you come to work at a hotel like the Grand Forest, you can't expect your personal interests to be taken into consideration.'

'Oh, I don't think we need to be too hard-hearted,' said Mr Armitage. Suddenly, amazingly, he smiled, and just for a moment was transformed. 'I agree with Mr Vass, Miss MacKenzie. You may have the weekend off to go to your sister's wedding. Miss Newall, I believe you had something you wanted to discuss with me?'

As he moved away, followed by the head housekeeper, concealing her chagrin with obvious effort, Lesley turned to Mr Vass.

'Thank you,' she said simply.

'Don't you worry about working here, Miss MacKenzie,' he told her, smiling. 'It's not as bad as Miss Newall makes out.'

'I think I know that, Mr Vass.'

Chapter Twenty-Four

There was dancing at Carrie's wedding. Ned played the fiddle, and Tam MacGregor, a friend of his, played the accordion; everyone had a wonderful time. Even after the ecstatic Carrie and Joe had been waved off to the train for their honeymoon in Berwick, the guests danced on, until Ned and Tam played 'Auld Lang Syne' and put their instruments away. The wedding party was over.

'Back to the Highlands, is it?' Adam Kay asked Lesley, as they left the dance floor to join guests making their farewells to Peg and Sam. 'Long way for you to come.'

'Wouldn't have missed it for the world,' Lesley answered, throwing a shawl over her thin bridesmaid's dress. 'And the hotel folk were nice. Gave me the weekend off.'

'You happy there? No' homesick?' Adam grinned. 'Silly question, eh? Why would you be homesick for poor old Leith?'

She reached up and whispered in his ear. 'I'll let you into a secret, Adam, I was, then. I cried ma eyes out for weeks!'

'Never!'

'True.'

'But you're all right, now?'

Before Lesley could answer, Janie Scot had joined them, rather out of breath from dancing with Joe's brother, Kenny, who was home on leave from the merchant navy.

'How's it going, then, Lesley? Happy with the nobs?'

'I'm happy with the folk I see at work, Janie. Don't actually mix much with the guests.'

Janie shrugged and put her arm in Adam's. 'Where were you for the last waltz, Adam?'

'Looking for you.'

'I got caught by Kenny. Och, he's a wild one! Just look at ma best shoes! He was more on ma feet than his own!'

Lesley was drifting away, to be with Auntie Peg, who was looking weary but so happy. Even so, she had a hankie to her eyes.

'Oh, Lesley, is it no' lovely? Carrie married! And looked such a picture, too!'

'Why are you crying, Auntie Peg, if you're so happy?' asked Lesley, laughing.

'Women always cry at weddings, eh? Sam, I think we'll be away. Most folk have gone now.'

'Thank the Lord,' Sam said fervently. 'I need a rest.'

'You'll come back to us for a bit, Lesley? Ned's coming.'

'I'll just nip home and change first. This dress is no' so warm.'

'But you looked a picture, too, Lesley, my word, you did!' Peg gave her a hug. 'Thank the Lord the hotel let you come, eh?'

'They were very kind.'

Peg's eyes rested on Lesley's face. 'And you've got over your homesickness?'

'Auntie Peg! I never told you I was homesick!'

'Aye, but you were, though. All thae letters you wrote us, I used to read between the lines. I used to say to Carrie, "She's missing us, but she'll never let on!"'

Lesley blushed. 'You're right, then, Auntie Peg, I did miss you. I missed everything.'

'But you're all right, now, pet?'

'I'm all right, now.'

*

Ned went back with Lesley to Number Fifteen, for he also wanted to change from his wedding clothes.

'This'll be sad for you, eh?' he asked, as they entered the flat that had always been in Auntie Peg's tenancy and now was Joe Halliday's. 'End of things, in a way?'

'Oh, yes, the end of things.' Lesley flopped into a chair and looked around. All as neat as a pin. She and Carrie had spent the morning tidying, though the Lord knew what the place would be like when she returned from honeymoon, Carrie had said, with Ned in charge. 'I suppose Carrie and Joe'll be moving into Auntie Peg's room, then?'

'That's the plan.'

'And you'll be taking our old room?'

Ned was walking about, whistling. He stopped and looked at Carrie. 'As a matter of fact, no.'

'You're sleeping in here still? There's no need to do that.'

'No' sleeping here, either.'

Lesley fixed her eyes on Ned. He seemed strange. Tense. As though he were hugging a secret. One that was giving him pleasure. She had the feeling that at any moment he was going to tell it to her.

'What's up, Ned? Are you getting married yourself, or something?'

'Or something!' He laughed. 'Now you know I'm no' getting married just yet. Listen, I'll get out of ma good suit and tell you what's going on.'

They were in their everyday clothes, ready to go round to Auntie Peg's, both on tenterhooks, Lesley because she was dying to know Ned's secret, he because he was dying to tell her. With a sudden grand flourish, he produced a suitcase.

'Here you are, Lesley. This'll give you a clue.'

'You're going away? Where? Tell me, Ned!'

'Oh, this beats all!' He lit a cigarette and shook his head. 'I'm going with you, Lesley. I'm going to the Hotel Grand Forest.'

If he had expected his news to be sensational, it was. Lesley could feel herself turning pale with the shock of his announcement. Ned at the Grand Forest? She couldn't believe it, and in a way didn't want to. No, it wasn't his sort of place, he wouldn't like it. But what was he going to do? Play the fiddle? How had he applied? When had he applied?

'Tell me what you're talking about,' she said quietly. 'Go on, Ned, tell me.'

He had lost colour, too, and was self-conscious as he sat on the sofa, smoking his cigarette, his eyes meeting hers and glancing away. She could tell that in spite of his longing to give her his news, he was uncertain how she was going to take it. That wasn't surprising, as she was so uncertain herself.

'Come on,' she said impatiently. 'Tell me why you're going to the Grand Forest.'

'All right, then. I'm the fiddler for the new trio.'

'Trio?'

'Aye. You know – piano, violin, cello?' He looked at her with his head on one side. 'Entertain folk with music?'

'I know what a trio is,' she said sharply. 'What I want to know is how you got into one at the Grand Forest?'

'Saw an advert in the *Scotsman*. Picked it up in the station buffet after Auntie Peg and me had seen you off. Can you credit it? I say it was meant, eh? I was meant to get the job.'

'Go on,' Lesley told him.

'Well, seemingly the hotel's usual trio had let 'em down, taken a job in the south somewhere, so they had to find another pretty quick. They found a pianist and a cellist locally, needed a fiddler. I'm it.'

Lesley hesitated for a moment. 'Ned, that's grand,' she said slowly. 'But – well – I don't know what to say.'

'A bit of a shock, eh?' He gave a short laugh. 'Same for me.'

'Why didn't you tell me before?'

'I was only given the job last week.'

'You could've let me know you were applying.'

'Never told anybody. Didn't think I'd a snowball in hell's chance.'

'You didn't come up to Glenmar for interview?'

'Audition,' he corrected. 'No, Mr Armitage saw me here in Edinburgh.'

'Mr Armitage?' For no reason she could think of, Lesley was embarrassed at the thought of the assistant hotel manager's meeting her brother. And he'd never said a word to her? 'He heard you play, Ned?'

'Well, his cousin did, a fella from the university. That's where we had to go for the audition, me and three others.'

'And they chose you?' Lesley felt a quick rush of pride. 'Oh, Ned, that's good, that's wonderful!' She went to him and kissed his cheek. 'I'm proud of you, I really am!'

He put out his cigarette and gave a sheepish grin.

'I'm sort of proud of maself, to tell you the truth. I mean, I'd nothing on paper, no exam certificates, or anything. Auntie Peg had paid for me to have lessons – a shilling a time, do you remember? And old Mr Goudie was good, taught me well. But after that, I'd only played in pubs. You could've knocked me down with a feather, when they gave me the job.'

'They must've liked your playing, Ned.'

'Said I'd a very good tone and excellent sight reading. Said I'd be able to play anything that was required. Well, it's just light stuff, you ken. No Beethoven.'

'And you're coming back with me?' Lesley asked wonderingly. 'So soon?'

'They needed me as soon as possible. Seems they'd have had the auditions earlier, only this university fella couldn't fit 'em in, so they've been managing with just the pianist and the cellist.'

'Kirstie and Rob Murray. Yes, I've heard them. They're very good.'

'Wait till there's three of us!'

Lesley stood up and buttoned on her coat.

'We'd better get along to Auntie Peg's, Ned. Does she know you're leaving?'

'Aye, I told her today.'

So, she's another who's never said a word, thought Lesley. Is all the world keeping secrets from me?

Ned, seeing the look on her face, said quickly, 'I asked Auntie Peg not to say anything to you. I wanted to tell you maself.'

Lesley shrugged. 'Just took your time about it. I feel a bit of a fool to tell you the truth. I mean, I should've known what was going on.'

'Och, it's just the way things turned out. And I never told Carrie. I thought it'd be a nice surprise for her and Joe, to come back and have the place to themselves.' Ned, pulling on his cap, moved to the door and looked back. 'Listen, you're no' mad at me, eh? For coming to work at the same hotel?'

'Why should I be mad at you? That's silly!'

'Well, I might cramp your style.'

'What style? Look, I'm glad you're coming, honest I am. Just as long as it's right for you. The Grand Forest's a lovely hotel, but it might no' be your sort of place.'

'Three meals a day, damn' good pay, doing what I like? I'd say it was ma sort of place.'

'There aren't many pubs in Glenmar, you ken.'

'So? The Grand Forest's no' a temperance hotel, is it?'

'No.' She smiled. 'A lot o' spa hotels are, but the Grand Forest is well and truly licensed.'

'Well, then, I won't be looking round for pubs. Come on, let's away to Auntie Peg's. And think about having me for company on that train back to Glenmar. Now that'll be grand, eh?'

'Grand,' Lesley agreed, and put on her hat. As they made their way down the gaslit stair, Ned caught her smiling.

'What's funny, Lesley?'

'I'm thinking of the faces of all the folk I know, when I walk in with you!'

'They won't all be surprised. Mr Armitage knows you're ma sister.'

'He does? How?'

'He asked me.'

'I saw him just before I left. He never said anything about you.'

'Bit of a dour one, eh?'

'Been kind to me, Ned.'

'Hey, and me!' Ned banged the house door and they set off together up the lighted Kirkgate. 'Gave me a job.'

Chapter Twenty-Five

Lesley's arrival back at the Grand Forest with Ned in tow created just the stir she had expected. While Mr Armitage remained impassive, only nodding to her and Ned on their first evening, all her colleagues were agog. Why all the secrecy? Why'd she never said he was coming?

'I swear I didn't know!' she declared while Ned was being shown his room by Moyra. 'It was just as much a surprise to me as it was to you.'

'Surprise?' Nick echoed. 'It was a damn' great shock when I saw you coming in with that new fella. I thought mebbe you'd gone home to get married yourself.'

'Oh, honestly!' Lesley laughed at that, though she had a few misgivings about the look in Nick's eye. She'd only been out with him when others were around, but he'd already angled more than once to take her somewhere on her own. Trouble was, he was another who wasn't Mr Right, as Carrie would have put it. 'Why are you so choosy?' Carrie had asked, but surely Lesley had a right to be choosy? She wasn't ready to be anything else.

'But how come you never told us your brother was so handsome?' Ella was asking.

'Handsome?' Lesley stared. 'Ned?'

'You must admit, he is.'

'Never thought about it. I suppose he's no' bad-looking in a way—'

'So romantic,' murmured Ishbel. 'Just the way you'd expect a musician to look, eh?'

'He'll have all the old ladies swooning,' put in Alison Gow, laughing, and Bill grinned.

'Seems to have you girls swooning already, if you ask me.'

'Let's see how he gets on with the Murrays,' Nick said coolly.

Ned got on very well with the Murrays, and everyone else at the Hotel Grand Forest; even Mr Armitage and the grumpy head porter; even Sadie Newall. In fact, it was a revelation to Lesley, to see the way he slipped into his new life as though to the manner born.

'To the hotel born,' he said, with a laugh, when she told him this in the village shop, as he studied postcards on their first free time together. 'Aye, this is a grand place, eh?'

'I wasn't sure you'd like it. I mean, it's very different from Leith.'

'You wanted a change from Leith, maybe I wanted a change and all.'

'Well, I love it here, now I've settled in. It's another world. But sometimes I canna help feeling guilty.'

Ned bought his postcards and they left the shop to stroll around the square, for all the world as though they were guests taking the cure. The November day was chill, the sky over the hills steel grey, the only colours in evidence the dark green of the evergreens. Lesley had already pointed out the two pump rooms and the pavilion; now they walked round the empty bandstand where the leaves blew, and Ned pulled his cap more firmly over his ears.

'How d'you mean, guilty?' he asked.

'Well, when you see all this money – all this luxury – canna help thinking of the bairns back home.'

'No boots?' said Ned.

'Aye. And you think, why so much for some? So little for others?'

'Way of the world.'

'I know, but you wonder, maybe it shouldn't be.'

'Don't see you going back to Leith, though,' Ned said after a pause.

'No, that's why I feel guilty. I like it here. Seeing the way other folk live.'

'You can see that in Edinburgh, any day.'

'I know, but here it's all there is. It's all around us. There's this lovely scenery and everybody's got money and good clothes, they all just stroll about and eat delicious food, play cards, chat. D'you think it's wrong, to want a part of that, Ned?'

'No, it's natural.'

'If we were like Janie Scott, we'd never work here, you ken.'

'Aye, well we're no' Janie Scott. Way I see it, I'll get experience here, then I'll move on, make some money and do something to help the folks in Leith.' Ned smiled and clapped Lesley on the back. 'In the meantime, have a good time, eh?'

A few evenings later, in the Palm Court after dinner, Lesley snatched a moment from serving coffee to watch Ned and the Murrays playing their way through a selection from Leslie Stewart's *Florodora*. Though Rob and Kirstie were both excellent musicians, even if Rob was on the solid side and Kirstie rather over-dramatic, there was no doubt that Ned was the star.

Oh, yes, thought Lesley, he carries them, he draws folk to him, he makes them listen. All those years of practising scales and studies in Auntie Peg's room had paid off, it seemed, yet there was more to Ned's mastery than a good technique. Looking at him, in the dress suit he'd bought for nineteen shillings and elevenpence in the Kirkgate, a lock of hair falling on his brow, his dark eyes shining, Lesley realised afresh that Ned was indeed handsome, was in fact very attractive, probably would have all the old ladies swooning over their coffee cups. Not just old ladies, either.

'*Florodora*,' Nick whispered, pausing at Lesley's side, an empty tray in his hand. 'Good tunes, eh?' He warbled under his breath. '"Tell me pretty maiden, are there any more at home like you?"'

'"There are a few, kind sir,"' Lesley sang back, smiling. '"But simple girls and proper, too."'

'Wish there was just one more like you,' he said quietly. 'One who'd take a bit of notice of me.'

Up went Kirstie's hands, and down went Rob's bow, as Ned's own bow leapt into the air with a last flourish, and then the selections from *Florodora* were over and the trio members were taking their applause.

'You're not saying anything, Lesley,' pressed Nick, under cover of the clapping.

'Well, what can I say, Nick? Look, we'd better get on.'

'He is good-looking, eh?' Nick murmured, studying Ned, who was putting more music on his stand. 'Ella's already got her eye on him, so has Moyra.'

'You think so?'

'You know so. I'll tell you something else about him, he can certainly put it away.'

'Put what away?'

'Come on, the drink. When all you girls have gone up for your beauty sleep, we fellas have the odd jar, you ken. Our perk, if you like. Your Ned has more than the odd one, I can tell you.'

'He's always been able to carry his drink,' Lesley said uneasily.

'Oh, I'm no' saying he can't. Just hoping he doesn't give himself too much of a burden.'

As Ned nodded to Rob and Kirstie and they moved into a melody from *The Merry Widow*, Lesley turned back to the coffee trays, leaving Nick still watching the trio, until Bill came up and said old Vass was spluttering. Colonel Fenn wanted a brandy, better get it over to him before Vass blew up.

'Nothing wrong, Miss MacKenzie?' asked Mr Armitage, looming up as he had a habit of doing when Lesley was least at her best.

'I'm quite all right, thank you, sir.'

'Look a little flustered.'

'No, no. I'm just serving the after-dinner coffee.'

The assistant manager's eyes went to the trio in the distance and rested on Ned.

'Your brother settling in well, do you think?'

'He seems to be very happy, thank you, sir.'

'It will be a help to him, no doubt, to have you here.'

Lesley managed a smile. 'Oh, I don't think he depends on me. He isn't homesick.'

'As you were?'

Her blue eyes widened. 'Didn't think you knew that, sir.'

'It's my job to know things. You're feeling better now?'

'Much better, thank you, sir.'

'A long winter ahead. You won't mind that?'

'No, sir. I like working here, whatever the weather.'

It was Mr Armitage's turn to smile. 'Well, you know what Shelley said, Miss MacKenzie. "If winter comes, can spring be far behind?"'

As he moved away to speak to a group of guests, Ella came up and knocked Lesley in the ribs.

'I can't believe it!' she whispered. 'You getting more than four words out of Mr Armitage? What's your secret?'

'He was just saying it'll be nice when spring comes.'

'Oh, yes? Well, I'm looking forward to that meself.'

Chapter Twenty-Six

Spring was in fact a long way off. It was true that the Glenmar valley was sheltered and that the winter was not quite as severe as it was elsewhere, but it was cold enough, and there was snow on the blue hills most mornings; sometimes even flurries of snow in the valley itself.

'You'll be glad of them flannel nighties your auntie made you, after all,' Ella told Lesley with a laugh. 'Oh, I wish they'd put some more heating on this top floor!'

Lesley was wondering when they might qualify for some holiday. She would have liked to go home for Christmas or Hogmanay, knowing how disappointed Peg and Carrie would be without either herself or Ned, but there'd been no prospect of leave, the hotel was full.

'Wouldn't you think these rich folk would rather stay at home?' Ishbel had asked irritably. 'But no, they have to come and land on us, and we have to work twice as hard.'

'That's what hotels are for,' Bill told her.

'But no' spa hotels, eh? Why go through all that dosing and then go and stuff yourself wi' Christmas food?'

Never mind, there'd been a grand Christmas party for the staff, with a band paid for by Mr Wilcox who'd decreed that the trio should have a good time too, though it never troubled Ned to play for anything. Still, he was able to keep his admirers happy, dancing with them all in turn, while Nick danced with Lesley as often as he could, and Mr Wilcox danced with Mrs Wilcox, who lived in London, but had come up specially for the occasion. Paul Armitage also danced with Lesley, and perhaps neither was surprised when Sadie Newall cut in, saying the waltz was a 'ladies' excuse me', though no one else knew that.

'Poor old Sadie,' Nick murmured, back with Lesley and dancing cheek to cheek. 'She doesn't stand a chance when you're around.'

'Don't talk such rubbish, Nick!'

'Aye, well I've got ma theories. Old Armitage has got his eye on you, Lesley. You mark ma words.'

'You're always saying folk have got their eyes on other folk.'

'And they usually have!' Nick's bright gaze went to Ned, dancing with Ella. 'But maybe you should keep your eye on Ned, Lesley. I'm no' joking. He's had enough tonight. Don't want Mr Wilcox to see him the worse for wear, eh? Or Mr Armitage?'

Lesley stopped, pulled herself from Nick's clasp and walked swiftly away. When he followed, she looked at him with flashing eyes.

'I just wish you'd leave Ned alone, Nick. He isn't drunk, he's never drunk, so just stop hinting that he is.'

'Lesley, I'm only thinking of him. I don't want him to get into hot water, that's all it is, honest!'

'All right, but just forget it now, will you?' Lesley glanced around. 'Mr Armitage is staring at us.'

Leaving Nick to gaze miserably after her, Lesley left him, and searched the room for Ned. He was by then talking with Bill, but she drew him to one side and told him what Nick had said.

'Nick says I've had enough?' Ned asked in a furious whisper. 'Who the hell gives him the right to say how much I can drink?'

'He's thinking you might get into trouble with Mr Wilcox, or Mr Armitage. Please, Ned, just take care, eh?'

'Do I look drunk to you?' He'd stared belligerently into her eyes.

'No, I'm no' saying you're drunk, Ned.' Lesley put her hand on his arm. 'But if you have had a lot, couldn't you call it a day? Just to be sure?'

'Look, it's Christmas, every fella has a drink or two at Christmas. I'm no' taking orders from Nick and you can tell him that from me.'

There was no more to be said, and in fact they'd been lucky. Ned had had too much to drink – Lesley had been able to tell – but he'd carried it, as he always did, and there had been no disaster. All the same, Lesley knew Nick had been right to give his warning and felt bad she'd been angry with him. Ned would have to watch his step for the future, and she would have to keep her eye on him.

To make things up with Nick, she danced the last waltz with him, and still felt bad, to see how just one last dance with her could give him so much pleasure. Being in love appeared to be no fun at all, as far as she could see.

After Christmas and Hogmanay had come and gone, the winter had set in, but the bright spot for Lesley was that Ned appeared to have taken heed of what had been said and had cut down his drinking. He was practising more, rehearsing more, 'acting quite the slave driver', as Kirstie said, with a smile. 'But don't worry, Lesley, he's doing well. I think the managers are pleased with him, and the guests certainly are. My goodness, he gets some compliments!'

By the time spring finally arrived, with daffodils in the hotel gardens and new leaves on the birches, Lesley had almost forgotten her worries over her brother. In fact, it was a happy time all round, with the young people on the hotel staff getting to know, at its best, the remote and different land that was now their home.

In twos and threes, on their time off, they would walk in the forests, or climb the hills, to look over to Cromarty

Firth and the mountains of Wester Ross. Or, they'd hire bikes from the village and visit the local beauty spots, the little lochs and waterfalls, the old towns of the Black Isle.

And if Nick had had to accept that Lesley was never going to be his girl, and Ella and Moyra had accepted that Ned was not going to be their young man, it didn't seem to matter. Life was pleasant, anyway, and they were all having a pretty good time, especially as they'd all been told they'd successfully completed their probation periods. No one would be asked to leave.

In the middle of June, Ned and Lesley did have a holiday back in Leith, where Auntie Peg spoiled them and Carrie said, no, she wasn't 'expecting' yet, but was hoping and knitting just in case.

'Any news of Adam and Janie?' Lesley had asked. 'Are they engaged, or anything?'

'Walking out, we think,' Auntie Peg told them. 'No' sure, mind.'

'Just suit each other, they will,' Sam muttered, and Peg said that that was very true.

'Everything all right with you?' Lesley asked her aunt later.

'You mean with Sam and me? Och, we're fine. He gets a bit difficult over grocery bills, you ken—'

'Grocery bills?'

'Well, he expects me to spend exactly what Aggie spent, but I've worked out ways of doing the accounts that keep him happy.' Peg had smiled. 'You'll find, when you get wed, Lesley, there's ways and means of making a man happy.'

'Should've thought it'd be his job to make ME happy!' Lesley had retorted.

How small everything seemed back in the flat in the Kirkgate!

'It's just after the big rooms at the hotel,' Lesley told

Ned. 'Being back in ma little bedroom I canna think how I used to fit everything in. I mean, Ella and me at least have a proper wardrobe.'

'And what about me?' Ned had asked. 'Back in the pull-down bed in the living room?'

'And going out for a pint again,' said Lesley.

'Now don't start, Lesley! I've behaved maself for long enough.'

'Yes, you've been very good. Make sure you're the same when we get back, eh?'

On the day they returned to Glenmar, several new guests also arrived on the spa express from Aviemore, and were driven to the Grand Forest in the hotel bus by Colum MacNee. Amongst them were a Mrs Meredith from London, a 'regular' at the hotel, with Miss Atkinson, her maid, and her son, Christopher, who was twenty-three and making his first visit. Miss Atkinson took her meals with other guests' attendants, but the Merediths were allocated one of Lesley's tables in the main dining room. That meant she would be seeing quite a lot of them in the future.

Chapter Twenty-Seven

'Mrs Meredith's got bad rheumatism,' Ella remarked to Lesley in the dining room one morning. 'See her stick? Veronica says she comes up here every year and stays for weeks. Very good-looking, ain't she?'

'And gracious,' said Lesley. She studied Mrs Meredith, who was slim and elegant, with what were known as 'fine' dark eyes under well-shaped brows. 'What's wrong with the son?'

Young Mr Meredith was less striking than his mother, but just as pleasant; always smiled at Lesley as though she were doing him a favour when she served him.

'Dunno,' Ella replied. 'He seems fit enough. But some people just come up for the air and the golf.'

'He has a nice face, hasn't he?'

'Anybody with his sort of money has a nice face,' Ella answered cynically. 'Veronica says the father's a stockbroker, and rolling in it.'

'Veronica would know.'

One evening in late June, Lesley was again on duty in the Palm Court after dinner. The glass doors were open to the air, the trio was playing as usual, the guests were taking coffee and chatting, or getting down to the serious business of auction bridge.

Mrs Meredith was one of the card players. She played

every night, always with the same friends, Mr and Mrs Powell and Colonel Fenn. There was no sign of Mrs Meredith's son.

'Coffee, madam?' asked Lesley, looking around the four faces. 'Sir?'

All said they would take coffee, and the gentlemen also asked for brandy.

'What d'you think of this news from Sarajevo?' Colonel Fenn, long retired from a Highland regiment, asked Mr Powell, as Lesley served their brandy. Mr Powell, middle-aged and greying, and at the spa for what he described as a 'gammy leg', shook his head.

'Bad business. Could be trouble.'

'Where on earth is Sarajevo?' asked Mrs Powell.

'Bosnia, it's the capital,' Colonel Fenn told her. 'Archduke Ferdinand of Austria's just been assassinated there by a young Serb.'

'His wife was shot, too,' said Mrs Meredith. 'I notice you don't mention her.'

'What matters is that Austria could go to war with the Serbs over this.'

'Men!' exclaimed Mrs Powell. 'Always looking for an excuse for war.' She turned to Mrs Meredith. 'Where's Christopher? I'd rather hoped he would take Marcia to the pavilion this evening, but he seems to have disappeared.'

'He's around somewhere,' Mrs Meredith answered, finishing her coffee. 'Shall we cut for partners?'

Lesley moved on, wondering who Marcia might be, then recalled a dark-haired girl with heavy-lidded eyes who sat around the hotel in bored fashion while her mother took the cure. It was easy to remember her because she was young. There weren't many young guests at the Grand Forest.

As no one seemed to require anything at that moment, Lesley stood by the open doors, smelling the scent of the flowers wafting through and listening to the trio. They were playing selections from *Florodora* again, always a great favourite, and Lesley, forgetting where she was, began to hum and then to murmur the words she and Nick had sung before:

'"Tell me, pretty maiden, Are there any more at home like you? There are a few, kind sir, But simple girls and proper, too ..."'

'That's nice to know,' said a man's mellow voice, and as a flame of colour rushed to Lesley's brow, she clapped her hand to her mouth and swung round. Christopher Meredith, elegant in white tie and tails, was standing at the glass door, smiling at her.

'Oh, I'm sorry, sir,' she stammered, and he laughed.

'Don't be, it was charming. You should sing some more. I like *Florodora*.'

'May I get you something, sir?'

As he shook his head and thanked her, she thought again how pleasant he was, how nice-looking, by which she didn't mean good-looking. He had such a broad, good-natured face, such steady blue eyes and a generous mouth. You'd know where you were with this man, thought Lesley, still so embarrassed she could feel her face burning, and suddenly realised that while she had been looking at him, he had been looking at her.

'Perhaps I will have something,' he said quickly. 'A whisky.'

'Whisky and soda, sir?'

'Yes, that'll be fine.'

When she returned with his drink on a tray, he took it with another of his smiles.

'Do you realise you and I are the only young people here?'

Where's Marcia, then? she wanted to ask, but contented herself with looking towards Ella and Nick and other waiters hurrying by with trays. He followed her glance.

'Oh, I'm sorry! Of course, your colleagues are young, too. So, you have someone to talk to, unlike me. Do you mind if I ask your name?'

'Lesley MacKenzie, sir,' she answered, offering up a

silent prayer that he was not going to call her bonnie Lesley. But then she remembered that he was English, and probably didn't know Rabbie Burns's poem. In fact, he made no comment on her name at all, but politely introduced himself.

'Christopher Meredith. But then, you probably know my name, don't you? I expect you know the names of all the people here.'

'Will you excuse me, sir?' asked Lesley, wondering if any guest had ever introduced himself to a waitress before, and thinking she had better go before she landed in trouble for wasting time. Even as the thought came into her head, she saw Mr Armitage's gaze on her from across the room, and almost ran to take an order for drinks from a gentleman coming in from the dining room.

'You seemed to be finding plenty to talk about,' Nick said at the end of the evening, catching her arm in the corridor outside the staff dining room. 'I mean, to that fair chap.'

'What fair chap?'

'You ken fine who I mean. His mother's that good-looking woman, always playing bridge.'

'Mr Meredith? I'd say his hair was light brown.'

Nick's eyes flashed. 'Stop teasing, Lesley! You know what I'm on about. That fella was trying to make up to you, everybody could see!'

'What do you mean?' she cried angrily. 'We exchanged a few words, then he asked for a whisky and I gave it to him. Am I no' even allowed to speak to a guest now?'

'You'd better watch your step,' Nick said in a low voice. 'You know what some men are like in hotels. Call themselves gentlemen when they're only out for one thing.'

'For your information, I've worked in hotels long enough to take care of maself,' Lesley rapped. 'And I think it's terrible of you, Nick, to take a man's reputation away for no reason. Mr Meredith is decent and nice. Everybody can see that, if they can see anything.'

Nick, trembling, stared at her for a moment, then turned and left her, slamming a door behind him.

'Phew!' cried Ned, coming through the door a moment later, as Lesley stood with exasperated tears pricking her eyes. 'What was all that about? Have you been upsetting Nick, then?'

'He's been upsetting me.'

Ned waved a finger at her. 'Now, Lesley, I saw you talking to that nice young Mr Meredith!'

'Do I live in a goldfish bowl?' she cried, and slapped his hand down. 'Ned, you've been drinking again, haven't you?'

'Aye, I've been dry for too long. And don't start looking down your nose at me again, Lesley, because I've had enough of that.'

It was Lesley's turn to run out and slam a door. And she kept on running until she reached her room on the top floor, where she tore off her cap and apron and collapsed on her bed.

'Like that, is it?' asked Ella coming in from the bathroom, with a towel round her neck and her hair in a damp plait.

'I've had a row with Nick,' Lesley told her, with a groan.

'I suppose he saw you talking to Mr Meredith?'

'Oh, not you as well, Ella! Did everybody in this hotel see me talking to Mr Meredith? Honestly, it was only for a couple of minutes, and the whole place knows about it.'

Ella shrugged and draped her towel over a rail. 'You know what it's like in hotels. Guests and staff aren't supposed to mix.'

'We weren't MIXING! We said a few words and I brought him a whisky. What's all the fuss about?'

'Yes, but you were by the window where everybody could see you. And he was smiling at you as though—'

'As though what?'

'Well, you were a guest, same as him.'

Lesley's colour rose again. 'And that's the end of the world, is it? For a hotel guest to talk to a waitress as though she's a human being?'

'Look, I feel the same as you.' Ella sat beside Lesley on her bed. 'It makes me furious the way we're thought of, but that's the way things are. And I suppose you couldn't run a hotel properly if they were any different.'

Lesley leaped up. 'Well, I'm no' going to stop talking to Mr Meredith if he wants to talk to me, and that's all there is to it. And I'm certainly no' having Nick Lithgow telling me what to do.'

'Poor lad, Lesley. Can't you see he's unhappy?'

'I thought he'd understood,' Lesley said after a pause. 'There's nothing between us.'

'He can't help his feelings, whatever he understands.'

'No.' Lesley pulled the pins from her hair and took up her hair brush. 'Maybe I should try to be more understanding maself. Och, what a mess!' She looked back at Ella. 'And Ned's drinking again. That's another thing to worry about.'

A shadow crossed Ella's face. 'Needs a good woman to keep him in check,' she said lightly.

'He does. Could you be the one?'

'I think there'd be more than one taker.'

Lesley put down her brush and sighed. 'I'll go and see if the bathroom's free. At least, I've got that to be grateful for, eh?'

'The bathroom?' Ella asked, smiling.

'Aye. Well, if you'd ever had to fill up a zinc bath from kettles, you'd be grateful too.'

'I used to do that very thing,' said Ella.

Chapter Twenty-Eight

Nick refused to be placated. At staff breakfast the following morning, he shrugged off Lesley's hand from his arm and asked her to leave him alone.

'But it's silly to quarrel over nothing, Nick.'

'I said, just leave me alone.'

'Come and sit over here, Nick!' called Ishbel, and Lesley, her eyes glinting, moved away.

Ella joined her. 'I've just thought, Lesley, if Mr Meredith's usually with his mother, he won't be able to talk to you.'

'And that's what you're hoping, is it?'

'Would be safer.'

'Oh, well, I like a bit o' danger. I might actually speak to Mr Meredith maself!'

Yet, when she entered the main dining room and saw him sitting alone at his table in the window, Lesley's heart failed her. He was early. There were hardly any other guests present. In fact, he shouldn't have been there himself, but at the pump room, taking the spa waters with his mother.

He was wearing a tweed suit and a striped tie, his hair well brushed and still a little damp, as though he had not long left his bath, his face smoothly shaven. As soon as he saw her, he rose to his feet, which made her catch her breath and look round, to see if anyone else had seen him treating her again as if she were a guest. Luckily, there was no one.

'Good morning, Miss MacKenzie!' he cried, and she could scarcely meet his eyes. Miss MacKenzie? She felt so flattered. No other hotel guest had ever called her that.

'Good morning, Mr Meredith,' she answered, wondering that she could manage to sound so composed. 'Aren't you early this morning?'

'I skipped the pump room, I'm afraid.' He shook out his table napkin. 'I don't need those waters, you know, and they're absolutely foul. As well as hot!'

'I know, I've tried them.' She laughed as she passed him the breakfast menu. 'Once.'

His eyes were resting on her face, he wasn't bothering with the menu.

'I think I'll just take porridge, please, and grilled bacon.'

'With eggs, sir? Or mushrooms?'

'No, thanks, just make it the bacon.'

'Very good, sir.'

'It's a wonderful morning, isn't it?' He waved a hand to the sunlit garden behind him. 'I should go walking.'

'Oh, yes, it'd be a lovely day for that.'

By the time he'd reached the toast and marmalade stage of his breakfast, there were a few more people in the dining room but not in Lesley's section. From the corner of her eye, she could see Ella bustling about, and Mr Vass in conversation with Bill, but thank heavens, there was no sign of Nick.

'More coffee, sir?' she asked Mr Meredith.

'Oh, please.' He buttered a last piece of toast. 'No, I'm afraid I've rather let my poor mother down this morning. She thinks if I drink the water and let myself be lowered into a tub of ghastly peat, I'll soon be fit and well.'

'You've been ill, sir?'

'Yes.' He smiled. 'Nearly died, though it's hard to believe. All I had was scarlet fever.'

149

'Scarlet fever?' Lesley lowered her eyes. 'I would believe it.'

'You've had it?'

'A long time ago. We all had it, us bairns. Then our mother caught it and she died.'

'I'm sorry.' He reached out as though he would have touched her hand, then drew back. 'I'm sorry I mentioned it.'

'You weren't to know, sir. Anyway, you nearly died yourself.'

'I'm convalescent now. Breathing in this wonderful air. Walking and all that.' He stood up. 'Listen, I hope you won't mind if I ask you this – but would you go walking with me some time?'

She raised her eyes to his face. 'You know I canna do that, sir.'

'Why not?'

'We're no' supposed to mix with the hotel guests.'

'That's ridiculous! What's it matter to anyone how you spend your free time?'

'I'm sorry, sir. It's out of the question.'

As Lesley began to pile his breakfast things on her tray, he stood watching her slim white hands.

'We needn't tell anyone,' he murmured. 'If you were to get an afternoon off some time, we could just meet in the woods.' At the look in her eye, he added hastily, 'Just for walking, Miss MacKenzie. Please, tell me when you could come.'

'I get a couple of hours off tomorrow afternoon,' she said in a low voice. 'From two till four. Then I've to be back for the afternoon teas.'

'Well, then. Let's say we'll meet in the woods at the back of the hotel at two o'clock?'

'I'm no' promising.'

'I'll be there, anyway.'

'What if it's raining?'

'I'll be there in the rain.'

As Lesley arrived back at the doors to the kitchens, she might have been relieved not to see Nick, if Mr Armitage had not been standing waiting for her. His eyes on her were quite expressionless.

'Miss MacKenzie, I think you should beware of letting certain guests monopolise your attention.'

'There's no one else at my tables, sir.'

'Even so. You should be ready and waiting for guests to arrive, not indulging in chit-chat with one particular person.'

'I'm sorry, sir.'

He hesitated. 'I do understand, that it was probably Mr Meredith who was detaining you, rather than the other way round. But it's necessary to avoid that sort of thing, you see.'

'Yes, sir.'

Taking her tray into the kitchens, Lesley set her mouth in a hard uncompromising line. If the sky fell in, she would be in the woods at two o'clock tomorrow, she promised herself. And just let Mr Paul Armitage try to stop her!

Chapter Twenty-Nine

It did not rain the following afternoon. In fact, the weather was perfect, sunny and warm.

'Isn't it grand?' asked Ishbel, who was also free for the afternoon. 'Where shall we go, Lesley?'

'I'm no' sure. I might just go down to the Square, listen to the band.'

'I'll come with you.'

'No! I mean, I've just remembered, I've letters to write.' Lesley gave a strained smile. 'Sorry, Ishbel.'

Ishbel gave her a long, disbelieving stare. 'Are you mad at me?' she asked. 'Getting Nick to sit with me yesterday? I felt that sorry for him, you ken. You've treated him badly, Lesley.'

'No, I haven't! I've never promised Nick anything and he knows it. Why should I be mad if he sits with you?'

'Well, you don't want to come out with me, do you?'

'Next time,' Lesley said, hurriedly making for the stairs to her room. 'Next time we're off, we'll go out together, eh?'

Now she would have to get out of the hotel by the side entrance and hope Ishbel didn't see her. Suppose she even followed her? Lesley's heart was thudding as she changed from her uniform into a cool white linen blouse and skirt, and put on her summer straw hat with its trimming of corn-flowers. How did she look? She hadn't time even to glance in her mirror. She had no watch, but she knew it was almost two. There, one of the hotel clocks was striking, and she was only just on her way! Would he wait?

He had waited. She could see him ahead, as she ran through the bars of sunlight slanting through the newly green trees. How pretty everything was! How strange she should even notice.

'You came!' He ran to meet her. 'I didn't think you would.'

'Well, it isn't raining.'

'But you said you wouldn't promise, didn't you?'

'I am here, though.'

'Yes,' he agreed softly. 'You're here.'

She felt better, now that she was with him. Not so worried, so churned up inside. Yet, she was actually more vulnerable. Anyone from the hotel seeing her with him – well, she could imagine Mr Armitage's face when he got to hear of it.

'Let's just walk on, shall we, Lesley? You don't mind if I call you Lesley?'

No, she didn't mind, not now. Because he had first called her Miss MacKenzie.

'And you must call me Christopher.'

'I'm no' sure I can do that, Mr Meredith.'

'Please don't call me that. Or, sir.'

'It could be difficult for me. I mean, at work.'

'We needn't think about work at the moment.'

That's where you're wrong, she thought. She had to think about work all the time.

They walked on through the quiet woods, each very calm, just enjoying the beauty of their surroundings. So it seemed.

'It's very good of you,' Christopher said at last. 'To come out with me like this. I really haven't anyone, you know, for a companion.'

'Isn't there Miss Powell?' Lesley couldn't help asking.

'Miss Powell?' He seemed taken aback. 'You know her?'

'I've just seen her in the hotel.'

'Yes, well – poor Marcia – she's very bored. Her mother drags her everywhere.'

'She might like to go for a walk some time.'

'I don't think she's a great one for walking. Anyway, you're with me now, and I'm very grateful.'

'No need to be grateful. I like to get out of the hotel, get some fresh air.'

'I expect you know all the places to see round here, don't you? Scenic spots, that sort of thing?'

'Yes, I think so.'

'Would you show them to me?'

'I don't get much time, Mr Meredith.' She hesitated. 'Besides, it wouldn't be right.'

'Because I'm a guest at the hotel and you work there?' He shook his head, as they both stood still beneath the trees and the dappled sunlight moved across their faces. 'I'm not accepting that, Lesley. I don't believe you want to accept it, either.'

She smiled wryly. 'For me, it's no' a matter of choice. I like working here. I don't want to lose ma job.'

'You shouldn't have to worry about that.'

'No, but I do. Look, I think I'd better be going back. I'm worried about the time.'

'All I'm asking is that we meet sometimes when you have time off. You must surely have days off?'

'Well, we have a rota. But it wouldn't be easy for me to meet you.'

'You'd like to, though?'

Oh, God, yes, she'd like to. She made no answer, knowing he could read it in her face.

'Please say you will!' He took her hands. 'We needn't leave together, we could arrange to meet away from the hotel. Just tell me the day.'

'Can you tell me what time it is, please? I'm really worrying about getting back.'

He sighed, and took out his watch. 'You're all right, you've plenty of time, but I don't want you to be worried. We'll go back.'

They walked slowly back towards the hotel, hand in hand, but at the end of the woods, Lesley loosed her hand from his.

'Maybe you should wait here? While I go on ahead?'

He nodded. 'But promise to tell me first when we can meet again. I bet you know, don't you? About your next day off?'

'It's no' a whole day,' she said reluctantly. 'Next Tuesday, I'm free after the luncheons until seven o'clock.'

'Tuesday.' His eyes shone. 'I think I can just about get through till then. Where shall we meet? At the bandstand?'

'No, too many people would see.'

'Where, then?'

'At the end of the village, there's a seat, by a milestone.'

'When? Two o'clock?'

'Oh, later. About three? I canna say for sure.'

'I'll wait.' He pressed her hand. 'Thank you, Lesley.'

'Will you be taking tea?' she asked hesitantly. 'Shall I see you in the Palm Court?'

'No, I don't think so. Not today.'

As she turned and ran from him, she guessed he didn't want to see her back in her black dress and apron, serving other people. Not when he'd asked her to call him Christopher.

Chapter Thirty

That was the start of a heady, delirious time that gripped Lesley like a fever. She really did feel almost ill, and knew her eyes appeared large and sometimes strange, but that she was, at the same time, prettier than ever. Perhaps, even beautiful. Yes, she could read it in people's faces, that that was what they saw, and they didn't know why.

Except for Ella. She'd had to tell Ella about Christopher Meredith. She'd had to tell somebody. Besides, Ella had wanted to know why she was never free to go out with her on their time off, and once she did know, she'd been able to cover for Lesley and make up excuses why she'd suddenly become so elusive. It had helped that Ishbel had set her cap at Nick and persuaded him to go out with her, so that neither of them looked around for Lesley, and while Nick didn't know what was going on, neither did Ned. But then Ned was not at his sharpest those days, and if Lesley had not had other things on her mind, she would have been worrying about him.

Other things on her mind? Christopher was on her mind, only Christopher. And, perhaps, in the middle of the night, fear of the future. What would happen when he went away? She wouldn't think of that.

'You are a fool, Lesley,' Ella told her once. 'You're storing up trouble for yourself.'

'I canna help it, Ella. There's nothing I can do.'

'What happens if his mother finds out about you?'

'She won't. She's always so busy with the cure and her friends and bridge, and everything. And in the afternoons, she rests.'

'H'm.' Ella was dubious. 'So – has he ever promised you anything?'

'No.'

'Has he ever said he loved you?'

Yes, oh, yes!

'I don't want to talk about it, Ella.'

'You will be careful, Lesley? You know what I mean?'

'You don't need to worry, Ella.'

'Worry? I worry about you all the time.'

Of course, Christopher had said he loved her! Not on their second day out together, when they'd climbed the hills and looked across to the magnificent scenery of Wester Ross. That had been a day of getting to know each other, when Christopher had told Lesley something of his life – school, Cambridge, working for his father, and she'd told him about Auntie Peg and Carrie and Joe, and living in Leith – and had burst out laughing when he'd said he thought at first she was a Highlander.

'A Highlander! Me? Could you no' tell from ma voice where I came from?'

'I don't know about Scottish accents,' he'd said apologetically. 'I thought if you worked here, you must be a Highlander.'

'Och, no, Ned and me've only been here a few months.'

Then he'd had to hear all about Ned and had been astonished that he was the violinist in the trio, and said all credit was due to him, to have worked so hard, saved up for his fiddle and finished up a musician.

'But Auntie Peg helped,' Lesley had explained. 'She always helped. I don't know what we'd have done without her, after ma folks died.'

Christopher had listened attentively, while she told him about her father's dying at sea and her mother, who'd been a waitress, dying of the scarlet fever. But of course he'd known about that.

'She was a very good waitress, Auntie Peg said, with lovely white hands.'

'Like yours.' Christopher had taken Lesley's hands in his. 'You know I noticed them on that first day you gave Mother and me breakfast? First I noticed your hands, then I noticed you. And you never noticed me at all, did you?'

'I remember thinking that your mother was very good-looking.'

'But not me?' He'd smiled at that. 'I'm like my father, people say. If my sister had lived, she might have been like my mother, I suppose.'

'You had a sister?'

'Yes, Polly. Died when she was four.'

'Oh, that's so sad. I'm sorry, Christopher.'

It was the first time she'd used his name, and it had seemed natural after that, to go into his arms, to rest her head on his shoulder, and then to let their mouths meet in a long sweet kiss.

'Oh, Lesley,' Christopher whispered. 'Ever since that first breakfast, I've dreamed of being with you like this. Could you not take your hat off? Let me see your pretty hair?'

She'd glanced round, but they were quite alone on the hilltop, there was no one to watch as she took off her hat and let Christopher take down her hair and tumble it round her shoulders.

'So beautiful ... You will come out with me again, Lesley? You promise?'

They'd walked, they'd cycled, they'd taken bus trips. Christopher said he would have liked to hire a car, but garages were few and far between and they couldn't risk breaking down, or not finding petrol. Though Lesley admitted that she would have been thrilled to go for drives, it didn't matter that they couldn't have a motor, for the weather was glorious and all they cared about, of course, was being together.

Because of Lesley's necessity to be back at certain times, they couldn't go too far afield, and it was on one of their short walks to a little local waterfall that Christopher told Lesley he loved her.

What did that mean, she wondered, as feelings of joy consumed her anyway. But still she couldn't help thinking of how things would have been back home. In Leith, if a man mentioned love, that would mean, not a ring, for few could afford one, but a definite engagement. Families would be told, a wedding date fixed, and there you were, settled.

Lesley, though floating on a golden cloud, could not imagine any of that happening for herself and Christopher. At the same time, it must. That was what being in love meant – wanting to spend your life with the beloved. That was what she wanted, anyway, and when she looked at Christopher's dear face, she couldn't imagine his not wanting the same.

Look how well he respected her, never asking her to go to his room, as some fellows would have done. Oh, yes, everyone who worked in hotels knew that that happened. Chambermaids, waitresses – they were considered fair game by some male guests, but what Lesley and Christopher had was something different. She was not just a girl he wanted to take to bed, he was in love with her, he'd said so.

In the beautiful July weather of 1914, it seemed to Lesley it would be best not to look too far into the future. Everything seemed so splendid, anyway. Not a cloud in the sky. Some of the hotel guests who read the papers seemed anxious about things that were happening in Europe. Austria-Hungary was mobilising armies near the Serbian border, Russia and Germany were becoming involved, but all that was very far away. Didn't affect Great Britain, anyway.

Chapter Thirty-One

When it was at last Lesley's turn for a whole day off, she and Christopher took the bus to Inverness. Here, before going to the loch, they went window shopping, which for Lesley was quite usual. Window shopping was mostly what she did when she went to shops. But it seemed that Christopher had other ideas.

'I'm going to buy you a little present,' he told her. 'A brooch.'

'No, don't, Christopher! You don't need to buy me presents. Honestly.'

'Nothing expensive. Just a keepsake. And I do want to give you something.'

But the brooch was expensive. A twist of gold in the shape of a heart, set with little pearls. The assistant in the jeweller's pinned it to Lesley's white blouse, and stepped back with pride to see the effect, while Christopher took large crisp five-pound notes from his wallet to pay the bill.

'What's the matter?' he asked, stricken by the look on her face outside the shop. 'You're not pleased with me. What have I done?'

'I don't want you to think I'm the sort of person you have to give presents to,' she said obstinately. 'And you know I canna give you anything back. No' like this.'

'It's in the shape of a heart, Lesley. You can give me something just like that.'

161

She coloured and was silent as they walked along the dusty pavements, moving in and out of the crowds of tourists, and Christopher grasped her arm.

'Please, Lesley, don't be angry with me. If you don't want the brooch, we can throw it in the loch. I just want to make you happy.'

'I am happy,' she told him, her lip trembling. 'I will keep the brooch, I'll always keep it. Thank you, Christopher.'

'Oh, thank God!' he cried lightly. 'I couldn't have borne to upset you. Now, one more shop, and then we go looking for Nessie!'

'One more shop?'

'Don't worry. I only want a camera.'

He has no idea, she thought, indulgently, yet with a certain regret, as she waited for him. He has no idea at all, of how most folk live. He wants a brooch, he buys one. He wants a camera, he buys one. Out comes his wallet and he doesn't have to think twice. How many bairns' dinners could she have bought for the cost of this brooch?

'Found one!' cried Christopher, leaving a photographic shop with his purchase of a box camera. 'I've got a Brownie like this at home, but I forgot to bring it. And I've been so desperate to take your photograph, Lesley.'

'Oh, please, show me how to take one of you!' she cried.

They spent an idyllic time by Loch Ness, looking out for the monster across the broad smooth waters, giving up and taking photographs of themselves. Christopher photographed Lesley, she photographed him, and an obliging passer-by took them both together.

'Now,' said Christopher, putting away his camera. 'Let's go back and find a place to eat. I'm so hungry, I could eat Nessie, couldn't you?'

They found a very pleasant little hotel, where they had a Scottish high tea because they'd missed lunch, and Lesley looked with sympathy at their elderly waitress whose feet were obviously aching, and said she wished she could have given her a hand.

'Your day off, remember!' said Christopher. 'My word, this is a very good meal. I'm not sure I don't prefer it to the dinner at the Grand Forest.'

'Did you tell your mother you wouldn't be taking dinner tonight?'

'Oh, yes. She said she'd have it with the Powells.'

'Your mother hasn't noticed you're never around? I mean, you never take the waters or have the peat baths, or anything.'

'She's just pleased that I'm out so much,' Christopher answered with a grin. 'Breathing in the wonderful air. Thing is, I look so well, I'm afraid she'll soon tell me to get back to London and Dad's office.'

Lesley set down her knife and fork. 'You're going home?' she whispered.

'No!' He reached across the table for her and. 'No, I'm certainly not going home. Not for a long while yet. I'm still convalescent. I need more time at the spa.'

She was laughing at him, her heart lifting, when he looked beyond her shoulder and said, quietly,

'Don't look now, but I think there are some people we know.'

'Who?' The blood was draining from Lesley's face. 'Who are they?'

He lowered his eyes. 'They're coming over.'

'Good afternoon, Miss MacKenzie,' came Sadie Newall's voice. 'And isn't it Mr Meredith?'

Chapter Thirty-Two

Miss Newall's face was flushed and rather moist, her eyes, as she looked down at the two young people, were sparkling. Standing next to her, and looking on with interest, was a dark-haired young woman with a thin nose and pale green eyes.

'Good afternoon, Mr Meredith, Miss MacKenzie,' Miss Newall said smoothly. 'No need for me to introduce Miss Atkinson, of course.'

'Good afternoon, Mr Christopher,' said Miss Atkinson. 'And Miss MacKenzie, how nice!'

Christopher, rising to his feet, murmured something in acknowledgement, but Lesley was struck dumb. Miss Atkinson, Mrs Meredith's maid! And Miss Newall! Of all the people from the Grand Forest, the last she would have wanted to meet.

'Your day off, Miss MacKenzie?' Miss Newall asked sweetly. 'Mine, too, and Mrs Meredith kindly gave Miss Atkinson the day off too, so that we could take a little trip. Fancy bumping into you two!'

'Fancy,' whispered Lesley.

'Well, we mustn't interrupt your meal, and we have to catch our bus. Goodbye, Miss MacKenzie, Mr Meredith. We'll meet at the hotel.'

As soon as the two women had left the dining room, Lesley's eyes went to Christopher's.

'Disaster,' she said in a whisper. 'Those two seeing us, it couldn't be worse!'

'I don't think Clara Atkinson will say anything.'

'She could, couldn't she?'

'I don't think she will, though.'

'Aye, well if she doesn't, that leaves Sadie Newall. There's no love lost between her and me, so my guess is, soon as she gets back, she'll go straight to Mr Armitage.'

'What of it? What can she say? She saw us having a meal. It's not a crime, is it?'

'You know the situation, Christopher. Why d'you keep talking as if ma job doesn't matter?'

He leaned forward. 'Because you're not going to lose your job over this. It's not as if Miss Newall or Miss Atkinson saw us – well, kissing or anything.'

'The hotel doesn't allow the staff to be friendly with the guests. I tell you, I'll be in trouble!'

'Mr Armitage is a sensible man, he won't sack you over this, I promise you.'

'As though you'd know what he'd do,' Lesley said bitterly. 'As though you know anything about ma life away from you.'

Christopher flushed a deep dark red and looked down at his plate. 'Shall I get the bill? I think we might as well go.'

Outside in the still warm evening, Lesley caught at his hand.

'I'm sorry. I shouldn't have spoken to you like that. It's just that I'm worried, you ken.'

'I understand, my darling. Of course I do.' Christopher was all smiles. 'But if Mr Armitage says anything to you, just refer him to me. I'll tell him it was all my fault, I'll see that you're not in trouble.'

She smiled and let him think he had reassured her, but of course she knew that whatever happened, it would not be his fault. Guests at the Hotel Grand Forest were never to blame.

*

165

It was a great relief to them both that Miss Newall and Miss Atkinson were not passengers on their bus back to Glenmar. They were able to sit close together, holding hands, and try to enjoy the remnants of their perfect day, but when they had left the bus and were approaching the Grand Forest, Lesley's spirits plummeted.

The hotel was so beautiful, there at the head of the village, its windows glittering in the last of the evening sun, why should she have to dread returning? She'd been so happy, and she had a right to be happy. As Christopher had said, she'd committed no crime. Why should she be penalised? She set her mouth obstinately, and as they reached the gardens where the guests were strolling, straightened her shoulders.

'If Mr Armitage does say anything to me, I still won't give you up,' she told Christopher. 'I won't!'

'I've told you, if he says anything to you, just refer him to me.' Christopher pressed her arm. 'Now – do we go in together?'

Lesley hesitated. 'I'd better no' break all the rules at once,' she said dryly. 'I'm no' supposed to go in the front entrance, you ken, old Colum MacNee would kill me.'

'Oh, for heaven's sake—'

'It's all right, I'll go round the back. But we'd better say goodnight now, Christopher.'

Always saying goodnight. Hadn't Carrie once said Lesley didn't know what it was like, to be always saying goodnight? She knew now.

'We've had such a lovely day,' she whispered, touching Christopher's lapel. 'I don't want it to end.'

'There'll be plenty of other days like this, my darling.'

He was hesitating, looking from her to the gardens where the lights were appearing in the dusk, and she gave him a little push.

'Go on, Christopher. I'll see you in the morning.'

Before he could speak again, she left him, walking fast round the hotel and into the back lobby, where Nick

Lithgow stepped from the shadows and seized her by the arm.

'Lesley, where've you been? I've been looking out for you!'

'Oh, Nick, you're not going to make a scene, are you? And shouldn't you be in the dining room?'

'I finished early tonight, and just as well. Look, you've got to come quick. Ned's in trouble!'

Chapter Thirty-Three

He was in a storeroom off the wine cellars, Nick told Lesley as he took her hand and ran with her through the basement of the hotel. Nick and Bill had got him in there for the minute, because they'd had to get him somewhere out of sight, he wasn't fit to play in the trio. In fact, Nick had only just got him away before he'd made a spectacle of himself. But now Bill had had to go back on duty and Lesley would have to give a hand, getting Ned up to his room.

'The damn' silly fool,' gasped Nick. 'Drinking spirits, you ken, and thinking they were beer. He's no' got the sense he was born with, and if Mr Armitage finds out, you know what'll happen!'

That would be the two of them, thought Lesley, brother and sister both, on the train back to Leith. Oh, why was everything collapsing around them, when they'd been doing so well?

'Here he is,' Nick said grimly, opening the door to the storeroom. 'Ned, Ned, wake up! Here's Lesley!'

Ned, who was sitting on the floor with his back to a white-washed wall, made no response. He was breathing heavily, his eyes closed.

'Oh, Ned ...' Lesley dropped to her knees beside him and took his hands. 'Oh, God, you're right, Nick, he's a fool. To do this to himself ... But he could always handle it, he always had a good head, everybody said so.'

'Aye, but, like I say, he's switched to whisky. There's no' many could stay sober who drink what he drinks.'

'I knew he'd started up again, but I never thought he was on whisky.' Lesley looked up at Nick, her face ashen pale. 'Where'd he get it from?'

'He's got his sources here. Always has had. Friendly with Ivor, you ken, one o' the wine waiters, and Ivor's got keys. Did he never say?'

She shook her head. 'We didn't talk all that often.'

'Especially no' lately,' Nick said curtly. 'You've no' been talking to any of us, have you?'

Lesley got to her feet, her eyes filling with tears. 'You're right to say that to me, Nick. If I'd had ma eyes open, if I'd been looking out for Ned, this'd never have happened.'

Nick put his arms around her. 'Don't say that,' he said gently. 'You shouldn't blame yourself. Ned's a grown man, he should look out for himself, eh?'

She pulled herself away and stood looking down at her brother. 'How do we get him upstairs, though? And where's Mr Armitage now? Are you sure he didn't see what happened?'

'It was bit of a luck, he was in his office at the time. Kirstie called me over – it was just before I went off – and said Ned had been insisting on playing but he could hardly hold his bow. He must have had a skinful in the afternoon, because he wasn't too bad, she said, at lunchtime.'

'Drinking in the afternoon.' Lesley shook her head, looking down at the still sleeping Ned. 'Why does he do it, Nick? Why does he need to do it?'

'You know what drinkers are. Nothing matters but the bottle. Aye, well, I was telling you – Kirstie and Rob had stopped playing, pretending they were taking a break. They'd managed to make Ned leave the platform with them, then I persuaded him to come with me. He still looked all right, then, and I don't think anybody noticed, but soon as I got him out o' the dining room, he started wavering about and I had to run for Bill. We were terrified

Mr Wilcox or Mr Armitage would appear, and we tried to get to the service lift, but there was somebody in it, so we got him down here.'

'And now we have to get him upstairs. Nick, I don't think I can do it.'

'I'm going to try for the lift again. It's no' far, you wait here.'

In a minute or two, Nick was back. The lift was empty.

'I'll try to get him to wake up, just enough to walk to the lift.'

But though Nick shook him and slapped his face, Ned only groaned a little and did not wake.

'All right, I'll take his shoulders – Lesley, you take his feet. Come on, he's no' so heavy – you can do it—'

But Ned was like a dead man, and both Lesley and Nick felt they were gasping their hearts out by the time they got into the lift.

'You squash in beside him,' Nick ordered Lesley. 'I'll run up the stairs and see you at the top. All right?'

'All right.'

It seemed a nightmare, getting Ned up in the lift, out of it, along the landing, into his room and on to his bed, where they left him for a moment or two until they got their breath back.

'Just as long as he's no' sick,' said Nick, and Lesley cried out.

'Well, it's what happens. Thank God, he's got no room-mate, eh? This place is a sight.' Nick looked around with distaste. 'Things lying about everywhere, and just smell that whisky! How about if you tidy up, Lesley, while I get Ned out of his dress suit, before he ruins it?'

While Nick struggled to undress Ned and get him into a nightshirt, Lesley ran around the bedroom, opening windows, hanging up clothes, finally wringing out Ned's sponge in his water jug and wiping his face. With another groan, Ned came to and made to sit up, then fell back on his pillow.

'Oh, God!' He put his hand to his head, then gradually focused his eyes on Lesley's face. 'Lesley, what the hell's going on? Why've you put me to bed?'

'You were drunk, Ned,' said Nick shortly. 'We had to put you to bed. You couldn't play your fiddle.'

'Couldn't play?' Ned tried to sit up and again fell back. 'Of course I could play! Who stopped me? Nick, was it you?'

'Nobody stopped you, Ned, you couldn't do it,' Nick told him. 'You must've been drinking all afternoon, you bloody fool. Now, you'd better just sleep it off and see you're all right tomorrow, or it'll be the next train home for you.'

For some time, Ned gazed at him, trying it seemed to follow what he was saying, then he closed his eyes and again dropped into a heavy sleep. Lesley sighed, straightened the pillow under his head, and turned to Nick.

'I canna thank you enough, Nick. You've been a real friend. Ned'll be that grateful in the morning, when he comes round, and ashamed too, I expect.'

'I'm glad I could help.' Nick's eyes were fixed on Lesley's face. 'But he's going to have to do something about the drink, you ken. Next time, he'll no' be so lucky.'

'I know. I'll talk to him.'

There was a moment of silence. Lesley, ill at ease, looked away, but Nick leaned forward and touched the brooch on her blouse.

'Did he give you that?' he asked quietly. 'Mr Meredith?'

'You know about him?'

'Everybody knows about him and you.'

'That's no' true!'

'All right, I know. Just looking at you serving him coffee, I knew. I've always known.'

'He loves me, Nick. He does.'

'And what's the brooch for?'

'What's it for? It's a keepsake, that's all.'

'He's going away?'

'No. Well, I suppose he will be—'

'You bet he will.' Nick smiled. 'Gents like him don't marry waitresses. Has he ever mentioned marriage?'

'Nick, I'm very grateful for what you did for Ned, but I think we should go now. Just let him sleep, eh?'

'Yes,' Nick agreed tiredly. 'Let's just go. There's no point talking, anyway.'

'I think he'll be all right now, and I've tidied everything up.' Lesley looked around the room. 'Goodnight, then, Nick, and thanks again.'

He made no answer and she opened Ned's door. Outside, his hand raised to knock, stood Mr Armitage.

Chapter Thirty-Four

His eyes went from Lesley to Nick and past them to the bed where Ned lay. He was, as usual, very composed.

'I came to see your brother, Miss MacKenzie. I heard he was unwell.'

'We came up to see him, too,' Nick said swiftly. 'When Kirstie said he couldn't play this evening.'

'Yes, Mrs Murray told me that too, after I'd found her and her husband playing duets. How is he?'

Paul Armitage's eyes were now seeking Lesley's, but she was not meeting them.

'It's just a bit of a headache,' she said in a low voice. 'Maybe a slight temperature.'

'Perhaps I'd better have a look at him.'

'He's all right, sir,' said Nick. 'Better no' risk a fever, eh? I mean, if he has one?'

'I don't catch fevers,' Mr Armitage returned, striding past Lesley and Nick to gaze down at the sleeping and snoring Ned. Certainly, Ned's face was flushed. It was possible that he had a fever, thought Lesley. If you couldn't smell the whisky.

'I think he'll live,' Mr Armitage murmured. 'No need to call a doctor.' He glanced at the two watching faces. 'Shall we step outside?'

In the corridor, Lesley and Nick stood waiting as Mr Armitage ran a finger round the collar of his dress shirt.

'Unconscionably warm tonight, isn't it?' he asked. 'What a summer we're having! Miss MacKenzie, I believe it was your day off today?'

'Yes, sir.'

'I wonder if I might have a word with you, in my office? Will you excuse us, Mr Lithgow?'

'Certainly, Mr Armitage.'

Nick, with just one brief glance at Lesley, marched away down the corridor, while she, quite hollow inside, faced the assistant manager.

'Shall we take the lift?' he asked.

'I'd rather use the stairs, if you don't mind.'

Anything would be better, she thought, than standing close to Mr Armitage in the lift, waiting for the blow to fall.

His office was on the ground floor at the side of the hotel, overlooking the gardens. It was a handsome room, lined with bookshelves, and furnished with a large desk, filing cabinets, and several easy chairs. Lesley had been in it only once before, shortly after her arrival, and had admired it. Now nothing in it existed for her, except the assistant manager himself.

'Please sit down, Miss MacKenzie,' he told her, politely placing a chair for her before taking his own seat at his desk and switching on a lamp.

Lesley sat down and folded her hands. I'll be calm, she thought, I'll be like him. I won't let him upset me. But was he going to talk about her? Or, Ned? Or, both? Would they really be packing their boxes tomorrow?

Mr Armitage cleared his throat, and it seemed to her that he was not quite as calm as he usually was. Should she make it easy for him? Should she say, 'I know you know about me and Mr Meredith? What are you going to do about it?'

'Miss MacKenzie,' Mr Armitage said gently. 'I think I should tell you that I know about your particular friendship with Mr Meredith.'

All her bravado died away, and a flush rose to the roots of her bright hair. 'Miss Newall told you about us, I suppose?'

'She did, as soon as she returned from Inverness. But I already knew.'

'I see. You saw us together.'

He smiled a little. 'Only in the dining room. That was enough.'

'I don't see how!'

'But then you couldn't see your own face. I saw yours and I saw Mr Meredith's. As I say, it was enough.'

Exactly what Nick had told her. 'Just looking at you serving him his coffee, I knew . . .'

Oh, why did we bother trying to hide what we were feeling? Lesley asked herself, bowing her head. Seemed everybody knew, everybody could see.

'Why didn't you speak to me?' she asked, raising her eyes to him.

'I should have done. It was my duty.'

'But you never did.'

'No. I suppose I thought Mr Meredith would depart and no harm would be done. He's not ill, just convalescent, it was never intended that he should stay as long as his mother.'

'He told me this very day that he was not going home yet.'

'That was in Inverness, where Miss Newall saw you?'

'Yes. We had a grand day, a lovely day, but when she saw us together, I knew she'd come straight to you and that you'd tell me I had to give him up.' Lesley's voice broke a little. 'It's no' fair, Mr Armitage. Why should the hotel make these rules? Christopher and me – we love each other!'

'He's told you he loves you?'

'Yes! And I believe him. Because what we have – it's a lot more than just some sort of hotel fling, you know. Girls going to men's rooms and such. It's no' like that at all for us, Mr Armitage – it's the real thing!'

He gave a long troubled sigh. 'Miss MacKenzie – Lesley – will you listen to me?'

She stared at him wonderingly. Lesley? He was calling her Lesley now? It should perhaps have meant as much as Christopher calling her Miss MacKenzie. A turning upside down of all that was usual. But it didn't mean anything at all.

'I will listen,' she said carefully.

'Well, then – I'm quite prepared to believe that Christopher Meredith loves you, but I tell you now that he will never marry you. His parents would never permit it.'

'You're saying I'm no' good enough for him?'

'No, I'm not. I'm saying that marriage needs more than love. It involves families and interests, and a way of life. People have to fit in. You and Christopher come from different worlds, that's all his parents will see. And if they cut him off, what happens then?'

'He has a job, he doesn't need their money.'

'He works for his father.'

'Well, he could get a different job.'

'He could. Maybe a certain type of man would. But are you sure that Mr Meredith will want to do that? Will he want to change his whole way of life for you?'

'Yes!' she cried. 'Yes, I'm sure!'

'My poor girl,' said Mr Armitage.

For a long moment, they sat in silence, then they both stood up.

'What will you do?' asked Lesley, staring into his compassionate dark eyes. 'Will you ask me to leave?'

'No.'

'Why? If I'm breaking the hotel rules?'

'I've told you that Mr Meredith will almost certainly be leaving very soon.' Mr Armitage came to her and put his hand lightly on her shoulder. 'And when he goes, I don't think he will take you with him.'

Lesley shook herself free from his gentle hold, and averted her face so that she need no longer meet those eyes of his, filled with the pity she did not want.

'Goodnight, Mr Armitage.'

'Goodnight, Lesley.' As she moved to the door, he called after her. 'Perhaps you could give your brother a message from me?'

'Ned?'

'Tell him, I know about his drinking and I shall speak to him in the morning.'

'You're going to send him away?' she cried, as a little more of her world collapsed. 'Oh, please don't do that! I know he's let you down, but if you send him home, I don't know what'll happen—'

'I'm not sending him away. I'm going to speak to him in the morning. Just give him the message, please.'

As Mr Armitage moved a paper or two on his desk, Lesley stared at him with wild blue eyes, but he did not raise his head and after a little while, she left him.

Chapter Thirty-Five

The following day was 29 July. The weather was again fine and warm. As Mr Armitage had said, what a summer they were having! At breakfast, the women guests were in their lightest dresses, the men in linen coats and pale trousers; only the dining-room staff were suffering in their usual dark clothes, but then they were so used to discomfort of one sort or another, it didn't occur to them to complain.

'No newspapers yet, I suppose?' Colonel Fenn asked Mr Vass. 'I need to know what's happening abroad.'

'I'm sorry, sir, as you know the papers are usually late. It'll be lunchtime, I expect, before we get *The Times* and *Morning Post*.'

'That's the one snag with the Highlands, eh? Everything's late.'

'I'll see you get the papers the minute they arrive, Colonel,' Mr Vass promised smoothly, and gave the nod to Lesley to bring the colonel's porridge, for of course there was no question of his changing to grapefruit, even if the temperature was climbing. The ladies might be happy with fruit, but if he had to get that god-awful water down his throat, he needed a proper breakfast afterwards.

'My goodness, bonnie Lesley, you're pale this morning,' Mr Vass told Lesley in the kitchens, when she had returned from serving Colonel Fenn. 'Nothing wrong, is there? Not sickening for something?'

'No, Mr Vass. I'm quite all right.'

'You don't look all right,' said Nick in a low voice, as Mr Vass moved away. 'What did Mr Armitage say to you last night, then?'

'I don't want to talk about it, Nick.'

'You're no' packing your box, though?'

'Not yet.'

'And neither is Ned. Have you seen him this morning?'

Yes, she had seen him. He'd been waiting, pale and red-eyed, outside her door when she'd emerged with Ella, feeling terrible, so he said. Ella, it was plain, would have liked to throw her plump arms around him, but at the glances that were exchanged between brother and sister, had tactfully removed herself.

'Oh, God, Lesley, I'm sorry,' Ned sighed. 'Nick's just told me you folks had to put me to bed last night. I don't know what happened, I'm no' usually so bad, eh? I mean, how often do you see me drunk?'

'You're going to have to apologise to Kirstie and Rob, Ned. And Bill.'

He put his hand to his brow. 'Anyone else?'

'Mr Armitage.'

'Mr Armitage? Hell, did he see me and all?'

'Only when you were in bed. But he's sent you a message.'

'What?' Ned asked fearfully. 'What's he say?'

'He told me to tell you that he knows about your drinking and he's going to speak to you this morning.'

'He knows about ma drinking? That's it, then? I'm on ma way. First stop, Leith.'

'He said he's no' sending you home, but I think you can prepare yourself for a bad time. Now, I've got to go to breakfast—'

'Breakfast! No' for me!' Ned, turning green, closed his eyes, then opened them. 'To tell you the truth, you look as though you've been having a bad time yourself. What's up?'

He didn't know? At least, then, there was one person who hadn't seen her love for Christopher written in her face.

'I'll tell you about it later, Ned. You've got enough on your mind just now.'

'No, no, we're family, tell me now.'

She told him, as briefly as she could, and watched the incredulity swim into his eyes.

'Oh, Lesley, what a mess, eh? How'd you ever let yourself get involved with somebody like that?' He put his arms around her. 'Poor lassie ... why'd you never tell me what was going on?'

'What would you have said? You'd have told me to give Christopher up, wouldn't you? Like Mr Armitage.'

'I'm a fine one to tell anybody what to do.'

'Sometimes, I think of Auntie Peg,' Lesley said in a whisper. 'And I wonder what she'd think of me. Risking ma job, breaking rules, no' her way, eh?'

'Don't mention Auntie Peg,' he answered with a groan. 'I ken fine what she'd have thought o' me. But she'd have understood about you, Lesley. She knows, when folk fall in love, they fall in love. There's nothing anyone can do.'

'You'd better find Mr Armitage,' Lesley said, freeing herself from her brother's clasp. 'Good luck, Ned.'

'Think you need a bit of luck yourself.'

He pressed her hand and they went their separate ways.

Lesley had found Sadie Newall at the staff dining table, sitting with Clara Atkinson, and at once prepared herself for an attack.

'Good morning, Miss MacKenzie!' the housekeeper had cried, her pale eyes gleaming. 'And how are you this morning?'

'Extremely well, thank you,' Lesley replied.

'You're looking rather pale. Nothing wrong, I hope?'

'Nothing at all. Mind passing me the toast?'

As Miss Atkinson obligingly passed the toast rack, Miss

Newall frowned. 'Nice you have such a good appetite. I believe you might be seeing Mr Armitage this morning? He told me he would be speaking to you.'

'I saw him last night.' Lesley buttered her toast. 'He was very nice, very understanding.'

At the look of defeat on the older woman's face, she could almost have felt sorry for her. Certainly, she felt no triumph. With Miss Atkinson's green eyes meeting hers, she knew she had no reason for that.

'Where is he, then?' Nick was asking, standing with his tray, oblivious of Mr Vass's dark glances.

'You mean Ned?' asked Lesley.

'I mean Mr Meredith. Isn't he early usually?'

'I don't know where he is,' she said desolately. 'He must have been delayed.'

She went back into the dining room, her eyes going everywhere in case Christopher was sitting somewhere other than his usual place, which was of course ridiculous, for why should he sit somewhere else when his table was ready and waiting?

'It's Russia I'm worrying about,' Colonel Fenn was booming to Mr Powell, while Mrs Powell and Marcia drank fruit juice with sighs of boredom. 'Now, if Austria–Hungary declares war on the Serbs, Russia will side with the Serbs and Germany will side with Austria, and then the fat will be in the fire.'

'You think Germany will get involved?'

'They're already involved! They'll declare war on Russia, and then France, and if they go through Belgium to get to France, that'll be us involved too.' Colonel Fenn crunched toast. 'We can't let Belgium down, we've guaranteed her neutrality. We must honour our commitments.'

'I wish to God we knew what was happening,' said Mr Powell.

'Could we at least have breakfast in peace?' asked Mrs Powell.

'Peace, yes, that might be in short supply,' said the colonel, rather pleased with his repartee. 'In the future, I mean.'

But Mrs Powell's eyes had brightened. 'Here's Beatrice!' she cried, as Mrs Meredith, cool and attractive in pale green, came into the dining room. 'Now, I wonder why she's so late? I didn't see her at the pump room.'

'Christopher's with her,' Marcia observed, also brightening. 'But he never goes to the pump room, does he?'

From the Merediths' table in the window, Lesley looked straight into Christopher's eyes and with no more than a murmured good morning to his mother's friends, he moved like an arrow to her side.

'How are you? Oh, you look so pale! Have you seen Mr Armitage? What did he say?'

'Christopher, folk are looking.' Lesley straightened cutlery on the breakfast table. 'I did see him and he's no' sending me away. He was – very nice.'

'Thank God for that, I've been so worried!'

'Where've you been? Why'd you no' come early, like you usually do?'

Christopher sat down and picked up the breakfast menu. 'Fruit juice,' he murmured. 'And scrambled eggs.' He raised his eyes. 'What happened was that my father sent a telegram. There's been bad news. Austria's declared war on the Serbs. He's thinking we should go home. Mother and I have been discussing it.'

'Fruit juice, scrambled eggs,' Lesley repeated dazedly. 'You're going home, then?'

'I don't know, I don't know what we'll do.'

'What are you going to do, Beatrice?' Mrs Powell was asking Mrs Meredith. 'Shall you go home?'

'I don't know, I really don't know. I mean, it may not be necessary.'

'Exactly! I absolutely don't see our country going to war over Belgium, whatever you say, Colonel Fenn!'

182

Colonel Fenn, who with Mr Powell, had courteously risen at Mrs Meredith's approach, sat down again and shook his grey head. 'I tell you, it will happen. We signed a treaty with Belgium, we can't go back on the terms.'

'Well, there's a dance arranged at the pavilion and Marcia wants to go,' Mrs Powell declared. 'And I think we should at least wait for that. Christopher might want to attend, if he's not too interested in that waitress he's always looking at.'

'What waitress?' Mrs Meredith's beautiful eyes went to Lesley, who was still standing at Christopher's table. 'Oh, the strawberry-blonde. Yes, she's a sweet-looking girl, isn't she? I think he's quite fond of her, but it doesn't mean anything.' She began to move away towards her table, leaning heavily on her stick. 'I'll see you all after breakfast, shall I?'

'You won't see me,' said Colonel Fenn. 'I'm looking up trains home. If the balloon's going up, I want to be in London. This is no place to be, if we're going to war.'

'What can I get you, madam?' Lesley was asking Mrs Meredith, who sighed and waved away the menu.

'Only grapefruit and toast, please. It's so warm already, isn't it? And this room is like an oven. Christopher, tell Mr Vass to have the windows opened.'

As the waiters ran to open the windows and Lesley went to the kitchens, Mrs Meredith looked at her son.

'We've decided to wait until the pavilion dance before we leave, Christopher. Then perhaps you could arrange to say goodbye to the pretty waitress. And do be gentle about it. I don't want her hurt.'

His head shot up, his blue eyes stared. 'You know? How long have you known?'

'Oh, for heaven's sake, Christopher! Of course I know. Mothers always know.'

'Especially when they have helpful ladies' maids.'

As his mother only raised her eyebrows, his eyes went to the service door, through which Lesley would appear

183

with their orders. 'What happens if I don't say goodbye?' he wanted to ask, but Lesley was carrying over their tray, her white hands were setting out their grapefruit and juice, their usual pot of coffee, cups, spoons, and they were unfolding their napkins.

In the end, he said nothing.

Chapter Thirty-Six

In the peace of the Highlands, sweltering in the sun, it was hard to imagine the frenzied activity taking place elsewhere in Europe. The mobilisation of armies, the telegrams, conferences, demands, replies, the final ultimatums. But news filtered through, from friends and relatives, from the newspapers, late though they might be. Even to the hotel guests of Glenmar, it was becoming increasingly obvious that unless a miracle happened, war in Europe was on its way.

Colonel Fenn had already left for home on 30 July, the day the Tsar of Russia ordered total mobilisation. When, the following day, Austria followed suit, certain other guests were already packing. Mr Wilcox, having received telephone calls from the company which owned the Grand Forest, was almost at the end of his tether.

'My God, Paul, what are we going to do?' he asked his assistant manager. 'London says it looks like we'll be at war within a day or two. We're going to have to close the hotel!'

'I imagine all the hotels here will be closing,' Paul Armitage told him. 'Who is going to take the waters if there's a war on?'

'But what'll happen to us? You're all right, you're not even thirty, but I'm in my forties. What am I going to do for a living?'

'I'm afraid I don't know. There'll be no problem for me, I suppose. I'll be joining up.' At the look on the manager's face, Paul tried to cheer him with some small hope. 'Look, it still might not come to war. We haven't declared yet, remember.'

'Any moment now, they say Germany will declare war on France and invade Belgium. We'll have to move then, Paul. There's no other course.'

'Let's wait and see if Germany does invade Belgium. In the meantime, do we get the pavilion to cancel the dance?'

'Oh, let it go ahead,' the manager groaned. 'It might keep a few people here for a while longer.'

'You're going to the dance?' Lesley cried, when she and Christopher met in the woods again as arranged. 'I can't believe it! Why would you want to go to a dance, for heaven's sake? The way things are?'

'I promised my mother I would,' he said apologetically. 'I know it seems all wrong, but this might be the last dance we have for a very long time.'

'So you'll be dancing with Marcia,' Lesley said bitterly. 'You say you love me, and yet you want to dance with someone else.'

'I don't want to dance with her, if I do, it will only be as a courtesy.' Christopher held Lesley close and covered her face with kisses. 'The whole thing is a courtesy, that's all it is. I'll dance with my mother and her old friends, I'll have done my duty and I'll come away.'

'And then what? You'll go back to London?'

'I'll have to, my darling. If there's a war, I'm going to volunteer.'

The blood left her face, left her whole body, so it seemed, and she leaned against him like a child's rag doll.

'You're going to the war? Oh, Christopher, no! You don't have to! There's a proper army, all professional soldiers, they won't need you.'

'They will, they'll need all the men they can get.

Besides, I want to go. I want to do something for my country. I'll think of it as my duty.'

'Duty,' she wept. 'Oh, no, I canna bear it. Think o' your family – how will they take it? You're all they've got.'

'I know, I feel bad about it. But it's what they'll want me to do. They'll understand.'

'You're all I've got,' she whispered. 'And I won't understand.'

'I'll come back for you,' he said steadily. 'I promise.'

'Come back?'

'Yes. And if you'll have me, we'll be married.'

It was the best and worst day of her life. He wanted to marry her, he wanted to be with her always. And he was going to the war. He might never come back. She would be like Auntie Peg, grieving alone for years and years, but unlike Auntie Peg, she would never marry anyone else. Everything she had or could ever want was contained in this man who held her close.

'They say they're going to shut the hotel,' she murmured. 'How will you find me? I don't know where I'll be.'

'I'll find you wherever you are. Besides, we're going to write to each other, aren't we? You'll tell me where you are.'

'Maybe you won't have to go!' she cried. 'Maybe there won't be a war after all.'

The dance at the pavilion took place on the evening of 1 August, attended by most of the guests left at the spa. All were beautifully dressed, of course, and determined to make the event a special occasion. Perhaps because they already knew it was. The last dance before the coming of war . . . Even if it were true, as some thought, that the war would be over by Christmas, the dance was still going to be different from any other.

Dinner was early at the Grand Forest and afterwards the staff found themselves standing around with very little to do. The trio had been told it would not be required, there being no one to listen to it, except one or two very elderly guests who had already said they would depart to their beds, and it wasn't long before someone suggested they should all go over to the pavilion and take a peek at the dancing.

'We'll get shot,' said Bill. 'Well, I mean, lose our jobs.'

'We're probably going to lose 'em anyway,' said Nick. 'If they're closing the hotel.'

'We needn't all go together,' said Ella. 'We could take it in turns.'

'Aye, and then come back and serve ourselves coffee, or, better still, brandy,' said Bill, laughing.

'No brandy for me,' said Ned harshly, and no tactless voice was raised to ask why. Rumour had already made its rounds, and most people knew that Mr Armitage had 'spoken' to Ned, and that Ned had promised to try to give up drinking.

Ella and Lesley went over to the pavilion together, Ella taking Lesley's arm and walking her smartly through the scented summer air behind Nick and Ned, Ishbel and Moyra.

'You're very quiet, Lesley,' Ella told her. 'I was beginning to wonder if you were going to come.'

'I suppose I wasn't keen.'

'Didn't want to see Mr Meredith dancing with other girls?' Ella asked sympathetically.

'I don't really have to worry about that.'

'Oh? What are you keeping from me, Lesley?'

'Och, I'll have to tell you! I'm dying to tell you.' Lesley's eyes were glittering in the dusk. 'Ella, he's asked me to marry him. Ssh, don't let the others hear. Ned's the only other one I've told.'

Ella's mouth dropped open. 'Never! I mean, oh, my God, that's wonderful! He has, he's really asked you!'

'Yes, but we can't marry before he goes away, there won't be time. He's going to join up, you see, but he's going to come back for me, he's promised. I tell you, Ella, I don't know whether I'm on ma head or ma heels.'

'I don't like to ask, but has he told his mother?'

Lesley shrugged. 'I don't know. It won't matter, if she doesn't approve, we're going to be married, anyway.'

'In fact, you're engaged. That'll be something to tell Mr Armitage, eh? You are going to tell him?'

'Oh, yes, I'll tell him. But will he believe me?'

'Why shouldn't he, if it's true?' Ella corrected herself. 'When it's true, I mean.'

The curtains of the pavilion's long windows were drawn back, so that the watchers outside could look directly into the ballroom. They could see the band in the corner, and hear it too, even through the glass. They could see the dancers, the men in white tie and tails, the women like perfect rainbows of colour, all dipping and smiling and turning their heads. Round the walls sat the older people, Mrs Meredith and Mrs Powell among them, and as Christopher whirled by with Marcia, both women exchanged glances and gracefully waved their fans.

'Well, there he is,' said Ned, joining Lesley. 'Looks smart, eh?'

'Yes, he does,' Lesley agreed.

'I canna get over what you told me, you ken. I mean, marraige, eh? That's something different!'

'I can see everybody's going to be very surprised,' Lesley said dryly.

'Och, you know why. Folk like us, we don't marry folk like the Merediths. I mean, can you see me marrying Miss Powell?'

Lesley smiled, but her heart was twisting a little, as she watched Christopher, so elegant, so suddenly far away, holding Marcia Powell in his arms. The fact that Marcia was there in the ballroom, and she, Lesley, was not, seemed to sum up all that Ned had said; all that she knew in any case.

'Mind you, Miss Powell's no' so bad,' Ned said consideringly. 'Quite pretty, when she's all dressed up.'

'Yes, quite pretty.' Lesley turned away. 'But I think I've seen enough for now.'

They had all seen enough, those who had been watching the dancing, and they walked slowly back to the hotel without speaking, the music echoing in their ears. If war did come, if the hotels were closed, where would they all end up? The future was blank, just an empty hole. But one thing seemed certain, they had just watched something special coming to an end. There might be other dances in the future, but not like that one. That dance was over, while its dancers still danced on.

Two days later, on 3 August, Germany declared war on France, and on 4 August, marched into Belgium. Great Britain, having earlier sent an ultimatum to Germany demanding there be no invasion of Belgium, waited for a reply and the promise to withdraw. Eleven pm was the deadline. When no reply had been received by that hour, Great Britain declared war on Germany.

Chapter Thirty-Seven

People were beginning to leave. From the hotels and boarding houses of Glenmar, a steady stream of guests was catching trains, or taking buses, or even taxis and hired cars. The pump rooms and the pavilion had already closed, and no band played in the main square. Already, the little Highland spa was taking on the look of a ghost town.

'It's the end,' said Mr Wilcox, looking down from his window at guests being shepherded into the station transport by Colum MacNee. 'We shall never recover, Paul. Things will never be the same again.'

'It's a mistake to think like that, Mr Wilcox, if you don't mind my saying so,' Paul Armitage told him. 'If the war is soon over, the spa can open up again, with very little lost.'

'Who's to say the war will be soon over? The company doesn't think so.'

'They've asked you to stay on for a while, haven't they?'

'Yes, and you know why. To superintend the removal of the hotel effects. The Grand Forest has already been commandeered for a military hospital. You think that sounds as though the war is going to be over by Christmas?'

'Sounds as though the authorities are just making sure they'll have what they need – if they need it.'

Mr Wilcox lit a cigarette and shook his head. 'I notice you're still set on volunteering. Hardly worth your while, is it, if the war's going to end before you get there?'

'I'd better go back to work,' Paul said patiently. 'I've a lot of reassuring to do downstairs.'

And upstairs, he thought, leaving the manager's office. Poor old Wilcox had been hit so hard by events he'd never believed could happen in his worst nightmares, he was finding it almost impossible to adjust. But then he wasn't alone in that.

While guests continued to besiege Veronica and Alison at Reception for information and timetables, the kitchen and dining-room staff were still serving meals, although Mr Chater and Mr Vass kept threatening to depart. For what sort of food could be provided in the circumstances? What sort of service, when everything was at sixes and sevens?

'I am an artist!' exclaimed Vincent Chater. 'I can't be expected to produce good food when this whole place is closing down around me. I should be back in London, at the Savoy.'

'And what is there for me to do?' cried Mr Vass. 'Serve people who are not even properly dressed? No one is taking the trouble to put on white tie, no one is caring what they eat!'

'Please, let's just try to keep things going until we close,' said Paul Armitage. 'We are at war, we can't expect things to be the same.'

'What's going to happen to us, Mr Armitage?' asked Bill. 'I mean, most of us fellows are thinking of joining up, but will we have jobs to come back to?'

'I can't answer that at the moment, I'm afraid. Mr Wilcox will be sorting the matter out with the London office. In the meantime, we'll just keep a skeleton service going here.'

'Skeleton is right,' muttered Nick. 'This place feels like a home for ghosts already.'

'Soon as the hotel guests have gone, you can all be on your way,' Mr Armitage told him.

'Aye, it'll be Leith for me,' said Ned. 'The trio's disbanded, Kirstie and Rob have gone home, I might as well go back and join up.'

'And you such a lovely violinist!' cried Ella. 'Do you have to go, Ned?'

'Duty calls. All the lads'll be going.'

'They say the Territorials from here are leaving tomorrow,' Bill murmured. 'Can't wait!'

'I'm no' that keen,' said Nick, and when Mr Armitage had moved away, Ishbel slipped her hand in his.

Paul Armitage was looking for Lesley. He had not seen her to speak to since she'd told him that Christopher Meredith had asked her to marry him. How happy she'd been to tell him that! And he'd said he was happy for her. She would not, he knew, be so happy now. The Merediths were leaving tomorrow.

He found her at a window in the Palm Court, looking out at the hotel gardens baking in the sun that never seemed to want to go in. Day after day, the glorious summer weather had continued, as though nature was saying, look, this is what I can do, make everything beautiful, while you people can only run around planning death and destruction. For Paul had no illusions about what war meant. The Territorials might be marching away as though to just another pleasant manoeuvre; when he went, he knew what he would be facing.

It was almost the time when afternoon tea had been served, to the accompaniment of music from the trio. Only a few days ago, this lofty hall would have been filling up with well-dressed people, chatting about their treatments or their golf scores, while the staff bore in trays of tiny sandwiches, buttered scones and muffins, trolley loads of exquisite pastries, almond cakes, chocolate cakes, and silver-plated pots of tea. Now, the room was empty, except for Lesley at the window, and she was very still.

'Looks like no one wants tea today?' Paul murmured, coming to stand next to her.

'I think they're packing. There's only a handful of folk still here, anyway, and they're all leaving tomorrow.'

'Including Mrs Meredith and her son.'

She looked down at her hands on the window sill. 'They'd have left sooner, only Mrs Meredith had a bit of a flare-up of her arthritis.'

'I understand she's rather better now.'

'Yes, she'll be able to manage the train.'

'Next to go will be us,' he said after a pause. 'Had you heard this hotel is going to become a military hospital?'

'A hospital?' She stared. 'I canna believe it. What'll happen to all the things? The furniture and everything?'

'Go into store. Mr Wilcox is going to superintend the transition.'

'They really think there'll be a lot of casualties?'

He smiled faintly. 'There are usually casualties in a war, Lesley.'

'Yes, but they said it'd be over by Christmas.'

'We'll have to see how it goes.'

'Maybe I'll look for war work, then, if it's all going to last a long time.'

'Might you not be getting married?'

She hesitated. 'I don't think there'll be time before Christopher goes to war. He's hoping to join a Guards regiment very soon.'

'The Guards? I'm not looking for anything so grand. Just anybody who'll take me.' He looked up and smiled. 'Seems like we have a taker for tea, after all.'

Old Mrs Gillespie, one of the regular visitors to the spa, was slowly advancing into the Palm Court, tapping her stick and looking about her.

'Is there to be no tea today?' she called in a high-pitched English voice. 'Where is everybody?'

'Tea is just about to be served, madam,' said Paul, holding a chair for her at one of the tables. 'See, you have your very own waitress!'

'Ah, yes, the girl with the pretty hair. Fetch me

194

something nice, my dear, won't you? At my age, something nice for tea is all one can look forward to, you know.'

Chapter Thirty-Eight

On his last evening at the Grand Forest, Christopher dined alone, his mother having decided to keep to her room and save her strength. Like the few other guests dotted around the great dining room, he was in casual clothes – in his case, a light suit, somewhat wrinkled. But his hair was as well brushed as ever, and he still gave the impression of having just left a wonderfully refreshing bath.

Although Bill and Ivor served his meal, Lesley was on hand to pour his coffee when he moved to the Palm Court, and as her eyes met his, a thrill of feeling ran between them.

'Never mind this coffee, let's get out of here,' he said urgently. 'There's hardly anyone about – surely, you're not needed?'

'Give me a few minutes to change,' she responded. 'Meet me in the gardens.'

It was still so light outside, they felt themselves brilliantly on view, and decided to make for the woods again. There, in the shadows of the full-leaved trees, they kissed and swayed in an agony of bitter-sweet joy. Their last night together . . . the knowledge seemed impossible to bear.

When at last they drew apart and stood trembling at arms' length, Lesley looked long into Christopher's face.

'Tell me something,' she whispered.

'Anything!'

'Are we truly engaged?'

'Of course, we are. Are you thinking you've no ring? My darling, I'll buy you a ring as soon as I get back to London.'

'I'm thinking that I won't be with you in London.'

'No, but you know I have to see about getting into a regiment.' He drew her to him, smoothing the hair from her brow, and kissed her. 'We're living in difficult times, you see. Nothing is usual.'

'I wouldn't expect to stay with your folks. I'd get a room somewhere, I could pay for it maself, I've a few pounds saved up—'

'Oh, Lesley!'

'No, it's what I want to do. And then I'd be able to see you until you went away. I mean, it's no' right, you should go to London and I should go to Leith, when we're engaged, is it?'

'Lesley, darling, it's a lovely idea, but it's just not practical. Do you think I hadn't thought of something like that myself? But it wouldn't work. I'll have to be busy most of the time, seeing my uncle's contacts – you remember I said he was the one who was going to try to get me a commission? And you'd be on your own – it wouldn't be fair.'

'I don't care, I don't care.'

'Look, I promise you, as soon as I've got things sorted out, I'll arrange for you to come down.'

'To say goodbye?' she asked hollowly.

He held her without speaking.

'And you still haven't told your folks about me, have you?' she whispered. 'Not even your mother?'

He shook his head. 'No, I haven't said anything. She's been so unwell, in so much pain, from the arthritis. It's rheumatoid, you know, she's had it since she was young, there's not much they can do.'

'I'm very sorry, Christopher, but are you saying it'd make her worse to be told about me?'

'She does know we've been seeing each other.'

'Oh? Who told her?' Lesley's mouth twisted a little. 'Let me guess – it was Miss Atkinson, right? You thought she wouldn't say anything, I was sure she would.'

'Mother seemed to know, anyway.'

'Well, if she knows as much as that, couldn't you tell her we're going to be married?'

'There are difficulties,' he answered reluctantly.

Lesley stared at him. 'I see. Maybe too many.'

'No!' He flung his arms around her. 'It's just that everything seems to have come at once – the war – mother's being unwell – the time's not right. But I love you and I'm not going to give you up, whatever they say. It's me you're marrying, not them.'

The words were sweet to her ears, they made her feel a little better, but not completely better.

'Couldn't we tell your mother tonight?' she asked. 'Just to – make a start.'

'She'll be resting. She told me she was going to have an early dinner and go to bed. There's the long journey tomorrow.'

'All right, we'll leave it then.' Lesley's voice was toneless. 'I think we should go back now. I shouldn't be away too long.'

'Ah, no, it's our last night.' He drew her back to him. 'Don't go yet, please. We have to exchange our addresses, remember.'

She brightened, as he wrote his London address on a page from his diary and tore it out for her. 'Now, yours,' he said cheerfully, and it seemed so strange to watch him write 15, The Kirkgate, Leith, and know that that would go with him wherever he went.

'Oh, I do love you, Christopher!' she cried suddenly, and kissed him hard. 'If only I was called Marcia!'

'Good God, I'm glad you're not! But, look, I want you to see these.' He took a package from his breast pocket. 'You remember our day in Inverness?'

'I'll never forget it.'

'Well, these are the photographs we took. I've just had them developed.'

Photographs. She'd forgotten all about them. But there they were – memories frozen, memories to keep, for ever.

'Oh, Christopher!'

'They're mostly of you. See, that's you by the loch, that's another of you by the loch, that's you on a seat—'

'Where are you?' she cried impatiently. 'I took one of you, didn't I?'

'Wait a bit, it's here somewhere. Yes, this is it. A bit dark, I'm afraid.' He smiled. 'Weather looks thundery.'

'There wasn't a cloud in the sky,' she whispered, gazing at the photograph. It showed Christopher, hat in hand, standing in front of the loch, his smile very broad, his hair, normally so smoothly brushed, rather on end. He looked very young and very happy, and as she looked from the likeness to the real man, watching her with so much love in his eyes, she wanted to cry. That moment when she had caught him on camera had slipped away for ever. But she had the memory and she had the photograph.

'Christopher, it's lovely,' she said quietly.

'Steady on! I've never been called that before!'

'I'll keep it for ever.'

'And I'll keep yours. But there's one more. Remember that fellow took us together?'

The unknown man's photograph was clearer than hers, and showed the two of them, again with the loch as background. Christopher had his arm around Lesley's shoulders, and they were looking, not towards the camera, but into each other's faces. Quite unmistakable was the feeling they shared, and as she looked at it, smiling now, Lesley knew how Paul and Nick and others had needed no telling that she and Christopher were in love.

'Who'll keep this one?' she asked.

'You can have it, I have my pictures of you. Wish they'd been in colour, to show your beautiful hair.'

'They're perfect as they are.' Lesley looked about her, at the subtle change in the light that told her it was getting late. 'Christopher, I have to go. In fact, I've stayed too long, already.'

'What does it matter now? You're all going to leave, anyway, it doesn't matter about your job any more.'

She shook her head. 'I still canna stay out all night.'

'Can't you?'

Their eyes met and for a moment they were as motionless as their images in the photographs Christopher had returned to his pocket.

'You think we can stay here, in the woods?' Lesley asked, catching her breath and laughing.

'No, I was joking, of course.'

She said in a whisper, 'I could come to your room.'

'Now you're joking.' His voice was shaking. 'Aren't you?'

'I don't know. We are engaged.'

'I couldn't let you do that, Lesley. No, it's out of the question. It wouldn't be fair.'

'I might never see you again!'

'You will, you will.' He gathered her into his arms, and for a while they clung together, not kissing, just letting their dread of the unknown flow over them.

'I'll have to go,' said Lesley, at last, and slowly, as though injured, they made their way back to the door of the hotel dining room. It was almost dark now, and there was no one about, but inside there were a couple of men smoking and talking in low tones, while Colum MacNee stood waiting to put out lights.

'Goodnight, my darling,' Christopher said. 'Don't come to the station tomorrow, I don't think I could bear it.'

'I'm coming, I have to come.'

He sighed. 'All right, then, we'll say goodbye there. You're going up now?'

'Yes, but please may I have ma photos?'

'Oh, yes, I almost forgot! You keep the package. I'll put mine in my wallet.'

They parted at last, with Lesley trailing away, turning often to look back at Christopher, oblivious of old Colum's inquisitive stare. The climb to the top floor had never seemed so long and when she reached her room, she was wishing with all her heart and soul that Ella would not be there. Oh, just not to have to talk about Christopher! Just to be quiet, on her own, to look at his photograph again! And then she found the room was empty. Ella must have gone to the bathroom, her clothes were neatly folded on the chair by her bed.

Poor Ella, she'll have given me up, thought Lesley, and sat for a moment or two on her own bed. A door banged and she leaped to her feet, but it was not Ella returning. After a moment, she moved to put her photographs in her bag on the chest of drawers. Then she let herself out of her room and ran like the wind to the stairs.

All was quiet on the wide corridor of the second floor, but then it would be quiet, with so many of the guests' rooms unoccupied. But Number 208 was occupied, she knew that. She'd always known Christopher's room number, had in fact once gone to the room when she'd known he wasn't there, and had looked at his brushes on the dressing table, and his beautiful clothes in the wardrobe. Giving herself no time to think, she now sped down the long expanse of carpet, under the dimmed ceiling lights, to Number 208 again. There was no one about, no one at all to see her, as she tapped on the door.

When he opened it, she didn't speak. Nor did he. He only stretched out his arms and drew her in.

Chapter Thirty-Nine

Christopher seemed stunned, yet not too stunned to hold Lesley fast, in case she did not stay.

'You came?' he kept saying. 'You came to me?'

'Yes, I said I would.'

'But I said you shouldn't!'

'You don't want me to go?'

'Oh, God, no. How could I?' He held her closer. 'I'm only flesh and blood.'

He eyes, moving beyond him, had found his suitcases, open on the floor, and her heart lurched. She'd been right to come. Tomorrow, he and those suitcases would be gone. This was their last chance.

'It's our last chance,' she whispered to him. 'To be together. It might be all we'll ever have.'

'Don't say that, don't say that.'

They clung together, kissing and caressing, then Christopher began to take down Lesley's hair, while she held the pins, and when he had finished, she laid them on his dressing table, as though she had always shared his dressing table and there was nothing strange about it. Yet what could be stranger than to come to his room late at night with the intention of making love? She should have been amazed at herself, yet it all seemed so natural.

'Are you sure you want to do this?' he asked, hoarsely, when they had thrown their clothes aside. 'I have to know.'

'I'm sure.'

'Well, I've only got a single bed.' He pointed to it, with an attempt at laughter. 'And the sheets are starched.'

'Let's no' mind the sheets. But will you put out the light?'

'Ah, why? You're so beautiful, Lesley. Couldn't we keep it on, so that I can see you?'

'You could just put it out for now.'

So it was in the dark that she had her first experience of love, though all that mattered to her was that it was with Christopher. Many women's first time was with their husbands, and it was the same for her. Christopher was her husband. Or, he would be. This was her wedding night.

He was worried about her, but she told him there was no need. She was in heaven.

'Me, too,' he said fervently. 'I still can't believe you're here, with me like this, I think I'm dreaming.'

'We're in the same dream, then.'

'Why did you come?' he pressed. 'Why did you take such a risk?'

'Because I wanted to and because you never asked me to. You respected me, Christopher, you even called me Miss MacKenzie.'

'Called you Miss MacKenzie?' He smiled in the darkness. 'Was that important?'

'It was to me.' But a great weight was settling round her heart. Time was passing, soon it would be morning. Before then, she had to leave him and she didn't know how she could.

'Christopher, I have to go!' she cried in anguish.

'Let me put on the light now,' he urged. 'Let me see you, Lesley, please.'

For a little while, as they delighted in each other's bodies, they were able to forget the time, but Christopher's little bedside clock ticked on, and Lesley's eyes could not at last evade it. It was the hardest thing she'd ever done, to loosen herself from his grasp and slide from his bed, but she found the courage, she did it.

'I have to get dressed,' she said desolately. 'I have to go back to ma room. Lord knows what Ella's thinking.'

'She'll be asleep, she won't know, you could stay a little longer.'

'The longer I stay, the worse it'll be to go.'

'I know, I know.' Christopher tied on his dressing gown, as Lesley fast got into her clothes. 'You're the brave one, Lesley.'

'Brave?' She gave a brief smile, as she pinned up her hair. 'I'm no' brave. Inside, I'm crying ma eyes out.'

'Well, that's what being brave means, isn't it? Keeping feelings on the inside.'

'I canna promise I'll be able to do it tomorrow.'

'At the station? I really don't want you to come. It'll be terrible, Lesley. Imagine it. My mother there, and the Territorials – they're taking the same train, I've been told. How can we say goodbye?'

'I'm coming,' she said obstinately. 'Don't try to stop me.'

'All right, if it's what you really want to do.'

'It is.'

He touched the little brooch she had fastened to her blouse. 'I haven't forgotten the ring,' he said softly. 'I wish I'd bought one in Inverness. But I'll get one in London.'

'I don't care about a ring, Christopher. Folk I know hardly ever have rings.'

'I want you to have one, to wear while I'm away.'

As she turned aside, her lip trembling, he caught at her hand. 'And there's something else I mean to do. I'm going to tell my mother about us tomorrow.'

'Your mother?'

'Yes, you were right. She should be told. It's only fair, to you, and her.'

'Maybe it'd be too much, Christopher.'

'You did ask me to tell her.'

'I know, but she's no' well and you're going away. I don't want to be the one to upset her.'

'I'm going to tell her,' he repeated. 'I think now, I should.'

As he drew her to him once again, she saw the anxiety in his eyes. 'Don't look so worried,' she murmured. 'You needn't tell her yet.'

'It's you I'm worrying about, Lesley.' He held her close. 'We shouldn't have made love, I shouldn't have let you take the risk.'

'Look, I'm all right!'

'But supposing – you know – anything happens?'

She had been trying to put from her mind the thought that anything might.

'No point in worrying,' she told him. 'At least, till we have to.'

'Lesley, I promise you, I won't let you down.'

'I know. I trust you. We're going to be married, aren't we?'

'Of course we are.'

'Well, then.'

They kissed again, long and sadly, and finally drew apart. Christopher opened his door and looked out into the corridor. It was silent and empty.

'Till tomorrow,' he whispered.

'Yes. Tomorrow.'

Lesley moved away, walking slowly, then faster, and at the end of the corridor looked back, to see him still at his door. He raised his hand and she raised hers, then she began to climb the stairs to the next floor. After standing for some moments without moving, Christopher turned and went back into his room.

In her own room on the top floor, Lesley sat on her bed in the dark, making no attempt to undress again, only fingering the brooch on her blouse and letting her desolation wash over her.

'Is that you, Lesley?' cried Ella sitting up with a start.

'Yes, it's me.'

'Where've you been? I was that worried—'

'Ella, don't say anything, eh?'

'All right, dear. Goodnight, then.'

'Goodnight,' said Lesley.

Chapter Forty

The following morning, before he went down to the dining room for his last breakfast at the Grand Forest, Christopher went to see his mother in her room. She was up and dressed in her travelling costume, her hat lying ready on the bed, and was sitting at a table in the window, pouring coffee. He thought she looked better, but not well; there were signs of pain around her mouth, her eyes were shadowed.

'How are you, Mother?' he asked, kissing her cheek, and she instantly put on a show of radiance.

'Much better, Christopher, thank you.'

'All set for the trip?'

'Oh, yes, I'll do very well. I shall be sorry to leave Glenmar, you know, I'm sure it was doing me good, but I'll be glad to get back to London. To be with your father, at this time.' Mrs Meredith dabbed at her lips. 'Would you like coffee, dear? I can easily ring for another cup.'

'No, thanks, I'm just going down to breakfast.' Christopher looked round his mother's handsome room, with its excellent view of the spa and the hills. 'Miss Atkinson not about?'

'She's at breakfast.'

'I suppose she'll be seeing to your luggage?'

'My dear, it's already gone down. Clara is very efficient.'

'Isn't she?' Christopher continued to look out at his

mother's view. Some young men were gathering at the bandstand, laughing and larking about, while a number of women talked together, and children played. The Territorials, who would shortly be on their way to the station, he thought. Didn't seem worried, did they? But one or two of the women had already taken out handkerchiefs.

'Mother?' he turned back, to face her. 'Mind if I have a word?'

'I can guess what it's about. Our pretty waitress?'

'Always seem to know what I have in my mind, don't you?' he asked, lightly. 'Yes, it's about Lesley. Miss MacKenzie. I want to tell you straight out, no beating about the bush, I love her and I want to marry her.'

'Oh, dear.' His mother gazed at him sympathetically. 'It's the war, isn't it? Making you think you must do the right thing? There's no need, Christopher. Miss MacKenzie will not expect you to marry her.'

'I don't understand the way you're talking, Mother. I'm not trying to do the right thing. I'm marrying her because I want to. We love each other.'

'You think so, dear, but it's only a holiday affair, isn't it? They never last. Your young friend will understand that, I'm sure. She'll know marriage with you is out of the question.'

'Just because she comes from a different background?'

'Yes.' Mrs Meredith's look was still very sympathetic, very understanding. 'Don't say these things don't matter, you know that they do. And poor girl, so does she. You'd be doing her no kindness, exposing her to a life she's not used to. People can be so very cruel.'

'It needn't be like that.'

'Oh? You want to change the world to suit your sweetheart?'

'I was only meaning that Lesley could adapt to my sort of life. She's bright enough.'

'And very pretty. But still not for you, Christopher. I'm sorry.'

Christopher's gaze on his mother was sombre. 'So, you won't help me to speak to Father?'

'Your father?' For the first time, his mother's composure cracked a little. 'Oh, no, you mustn't speak to your father, Christopher! He has enough to worry about, with your going to the war. Promise me you won't say a word!'

'He'll have to be told sooner or later. I mean what I say, I am going to marry Lesley.' As his mother made no answer, Christopher cried urgently, 'Why can't you understand? Weren't you ever in love yourself?'

'Of course I was, and I do understand.' Mrs Meredith's face changed a little. 'But you have to think of what you'll live on, if your father withdraws your allowance. Or asks you to leave your post.'

'He wouldn't do that.'

'He might, if it brings you to your senses.'

'I've a little money from Grandfather's trust fund.'

'It won't be enough, Christopher.'

He shrugged. 'Won't matter while the war is on, anyway. I'll have my army pay.'

As she winced and bowed her head, he went to her and put his arm around her. 'Mother, it's all right, I'll be coming back. Don't worry about me.'

'Don't worry? There are men being killed at this very moment in Belgium. Germans and Belgians, yes. Men. Somebody's sons. Why should you be safe?'

He was silent; he had no answer.

'I don't know how you can think of your own happiness at this time!' his mother added, dabbing at her eyes with a lace handkerchief.

'It's just the time to think of it.' Christopher touched her hand. 'Look, please try to understand, Lesley and I do truly love each other. For both of us, it's the real thing.'

Mrs Meredith lowered her handkerchief and gave a tired smile. 'My dear boy, doesn't everyone think that at the beginning?'

*

As soon as he went into the almost empty dining room, he saw Lesley, standing tall and straight beside his table, waiting for him. He caught his breath, remembering; knew she was remembering, too.

'How are you?' he whispered, as he took his seat.

'Still in heaven. What about you?'

He smiled. 'The same. Listen, don't worry about breakfast for me. I'm not hungry. Just coffee'll do.'

She smiled. 'I'll bring porridge and grilled bacon, just as usual. You're travelling today, remember.'

'Why don't you sit down and have breakfast with me? To hell with Mr Armitage!'

'Ssh, he's just over there.'

But she managed a smile as she passed the assistant manager. One day, yes, she would sit down to breakfast with Christopher, and every other meal, too. And no one would think it strange.

'I suppose you want to go to the station this morning?' Paul asked her, holding open the service door.

'Yes, sir, if that's all right.'

'You might as well, there'll be no guests left here to serve.'

She thanked him and went on in to the kitchens to give her order for Christopher's breakfast.

'Thank God,' said an assistant chef. 'Something to do!'

'Where's Mr Chater?'

'Packing. He's leaving tomorrow.'

'When do we get away, do you think?' asked Bill, who was standing around with Nick and other waiters, while Ishbel was drinking coffee with Ella, whose compassionate eyes Lesley was refusing to meet. Nick shrugged and said it couldn't be too soon for him.

'You going to see him off?' Ella murmured to Lesley, as the chef served Christopher's porridge into an elegant bowl.

'Yes, I'm going to the station.'

'What about his mother? She'll be there.'

'She can't stop me saying goodbye, can she?'

'Another thing,' said Christopher, as she placed the porridge in front of him. 'I've told my mother about us.'

Lesley grew cold. 'What did she say?'

He hesitated. 'She seemed to be more worried about the war.'

'She must have said something about me, Christopher!'

'Well, she thought maybe you wouldn't be happy marrying me – having to live a different sort of life.'

Lesley gave a sardonic smile. 'I see.'

'The truth is, we'd be happy with each other anywhere, wouldn't we?'

'Yes, that's the truth. I'll get the bacon.'

When he had finished his breakfast, she walked with him from the dining room, not bothering to check if Paul Armitage or anyone else was watching.

'I'm going up now for Mother and Miss Atkinson,' said Christopher. 'We have a taxi due, we're not taking the hotel bus.'

'And the train's at ten?'

He nodded. 'Come earlier than that.'

'I'll follow your taxi.'

Their eyes locked. The memory of last night's lovemaking held them in such sweet thrall, they could scarcely find the will to separate, but Christopher at last turned away for the lift and Lesley ran upstairs to change. She was not, of course, going to be seen at the station in her waitress's black dress. Her heart and mind might be Christopher's, but she still wanted to look her best for his mother's eyes.

Chapter Forty-One

The Territorials were marching down the hill to the station, accompanied by a small pipe band, their families, and small children noisily whooping and enjoying the excitement. The young men were enjoying it, too. Although red-faced and sweating, for the day was fearsomely hot, they looked as though they were going on holiday. This war, it was all a bit of fun. Over by Christmas. They'd soon be home again.

'Poor boys,' murmured Mrs Meredith, watching the reservists break ranks from her seat on the platform. Her face beneath her parasol was strained.

'They look happy enough,' said Clara Atkinson.

'Their mothers don't look happy.'

Christopher was striding up and down, edgily waiting for the sight of Lesley. His face too was red and moist and he kept taking off his hat and running his hand through his hair.

'Sit down, dear,' said his mother, watching him.

'Plenty of time to sit down in the train.'

'When it comes,' sighed Miss Atkinson. She narrowed her eyes at their porter in the distance, checking again that he had all their cases. Fortunately, Mrs Meredith's dress trunk had already been sent off, and should be waiting for them in London.

'Have you the tip for the porter?' Mrs Meredith asked her.

'Yes, Mrs Meredith.'

'I've a shilling, anyway,' Christopher muttered, then took off his hat again and stood very still. Lesley was in sight and running towards them. 'Mother, Miss MacKenzie's here. She's come to see us off.'

Mrs Meredith turned her head. 'How kind.'

Lesley came forward. She was wearing her white blouse and blue skirt, with her straw hat trimmed with corn-flowers, and was holding herself very erect, as though to show she had her feelings well under control. Only her eyes, so vividly blue, gave her away; they were anguished.

'Good morning, Mrs Meredith,' she said quietly. 'Miss Atkinson.'

Both women inclined their heads. Christopher indicated the platform bench.

'Would you like to sit down, Lesley?'

'I'm all right, thank you.'

Her eyes were fixed on Mrs Meredith, who looked up at her with a pleasant smile.

'And what is going to happen to you, my dear?' she asked. 'Now that the hotel is closing? I do hope you will be able to find another post.'

Christopher stiffened and replaced his hat. 'It need only be temporary,' he said shortly. 'I've told you something of Lesley's plans.'

Miss Atkinson looked interested. 'War work, perhaps? They say a lot of girls are going into munition factories.'

'Miss MacKenzie is not going into a munition factory,' Christopher said shortly.

'I'm no' quite sure yet, what I'll do,' said Lesley.

Mrs Meredith smiled again. 'Well, whatever it is, my dear, I wish you every success.'

How plain she makes her views without saying an unfriendly word, thought Lesley. She's really nice, really polite, but all the time she's hoping I will just go away. That Christopher will go to war and forget me. That she'll never see me again.

213

Another hotel bus had arrived and more people were streaming on to the platform, exchanging greetings with those who were already there and exclaiming about the heat. The reservists were still talking and laughing, while their mothers put on brave faces and the children ran about, dodging between grown-ups' legs and getting in everyone's way. Over them all, a relentless sun beat down.

'Train's coming!' cried a voice, and a wave of excitement swept the platform. Porters began picking up luggage, people moved forward, the reservists gathered up their packs and kissed their mothers, who were now openly crying. Mrs Meredith put down her parasol and slowly rose, leaning on her stick.

'Can I help?' asked Lesley quickly, but Christopher was already giving his arm to his mother and Miss Atkinson was gathering up their belongings. The train for Aviemore was clanking to a halt, the porters were opening doors, and Lesley stood back. There was no role for her here.

'Goodbye, my dear,' Mrs Meredith said kindly. 'And I wish you the very best of luck for the future. Now, I think we have seats arranged, don't we, Christopher?'

'First Class this way!' called the Merediths' porter, and Christopher, shepherding his mother to their compartment, looked back in agony at Lesley.

'Wait!' he mouthed, but there was no question of her doing anything else. She would not leave without their last goodbye, she would not leave until the train had carried him finally from her view.

In a moment, he was back, diving through the waving mothers, to take her in his arms.

'Don't worry, don't worry, I'll come home to you, you'll see, and I'll write, I'll be in touch!'

Their mouths met in a last intense kiss, which was over before the onlookers could become too interested, and as they pulled themselves apart, their eyes made their last tragic farewells.

'The guard's looking at his watch,' Lesley murmured

with a sob. 'You'd better go, Christopher.'

He pressed her hand, still making no move.

'Taking this train, sir?' roared the guard.

'Oh, God, yes,' he answered and ran. As soon as he was aboard, the guard brought down his flag and the train began to move. The children ran alongside, the young men waved, and Christopher waved, until the train had moved quite away and Lesley and the waiting mothers could no longer see anything for tears.

Chapter Forty-Two

The Hotel Grand Forest was empty now, except for the staff. But it was the guests, not the staff, who were the life-blood of the hotel, and there were no guests. In every hotel and boarding house in the spa, it was the same. No guests, only staff, moving round echoing rooms, feeling hollow, feeling strange. Soon, the staff would be gone too, leaving Glenmar to revert to its old role of quiet little village. Until the workmen arrived to transform the Grand Forest into a military hospital. Until the patients arrived.

'I find this very depressing,' said George Wilcox, standing in the Palm Court with Paul Armitage. 'Not to say heart-breaking.'

They were taking a last look at the vast hall, seeing it as it had always been, knowing that the following day the packers would arrive to strip this and every room in the hotel. Carpets would be rolled up, curtains taken down, furniture, china, glass, pictures, chandeliers, the piano – all would be wrapped and removed to Edinburgh for storage. Only the wine in the cellars would remain, but that would be locked well away for the duration of the war.

Mr Chater, the head chef, would not be there to see the removal of his precious pans and kitchen equipment, he having already taken himself down to a London hotel. Mr

Vass had gone, too, but only to Edinburgh, where he had obtained a post at the Caledonian.

Lucky devil, thought Mr Wilcox. He himself was staying on in the village from where he would superintend the closure of the hotel with the aid of Miss Newall and Moyra Gillan; then he would be looking for a job. The rest of the staff would be leaving tomorrow. This was their last night.

'Heartbreaking,' said Mr Wilcox again, shaking his head.

'I'm afraid there's going to be a lot of heartbreak around before the war is over,' said Paul.

'Oh, I'm not comparing this to what's happening to Europe. But for us to see the end of all our work – you must admit, Paul, it's hard.'

'It's hard,' Paul admitted.

On that last night, the staff had a scratch supper of cold ham and salad in their dining room. Mr Wilcox, accompanied by Mr Armitage, looked in to thank them for all they'd done and to wish them all the best for the future, especially those who would be joining up. After the war, he could promise them that the hotel would be re-opened, everything would be as it had been before. Somehow they knew, he didn't believe a word of it.

'Nothing should have been changed in the first place!' cried Sadie Newall, when the manager and his assistant had left them. 'Imagine, this beautiful hotel being turned into a hospital! And where are all the casualties coming from? Everyone knows the war will be over by Christmas.'

'Seemingly the Jerries are doing pretty well in Belgium,' Bill Souter remarked. 'And our chaps are no' even there yet.'

'The government's appealing for more volunteers,' put in Nick. 'Looks like we'll be some of 'em.'

'Oh, Nick!' groaned Ishbel. 'You said you were no' keen!'

'I'm still no' keen. Thing is, you don't want to go to

217

war, but you don't want NOT to, if you understand me.'

'Canna be left out,' said Bill.

'Duty calls,' Ella murmured. 'Isn't that what you once said, Ned?'

'Aye, I said that,' he agreed.

He looked pale and ill, but no one was surprised. Poor laddie, eh? Struggling not to take a drink? Lesley, sitting next to him and looking almost as pale, wanted to reach out and touch his hand, but he would probably have pulled his hand away. He did not appreciate sympathy, which Moyra and Ella had already divined and had been careful not to offer any.

'What are you joining?' asked Bill easily. 'I might try for the Black Watch.'

Ned shrugged. 'I'll have to think about it.' He drank from his glass of tonic water. 'Canna wait to get away now, anyway. Thank God, we're leaving tomorrow.'

After supper, which the remaining kitchen staff graciously agreed to clear away, no one knew what to do. They wandered around the empty rooms, so recently filled with elegant guests, and opened the french windows to the gardens, where they strolled and smoked and wondered if old Wilcox was watching them from his window. Couldn't say anything, could he? They'll all be gone next day.

'Feel like we're in a ship that's drifting,' said Bill. 'No engine, no lifeboats.'

'And no captain,' said Nick. 'Abandon ship!'

They laughed and sat in the evening sun, until someone suggested that they should push the tables back in the main dining room and have a little dance. Ned could play for them. But Ned said he was going to bed, his head was throbbing like the devil. Miss Newall, too, said she'd go up and finish her packing, she'd no heart for sitting around chatting.

'Unless it's to Mr Armitage,' Ella whispered to Lesley.

But there was no sign of Mr Armitage.

'Tell you what, let's play cards,' said Ivor Greig, after Ned had left them. 'Come on, we'll be like thae bridge players, eh? Bill, kindly bring me a brandy, and make it a double!'

'Hey, that reminds me – what's going to happen to all the wine, then? They're no' trying to move that, eh?'

'No, they're leaving it locked up,' Ivor made a face. 'All us wine waiters have had to surrender our keys.'

'No brandy, then?'

'Just in imagination. Listen, who knows where the cards are?'

'It'll have to be whist, if I play,' said Ishbel. 'I canna play bridge.'

'Whist it is, and we'll have a little flutter, eh? Make it more exciting.'

Chapter Forty-Three

Lesley, who had no desire to play cards, followed Ned, as the eyes of Ella and Moyra followed her, but they made no move to go with her. By the time she caught him, he was outside his room and gave her a sharp look when she called his name.

'What's wrong? You want to check up on me? No bottles under the bed, I promise you.'

'Ned, I'm no' checking up on you. I just wanted to see how you are.'

'You've no' had much time to ask me that before, of course.'

'I'm sorry.'

Ned's expression softened. 'I shouldn't've said anything. You've got your troubles. Don't think I don't sympathise.' He opened the door to his room. 'Come on in, for a minute. See, it's tidy, eh? I'm all packed and ready to go.'

While he sank on to his bed, Lesley sat on his one chair and remembered the last time she'd been in this room. What a state it had been in! And Ned had been even worse. Now the room was spartan in its stripped neatness and Ned was no longer drunk, but he didn't look well. What would Auntie Peg say about his pallor? Or her own? Peg's eyes wouldn't miss a thing.

'Is it very bad?' she asked Ned quietly. 'Giving up the drink?'

'Aye.'

'I can imagine what it must be like.'

'No, you canna imagine. If you're no' a drinker, you canna imagine.'

'Is there anything I can do to help?'

He shook his head. 'Only person who's been helpful is Mr Armitage. He gave me the address of a place in Edinburgh where you can go and they sorta talk you through it.'

'A temperance place?'

'No, they don't make you sign the pledge, or anything, they just try to help you no' to take another drink.'

'Mr Armitage doesn't drink himself, does he?'

'Lord, no! He'd never give in to anything like drinking. But he's been a good friend to me, Lesley, he's a nice chap.'

'Will you try this place in Edinburgh?'

'I think I might.'

'What about the war? You won't go, will you? You needn't. You're a musician.'

He smiled grimly. 'Think that matters?'

Lesley slowly stood up. 'Well, I'll see you in the morning.' She paused at the door. 'Funny to think that this is our last night here, eh? Tomorrow night, we'll be back in Leith.'

Ned, holding his aching head, swung off his bed and came to stand at the door with her. 'I'm looking forward to it. Seeing everybody again.' He turned back to his room. 'Goodnight, Lesley.'

'Ned—'

'What?'

'I was thinking – maybe you'd like to write to Ella? I could give you her address.'

'Ella? There'd be no point. We're no' likely to meet again.'

'I thought you might be fond of her.'

'I am, but I'm no' a suitable fella for any girl just now. Got to sort maself out, Lesley.'

221

'So, Moyra's no' the one, either?'

'Look, stop matchmaking. I told you a long time ago I wasn't ready for anything serious.'

'I think Ella could be a grand help to you, Ned. She's steady and true. You could rely on her.'

Ned fixed Lesley with a dark, brooding gaze.

'And how about your Christopher? Can you rely on him?'

'We are not talking about Christopher!' Lesley cried spiritedly. 'Goodnight, Ned!'

Breathing hard, she ran down the main staircase. In the past, this had been strictly for the exclusive use of hotel guests, but who cared now? She certainly didn't. All she was conscious of was the ache in her heart which never eased, however much she tried to interest herself in other things. But what a fool she'd been to try to plead Ella's case with Ned! She should know by now that folk managed their own love affairs, and in any case it was true that Ned had his particular problems to solve.

'All ready for tomorrow, Lesley?' came Mr Armitage's voice, and she drew up with a start at the foot of the stairs.

'I'm sorry, I didn't see you, Mr Armitage.'

'Probably didn't recognise me, out of my tails.'

It was true, he did look different, in a light tweed suit instead of his formal dress clothes. Different, and younger. More human. He didn't make any comment about her coming down the main stairs.

'I've packed ma case,' she told him. 'And our boxes have already gone.'

Well, of course, he knew that. He knew everything.

'I've just been up to see Ned, Mr Armitage, and I'd like to thank you. He says you've been very helpful to him. It's good of you.'

'I was glad to do anything I could. Ned is worth helping. I believe he's got the chance now to be free of alcohol altogether.'

He took her arm and they crossed the vestibule, where Veronica and Alison would once have been at Reception, Colum MacNee would have been at the door, and Paul himself would have been greeting guests, smiling, answering questions, keeping his finger on the pulse of the hotel. Now, it was empty. The receptionists had left the day before, Colum had returned to his home in the village, and Paul was looking at Lesley.

'How are you?' he asked softly. 'You've been having a hard time, I think.'

'I'm all right, thanks.'

'When are you going to see Mr Meredith again?'

'I'm no' sure.' Lesley looked directly into Paul's eyes. 'But he's told his mother about us, so it's no secret any more.'

'I'm very pleased to hear it.'

'Och, she didn't exactly cheer. But it shows he's sincere.'

'Yes, indeed.' Paul hesitated, 'Well, I'll see you in the morning, bright and early, before the packers come.'

'Goodnight, Mr Armitage.'

'We're no longer employees of the Grand Forest,' he reminded her with a smile. 'Couldn't you call me Paul?'

Chapter Forty-Four

At breakfast on their last morning, Sadie Newall suddenly burst into tears.

'Och, it's so embarrassing, eh?' Ishbel murmured, watching the housekeeper hurrying from the dining room with a handkerchief pressed to her eyes. 'Crying like a bairn because the hotel's closing!'

'Poor old thing,' whispered Ella.

'She's only thirty-five,' said Moyra, rising to run after Miss Newall.

'Well, there you are.' Ella, buttering an oatcake, laughed a little.

'Canna help feeling sorry for her,' said Lesley. 'This hotel has been her whole life, and now it's been taken from her.'

'Aye, and her chance to get her hooks into you know who,' said Ishbel. 'Mr Armitage must be glad to be joining up, eh? To get away from her?'

'Speak of the devil, here he is,' Ella warned, as Paul came swiftly into the dining room and raised his hand for attention.

'Just a few last words – when you've finished breakfast, would you please strip your beds and make sure your rooms are clear? Miss Newall has put laundry baskets on the landing for the sheets and towels. Then assemble at the front entrance for the bus to the station.' Paul smiled briefly. 'Thank you.'

'He's no' bad-looking, you know,' said Ishbel, when Paul had left.

'Who?' Nick called down the table.

'Mr Armitage.'

'Mr Armitage? He's about as exciting as a plank o' wood.' Nick's eyes went to Lesley. 'Wouldn't you say, Lesley?'

'I've never thought about him.'

Nick made no reply but, as the hotel staff began to make their way upstairs, contrived to walk with her.

'Is everything all right?' he asked in a low voice. 'I mean, with you and that fella Meredith?'

Lesley flashed a look at him. 'Everything's fine.'

'I just want you to be happy, you ken.'

'Well, I am. I expect you know, we're engaged.'

'Yes. Word gets around.' He gave a sudden smile. 'I think I might end up engaged maself.'

'To Ishbel? Nick, that's wonderful!' Lesley, somewhat relieved, kissed his cheek, at which he looked round quickly to see if Ishbel was watching, but she had gone on ahead.

'I'm really happy for you both,' Lesley said warmly. 'Be sure to invite me to the wedding, eh?'

'Aye.' He gave her a sideways glance. 'And how about your wedding, then?'

'No plans yet.'

'But he's in London?'

'Trying to join up.'

'Like the rest of us.' Nick stopped and took Lesley's hand. 'All the best, then. I mean that, Lesley.'

'I know.' She pressed the hand in hers. 'Good luck, Nick.'

As she looked into his quick bright eyes, something squeezed her heart. Going where he was going, he would very likely need more luck than she did. And the same would be true of all of them, all the young waiters and chefs leaving this hotel, streaming off to enlist, all the young men queuing at the recruiting offices, Christopher, too. Oh, better not think of Christopher, or she might disgrace herself, like poor Miss Newall.

'Good luck,' she said again to Nick, and went on to her room.

'Got the sheets off!' Ella cried cheerfully. 'Help me put 'em in that basket outside.'

'Who's going to do this laundry?' asked Lesley, as they heaved their sheets and towels into the basket on the landing and returned to their room.

'Miss Newall's organising it. Her last chance to organise something for the dear old Grand Forest.'

'I wonder what she'll do now?'

'Probably join something where she can boss people about. You ready to go, Lesley?'

'One last look.'

Lesley moved to the window and leaned on the sill, gazing out at the familiar view. She remembered her first sight of it, blurred by the tears she would not shed; the beauty of it, the tranquillity, that was so far removed from the Kirkgate. Then, she had only wanted the Kirkgate. Now, this view was a part of her. And she must leave it, because of war. It was hard to understand.

'Remember how homesick I used to be?' she called back to Ella, her eyes moving across to the hills, shimmering in the summer heat, and back to the pump rooms, empty now. 'I remember thinking, for two pins I'd go home. And now I am going home.'

'Maybe not for long.' Ella was opening and shutting drawers and checking the wardrobe. 'All clear here. I think we should be going down.'

Not looking in the mirror, Lesley put on her hat. She didn't want to see herself in this same hat with the corn-flowers, the one she'd worn at the station, saying goodbye to Christopher. She didn't want to go again to the station, either, but of course she'd no choice. Don't think of it, she told herself. Don't think of that last kiss, or waving goodbye, or seeing that train steaming away. Not until you're on your own. For it was only when she was on her own that she unfolded all the memories, smoothed them out and studied them, taking comfort.

'We've had some good times here, Ella,' she said, taking a deep breath. 'You've been a grand friend, I won't forget you.'

Ella hesitated for a moment. 'If you ever need me, Lesley, you know where to find me. You've got me mum's address, eh?'

'If I need you?'

'Well, you never know, dear, what'll happen.'

Ella's eyes were wary, Lesley's understanding.

'You should trust Christopher, Ella. I do.'

'Yes, I'm sure.'

'All right, I did sleep with him the other night. But we're going to be married. There's no need to worry.'

'I'm only saying, if you need me, I'll be there.'

'I appreciate that, Ella, I really do.' Lesley threw her arms round Ella's plump shoulders. 'Will you write to me? Keep in touch?'

'It's a promise. Now, we'd better go.'

They came out of the front entrance together into a crowd of hotel workers standing by the bus. From under his shaggy brows, Colum MacNee, up from the village, was glowering at everyone for no reason at all, except that he liked glowering, and Mr Wilcox was looking depressed, Miss Newall tragic, and Mr Armitage calm as ever.

'Time to be leaving,' he said cheerfully. 'Better get the luggage in, Colum.'

'Aye, if these laddies care to give a hond,' Colum retorted. 'I'll not be after straining ma back, I'm telling you!'

'We'll all give a hand, no need to worry.'

'Honestly, is he a porter, or is he not?' Ishbel murmured.

'If we were guests, he'd be putting our luggage in quick enough, eh?'

'Och, he's no' so bad,' said Bill, swinging up cases. 'I never minded old Colum. He's staying on, you ken – porter and handyman for the hospital.'

'Lucky hospital,' said Ishbel. 'Nick, shall we get in the bus now? I just want away.'

Ned, picking up his violin case from where he'd left it at the entrance, saw Moyra standing there, her large grey eyes steady on his face. She, of course, was not leaving, and was waiting to say goodbye. On an impulse, he stooped and kissed her cheek.

'Goodbye, Moyra, and all the best.'

'Goodbye, Ned,' she said quietly.

'Hope you find a job you like,' he said after a moment.

'I'm thinking of doing war work when we've finished here. Making munitions, maybe.'

'That'll be hard. Too hard for you, Moyra.'

She shrugged. 'I don't mind hard work.'

'Well, take care of yourself, anyway, eh?'

'And you, Ned.'

'Aye.' He smiled uneasily and walked back to the bus where Ella was standing, watching. He glanced round for Lesley and called to her to come.

She was looking back at the hotel. Images filled her mind. Did no one else see them? Did no one else hear the music? 'Tell me pretty maiden, Are there any more at home like you? There are a few, kind sir, But simple girls and proper, too ...'

'Lesley, come on!' Ned cried impatiently.

'Lesley, we're waiting for you,' said Paul Armitage, not impatiently at all.

'I'm coming,' said Lesley, and climbed on the bus.

Colum started the engine and everyone cheered. Mr Wilcox raised his hand. Moyra waved. Miss Newall dabbed her eyes.

'Goodbye, goodbye!' cried the hotel workers, and

228

'Goodbye!' cried those who were left.

'Good luck!' cried Ishbel, and Nick raised his eyebrows. 'Who's the good luck for?'

'Don't know. Must be somebody who wants it.'

Down the drive went the bus and turned left for the station, just as the first of a line of great furniture vans from Edinburgh hove into sight. The packers had arrived.

Part Three

Chapter Forty-Five

It was the week before Christmas, 1914. Peg MacNab had come over to the old flat in the Kirkgate where she was planning to give Carrie a hand with the tea. Poor girl, she could do with a bit of help, now that she was in the family way. Only three months on but still feeling sick, and she'd Ned and Lesley in the house as well. Of course, Lesley did what she could, but she was back at the Princess Louise and didn't get much time, and Ned was playing his fiddle at the Royal Albert, and wouldn't be expected to do anything anyway.

Peg was secretly worried about Ned, and Lesley, too, come to that. Being up at that grand hotel in the Highlands didn't seem to have done either of them much good. Both were that pale, eh? And so often sitting, lost in thought, when everybody else was talking around them.

Mind, Lesley'd cheered up when she'd gone down to London early in December and come back with a ring that had set everybody's eyes blinking! Seemed everything she'd said about the gentleman she'd taken up with was true, though Peg and Carrie couldn't really believe it. But he'd sent for her to say goodbye before he went to the front, and he'd put that ring on her finger, you couldn't deny it. Aye, but there was still his parents to reckon with, eh? Lesley'd no' be out of the wood until she'd a wedding ring to go with thae diamonds.

As for Ned, he'd been in a funny mood since he got back

from Glenmar. Always so cheerful before, now he was downright morose. Never went out drinking on his nights off from the Royal Albert, though he did go out sometimes without saying where he was going. Mostly, he just played his fiddle, or else sat looking at his hands. Och, Peg didn't know what to make of him, even if Sam was pleased and said it was his opinion that Ned had signed the pledge. But no one else liked to ask Ned if he had. He, who'd been as open as they came in the old days, was now a closed book.

And then there was the war to worry about. Over by Christmas, everybody'd said. Well, here it was, only a week to go, and the war was not over, nor likely to be in the near future. The troops were settling in, folk said, in the trenches, and that was after there'd been retreats from battles on both sides and the casualty lists were horrific. Mons, the Marne, Ypres – all strange names that had become familiar, all taking dreadful toll of young lives. Peg often sat and cried over the newspapers, though it did no good, she knew. You had to keep your spirits up, there was nothing else to do, and at least she could be grateful that neither Ned nor Joe had volunteered.

Peg was dicing carrots on that dark December afternoon when Ned and Joe came into the flat together. Carrie was lying down and Joe went straight in to see her, while Ned said, yes, he'd like a cup of tea if there was one in the pot.

'Cold out?' asked Peg, pouring his tea.

'Aye, and miserable.'

Ned held out his long, strong-fingered and graceful hands to the open door of range. He'd come from the Royal Albert Hotel where he played with another trio, and very pleased he'd been to get the job. Wouldn't have got it, either, he said, without his experience at the Grand Forest. That afternoon, he'd been playing for the tea dance that finished at five.

'How'd it go?' asked Peg.

'What?'

'The tea dance, o' course!'

'Oh.' He shrugged. 'Same as usual. Officers on leave and girls looking at me because I'm no' in uniform.'

'Why, what a piece o' nonsense, Ned! Why'd they be looking at you?'

'I'm a civilian, right? And a young man and fit. I should be at the front.' He stood up, rubbing his hands. 'I tell you, I can see it in their eyes, what they think.'

'But Ned, that's no' fair! Why should they single out you?'

'Think they'd expect Miss Brown and Mrs Perry to go to war?' Ned laughed without humour. 'They're the cellist and the pianist, you ken. Middle-aged ladies. I stick out like a sore thumb. Och, I'm away to wash ma hands.'

While Ned slammed into the scullery, Carrie, followed by Joe, came to get warm by the range.

'How are you feeling, pet?' Peg asked solicitously, pouring out more tea.

'All right, thanks.' Carrie sighed and sank into a chair. 'Six months to go, eh? Feels like six years.'

'Ah, Carrie, don't say that!' Joe said earnestly. 'It'll soon pass, you'll see!'

'Oh, and you'd know!' Carrie answered laughing. 'Trust you to be cheerful!'

'I'm no' always cheerful.' Joe stood, drinking his tea. 'When I think o' thae chaps over the Channel.'

There was a silence. Carrie and Peg exchanged glances.

'Well, I'm glad you're no' there,' Carrie said at last. 'I ken fine you're hankering to go, but you'd be crazy, eh?'

'Joe, you'd never go?' cried Peg. 'With Carrie expecting, and all? And then there's your Ma to think about, your Kenny's already away, remember.'

'As though I can forget.' Joe set down his cup. 'But I've no' said I was going. It's just that I canna help feeling bad, with Kenny and everybody doing ma fighting for me. When they come back, what'll they say to me? "What did you do in the war, Joe? Deliver Christmas cards?"'

'If they come back,' said Ned, from the doorway. 'IF

235

they come back, they might ask you that.'

Joe looked at him for a moment without speaking, then went to his bag he had thrown down in the corner.

'Talking of Christmas cards, I've got a couple for Lesley, and one for you, Ned. Lesley no' back yet?'

'She's working late tonight,' said Carrie, watching Ned open his Christmas card. She tried to smile. 'That from one o' your admirers, Ned?'

'No.' He held it out for her to see. 'It's a regimental card from Mr Armitage, the assistant manager at the Grand Forest. Used to be, I mean. He's in one of the London regiments now.'

'Whyever would he send you a Christmas card?' asked Peg. 'I mean, the assistant manager? Were you special friends?'

'He was very kind to me,' Ned answered after a pause. No one asked why he should have needed particular kindness. 'But he's probably sent one to Lesley as well.'

'Ah,' said Joe, grinning. 'I can imagine he'd be kind to Lesley, too. One of her cards is from London, like yours, Ned.'

'Aren't we nosey?' asked Carrie. 'Looking at the postmarks! I bet there's one from that Christopher Meredith.'

'Couldn't say, but the other one's from the Highlands. From a hotel friend, I expect.'

'There's no one at the hotel now,' Peg reminded him. 'It's been turned into a military hospital.'

Before this could produce more depressed looks from Joe and Ned, she hastily began to clear the table of cups and said she'd to get the carrots on. The hotpot was nearly ready and Sam would be over any minute. Better no' keep him waiting, they knew what he was like.

'Oh, no, mustn't keep Sam waiting,' Ned muttered under his breath, but Carrie put her finger over his lips and said she'd put Lesley's cards in her room, ready for her when she came in.

Chapter Forty-Six

Across town, in the restaurant at the Princess Louise, Lesley was shifting from foot to foot, as she stood by the service door watching the diners. So many chaps in uniform! The place was a sea of khaki, except for the occasional patch of navy. All young officers, of course – the private soldiers couldn't afford to eat here – and all lucky. Home for Christmas leave, it seemed, and dining with adoring girls. Yes, very lucky. But for how long?

Dread weighed like a stone in Lesley's breast, as she thought of Christopher, only a few weeks out, so of course no leave for him. But how lucky would he be? In the overheated room, she shivered and looked down at her ring for comfort. See how its diamonds caught the light! Folk she knew were dazzled by it, as she was herself. To think that she should own such a thing . . . But she would have thrown it in the Water of Leith tomorrow, if she could just have had Christopher back.

'Lesley, Lesley, somebody at Table Nineteen's trying to catch your eye!' cried Sally Abbott, skidding to a halt in front of her. 'You're no' daydreaming again, eh? Mr Hawkins is watching and all.'

How could Sally appear so calm? marvelled Lesley, hurrying to take Number Nineteen's order for another bottle of wine. (Hadn't he already had too much? But then most of the young men were drinking a lot, and who could blame them?) But Sally was engaged to Alex Mitchie and Alex was in the trenches and still alive, while his brother, George, was dead. Oh, poor George! A territorial, he had gone out early with the British Expeditionary Force and been killed in September at the battle of the Marne.

Lesley had just been given her old job back at the Louise when the news came through, and had cried for George as though he'd been the sweetheart he'd always wanted to be. But the truth was that George in her mind had become Christopher. She wept for George, who now had only a past, and for Christopher, who might, or might not, have a future. Three months had gone by, and now Christopher was at the front. There must be no more tears. She must be brave, calm, like Sally. But, oh God, how did Sally do it?

The restaurant closed at last. The young men, somewhat the worse for wear, took their girls home, while the waitresses cleared up and went out into the wintry streets, where there was little sign of the Christmas spirit. There were no waiters now, to joke and flirt; all were away on military service, leaving Mr Hawkins to say he didn't know what he'd do without his girls, and he hoped none of 'em would leave him for war work. All the same, Lesley was thinking of it and had enrolled in a first aid class on her evening off.

'Honestly, you're a devil for punishment,' Sally had said. 'Have you no' got enough work as it is?'

'I just feel I want to do something useful,' Lesley had told her. 'There's a place at one of the docks where the Red Cross look after the wounded coming into Leith. Maybe they need help there.'

'Aye, but that'll be voluntary, eh? You canna afford to give up your wages, Lesley.'

'I know, but when I think of Christopher at the front, I feel I shouldn't be just waiting on.'

'What about factory work?' Sally asked, on that December evening when they stood at her tram stop in Princes Street. 'That's needed, you ken, filling in for the men, and it's good money. Or would your young man no' approve?'

'Maybe not,' said Lesley.

'You'd never be able to flash that ring about in a factory, that's for sure!'

'No, I wouldn't.'

Sally's eyes gleamed under the streetlight. 'My, you're lucky, eh, to have a ring like that? I've no' got one at all.'

'You're lucky to have Alex, Sally, ring or no ring.'

'If I have.' Sally's look was suddenly desolate. 'You never know, eh? What's happening over there?'

Overcome by misery, Lesley left Sally and ran to Waverley for her train. It was only when she'd found a seat and could sit looking at her ring again that she managed to calm down. But it didn't help to know that Sally felt no better than she did.

Christopher had given her the ring at their last meeting in London. He'd been given a weekend's embarkation leave and had asked if she could come down? Could she come down? She would have grown wings to fly there, if there'd been no train, and even on the train, still felt as though she were flying. To see him again, even just for a day, for that was all they had, would be more than she'd ever hoped for, would be something to remember, to treasure, through all the wastes of time ahead.

Ella had been glad to offer her a bed at her mother's tiny terraced house in Hackney. 'Nothing fancy, dear,' she'd said. 'This is London's East End.'

As though Lesley had any eyes for surroundings that didn't include Christopher! But she was grateful to Ella and her mother, a plump, easy-going widow, and gave them shortbread, and also black bun, over which Mrs Bailey exclaimed and said she'd never seen a funnier looking cake, but it certainly tasted fine. Then Lesley, dressed in her best costume and a new raglan coat, went off for her golden day.

*

It had been spent in Richmond, where they'd walked in the park, gazing only at each other, and had lunch in a hotel, which might have been very good, only they hadn't the slightest idea what they'd been given to eat. Then Christopher, looking wonderfully well in his second lieutenant's uniform, had put the ring on Lesley's finger where it fitted perfectly and as she had almost dissolved into tears, had apologised because they could have so little time together.

'As though that's your fault!' she cried. 'I'm just so glad that we can have this day together!'

'Yes, but we might have had the whole weekend, if it hadn't been for my family.' He'd hesitated. 'Well, I had to think of them, you understand.'

'Your folks? Christopher, I do understand.' Lesley had covered his hand with hers. 'You're their son, eh? You're going to war, they've a right to be with you.'

He raised his eyes to hers. 'But I'd have given my soul to make love to you again. You know that, don't you? But maybe it's just as well we can't.' He tried to laugh. 'Maybe we should wait to be married, anyway. I was worried enough before.'

'I was all right, though.'

'Thank God. Imagine if there'd been a baby! How would you have managed?'

'Folk do,' she answered dryly. 'Sometimes I think I wouldn't have minded having your baby, Christopher.'

'Ah, darling, there'll be time, when we're properly together. When this war is over.'

Parting at the end of the day had been unbearable, but they had borne it, as people do bear things when they have no choice. They'd taken a taxi to Hackney, which would have caused some interest had it not been dark, but Lesley thanked God for the darkness, anyway, as their driver politely kept his eyes front and no one saw their last frantic kisses of goodbye. When Christopher had finally been driven away, Lesley had stood for some time, unable even to knock on Ella's door, but Ella must have heard the taxi leave, for she opened the door herself and took Lesley in.

Some time later, fortified by cups of tea, Lesley showed Ella and her mother her new ring. Both declared themselves speechless, though in fact had plenty to say, all of it praise.

'My word, I've never seen nothing like it in me life before!' cried Mrs Bailey. 'Well, not round here, anyway. Ellaline, have you ever seen stones like them?'

'Never. Except in a jeweller's winder.'

'Well, that's what I'm saying, dear. Anybody round here come home with a ring like that, we'd say they'd put a brick through a shop winder for it, wouldn't we? 'Course I know your young man didn't, dear.' Mrs Bailey patted Lesley's arm with a small fat hand. ''Cos Ellaline says he's a toff and he's got the money, but my advice, love, is to keep that ring covered up till you get home!'

'He means it, then?' Ella asked later, when she and Lesley were alone in Ella's room, which was about the size of Lesley's back in the Kirkgate. 'He means to marry you?'

'I told you he did. I told you I trusted him.'

'Seems you were right. Oh, Lesley, I'm that happy for you!'

After a pause, during which they hugged, Ella asked casually, 'How's Ned?'

Nearing Leith in the train that evening, Lesley wondered about Ned. As she had told Ella, he seemed to have conquered his drinking, perhaps with the help of the people he saw in Edinburgh from time to time. But he had never enlisted as she'd thought he would, and though the last thing she wanted was for him to go to war, it seemed to her that his not going was strange. One thing was sure, he was not the cheerful Ned they had all once known. How long would they have to wait to see that Ned again?

Chapter Forty-Seven

She could hear men's voices as she climbed the stairs to Number Fifteen, and thought to see Ned and Joe. But it was Adam Kay who was sitting smoking a cigarette with Ned, and who leaped to his feet as readily as Christopher, when he saw her at the door.

'Lesley! Grand to see you! We're just having a bit crack.'

'Joe and Carrie've gone to bed, got to keep our voices down,' said Ned, rising to push the kettle across the range. 'Want a cup o' cocoa?'

'Oh, tea, I think.' Lesley took off her coat and hat and slid into a chair. She smiled across at Adam and gave a long relaxed sigh. 'Isn't it nice to be waited on?'

'Had a long day?' Adam asked sympathetically.

'Aye – you wouldn't believe how busy we are. All officers on leave, trying to enjoy themselves.'

'Poor devils, eh?'

'Hey, what about the men?' asked Ned, laboriously making the tea. 'They canna afford to live it up when they're on leave.'

'Aye, but they say subalterns don't last more than five minutes at the front,' said Adam, then froze. 'Oh, God,' he said quietly. 'Lesley, I'm sorry.'

'It's all right.' She took the cup Ned gave her with a trembling hand. 'I know what they say, anyway.'

'Want a shortbread?' Ned asked hastily. 'Auntie Peg left some. Says if they cut supplies of butter again, she'll no' be able to make any more. And sugar's up to fourpence a pound, would you credit it?'

'Imports are the problem at the moment,' said Adam, taking a shortbread, though Lesley shook her head. 'Och, the docks are totally disrupted, to tell you the truth, and men keep leaving to join up when they're needed at work.' He hesitated. 'That's why I'm still here.'

Lesley and Ned looked at him, and he looked down at his cup.

'I'm supposed to be setting a good example, you ken.' He laughed shortly. 'Though what sort of example is it for me to stay out of uniform, when I'm no' even a docker?'

'But what can you do about it?' asked Lesley.

'I can join up, anyway. The union and Janie will just have to lump it.'

'Janie?' asked Lesley. 'What's she got to do with it?'

'Och, she's very anti-war. Thinks it's a crime it was ever started. Says it's all political and the fault of the government. The soldiers should just refuse to fight and then it'd all come to an end.'

'Maybe she's got a point.'

'Maybe, but I think she's had her head filled with hot air from a few journalists. She's shown me articles that I just canna accept. Germany's aggressive and won't stop trying to conquer France and Russia just because our lads come home.'

'So, you think you'll join up?' asked Ned, re-filling the teacups. 'What'll you try for?'

Adam shrugged. 'The Royal Scots, I suppose. It's local.'

Ned was silent for a moment. 'I wish to God I'd the courage to go with you,' he said at last.

'Why, Ned, what do you mean?' cried Lesley, as Adam fixed Ned with surprised grey eyes. 'You've got courage! What are you talking about?'

Ned stretched out his hands. 'These. These are what I'm

talking about. Ma hands.' He drew them back. 'I'm no' afraid of action, I'm no' afraid of dying, it's living without ma fiddle I canna face. If they ruined ma hands and I couldn't play – well, I'd be finished.'

'Ned, that's understandable,' Adam said quickly. 'Playing the fiddle, that's your whole life.'

'Understandable? Worrying about your hands when other fellas are dying?' Ned shook his head. 'No, I'm being bloody selfish and that's all there is to it.'

'Ned, don't talk like that,' said Lesley. 'Maybe there's something you could do where your hands'd be safe?'

'Oh, yes? Like when I wore gloves for ma french polishing? Lesley, you canna go to war and say you want to keep your hands safe. That'd be a laugh.'

'There's the navy,' Adam said. 'Might be less risk to your hands on a ship.'

Ned glanced at Lesley. 'Aye, Nick Lithgow's in the navy, you ken. Suppose I could risk drowning ... Och, I dunno, I'll have to join something, before some woman gives me a white feather.'

'Well, if she does, you tell her where to get off!' cried Lesley. 'The cheek of thae women, going round telling men to go to war when they don't have to go themselves.'

'Before this war is over, there'll be conscription brought in,' said Adam. 'You'll see, they won't be able to manage on volunteers.'

'Conscription,' repeated Lesley. 'You mean they'd make men join up? Could they do that?'

'Sure they could. We're one o' the few countries haven't got conscription now. But it'll come.'

'Joe wouldn't have to go, would he? He's desperate to enlist, but Carrie won't let him. Canna blame her, with a baby on the way.'

'They might exempt married men, but I should think everybody who's fit and no' too old will have to go. Unless they're needed for essential work.' Adam shrugged. 'That'll be the dockers. Just hope I can get away before somebody stops me. Thanks for the tea, Ned. I'll be on ma way.'

'Adam, stop a minute. When d'you think you might sign on?'

'After Hogmanay. Might as well have a last fling, eh?' Adam's eyes on Ned were grave. 'Coming with me, then?'

'What the hell – I think I will,' said Ned.

Lesley went with Adam to the door, where he looked with some unease into her troubled face.

'I didn't persuade him, Lesley. I think he really wants to go.'

'I know. He won't rest till he does.' Her voice shook. 'But, think of it – both of you – away together.'

'Aye. Well, think of me telling Janie.' Adam took Lesley's hand. 'There's something else – I hope I didn't upset you, saying what I did about the subalterns. I know your young man's at the front.'

'No, I told you, it was all right. We all know the situation.'

'Aye.' His eyes went to her ring. 'I'd like to see you happy, you ken.'

'I want the same for you and Janie.'

'Och, Janie's happy when she's busy. Collecting for the dependants of poor soldiers at the moment.' He grinned. 'Maybe it'll take her mind off me joining up.'

'Nothing'll do that, Adam.'

'No.' His grin faded. 'Goodnight, then, Lesley.' He raised his voice. 'Goodnight, Ned!'

'See you at Hogmanay!' called Ned. 'For that final fling!'

When Adam had gone, Lesley washed up the teacups and Ned began to pull down his bed from its alcove.

'You really want to go to the war, don't you?' Lesley asked quietly.

'Aye, I'll be able to face maself again.'

'You've been worrying about it for a long time. I thought it was just giving up the drink.'

'No, that's been hell, but I'm over the worst.' He gave a crooked smile. 'Comes to something when you have to go to war to feel better.'

'I wish you didn't have to go at all.'

'Hey, I've just remembered. There's a couple o' cards came for you today. One's from Mr Armitage.'

'Mr Armitage? How do you know?'

'Because I got one, and all. It's the same writing.'

'Well, I never sent him one. Are you sure, Ned?'

'Go and have a look. They're in your room.'

Lesley was soon back, with her cards in her hand.

'Yes, there's one from Mr Armitage,' she told Ned, showing it to him. 'Is it the same as yours?'

'No, mine was a regimental card. You've got a nice Christmas scene, eh? Robins and holly. What's he say, then? "Best wishes for Christmas and the New Year." Just what he said to me. No news, eh?'

'I canna think why he bothered to send me a card, but it's nice of him. Now this other one's from Moyra, and she's written a letter, as well.'

'Oh, yes?' asked Ned, damping down the range for the night. 'How's she getting on, then?'

'You'll never guess, she's still at the Grand Forest! Well, Glenmar Military Hospital it is now. She's some kind of aide to the nurses. And Miss Newall's there, too, doing housekeeping again. Seemingly, they were both asked to stay on when the hotel was finished.'

'Should've thought they'd want to get away, with the hotel all changed.'

'Miss Newall? She'd stay on at the Grand Forest whatever happened! And Moyra says she thinks of the job as kind of war work.' Lesley looked thoughtful. 'I'd have liked to do something like that.'

'What, looking after the wounded? Canna see you doing

that, Lesley. There'd be some terrible sights.'

'I wouldn't be nursing, just helping. Doing the chores, probably.'

'Well, then. Give it a miss.'

'I'm no' thinking of going, anyway. I'd be too far away, if Christopher got leave.'

'He due for some?'

'No.' Lesley's face was bleak. 'Not for a long time.'

Chapter Forty-Eight

True to their word, as soon as Hogmanay was over, Ned and Adam enlisted in the Royal Scots.

'You didn't consider the navy, then?' Lesley asked Ned, sighing.

'Och, you're no' going to be safe anywhere, so why worry? The infantry's as good as anything else.'

'You were worried before.'

'Aye, well, now I'm going along with what the lads say. If a bullet's got your number on it, there's nothing you can do, and if ma hands go, they go.'

Seeing the looks on the faces of the women watching him – Peg, Carrie and Lesley – Ned produced a strained smile and said he felt in his bones he'd be lucky. 'I'll be back, don't you worry, I'll be practising ma scales to drive you crazy, just the same as always.'

Next day he and Adam departed for training, much to the envy of Joe, who tightened his lips, but meeting Carrie's reproachful eyes, said nothing. Janie, who looked in at Number Fifteen that same evening, accompanied by Adam's father, was clearly simmering with rage.

'Ned's gone, then,' said Carrie, when everybody had finished the obligatory cup of tea.

'I've no' gone,' muttered Joe.

'Quite right, too,' Janie said sharply. 'You're best out of a war like this, Joe!'

'Think so?'

'Well, you tell me why you want to go.' Janie's flashing eyes held Joe's mild blue gaze. 'Come on, why'd you want to kill people? Shoot 'em? Run 'em through with a bayonet?'

'Now, now Janie,' said Jock Kay, as Lesley winced and Carrie closed her eyes. 'That's enough.'

'Why does nobody want to face facts?' cried Janie. 'Here's Adam and Ned off to war and Joe moaning because he's no' gone, and what it's about is killing. Killing other men because everybody else is killing 'em. You think about that Joe, and see if you want to do it!'

'We have to save Belgium,' Joe said after a pause. 'We have to stop the Germans taking over France.'

'Did you no' hear about the Christmas truce? When the Germans and the British swapped cigarettes and sang carols in No Man's Land? Thae Germans are just young fellas like you, Joe. Pushed into war by the Kaiser. All the soldiers should just lay down their arms and go home and that'd be the end of it.'

'It's no' as easy as that,' said Joe.

'No, and it's no good talking like that when Adam and Ned have just joined up!' cried Jock. 'They're brave laddies, and I'll no' have you runnin' them doon, Janie.'

'Oh, I'm no' doing that,' she said wearily. 'I just canna bear to think o' men risking their lives for nothing.'

A little later, she and Jock left, and as Jock slowly clumped his way up to his lonely flat, Lesley saw Janie to the front door.

'What you say makes sense, Janie,' she murmured. 'But you canna let the Germans just conquer France and Russia, can you? I mean, how d'you make the Germans lay down their arms?'

'German and British soldiers should lay down their arms together, then there'd be nothing the leaders could do.'

'I canna see it happening,' said Lesley.

'No,' Janie agreed with a sob. 'It'll no' happen. And Adam and Ned have gone, and our Hughie, and your young man and all. For God's sake, tell Carrie to keep Joe at home. At least, there'll be one spared.'

'Adam was saying they might bring in conscription.'

'Oh, then nobody'd be spared!' cried Janie, and hurried away into the night.

Nobody spared, thought Lesley, closing the front door. But Christopher was already at the front and had been spared so far. His letters, even though they gave no real news of himself, were what Lesley lived for, yet not a day went by that she did not fear for something from his mother. She was his next of kin but he had asked her, if anything happened to him, to let Lesley know and she had promised to do that. So, for Lesley, it would not be a telegram that would bring the end of the world, but an envelope with unknown handwriting and a London postmark.

Four months were to pass, before it came.

Chapter Forty-Nine

News came in March of a battle around a little French village called Neuve Chapelle, where British and Indian forces attacked German trenches. Its result was not decisive and the casualty lists were very high. How long before the telegrams began to arrive, wondered those at home, while Lesley looked for that envelope from London. When it did not come, she breathed again. But dread was everywhere, you couldn't expect to escape it.

Now that Adam had actually gone to war, Janie soothed her own dread by writing him long impassioned letters on every topic that came to mind, while Ella, who had taken up war work making uniforms, wrote to Ned. He wrote back, too, which was a surprise to Lesley, but she didn't read too much into it. All soldiers loved letters, and Ned would appreciate Ella's, but there would be no more to the correspondence than that.

Lesley herself, as she'd said she might, had found voluntary work for her afternoons off at the Red Cross clearing station for the wounded at Leith docks. Every time she went, she had to steel herself to face sights she could never have imagined, for the damage done by shells in this war was something new even for the professional nurses. Saddest to see were the blinded, but the suffering of all the men was intense, not least in those who appeared to have no physical wounds, though they often had physical symptoms.

'We call them the shell-shocked,' a nurse told Lesley. 'Some think they're malingerers, but they're not. It'll take a long time to get some of 'em back to the front.'

'Will they have to go?' asked Lesley, surprised.

'Why, of course! Anyone who recovers goes back. Every man is needed.'

Lesley asked where the shell-shock cases would be treated and was told there were special hospitals dealing in neurasthenia and mental problems, as well as wards set aside elsewhere.

'Most of our cases go to Craiglockhart here in Edinburgh,' the nurse added. 'But some go up to the Highlands, there's a very good doctor in a place up there.'

'Not Glenmar?' asked Lesley.

'Yes – do you know it?'

'Used to work there. Seems like a long time ago.'

After that conversation, Lesley took particular notice of the shell-shock cases, wondering if they would get well in the beautiful surroundings she had once known. But their faces were so blank, their eyes so strange, it was hard to think they would get well anywhere. The war had killed the bodies of many of their comrades; for these men, it was the spirit that had died.

One evening in early April, she came home from her usual stint at the clearing station to find Carrie puffing around, setting the table.

'Och, Carrie, you leave that to me!' she cried. 'Lie down on the sofa, before your ankles swell again.'

'You're tired, Lesley, I canna leave everything to you.'

'Who's tired? I feel fine. I'll start the veg, shall I?'

'Aye, I've put them out on the board.' Carrie lay back on the sofa with some relief. 'I'm that big, Lesley – d'you think I'm having twins?'

'No! Most folk put on weight like you, eh?'

Carrie's eyes were sombre. 'Always knew about the weight. Never expected all that sickness, though, and now

I've got heartburn and backache, and I don't know what. And I've no' even had the wean yet!'

'You'll be all right,' Lesley said, manufacturing confidence. 'Some women sail through the whole thing.'

'No' me.' Carrie sighed, then brightened as she heard Joe at the door. 'There's Joe! Push the kettle over to boil, Lesley, he'll want some tea.'

But Lesley did not push the kettle over. She had seen the look on Joe's face, she had seen the envelope in his hand, and was standing very still.

'It's all right, Lesley,' he said swiftly. 'It's from London but there's a message on the back.'

'Message?' she repeated faintly, as he made her sit down.

'"C is safe". That's what it says. His ma must've written it, so's no' to frighten you.'

'C is safe.' Lesley stared at the words written in an elegant pointed hand until they burnt into her brain, while Carrie, very pale, cried, 'Open it, Lesley, open the letter!'

The envelope was stiff, of very good quality, hard to open; inside, the writing paper, headed by the Merediths' London address, crackled in Lesley's shaking fingers.

'It is from his mother, eh?' asked Joe.

'Yes, it's from Christopher's mother.' Lesley's eyes were devouring the lines.

'And is he really all right?' asked Carrie, holding Joe's hand. 'Read it to us, Lesley!'

'Oh, I canna,' Lesley answered. 'No, I canna do that.'

'Let me read it, then. Lesley, give it here!'

Without argument, Lesley handed the letter to her sister, who began to read it aloud in a high stilted voice, perhaps the tone of voice she thought appropriate to Mrs Meredith, while Lesley sat staring at her hands on her knee.

'My dear Lesley,' Carrie read,

Please don't be alarmed, but Christopher is now home and in hospital. He is well in himself, but it appears

253

*that during a recent battle he was for a time buried
when a shell destroyed part of his trench. This has left
him with loss of memory, which is not unusual and
should be only temporary.*

*After a short time in a Hampshire hospital, it was
decided it might be helpful if he were moved to a place
he knew, and he is now in the military hospital at
Glenmar. You will no doubt be surprised by this, but
if you should wish to see him, we feel sure your visit
would be beneficial. I myself am unable to make the
journey at present, but Christopher's father is already
there.*

*I know you will join with me in our prayers for
Christopher's speedy recovery, and for all those fighting in this terrible war.*

I am, yours sincerely,
Beatrice Meredith

Carrie laid down the letter and looked from Joe to Lesley.
'Well, that's a change!' she declared. 'Now they want you
to be with him, Lesley. They're willing to accept you, if it
just gets their son better.'

'Aye, looks that way,' Joe agreed.

'Buried,' Lesley whispered. 'Mrs Meredith said he was
buried . . .'

'Soon rescued,' said Joe. 'And that loss of memory, it'll
be only temporary, like his ma says. When he sees you,
it'll come back, all right.'

'Will it?' Lesley stood up, twisting her hands. 'Imagine
what it'd feel like, to be buried. He wouldn't have known
he'd be rescued.'

'Well, he was rescued, and now he's safe,' said Carrie.
'That's what you have to remember.'

'I've seen some of the cases at the Red Cross centre.
They're safe, you ken, but they don't feel safe.'

Nor are any of us safe, thought Joe. This war touches us
all.

'When d'you think you'll go?' he asked Lesley, after a long silence.

She stared at him, as though his question were strange to her.

'Why, as soon as possible, Joe. Tomorrow.'

'You'll have to make arrangements,' said Carrie. 'You'll have to find somewhere to stay.'

'I'll make the arrangements. I'll find somewhere to stay.'

'Are you no' going round to tell Auntie Peg?'

'Aye, soon as tea's over.'

'Grand comfort, your Auntie Peg,' said Joe.

'You're all a comfort,' said Lesley, but was no longer looking for, or expecting, comfort.

Chapter Fifty

The April evening was light as day when Lesley arrived again at Glenmar. A number of soldiers had travelled with her from Aviemore, and though some had looked at her, none spoke. She guessed they were on their way to the hospital – one or two had sticks – but they didn't appear to be wounded. Shell-shock cases, then? On the station platform, they stood about, as she did, looking indecisive, but then the hotel bus came creaking up and Colum MacNee climbed out.

'Glenmar Hospital!' he shouted hoarsely, and the soldiers moved forward. To Lesley, it was like a parody of the old days. Everything so much the same; everything so tragically different.

'You are coming?' Colum asked her, making no sign that he recognised her.

'Mr MacNee, don't you remember me? Lesley MacKenzie? I've come to visit someone.'

'Aye, Mr Meredith.'

Her heart leaped. 'You've seen him?'

He shrugged. 'He's here. Thought you'd be coming, sooner or later. Better get in, you're keeping these laddies waiting.'

'I have to find somewhere to stay. Are there any boarding houses still open?'

'The Rose Down Guest House.' He snorted. 'Damn'

foolish name, but it's a comfortable place and Mrs MacRobie is a fine cook. Hand me your case, now, and I'll drop you off.'

Mrs MacRobie was tall and angular, with greying hair in a bun and a long colourless face, but she was welcoming enough. Aye, she had a room, just the one, there being so many folk up visiting their puir laddies at the Grand Forest.

'I am still calling it that,' she said with a smile. 'Though of course it is no hotel now.'

'I used to work there,' said Lesley, signing the register.

Mrs MacRobie's eyes brightened. 'Why, now I am sure I have seen you before! Walking in the Square, would it be? Fancy, and here you are back again!'

'I'm visiting at the hospital, too. A friend.'

'I am sorry for that, Miss MacKenzie. Now, I will be showing you your room and cooking you a little something, for you have missed my evening meal.'

'I'm no' hungry,' Lesley told her. 'I just want to get to the hospital. To see ma friend.'

Mrs MacRobie's eyes went to the ring on Lesley's finger, as she took off her gloves, and her long face softened. 'Take my advice, my dear, have a cup o' tea and a little rest before you see your friend. It will be better for you.'

Oh, God, all she wanted to do was run to the hospital, but it was true, she was exhausted and looked, as she could see in the bedroom mirror, like a woman distracted. It was no way to meet Christopher, no way to find the courage to face whatever she had to face. She must take the time to drink the tea the landlady had brought, to wash and change and do her hair, and try to look herself again.

'Ah, you are looking better!' cried Mrs MacRobie, when Lesley, in her hat and coat, went down to the entrance hall. 'And you are going to the hospital now? No need to tell you the way!'

Lesley, summoning a smile, opened the glass outer door

to leave, and stood transfixed. A man was on the step, about to enter. A well-dressed man, a prosperous man, and one she knew. It was Christopher, come to her. Christopher, fit and well. Her heart pounded, the blood rushed to her face and her head seemed to spin.

'Good evening, Mr Meredith,' said Mrs MacRobie. 'This is Miss MacKenzie, from Edinburgh. Miss MacKenzie – Mr Meredith, from London.'

He wasn't Christopher, he was Christopher's father, but so like, so painfully like. Oh, of course she could see now that he was older, in his fifties, certainly. There were lines at his blue eyes, strain showing at his generous mouth, but she would have known him anywhere.

'Miss MacKenzie?' His mellow voice was Christopher's, too, but as they stood and looked at each other, her first flush of delight faded, as it had to do. However like, this was not Christopher, and the courage she had for meeting Christopher could not be found for meeting his father.

'Miss Lesley MacKenzie?' Mr Meredith asked, as Mrs MacRobie watched them from under lowered lids.

'Yes, I'm Lesley MacKenzie. You're Christopher's father?'

'I am.' He put out his hand and Lesley shook it. 'I've been hoping you'd come. If you're going to the hospital, may I walk with you?'

'Oh, yes. Please do.'

'I'm afraid you may be a little too late to see my son tonight. They have an early dinner and then it's lights out.'

'Lights out,' she repeated desolately.

'But let's see what we can arrange,' he said quietly, and stepped back to allow her to precede him.

'Are you not wanting me to prepare you something, Mr Meredith?' cried Mrs MacRobie. 'You have missed your supper.'

'Thank you, Mrs MacRobie, I had something earlier,' he answered courteously. 'Though I was extremely sorry to miss your excellent meal.'

As Mrs MacRobie flushed with pleasure, Lesley thought, he's so like Christopher, isn't he? Always so polite. He treats everyone the same. And she felt a little better about walking with him. At least, if he gave her her marching orders, he would be nice about it. But then she remembered Carrie's words. 'Now they want you to be with him, they're willing to accept you, if it just gets their son better ...' She would soon know if that was true.

Lights were coming on in the houses as they walked slowly through the village, where outwardly not a great deal had changed. The pump rooms and the pavilion were, however, in darkness, and of course no visitors were strolling in the Square. Perhaps, during the day, there would be patients taking the air, sitting in the empty bandstand, wondering what this place had been like before the war put up the notices saying 'Closed'. Or, perhaps not. Perhaps for them, their present surroundings scarcely existed. Perhaps they still lived in their own world, which was the battlefield.

'It must feel strange for you, to be back,' Mr Meredith remarked.

'Yes, seems like a dream.' Or, a nightmare.

'My wife has stayed here many times, to take the cure, you know, but I only came once before. Some years ago, now.'

'I suppose you stayed at the Grand Forest?'

'Yes. It was a fine hotel.'

'The Rose Down is very comfortable, though.'

How stilted they sounded! But they were making conversation, going through the motions, before the real talk came. Glancing at him, she saw that he was hesitating; the real talk might be coming now.

'Miss MacKenzie, I want to say I'm sorry we've had to meet like this. My wife and I – we've been remiss. I apologise.'

What could she say to that? Did he think she'd expected to be invited to dinner? Stay in their house? Meet their friends? She would never have been invited to anything, she

259

knew, but she didn't care. Her eyes were fixed ahead, on the hotel in the distance, its whiteness glimmering in the dusk. Her mind was on Christopher.

'But I'm glad to meet you now,' Christopher's father was continuing awkwardly. 'We have great hopes, you know, that you will be able to help Christopher.'

'I want to do that,' she told him fiercely. 'More than anything in the world.'

His eyes widened a little, perhaps at her sudden passion, but he seemed grateful. At least, his look was approving. 'How much do you know?' he asked. 'About what happened?'

'Just what was in Mrs Meredith's letter.'

'Ah.' He swung his walking stick. 'My wife might not have given all the details.'

'She said Christopher was – buried.'

'He was. During the battle of Neuve Chapelle. But there was someone with him. One of his men. When they were found and dug out – that man – was dead.'

'Oh, no!' The image was so strong, Lesley felt almost as though she were suffocating herself. Christopher and a dead man, below the ground? Christopher alive, and the poor soldier dead, and Christopher perhaps knowing, seeing? She could scarcely bear to think of it.

'But Christopher was alive, with only a few cuts and bruises,' Mr Meredith went on. 'It seemed like a miracle. Seemed as though he'd been extraordinarily lucky.'

'Seemed,' murmured Lesley.

'Well, he was lucky. I think you'd have to say that. He was alive, after all. But when he was told at the field hospital that the guardsman was dead, he lost consciousness. When he came round, he didn't know who he was. All that had happened before he was buried had been wiped from his mind.'

'Everything?'

'Everything. Now, he doesn't remember his mother, or me, or where he went to school, or Cambridge.' Mr

Meredith shook his head. 'I'm afraid, to begin with, he won't remember you. But we're all hoping that you will help to change things, bring him back to himself.'

'I don't understand,' she said slowly. 'Why should his memory go? Could he no' face what happened?'

'That's what the doctors think. His amnesia is blotting out the horror. And possibly his guilt.'

'Guilt?' Lesley stared. 'What do you mean? What's he got to feel guilty about?'

'The death of the soldier. Because he is dead and Christopher is not. It's quite common, the doctors say, to feel guilt for having survived. Not remembering is a way of living with it.'

'Do the doctors really think he can get better?' Lesley asked, after a silence.

Mr Meredith's eyes held hers. 'Maybe with your help. We can only hope. And pray.'

They had reached the hotel, which, like the village, seemed little changed on the outside. Still had its long windows and look of opulence, still had its elegant steps and portico where guests had once arrived to be greeted by Paul Armitage, while Colum carried in their luggage. How long ago that seemed! A lifetime. Her hand to her lips, Lesley entered the Hotel Grand Forest, that was now the Glenmar Military Hospital, on the arm of Christopher's father, who seemed to have a charmed key to the hearts of the nurses sitting behind Veronica's old desk.

'Just like to see my son again, for a few moments, if that's all right?'

'It's awfully late, Mr Meredith, your son might be sleeping. We'll have to ask Sister.'

'It's not really so very late is it? And poor Miss MacKenzie has come so far.'

'Well, we're not sure—'

'And you know we are hoping great things from Miss MacKenzie.'

Whispers and glances at Lesley. Finally one nurse gave in. 'Just a few moments, then. And I mean it, Mr Meredith!'

'This way,' he said to Lesley. 'Christopher's room is on the third floor. At the moment, he's fortunate, he's on his own.'

They went up in the guests' lift which was now looking shabbier and much less grand, just as the first glimpses of the changed hotel also showed it to be shabbier and much less grand. There were partitions everywhere, and painted wooden floors, light bulbs without shades, doors swinging open without locks. No flowers or curtains, or comfortable armchairs. No feeling of comfort or luxury, but tremendous cleanliness, a smell of carbolic and food cooked long ago. Oh, yes, this was a hospital now.

'Christopher's room,' murmured his father, and Lesley felt a pang. She had come to Christopher's room once before. She had knocked on the door and he had opened it, his eyes had lit up, he had taken her in. But this door was a different door and though open, might not truly let her through.

Christopher was lying on his bed, wearing a shirt and uniform breeches and smoking a cigarette. He looked just the same. Serene blue eyes, wide unlined brow, hair scrupulously parted and combed.

'Christopher,' said his father. 'I've brought someone to see you.'

At once, he leaped to his feet, and Lesley, her legs suddenly weak as water, reached his side and took his hand in hers.

'Hello, Christopher,' she whispered. 'It's Lesley. Lesley MacKenzie.'

His smile was polite.

'Don't you know me?'

'I'm sorry, I'm afraid I don't.' His eyes were blank. 'Please forgive me. Where did we meet?'

Chapter Fifty-One

Nightmares. Everybody in the neurasthenic wards had nightmares, so the nurses said, Christopher, too, though he never remembered them. In those days that followed, Lesley had her own. For to be so close to Christopher and not be able to share her love was a nightmare, all right. It was to suffer the kind of terrible dream you only long to wake' from – although she was already awake.

On that first evening when she'd seen him, it had been almost impossible for her to believe that he couldn't recognise her. He looked so much the same, how could he not be the same? But when she'd told him they were engaged, he had looked so embarrassed and confused, she'd been ready to burst into tears. And when she'd showed him her ring and said he'd given it to her, he could only shake his head and look away. It was then that she realised he was not, after all, the man who had been her lover. Nor were his eyes serene. They were empty of all feeling, but that was not the same thing at all.

'He will never remember us,' she'd said to his father, as they walked unseeingly back to the guest house. 'I just feel he never will.'

'You mustn't be downhearted, Lesley,' Mr Meredith had told her, using her name for the first time, something she scarcely noticed. 'It's only what we expected to begin with, but the more you are with him, the more likely he'll be to recover.'

No, she couldn't see it. To her, it seemed true what the doctors thought, that he was shielding himself from a world he couldn't face, and she and his family were part of that world. Think of the pain he would suffer, if he had to enter it again! Was it right to make him do it? But, oh, God, she herself wanted him back so much, wanted him with her again as he had used to be. That wasn't wrong, was it?

'I have to leave in a day or so,' Mr Meredith was saying. 'I can't leave things in London too long, but I'll be back, of course, if I can. In the meantime, you'll stay, won't you?'

'Oh, yes, I'll stay.'

'Forgive me for mentioning this, but are you all right for money?'

'Yes, thank you. Quite all right.'

'Will you at least let me pay your bill at the Rose Down? Please, I want to help.'

She shook her head. 'I can manage.'

'But you may be here some time, and you've left your job.'

'Maybe I'll get something in Glenmar. Don't worry about it.'

'We're almost family, you know,' he said gravely. 'You would not be beholden to me.'

Almost family? There was a time when those words would have given her great joy, but they had come too late, they meant nothing to her now. Perhaps, if Christopher recovered and came through the war, they might take on meaning again, but as things were, she couldn't even hope for it.

Two days later, Mr Meredith left. They'd made two further frustrating visits to Christopher, and his doctor had arranged a meeting with Lesley.

'Let me know how that goes,' said Mr Meredith, before

264

he went for his train. 'Be sure to keep in touch. You are our lifeline.'

'I'm really sorry Mrs Meredith canna visit, but I will keep in touch, I promise.'

'Thank you.' He was hesitating again, and she knew he wanted to say something nice, something that would make her feel better about not having been thought 'suitable' for Christopher, but he knew and she knew that there was nothing he could say. In the end, he had shaken her hand and given her a peck on the cheek. He'd made his good-byes again, she'd promised again to keep in touch, and he'd left her, looking so weary, so grieved, she'd longed to run after him.

'It's all right,' she wanted to tell him. 'Don't worry. Christopher will be well again.'

But of course she'd made no move. What was the point? She couldn't give him hope when she had none herself.

In her room, she counted her money again, though it was a waste of time, she knew very well she hadn't enough to stay on at the Rose Down. Perhaps she had been foolish not to let Mr Meredith help her, but at this stage, she felt strongly that she should keep her independence. Let the Merediths see that she was not out for what she could get. If that meant finding work, so be it. Springing to her feet, she began to get ready for another visit to Christopher. But first, she had her appointment to keep with his doctor, and then she must ask about a job.

Chapter Fifty-Two

Major Quentin, Christopher's doctor, was not old but he had lost most of his hair, and what was left was grey. Thin and rather yellow in the face, he looked no better than his patients, except for his eyes, which were the sharpest Lesley had ever seen. Oh, those eyes would see beyond the emptiness of his patients' eyes! They would probe and find whatever was to be found, even if that didn't always lead to a cure. Major Quentin had not been able to cure Christopher yet.

'Come in, Miss MacKenzie!' he had cried cheerfully, when she had arrived at his office, and she was relieved to find that it was not Paul Armitage's old room, or anything grand like Mr Wilcox's, which would have made her nervous, but just a small room converted from a bedroom on the third floor. 'Please sit down. You see, I have cleared a chair for you.'

She had smiled then, for not much else had been cleared in the doctor's room, which was awash with files and papers, but there was no doubt in her mind that if he wanted to put his hand on anything, he could do so without a moment's hesitation.

'Now, you are Mr Meredith's fiancée, and it's wonderful that you are here. Actually, I call him Christopher, not Second-Lieutenant, or Mister. I never bother with ranks, though I'm supposed to have one myself, being in the

RAMC. Always wear my white coat over my uniform, to make the point.' He leaned forward, giving her the full searchlight effect of his gaze. 'Miss MacKenzie, first let me ask you how long you think you can stay.'

She stared, a little surprised. 'I'm no' sure. I was thinking of trying to get a job.'

'A job? Here? Are you a nurse?'

'No, I'm a waitress. But I've worked at the Red Cross clearing station in Leith, helping the nurses.'

'Have you indeed? Well, it's not my department, but I should've thought we could find you something. We normally depend on VADs for assistance – they're the volunteer nurses, you understand – but they're in short supply in this neck of the woods. So many are in France, anyway. Ask at the reception desk, they'll help you.'

When she had thanked him, he went on:

'Now, the second thing I want to say is that I know how distressing all this must be for you. A fiancé who doesn't even know who you are – that's hard to take.'

'Yes,' Lesley agreed huskily.

'But what you have to remember is that Christopher's condition is probably not going to be permanent. It's what we call hysterical amnesia, because it has no physical cause. He did have a little concussion, but not enough to explain what has happened to him.'

'Mr Meredith told me you thought he was blotting out something he didn't want to remember.'

'That's the theory. Christopher, like many others here, has come through a situation of great stress, and has reacted to protect himself. Quite subconsciously, of course. I think you understand me, Miss MacKenzie?'

'Yes, I think I do.'

'Because you are an intelligent young woman. I wanted to see you, to prepare you for what might happen when he recovers his memory.'

'You really believe he will?'

'Yes, I've told you, his memory loss will not be

permanent. If it doesn't return naturally, there are things we can try. Hypnosis, perhaps, or other treatments. But I think it will come back soon and quite suddenly, and then you must be prepared to help him through what might be a very bad patch. Now you understand why I wanted to know how long you could stay.'

'It'll be so hard for him!' she cried. 'I mean, reliving it all!'

'He must relive it,' Major Quentin said quietly. 'It's only by reliving it, and facing it, that he can know himself again. And know you, Miss MacKenzie.'

It was like looking through falling rain to a land where the sun was shining. Christopher to remember her? To remember all that they'd been to each other? But there was no sunshine yet, and when Major Quentin stood up and escorted her to the door, her own gaze was as sharp as his.

'If his memory does return, will he have to go back to fight?'

'Let's cross that bridge when we come to it.'

'He will, won't he?'

'Well, patients are assessed at regular intervals. If a man is fully recovered, then, yes, he usually returns to active duty.'

'All this effort to get them better,' she said bitterly. 'Just for them to go back to the front.'

'They are needed, you see. And most of them want to go. I think Christopher will.' As her eyes fell, Major Quentin put his hand on her arm. 'Would you rather have him stay as he is, Miss MacKenzie?'

She shook her head, and he smiled faintly as he removed his hand. 'Goodbye, for the present. Keep your spirits up, and your hopes, and see what you can do about that job.'

'Goodbye, and thank you, doctor – I mean, Major—'

'I told you, I don't bother about titles. Doctor will do.'

Chapter Fifty-Three

Outside the doctor's door, Lesley stood for a moment or two, gathering her thoughts, wondering which she should do first. Go to reception and ask about jobs, or visit Christopher? Reception, she decided, and was about to take the stairs down, when a voice she knew cried: 'Miss MacKenzie!'

It was Sadie Newall, looking just the same as ever, with a pile of towels over her arm and her narrow eyes devouring Lesley in the same old way. Yet, when she asked if Lesley was visiting Mr Meredith, she seemed strangely kind.

'I was so sorry to hear what had happened to him, you know. Oh, the poor young man! It's too terrible, what all these fellows are going through.'

'Yes, terrible,' Lesley murmured, wondering why words could express so little. Yet she appreciated Miss Newall's sympathy.

'We can only do what we can to help.' Sadie moved the towels from one arm to the other. 'Have you, I wonder, heard from Mr Armitage at all?'

'Mr Armitage? Only a card at Christmas.'

'Oh, well I had one, too.' Sadie flushed and smiled. 'Of course, he'd be too busy to write, and now I suppose he's in France. Well, I must get on, I have work to do.'

As Lesley walked with Sadie towards the stairs, she took

the opportunity to ask if it was likely she could get employment at the hospital.

'I need to be near Christopher, you see,' she explained. 'And I canna afford to stay much longer at the guest house. I've done a bit of first aid and care work, I could be useful.'

'Oh, I'm sure they'll take you on!' Sadie cried. 'They're having to employ civilian help because they're so short of VADs to help the QAs. I'm in charge of laundry and Moyra's making beds and washing patients and all that sort of thing. You could ask at reception now – I'll come with you, if you like.'

'That'd be very kind. And I'd like to have a word with Moyra, too, if I could.'

'I'll find her for you. Goodness, it's nice to see a face from the old days, Lesley. It brings it all back, meeting you.'

What on earth's got into Miss Newall, thought Lesley bemusedly. To be so friendly! But then it came to her. She had another man's ring on her finger and had had no more than a Christmas card from Paul Armitage. Poor Sadie! Still so much in love. Why not, though? Love needn't die because it wasn't returned.

In the end, things worked out well. Lesley filled out an application form and was told that if her references were acceptable, she would be considered for civilian work at the hospital. No nursing, of course, because she wasn't qualified, but she could roll bandages, make beds, do anything that was required to help the QAs or the VADs.

Afterwards, Moyra appeared and flung her arms round Lesley's neck, said she'd known Lesley would be coming as soon as she'd seen Mr Meredith admitted, and had been looking out for her. How was she? How was Ned? Oh, it was good he was still all right! Had Lesley heard that Nick was in the navy now and engaged to Ishbel? And Bill was fine and Mr Wilcox in some government ministry in London.

'Listen,' she finished, 'why should you not be invited to have your lunch with us today? We have it in our old dining room, where the nurses have their meals now. I mean, you're soon going to be one of us.'

A sister approved and Lesley enjoyed what was almost a convivial meal again in surroundings she knew, with Sadie and Moyra and a group of VADs.

'Some of those VADs are very grand,' Moyra whispered after lunch was over. 'They are not used to making beds or cleaning the sluice or anything of that sort, you know, but they are very good, they never complain.'

'Just not enough of them, that's the trouble,' said Sadie. 'So many are in the field hospitals in France.'

'That's what Major Quentin said.'

'Major Quentin? You've seen him?' Sadie shook her head. 'Now hasn't he got the sharpest eyes you've ever seen?'

'Sharper than yours, Sadie?' asked Moyra, laughing, as Lesley wondered at her daring.

Soon, though, she said she must go, she must visit Christopher, and a silence fell. Moyra walked with her from the dining room.

'It's so hard for you,' she said in a low voice. 'I hope Mr Meredith gets his memory back soon.'

It was only when Lesley had left her and was making her way to the third floor, that she remembered neither of them had mentioned Ella. Not that she herself spared Ella another thought, when she arrived at Christopher's room and opened his door.

Chapter Fifty-Four

They were in the woods again, behind the hospital that Lesley still thought of as the Hotel Grand Forest. The April afternoon was chill, but Christopher had undone his tunic and was not wearing his belt or his hat. He liked to feel free, he said, he didn't want to be burdened with a uniform that had no meaning for him. Lesley walked beside him, wearing her raglan coat and her blue hat. All the light-heartedness of her lunch with Moyra and the nurses had melted away, but that was only to be expected. With Christopher as he was, how could she feel light-hearted?

'You say we've been here before?' he asked, walking through piles of dry old leaves.

'Yes, we often came here. In fact, it was the first place we came to be on our own.'

At the tenderness in her voice, he glanced at her. 'Means something to you, then?'

'Yes. I told you, didn't I, that I was a waitress at the hotel, and you were a guest? I kept worrying that somebody would see us and report me, because we weren't supposed to go out with the guests.'

'As though it mattered!'

'Mattered if it meant risking your job. Earning a living was important to somebody like me.'

'I'm sorry.' He gave an apologetic smile. 'I've everything to learn, it seems.'

'I'm sorry, too. I shouldn't have snapped at you.'

For some time, they walked in silence. When they came to a fallen log, he took off his tunic to cover it and invited her to sit down.

'Oh, we canna sit on your tunic, Christopher! Anyway, you'll be cold!'

'I don't feel cold at all, and what the hell does my tunic matter?'

She took off her hat and unloosened her coat and they sat down. After a moment, Christopher put his arm around her in the old way, which only made her heart ache. He was trying to please her, but he didn't know her, he didn't love her, she wished they could just be like two strangers until he was himself again. Perhaps he guessed what she was feeling, for he took his arm away.

'Can't think why I don't remember you, Lesley. You're a very pretty girl.'

'You don't remember your folks, either.'

'No.' He shuddered a little. 'Can you imagine what that's like? To meet a lady who says she's your mother and have no recollection of her at all?'

'I canna imagine what that would be like.'

'Hell, is what it's like. But from what I've been told, everybody's living in some kind of hell at the moment. And nobody seems to know what it's all for.'

'It was to help Belgium, to begin with.'

'Belgium? Where's Belgium?'

Tears began to roll down her cheeks, as the seeming hopelessness of his situation overcame her, and he took out his handkerchief and wiped the tears away, then gently kissed her.

'Lesley, you should just go home, just leave me. There's nothing you can do.'

'I'll never do that!' she flared. 'I'm going to see you better, it's all I'm living for. The doctor said your memory'd come back and I'm going to be here when it does.'

'Let's go back,' he said, after a pause. 'We're only making ourselves sad, sitting here.'

273

They stood up and he shook out his tunic and put it on, and Lesley put on her hat.

'I hate it when you do that,' he told her. 'When you cover your hair. Didn't I once love the colour of your hair?'

'You once loved me,' she said quietly.

For a long time, he looked into her face. 'I have to tell you something, Lesley,' he said very slowly. 'I know it will hurt you, and I don't want to do it, but I have to, I can't shirk it. Because it will be for the best.'

'When folk say that, it never is,' she whispered, turning pale. 'Are you trying to say goodbye to me, Christopher?'

'I'm saying that even if my memory returns, I'll never be the same man you loved. I know that, I feel it. I can't explain it, but I know that you'll be better off without me.'

'That's no' true, that could never be true. You don't know how you'll feel when your memory comes back. Just now, you're depressed, anybody would be, but when you're yourself again, you'll feel different. You will, you will!'

'Let's go back,' he said again, taking her hand.

'When your memory returns, you'll know you love me,' she said desperately. 'Then you'll know we canna say goodbye.'

'I never said I wouldn't love you, Lesley.'

'What then? What then?'

'I said you'd be better off without me.'

'And we won't be married?'

'It would be for the best.'

'That is all a piece of nonsense!' she cried, striding away from him. 'Come on, we'll go back, have a cup of tea, and we'll no' speak of it again.'

Back at the hospital, they sat in the old Palm Court, which was now a place for the patients to sit and talk or read, and entertain their visitors. A ward-maid brought them tea in thick white cups, which made Lesley smile in the midst of

274

her misery, as she thought of the exquisite teas that had once been served here. Christopher, of course, would not remember them, or Ned's playing of the sweet old songs with Kirstie and Rob.

'Tell me, pretty maiden, are there any more at home like you?' She wouldn't think of that.

'Like a scone?' Christopher asked politely. 'They're not too bad. Rather hard, perhaps.'

'I forgot to tell you,' Lesley said, shaking her head at the large scone he was proffering. 'I may be coming to work here. Just as a nurses' aide, you ken. No' proper nursing.'

'You're going to work here?' His face was full of contrition. 'Oh, God, you need money? Look, you should have told me—'

'Christopher, don't worry. I want to work here, it'll be ma war work, sort of thing. And it'll mean I'll be near you.' Her blue eyes shone defiantly. 'And I am your fiancée, Christopher, so I should be near you.'

He sighed and pushed aside his plate. 'If it's what you want.'

'It is!'

'I'm grateful, then.' He managed a smile and stood up. 'Lesley, will you excuse me? I'm afraid I have to see Major Quentin now, for another of his little probes into my subconscious. Shall I see you tomorrow?'

'Yes, and the next day, and the next.'

He smiled again and left her, walking slowly, his tunic still hanging loosely, his head bowed. Lesley watched him until he was out of sight, then she too walked slowly away.

Chapter Fifty-Five

By the end of April, Lesley was installed as a civilian aide at the hospital, and if not actually enjoying the work, was finding it rewarding. She wore a green uniform dress, white apron and white cap, and shared a room with Moyra on the top floor. No fine views of the Square and the distant hills, but instead she could look out on to the woods, now in full new-green leaf, and for her they were even better. She and Christopher walked in those woods. They were special.

Lesley got on well with Moyra. She was not Ella, but still a friend from the old days, and although she was seeing a young man from the village, Lesley knew she still cared what happened to Ned. He and Adam were together in Gallipoli in the Dardanelles, where a second front had been opened up against Turkey. Sounded awful, said Moyra.

'Fighting Turks! They'll be worse than the Germans. Why are we fighting them, anyway?'

'They're on Germany's side,' Lesley answered. 'And stopping Russia having a supply route, so one of the patients told me.'

'It sounds a terrible thing to say, but I wish Ned could've been like Finlay. He has the asthma, you know, they will not accept him for the war.'

'I wish all the men could've been like that. But I suppose Finlay minds, eh?'

'Well, he is farming, and someone has to do it. So far, he has not been given a white feather.'

'Thank God for that!'

It was a relief to Lesley that Moyra had not asked about Ella, who wrote long letters full of her fears for Ned, now that he was in action. But then Moyra had her Finlay, who was the lucky one, even if he didn't think so.

The war news was bad, with the Germans using poison gas for the first time at Ypres, and sinking the Cunard liner, the *Lusitania*, off the Irish coast. But then on 22 May, Leith and the whole of Great Britain were stunned when a troop train, mainly carrying men of the Seventh Battalion, Royal Scots, was involved in a disastrous crash near Gretna, with the loss of more than two hundred lives. Many of the dead were Leithers – dockers and others – who had joined the Territorial Battalion in February. They had been on their way to Liverpool, bound for Gallipoli; now they were dead, without ever having left their own country. The irony seemed too hard to bear.

'I must go home!' cried Lesley, utterly distraught. 'I must go home. There'll be men we knew on that train!'

'But not Ned,' Moyra said soothingly. 'Not Ned's friend you told me about.'

'They could've been. They're in the Royal Scots. They might have been in that battalion.'

'But they weren't. Thank God, they weren't!'

Yes, Lesley thanked God that they weren't, but what of those who were? Should God be thanked for saving some and not others? Was there any pattern? Was everything just luck?

'I must go home,' she said again, and felt like a bird in a cage, beating her wings against the bars, for there was also Christopher to consider. He was no better. No natural return of his memory had happened and Major Quentin was about to try hypnosis. Lesley had promised to be there. All along, she had said she would be there, when Christopher's memory came back. But now she should be in Leith, with her own.

'Oh, God, Moyra, what'll I do?' she asked.

'Couldn't you ask the Major to postpone the treatment till you come back?'

'I don't like to, but perhaps I will. Soon as I've finished the beds, I'll see what he says.'

Working like an automaton, Lesley made beds on the main ward, finally reaching the last one, while the soldier whose bed it was sat on a chair and watched, singing to himself in a southern English accent,

'"If you want to find the old battalion, I know where they are, I know where they are..."'

Suddenly, he interrupted the song to tell Lesley that she was a very pretty girl. Yes, if he was ever himself again, he'd ask her out to the pub, that was a promise.

'Lovely,' said Lesley, trying to smile. 'Though there is no pub.'

'And I'm not meself, either.'

'You soon will be.'

'So they tell me. Then it'll be back to the old battalion, eh?'

'Maybe not.' Lesley was about to help him back into his bed when Sadie Newall, hurrying down the ward, drew her to one side.

'You've a phone call, Lesley. At Reception.'

'A phone call?' Lesley turned pale. 'Who is it?'

'They said it was your auntie. Away you go now and take it. I'll finish up here.'

Lesley was already on her way.

'Auntie Peg?'

'Is that you, Lesley?'

'Yes, yes, it's me. Auntie Peg, tell me quick, what's wrong?'

'Nothing's wrong. It's Carrie. She's had her baby. A grand little boy.'

'Oh, that's wonderful!' The one piece of good news. Lesley was ready to collapse with relief, as the nurse at Reception looked politely away. 'Oh, thank God! But is it no' early? How is she?'

'It's three weeks early, but she's fine. Oh, but Lesley, could you no' come home? We're in such a state here, you ken.'

'I'm coming, Auntie Peg.'

If she hurried, she could catch the one train of the day. First, she'd have to get permission to leave, of course. Then she'd have to get changed out of her uniform, throw a few things into a case, see Major Quentin and say goodbye to Christopher.

The doctor was very sympathetic. Of course, she must go home. Any Leither would want to be with family and friends at this time, and then Lesley had her sister to think about. Christopher would be all right. They could postpone treatment till her return.

'I do want to be there, if his memory comes back,' she said earnestly. 'I know he'll need me.'

'I'm not promising that anything I try will work, you know. He's not been a responsive patient so far. Still doesn't remember his nightmares, still doesn't really want to talk to me.'

'You thought his memory would've come back earlier, didn't you?'

Major Quentin sighed. 'My mistake, Lesley. We doctors are not infallible.'

'Well, I've been no help,' she said bitterly. 'You all expected him to remember me, but he didn't.'

'If he'd remembered you, he'd have had to remember everything else and obviously up till now he's not been ready. But don't lose heart, Lesley. It'll come, you'll see.'

She found Christopher in the Palm Court, as she still called it. He was reading a newspaper by a window overlooking the gardens. Someone still looked after them, or at least cut the lawns, and the spring shrubs were in full flower, but then they'd be in flower, anyway.

'Christopher?'

He looked up, and sprang to his feet. 'Hallo, are you going, then? Going back to Leith?'

'You've been reading about the train crash?'

'I can't believe it. Three trains involved! Human error, of course.' He smiled grimly. 'Like the war.'

'I have to see ma sister,' Lesley said quietly. 'She's just had her baby. A boy.'

He relaxed a little. 'Why, that's good news for a change. I hope you find her well.'

She gave him a desperate look. 'Christopher, can we no' go somewhere more private?'

He glanced at the other patients, who were sitting about, reading, or lying back with their eyes closed.

'If you like. Though no one's looking.'

'Please.'

They walked through the gardens and to the edge of the woods, Lesley fighting to control her nerves, Christopher quite calm. When they stepped into the shelter of the trees, she took his hands in hers.

'I won't be away long, I promise. And I'll be thinking of you all the time. Major Quentin says he'll postpone any treatment till I get back.'

'He might as well. Won't work, anyway.'

'Don't say that!'

He shrugged. 'I'll miss you, though.'

'Will you?'

'Yes, of course. You brighten my days.'

Tears stung her eyes as she reached up and kissed him on the lips, and he held her close for a moment, almost as though he loved her. When she had to draw away, he came with her to pick up her case from Reception.

'I'll walk with you to the station.'

'No, don't do that. You needn't, I don't want you to.'

'Why not?'

Because she would be remembering the last time they had said goodbye at the station, and didn't think she could bear the difference between then and now. She shook her head.

'All right, I'll just carry your case, I won't see you on to the train.'

The train was almost due in when they arrived at the platform, and this time they only shook hands as they said goodbye.

'I will be thinking of you,' he told her. 'Take care.'

'No, you take care, Christopher.'

'For what?'

'For me.'

She walked away with her case to wait for the train, and when she looked back, he was still there. Even when the train arrived and had moved off again, with Lesley squashed in to a small compartment filled with strangers, she had the idea he was still waiting. But she couldn't in fact see.

Chapter Fifty-Six

It was late when she finally arrived back at Number Fifteen, to be hugged and kissed by Auntie Peg, Joe and Sam, who were gathered in the living room, waiting for her.

'Now, I've got a meat and potato pie all ready,' Auntie Peg told her, brushing away a tear or two. 'And, from the look of you, I think you need it – you're that thin, eh! Do they no' make beef tea at that hospital of yours? You should take a bit, Lesley, get some flesh on your bones.'

'Can we no' put the kettle on?' asked Sam.

'Lesley'll be wanting to see the baby,' said Joe. He took her arm. 'Come on, I'll take you in.'

'Oh, you should see him!' cried Peg. 'He's the bonniest baby in the world, and the image of Joe!'

'Thanks very much,' said Joe, who was putting on the smiles with tremendous effort. It was obvious that in spite of the joy of the baby's arrival, the cloud of grief caused by the train crash hung over them all like a pall.

'Will Carrie no' be sleeping?' asked Lesley. 'It's so late.'

'No, she's desperate to see you, but if the baby's asleep, keep your voice down, eh?'

They tiptoed into the bedroom, where the gaslight burned low and Carrie lay in bed, propped up on pillows. In his crib, trimmed by his doting great-aunt, lay Lesley's new nephew, Donald Joseph, who was, Lesley at once declared in a whisper, the best sight she'd seen since she didn't know when.

'Och, he's lovely! And it's true what Auntie Peg says, he's the image of Joe! Can I pick him up, then?'

'Well, if he's asleep, could you wait a bit?' asked Carrie. 'First rule we've made is that if he's asleep, we leave him.'

'I'll just sit beside you, then. How are you, Carrie? What was it like?'

As Joe left them, the two sisters embraced, and Carrie, who was looking well, apart from the dark shadows under her eyes, made a face.

'No' so bad. Could've been worse. Anyway, he's worth it, eh? Ma Donald? D'you really think he looks like Joe?'

'Spitting image! Except for the dark hair. What a mop he's got, hasn't he?'

'That'll all come off, the nurse said. Then it'll come in fair, like Joe's. Or, maybe like yours.' Carrie studied her sister. 'Lesley, you're awful pale. And so thin! What's happened to you? Is it worry over your poor young man?'

'Might be.'

'He's no better?'

'The doctor says his memory could come back any time, but he's no' better yet.'

'I'm that sorry.' Carrie's expression was grave. 'Oh, Lesley, is it no' awful about thae poor laddies on the train? I'd just had Donald when the news came through and Joe was in such a state! There was so many he knew, from school, you ken, and Ned would've known 'em, too. There was that fellow who used to play the accordion, when Ned played the fiddle, he played at ma wedding, do you remember?'

'Oh, don't,' Lesley said, bending her head. 'I canna bear to think of them. Have to, though. Have to think of the families. And what'll Adam do when he hears? There must've been so many of his dockers.'

'Aye, poor Janie's been running around, seeing families, trying to help, and she's already got a great cut on her brow from the riots the other week.'

'What riots?'

'After the *Lusitania* went down, folk started attacking German shops, and there was that pork butcher's in Great Junction Street where Auntie Peg used to go, and when people started throwing things, Janie got involved, trying to stop 'em, and got hit on the head. Poor Janie! Just like Ned that time in the strike, but she only had some stitches, didn't have to stay in hospital.'

'People are so stupid,' said Lesley, rising and looking down at the sleeping baby. 'That pork butcher's shop has been here for years, the folk had nothing to do with the *Lusitania*. Listen, I'll go and get tidied up, and then I'll come back for another look at Donald. I'm sorry, I've no' had time to get him a present—'

'Who wants presents?' asked Carrie. 'I'm just so glad to see you, Lesley. The miserable thing is I'm no' allowed to get out of this bed! I've another week to stay here, would you credit it? And the nurse says, now if you put a toe out of that bed, you'll be in trouble!'

'I know that's what they say,' said Lesley. 'But it never seems right to me.'

'I take no notice,' declared Carrie. 'At any rate, I sneak out to the wc! I mean, I canna expect poor Auntie Peg to nurse me like I was ill.'

'Now I've come, I'll take care of you.' Lesley kissed her sister's cheek. 'That's what I'm here for.'

The meal that should have been so festive was subdued. Lesley confessed herself too tired to eat and said she'd like to get to bed, at which Joe gave a rueful smile.

'Canna promise you much sleep, Lesley. Not once Master Donald starts up.'

'Lesley could come and stay at our house,' suggested Sam, and Peg agreed.

'We've a bigger spare room, you ken, and it's nice and quiet.'

'No, no, I want to stay and help Carrie and Joe,' Lesley

told her. 'And give you a break, Auntie Peg.'

'Canna talk about breaks when you remember what's happening in this world,' Peg answered, her lip trembling. 'And what happened to thae laddies the other day.'

'They say they'll be giving 'em all a grand military funeral,' said Sam, after a silence. 'Even though they never got to war.'

'They were on a troop train, weren't they?' asked Joe sharply. 'They were as much at war as any lads at the front.'

Much later, when Peg and Sam had departed, and the baby had woken up roaring, been fed and gone back to sleep, Lesley looked in on Carrie and reported to Joe that she was asleep, too.

'Aye, poor lassie,' he murmured, damping down the range. 'She's tired out, but she'll no' admit it.'

'I'll see she gets some rest, Joe.'

'You could do with some rest yourself.'

'No, I'm very well. I might look thin, but I'm fit.'

'Just need a bit of happiness, to bring back the sparkle.'

'Think we all need that, Joe.'

'Aye, well, wee Donald's brought it to Carrie and me.' Joe hesitated. 'Only thing is, I shouldn't be here with him.'

Lesley put her hand on Joe's arm. 'Don't feel bad about being at home, Joe. You're needed.'

'Don't feel bad?' He shook his head. 'Lesley, I canna tell you how bad it is. I felt terrible before, but now, after Gretna, I canna bear it. All thae laddies gone, and me still here. They're asking for volunteers for the battalion, you ken, and I should go.'

'You've got duties here, Joe. Surely you wouldn't leave poor Carrie now?'

He looked away. 'Better get some sleep, Lesley. Before the baby wakes up again.'

Chapter Fifty-Seven

It took time to identify the dead in the train crash, but soon their photographs began to appear in the newspapers, together with details of their lives and families, and the names of the 246 injured. There would be an official inquiry, of course, but that would be for the future. Now the main concern lay in the planning of the military funerals and in discovering what help the relatives needed.

Whenever she could spare the time from doing the chores at Number Fifteen, Lesley visited the families of those who'd lost men she knew, and came back feeling so low in spirits, Peg said it was the worst possible thing for her to do. She had enough on her plate with her young man to worry about, so she had, but Lesley said at least he was alive.

'Aye, that's true,' sighed Peg. 'Our poor Roddie lost his brother in the crash, you ken. Makes him feel worse than ever.'

Lesley, remembering Sam's long thin assistant, asked what Roddie was doing, then? He hadn't joined up?

'They wouldn't take him,' Peg told her. 'Something wrong with his heart – not that any of us knew. Anyway, he went off to make munitions, felt really bad, and now he feels worse, because Dick's gone. But what can the poor laddie do? He's no coward.'

'I think Joe feels he's a coward,' Lesley said hesitantly.

'Joe?' Peg shook her head. 'No, he's afraid other folk think he is. His duty's to stay with Carrie, and he knows it.'

'She is feeling better. Desperate to get out of bed.'

'And then you'll be able to go back to the Highlands. And that's where you want to be, eh?'

'It is, but I had to come here, Auntie Peg. I had to be with Carrie, and I had to be with folk in Leith. I still want to stay for the funeral. I just wish Adam and Ned could've been here, too.'

'That battalion in the crash was going to join their battalion in the Dardanelles. And now what's left of it'll still be going.'

'Is that what they say?' cried Lesley.

'Aye, Sam heard the other day. They'll be away in June.' Peg tightened her lips. 'That's war, eh? You never get let off, whatever happens.'

'Whatever happens,' Lesley repeated, thinking of the shell-shocked patients who would be returning to the front if they passed their medical boards; thinking of Christopher, who would be joining them. If his memory ever returned.

At the funeral procession for some of the crash victims, Lesley found herself standing next to Janie Scott, whose stitched brow still glowed angrily and whose face was set with stark sorrow. As the gun carriages passed through the silent streets lined with soldiers, Janie did weep for a moment, but afterwards declared that they should not be weeping, they should be lobbying their MPs to bring this war to an end.

'Aye, because thae laddies'd never have been killed if they'd no' been going to war! And how long is it going to go on?' Janie's eyes glistened with the tears she wouldn't shed. 'Every day, more and more casualties reported and nobody seems to give a damn. It's like the top brass is playing with men's lives. So many here, so many there, win a few battles, lose a few battles, what does it matter? D'you no' agree with me?'

She looked from Joe to Sam, from Peg to Lesley, but Joe refused to look up and Sam only shook his head. Peg, wiping her eyes, said she didn't see what they could do, and Lesley nodded agreement.

'I'd like to stop the war tomorrow, but how? Writing to our MP will do no good, Janie, you ken that fine.'

'There's no' enough folk against it,' said Sam. 'Just see the way the dockers and the miners have been rushing off to enlist. And the men of the kirk are no' speaking out, either.'

'Women are against it!' cried Janie. 'You find me a woman that wants her man to go to war!'

'I'm away back to work,' Joe declared, his face darkening. 'I only got time off to watch the funeral.'

As he put on his cap and walked fast away, Sam turned to Peg.

'Thinks he should take their places, you ken.'

'Whose places?' demanded Janie.

'Why, thae lads of the Seventh Battalion, of course.'

'You mean, the dead?' Janie put her hand to the throbbing stitches in her brow. 'Och, what's the use o' talking, I'm wasting ma breath. I'll away back to work maself.'

'Poor Janie,' Peg murmured, watching her hurrying away. 'Nothing's ever right for her.'

'There's no' much right for any of us, if you ask me,' said Sam.

Three days later, Lesley left for Glenmar. Carrie was now up and about, relieved to be feeling well and fitting into her clothes again and, as Joe was not going anywhere, there seemed no need for Lesley to stay.

'Aye, away you go,' said Peg. 'I'll take care of things here, pet. You get yourself back to that laddie of yours. There might be some good news waiting, eh?'

'Maybe. I'll let you know, anyway.'

It was hard, saying goodbye again, this time to wee Donald as well, but goodbyes had become a feature of most people's lives at that time, you just had to get through them.

'No coming to the station, though,' Lesley ordered. 'Stations are such sad places, now.'

Joe, however, insisted on carrying her case and seeing her into the train, even managing to look cheerful as he waved goodbye, and Lesley had to admit he'd been a comfort. Taken her mind off the journey ahead and all the thoughts she knew would crowd her mind, just for a little while.

Chapter Fifty-Eight

Arriving at Glenmar was a repeat performance of the last time Lesley had come to find Christopher. Here she was, descending again from the train at Glenmar station, looking out for the bus, watching soldiers climb into it, being called by Colum MacNee.

'You are coming, Miss MacKenzie?'

Only this time, of course, she could say she was coming. This time she need not go looking for a place to stay. She had a place to stay, and a job. Nor need she worry about finding Christopher, for she knew where he was. But not how he would be.

The early summer evening was exquisite, warm and fragrant, the trees in full leaf, the gardens of the old Grand Forest filled with flowers. What did the new patients make of it, Lesley wondered? Were they happy, to know that such a world still existed? Or, angry, that they'd had to live in such a different world as the Western Front? That their comrades were still there? Perhaps they only cared about getting well. They showed no emotion as the QAs came out to greet the bus and gathered them in, and Lesley did not linger. She had to see Christopher.

As soon as she had quickly washed and changed, she flew to his room, thanking her lucky stars that Moyra was not about, so she needn't waste time talking. She did pass a nurse, who gave her a strange little smile, but she didn't have to stop and when she reached his door, knocked gently and let herself in.

For a moment, she thought she'd got the wrong room, or that Christopher had perhaps acquired a room-mate, for a young man she didn't know was sitting at the window, looking out at the view.

'Well, hallo!' he cried, swinging round at her entrance, and she saw that he looked a little like Nick Lithgow, with a narrow dark head and bright, intelligent eyes. Eyes that were studying her with a good deal of interest.

'I'm looking for Christopher,' Lesley said. 'Second-Lieutenant Meredith, I mean.'

'Meredith?' The young man, who was wearing a uniform shirt and breeches, reached for a stick and stood up. 'I'm afraid he's gone.'

'Gone?' Lesley smiled. 'That's no' possible. He's lost his memory. He's being treated here.'

'His memory came back.' The young man took a step forward, supporting himself with his stick. 'Look, can I help? My name's—'

What was he saying? It was as though a fog had come down between them. He was talking through it, but she couldn't hear him, couldn't even see him. Christopher's memory had come back? And she had not been with him?

'I'm sorry, I'm sorry!'

Who had said that? She didn't know, because she was running again, running away from the young man who wasn't Christopher, who was, she thought, standing in the corridor, calling to her, but she still couldn't hear. Anyway, she had to find Major Quentin. Major Quentin, who had let her down.

It wasn't quite time for dinner and the doctor was still in his office, writing up his notes. As soon as he saw Lesley in his doorway, he sprang to his feet and went to her.

'Lesley, you're back. Thank God for that. I've been waiting for you.'

'Where's Christopher, Major Quentin?'

She was swaying on her feet and so pale, he brought a chair and made her sit down. 'Nurse!' he called from his door. 'See if you can find somebody to bring us some tea, please.'

'I don't want tea,' said Lesley.

'If you don't have tea, you'll have to have brandy. You need something. Now – let me tell you what happened to Christopher.'

'You hypnotised him, and you said you wouldn't. You said I'd be there when his memory came back, and I wasn't. You broke your word.'

'I never hypnotised him, Lesley. His memory came back naturally, as I'd hoped it would.'

His tone was so gentle, she felt like breaking down in front of him, but he said no more until the tea came and she managed to cling on to a few shreds of control.

'I canna believe it,' she whispered, drinking the sweet, strong tea. 'What made it happen?'

'You know he had nightmares? Nightmares he could never remember? One morning, he woke up and he did remember. And when he remembered the nightmare – which was about being buried, as I'd expected – he remembered everything else. He knew who he was, he knew who you were, and his family. He knew what had happened to him, and to the guardsman who had died beside him.'

'How – how did he take it?'

'To begin with, I thought, very well. The nurses called me, of course, and I talked to him for some time. He said he felt fine, just as normal, but I told him there would be a backlash. I said he would need help, to face what he'd hidden for so long, but all he wanted to know was the date of the next board.'

'The medical board?'

'Yes, the board for assessing patients' fitness.'

'I see,' Lesley said without expression. 'He wanted to be passed fit.'

292

'That's right. I told him there wouldn't be another for six weeks. He said that that was too long to wait, and couldn't I get him on to a board elsewhere? I told him, no. He was my patient, he must wait to be assessed here.' Major Quentin cleared his throat and looked away from Lesley's eyes fixed on him. 'Next day, he walked out.'

'He could do that?' she cried. 'You let him do that?'

'You know that patients have always been free to go in and out of this hospital. It's not a prison. They go for walks, they buy a few things at the local shop. Apparently, Christopher just packed a small bag, walked down to the station and took the train south.'

'He went home, didn't he? Oh, God, he just went home, without a thought for me?'

'He didn't go home, he went to Carwood, the hospital in Hampshire where he was first admitted. And he didn't go without a thought for you. He left you a letter.'

When the doctor had put it into her hands, Lesley held it, just looking at it. The envelope was cheap, not the sort Christopher's mother would have used; he must have bought it at the village shop, with a writing pad. She could picture him, buying the stationery, going back to his room and writing the letter, before he walked out of the hospital and out of her life.

'You'd like to read it when you're alone?' Major Quentin asked.

'No, I want to read it now.'

He turned aside, busying himself with papers on his desk, while Lesley's desperate gaze ran down the words Christopher had left for her.

My dearest Lesley,
You will know by now that my memory has returned and that I'm quite recovered. I'm planning to go back to Carwood Hospital, where I hope to be given an earlier board than I could take here. Forgive me for not saying goodbye to you, it would make it harder for

me to go and I must go. I must be back with my men.
Please try to understand.

I want you to know that I still love you and always
will, but, as I told you, it's not possible now for me to
marry anyone. When I say I'm recovered, I mean,
physically, but I know I could never return to civilian
life. Some men talk of taking up their old lives again,
but others are like me. They can never be what they
once were.

My hope now is that you will meet someone who can
make you as happy as you deserve. I wish it could
have been me.
With all my love,
Christopher

When she had finished reading, Lesley folded the letter and
replaced it in its envelope. She raised her eyes to the
doctor, who was now looking at her.

'It's no surprise,' she said tonelessly. 'It's what he told
me before. We canna be married.'

'He told you that before?'

'Yes, he said he still loved me, but he couldn't marry
me, couldn't marry anyone, he'd changed too much. I
wouldn't listen, I said it was a piece of nonsense.' Her
voice had begun to tremble. 'Seemingly, it wasn't.'

Major Quentin drew up a chair. 'Lesley, I want you to
listen to me. Try not to be too cast down by this.
Christopher is like a lot of men who've experienced the
trenches, he thinks he can only relate to people who've
been through what he's been through. What he's seen has
been so horrible, he doesn't believe he could ever go back
to normal life, and you're part of that life, you see.'

'I could've helped him!'

'I know, I know, but all he wants now is to be back with
his battalion, his fellow officers, his men. He can't see
beyond the war, but once it's over, he'll think very differ-
ently, I'm sure of that.'

'Where is he now?' she asked, after she had sat quietly for a while. 'Still at this Carwood place?'

'Yes. Apparently, he made a telephone call from here. When they told him they had a board due in three weeks, he just decided he'd be on it. His parents have been informed and are visiting him, and I've transferred his case to one of the doctors there. He will see if Christopher's ready for the next board.'

'And if they think he's fit, he'll go back to the front.' Lesley stood up. She looked down at Christopher's letter still in her hand. 'I'll never see him again.'

'Lesley, I've tried to explain, you mustn't give up hope. There's every chance that when he comes back from the war, he'll be his old self, and then he'll look to you again. And need you.'

'He won't come back,' she said quietly. 'He doesn't want to.'

Chapter Fifty-Nine

By the beginning of July, Lesley was back at Number Fifteen and working again at the Princess Louise. There'd been no question in her mind of staying on at the hospital, which had become intolerable to her, with every part of her life there a reminder of Christopher. Major Quentin had informed her that he'd passed his board and returned to his unit, which was just what she'd expected.

'He got what he wanted, then,' she'd commented, shrugging, and the doctor had shaken his head. Later, when she went to say goodbye and thanked him for his kindness, he said he was sorry she was leaving, but quite understood her reasons.

'Don't forget what I told you, though. Never give up hope.'

But Lesley had already decided that hope was a luxury she couldn't afford.

Moyra and Sadie Newall saw her off from the station, Sadie expressing dismay when Lesley said she thought she would never see Glenmar again.

'Of course, you will!' cried Sadie, 'Why, when the war's over, you'll be back at the hotel.'

'Think it'll open again?' asked Moyra.

'Certainly, it will! Why, the whole spa's just waiting to open again, it's everyone's bread and butter, and you remember that we were all promised our jobs back.' Sadie's eyes gleamed at the thought. 'It's all that keeps me going, as a matter of fact, thinking of the Grand Forest opening again.'

Moyra and Lesley exchanged glances, but said nothing. Who knew what the situation would be when the war was over? If it ever was. And how many men would be coming back, to claim their old jobs?

'Keep in touch!' cried Moyra, as the train came in, and Sadie graciously kissed Lesley's cheek.

'Take care! Take care!' they called to one another, and then Lesley was being borne away, and not looking back.

Joe had lost no time in seeing the advantage to himself in having his sister-in-law back home.

'Lesley, you'll no' mind keeping an eye on Carrie for me?' he'd asked her. 'And wee Donald?'

'Oh, Joe, you're no' going to the war, are you?'

'Aye, I'm joining the Seventh. Now's ma chance.' His smile was a little guilty. 'You've given it to me, Lesley. But don't think I'm no' sorry about your laddie. Och, it's terrible, what happened to him, and to you, eh? He'll change his mind, Lesley, once he's got time to think, I can guarantee it.'

'He's back in France, and I don't want to talk about it, Joe. I'll be happy to watch out for Carrie and the wean, so you've no need to worry. Just as long as you know what you're facing, that's the thing.'

'Think I don't know?' Joe's look was bleak. 'Think I canna read the casualty lists? And Adam's been wounded, you ken.'

'Janie told me. She said it wasn't serious. I hope she's right.'

'Aye, we're all hoping that. At least, Ned's all right. So far.'

So far.

Carrie had borne Joe's departure very well, though Peg was devastated for her, and said she couldn't understand why a man would leave his wife and bairn when he needn't. Why, even if they brought in conscription, folk were saying the breadwinners would be left, and what was Joe, if no' a breadwinner? But Carrie said she'd decided she didn't want to be the one who'd held Joe back. He wouldn't be able to blame her, if he couldn't face his mates, eh?

'Small comfort, if he never comes back,' grunted Sam, though not in Carrie's hearing.

'We'll just have to hope for the best,' sighed Peg, and Lesley agreed. She might not be able to allow herself to hope for Christopher, but hope had to be kept alive for everyone else.

Chapter Sixty

One afternoon when she'd finished serving lunches at the Princess Louise, Lesley took a sandwich into Princes Street Gardens for her own short break. It was a relief to get into the fresh air, and to get away from Sally, who couldn't stop talking about her forthcoming wedding, except when she was commiserating with Lesley for no longer being engaged.

'What a good thing, you were able to keep the ring, though, eh?' she'd cried, making sure that that was the case, when first hearing what had happened. 'Imagine if your young man had wanted it back! And I'm glad you weren't daft enough to send it anyway.'

Lesley had flushed crimson. 'There'd have been no point. What would he have done with a diamond ring, going back to France?'

'Aye, well, some fellas are funny, you ken, wanting their stuff back. Alex'd never be like that. No' that I've got a ring, of course!' Sally had tossed her head. 'But I'll be having a wedding ring, on his next leave. You'll come to ma wedding, eh? It'll just be in the registry, canna be bothered with church weddings when there's a war on. Be cheaper, too.'

Ah, but it was nice to be alone for a little while, in the sunshine, Lesley reflected, watching the crowds passing to and fro, and the Castle on its rock, looking down. War or no war, some things didn't change. She was about to open her packet of cheese sandwiches, when she sensed a shadow looming and looking up, met the dark eyes of a tall man in officer's uniform.

'Lesley?' he asked, and of course she knew his voice. Knew his face, too, with a second look, though he seemed so different in khaki.

'Mr Armitage!' She leaped to her feet, pushing her sandwiches back in her bag.

'I thought we'd agreed you'd call me Paul.' He was smiling with what seemed to be genuine pleasure. 'I didn't dare to hope I'd meet you in a city this size, but here you are!'

'Yes, this is ma break.' She shielded her eyes from the sun to look at him. 'I'm working at the Princess Louise, where I was before. How is it you're in Edinburgh, then?'

'I've been spending some of my leave with my cousin. He's the one at the university, who heard Ned play.'

'Oh, I remember!' How long ago that seemed ... 'But he's no' with you today?'

'He has a rehearsal for a choral concert. I said I could amuse myself.' He was gazing at her intently. 'How is Ned, then?'

'All right, as far as I know. He's in Gallipoli.'

Paul's face darkened. 'Gallipoli. What a mistake that campaign's proving to be.'

'Mistake?'

'Well, misguided, some people think. I'm relieved to hear that Ned's safe, anyway.' He hesitated. 'Lesley, if you have time, couldn't I take you to lunch?'

'That's very kind, Mr Armitage – Paul – but I've to get back to work soon.'

'Perhaps we might sit down, then, just for a few minutes?'

As long as he doesn't ask me about Christopher, Lesley thought, as they sat together on her bench. But it seemed he already knew all there was to know.

300

'I was so very sorry to hear about Christopher's terrible experiences,' he told her, clearing his throat. 'And then your engagement ending. Miss Newall told me what had happened. She writes to me from time to time.'

Lesley was silent for so long, he touched her hand.

'You don't mind my mentioning it? I just wanted to let you know I've been thinking of you. I would have written, but didn't want to intrude. You don't think I'm intruding now?'

She shook her head, clasping her hands together on her lap, feeling the finger on her left hand where there had once been a ring.

'Is he back in France?' Paul asked gently.

'Yes, I don't know where.'

'Things might be different when the war's over.'

Tears were gathering in Lesley's eyes, but she was used to keeping them back, and stood up.

'Think I'd better be going, it's been nice seeing you again, Paul.' Her eyes went to the pips on his tunic. 'Are you a captain now?'

He smiled. 'For what it's worth.'

'When d'you go back?'

'I go back to my parents in London tomorrow. Return to France the following week.'

She shivered, thinking of it, and put out her hand.

'Good luck, then.'

He took her hand and put it in his arm. 'Thank you. May I walk back with you to the hotel?'

Outside the solid stone façade of the Princess Louise, she slipped her hand free, anxious to say goodbye again, but Paul was looking at the hotel with a professional eye.

'Well kept up,' he remarked. 'Must be doing good business?'

'Oh, yes, we're busy enough. It's no' the Grand Forest, of course.'

'I met Mr Wilcox recently. He said the company want to

301

re-open as soon as possible after the war. They're of the opinion people will be desperate to return for their treatments again, especially in our sort of hotel.'

'I suppose so.'

'You sound doubtful.'

'Well, at the moment, I canna see anything beyond the end of the war.'

'It will end one day, Lesley, then we'll all take up our lives again.'

'You think we'll win?'

'Of course, no question of it. And when it happens, I promise you, everything will return to normal.'

She wished she could believe him.

After he'd gone, she felt guilty, in case she'd seemed unfriendly. He'd been so kind in the past, to her and to Ned, and she could tell he'd wanted to be kind now. Asking her to lunch, and all that. She should have made it more obvious that she was glad to see him, especially as he was soon going back to the front. And she had been glad to see him, of course she had, it was just that she couldn't relate to anyone at the moment. Perhaps he understood. Oh, God, may he be safe, she prayed, and tried to put him from her mind as she flung herself into her afternoon's work. Thank heavens it was her evening off.

Back at Number Fifteen, she was pleased to find Auntie Peg dandling wee Donald on her knee, while Carrie stirred a pan on the range.

'How are you, pet?' asked Peg. 'Any better? I think you've got more colour. Carrie, do you no' think Lesley's got more colour today?'

'Anybody'd think I'd been ill,' said Lesley, sinking into a chair and leaning forward to touch the baby's dangling little foot.

'Aye, well, so you have. In a way.'

'I'm no' better, then.'

'Takes time. You just have to take each day as it comes.'

Carrie, spoon in hand, came over from the range. 'Lesley's young man is no' dead, Auntie Peg. He might still come back, you ken.'

'I'm just getting on with my life,' said Lesley quietly. 'It's all I can do.' She stood up. 'Are you staying for your tea, Auntie Peg?'

'No, I'm away back home. I'll just put the wean down, eh?'

'Forgot to tell you, Lesley, we got letters today,' said Carrie, her face twisting a little, for of course it had always been Joe who brought home their letters. 'There's one from Joe, and one from Ned.'

'Any news?' Lesley asked quickly.

'Good news. Joe's still doing his training, he's fine, and Ned's safe and says Adam's recovering very well.' Carrie passed the letters across. 'What a relief, eh?'

'Aye, it's grand,' said Peg, returning from putting Donald in his crib. 'We've to be grateful for what we have. Now, I'll have to run, or I'll be in trouble. Stayed too long, blethering.' She pinned on her hat and wrapped a shawl around her shoulders. 'You girls take care, mind, and I'll likely pop round tomorrow.'

'See you to the door, Auntie Peg,' said Lesley.

'Ma brave lassie,' Peg murmured, as they went down the stair. 'You've been through a lot and you're no' complaining. I'm proud of you.'

'Haven't got much to complain about, when you think of the lads at the front.'

'Lesley, you're a casualty of the war, just like your man.' Peg said deliberately. 'But there'll be good times again, you'll see. Think of them, and like I say, take one day at a time.'

'One day at a time,' Lesley repeated, and aunt and niece hugged at the swinging front door.

'Shall we read the letters again?' asked Carrie, when Lesley came back into the flat. 'The hotpot'll take a few minutes yet.'

'Yes, let's,' Lesley agreed, and the two sisters sat together, re-reading their letters, while wee Donald squirmed and snuffled in his crib, and outside the evening sun still shone over the Kirkgate.

Part Four

Part Four

Chapter Sixty-One

The years passed, and took their toll. It seemed as though the war would never end, the guns never stop firing. But at eleven o'clock on the morning of 11 November 1918, the war did end and the guns did stop firing, after delegations from Germany and the Allies signed the papers for an armistice. All the countries in the conflict had had enough. The world was once again at peace.

Later, on that momentous day, Peg and Sam were on their way to Number Fifteen to celebrate with Carrie and Joe, Sam wearing an anti-germ mask against the influenza that was going about, Peg refusing, because she said it was useless. But of course, they weren't arguing. Not today, not on this special day.

'Armistice,' Peg murmured as they battled through ecstatic crowds in the Kirkgate. 'Is it no' a lovely word, Sam?'

'Lovely word?' Sam adjusted his mask to speak. 'It's more than a word, Peggie.'

'Och, I ken that. It's got a grand meaning.'

'Truce, is what it means.'

'No' just a truce, Sam. Peace.'

'Maybe.' Sam shook his head. 'There's some think the Germans are just having a rest.'

'Never! The papers say they've lost too many men, and the Kaiser's away to exile. How could they start the war again?'

'I canna trust 'em. The way things have gone these past four years, I canna trust anybody. Even our own generals.'

'Let's no' get on to all that, Sam. Let's just remember the war's over.'

But Peg knew well enough that it wasn't possible just to do that. You had to think of the men who wouldn't be coming back, you had to go through the names on your own private roll-call. Everyone had one, eh?

Janie Scott's brother, Hughie; Billy MacSween and Ian MacSween; Lesley's young man, Mr Meredith, and thae waiters Ned and Lesley knew in the Highlands; Tam MacGregor, Rab Pringle, and all thae other laddies killed in the train crash. Names, names, names. Aye, give them all their due, and also the ones that had survived. For today was today. The day they'd thought would never come. Armistice Day.

As soon as she saw Peg, Carrie came running and flung herself into her arms, while Donald, now a handsome blond child of three, jigged up and down, wanting to be in Peg's arms, too, and Sam took off his mask and pulled up a chair next to Joe on the sofa.

'How are you, then, Joe? Leg giving you stick, eh?'

'It's no' so bad.' Joe, who had been invalided out of the army with a shattered hip, never wanted to talk about his injury. 'Canna think about that today, eh?'

'Oh, is it no' grand news, Auntie Peg?' Carrie was asking shakily. A little pulse beat in her brow, as it so often did since Joe had come home wounded. 'Och, I canna believe it!'

'Everybody's saying that,' said Sam. 'Is there a cup of tea in the pot?'

'Thought we'd have something stronger,' said Joe, now attempting one of his old grins. He looked the same, yet not the same, thought Peg, stooping to pick up Donald. No older, yet no longer the cheerful young postie who'd courted Carrie before the war. Of course, he was in constant pain with that hip that was never going to be truly healed. He'd already had an operation at a military hospital and was due for another at the Royal, but he'd never be walking round with the letters again. Carrie had said something might be found for him in the sorting office when he was better. Aye, whenever that was.

'We'll no' be needing drink to celebrate Armistice Day,' Sam was muttering. 'Never does any good, drink, as young Ned found out, eh?'

'Well, Ned's fine now,' Peg said quickly. 'And lucky, eh? Come through without a scratch and his hands as good as ever. It's a miracle, eh? Even Adam got hit in the shoulder.'

'Ned had the fever in Gallipoli,' Carrie called from the sink where she was filling the kettle. 'Joe says it was terrible, he remembers it.'

'Aye, a lot of the lads died,' said Joe. 'Now, of course, they've got the Spanish flu, over in France. Imagine, getting through a battle and dying from the flu!'

They were silent for a while, reflecting on that, until wee Donald began to cry because everything was too quiet, and Peg had to cuddle him and let him play with her handbag.

'Thank God, your Kenny was all right, eh, Joe?' she murmured, as Donald gurgled with pleasure over all the odd things he was finding, and Joe shook his head.

'What Ma would've done if anything had happened to him, I canna think.'

'Been bad enough over you,' remarked Carrie, but Joe drew his brows together and she said no more. He'd told her once that he was never going to complain about his hip, whatever happened. Not when so many of his pals were lying under white crosses in Gallipoli and France. 'Thank God you're not with them!' she'd wanted to say, but had kept silent then, too.

'When's Lesley getting home?' asked Sam, changing the subject. 'No' working late, is she? Tonight of all nights?'

'She is, then,' Carrie told him. 'And if I know the

Louise, it'll be packed to the doors, they'll be going mad in Edinburgh tonight.'

'Oh, poor Lesley!' cried Peg. 'She'll be feeling low today, it'll have brought it all back.'

'She won't be low,' said Joe. 'She'll be thinking o' the laddies coming home.'

'Aye, but her Christopher's no' coming home, is he?'

'Wasn't her Christopher, anyway,' remarked Sam.

Carrie flashed him a resentful look. 'He might've been,' she said coldly. 'You don't know how he'd have felt at the end of the war.'

'Never got past the Somme,' said Joe, and another silence fell, until everyone remembered that this was a celebration and began to talk again, while the kettle boiled.

Chapter Sixty-Two

Carrie was right. The Princess Louise, like every hotel and pub in Edinburgh and around the world, was packed to its doors with people savouring the relief and heady delight of that first Armistice. Nobody knew what they were eating or drinking, but even in the genteel surroundings of the Louise, there was singing and cheering and flags being waved, and the sort of atmosphere that would never come again in a life-time. At least, folk hoped it never would, even while they enjoyed it, for such euphoria could only follow terrible suffering, which must never be allowed to happen again. The war that had just ended must be the war to end wars.

'Never again,' men and women solemnly pledged, as they raised their glasses. 'Never again.'

'Never again,' agreed the waitresses, moving swiftly through the tables, avoiding kisses and the outstretched arms of those young officers who were already tipsy, as Mr Hawkins began to bite his lips and shake his head, saying he hoped things were not going to 'get out of hand'.

'Och, have a heart, Mr Hawkins, it's Armistice Night!' cried Sally, who was tipsy herself, not with alcohol but just the sheer relief of knowing that her husband, Alex, would now be safe. He'd already had one escape, when he'd been involved in a gas attack, but had taken no serious harm, and Sally had spent the last two years wondering if his luck could possibly hold. And it had, it had!

311

'Oh, Lesley, I'm in the seventh heaven tonight!' she whispered, as they waited to collect orders in the steamy kitchen. 'Whatever that is, eh? Where's the other six, is what I've always wondered.' But then her pretty face crumpled with contrition and she put a hand to her lips. 'Och, I'm sorry! Trust me to put ma big foot in it, blethering on about maself, when you've lost your man.'

Lesley's eyes were on the grilled turbot that was coming her way.

'Table twenty?' she called to Hector, an assistant chef, who was large and healthy and had in his time received many white feathers for being a civilian, yet with one leg shorter than the other could never have joined the army.

'Aye, hang on for the twist o' lemon,' he answered now. 'Off you go, bonnie Lesley!'

'What about ma steak?' cried Sally, still looking guiltily at Lesley.

'I'm away,' said Lesley, and in a low voice added, 'it's all right, Sally, I'm no' upset, I lost Christopher a long time ago.'

'But today's brought it all back, eh?'

'I don't mind, I don't mind. I want to think of him. I should.'

He had been present with her all that day, and going home in the train crowded with revellers, she closed her eyes and gave herself up to memories. In the two and a half years since his death in 1916, she had been, as Peg said, 'getting over it'. Healing had taken place, a skin had formed over the wound. Now, the Armistice had for a while opened up that wound again, and she must accept the pain, relive the day his mother's second letter came.

That time, there had been no comforting message on the envelope. No 'C is safe', to set her fears at rest. For, of course, Christopher wasn't safe. He had died as he had wished, saving one of his men, on 1 July, the first day of the battle of the Somme, making reparation for what he saw as his failure to save the guardsman who had died at Neuve Chapelle. He had been awarded a posthumous Military Cross.

How kind it had been of his mother to write, taking time from her own grief to tell Lesley of his death, even though he and Lesley had parted. Yet nothing she wrote could protect Lesley from the shock of knowing that what she'd expected had actually happened. All along, she'd felt sure that Christopher would never come back. As she'd told Dr Quentin, she was convinced he didn't want to. Therefore she was prepared. Until the letter came, when she realised she wasn't prepared at all. Many had learned the lesson before her, that expectation was quite different from reality, but the lesson was no less bitter, even so.

A few weeks later, balm had arrived when she received another letter, this time from Christopher's father. It was short and as kind as his wife's. Just a line or two, he wrote, to accompany the photograph that had been found in Christopher's wallet along with a picture of his parents, and recently forwarded from France.

'We thought you would like to have it, my dear,' wrote Mr Meredith. 'It may give you some comfort to know that Christopher had kept it with him.'

The photograph was of herself, taken by Christopher at Inverness. For a long time, she had not been able to look at it. Then she had placed it with her ring and her brooch and her own photographs of Christopher in her drawer, and yes, she had taken comfort. There was no pain of rejection then, only of loss. And in that, she was not alone.

Two and a half years later, she faced her loss again, but knew the pain would pass. Her life had to go on, even though Christopher's had ended, just as poor Bill Souter's had ended at Arras, Nick Lithgow's at Jutland, Ivor Greig's at Ypres. It twisted the heart to remember them, in what had seemed the perpetual sunshine of those days before the war. Such a long, hot summer ... There would never be such a summer again.

At least, Ned and Adam were safe, even if still in France, where they'd been sent at the end of the Gallipoli campaign. How soon would it be before she saw Ned again, with his fine hands that had never been hurt? Or Adam, with that chin of his and the grey eyes that could see so far? Or Paul Armitage? He'd come through with only a couple of minor injuries, as he'd told her himself in his occasional letters. It seemed unlikely that she would ever see him again, but she was glad to think that he was well.

'"Keep the hame fires burning",' someone sang drunkenly, as the train rattled into the shadows of Leith station. '"Turn the dark cloud inside oot, till the boys come hame!" Hey, we are hame, eh? How'd we get here, lads?'

'All change!' shouted the guard. 'Leith! Leith! All change, please!'

'You're lookin' awfu' doon, lassie,' a soldier said to Lesley, as she stood up to leave. 'D'you no' ken it's Armistice Day?'

'Aye,' she answered, finding a smile. 'I ken fine it's Armistice Day.'

Chapter Sixty-Three

'Till the boys come home,' the soldier had sung. And the thought of the boys coming home was in everyone's mind. Everyone wanted them home before the ink on the Armistice papers was even dry. But it wouldn't happen. Time would be taken. As Joe said, 'Fast in, but no' fast out.' Aye, they'd just have to be patient, and thank God the boys were coming home at all.

Meanwhile, the influenza continued to rage across the world, the toll of its victims so huge, they were said to outnumber all those killed in the war. In Leith, everybody knew somebody with the flu, and every daily paper brought more news of the men still in France going down with it. The dread of the telegram had not yet gone.

Lesley's particular fear was that Peg, who was older and so special to her, would be the one to fall ill. She made it her duty to watch closely for any symptoms, though what she would do if she detected any, she had no idea. There was no real treatment for the flu.

Sometimes, if she had a free evening, she and Peg would go late shopping in the Kirkgate when things were cheaper, and she would look at her aunt, stooped over displays of vegetables, spectacles slipping from her nose as she inspected sprouts and celery, sniffing and arguing over the price, and her heart would turn over at the thought of losing Peg as well as so much else. Still, she didn't like to say anything.

Peg was usually complaining about the difficulty of doing the messages when supplies were so short and rations so meagre. No' that she was saying she'd rather have the queues, mind, but all thae little bits o' this and that, two ounces here, and four ounces there, what good were they to her, cooking for Sam, who liked a lot of everything?

Rationing on a limited scale had been brought in during 1917, after the German U-boats had made food supplies precarious. No need to worry about the submarines now, of course, but rationing was still with them, and seemed to worry Peg more than the flu, which Lesley found hard to understand. When death might be round the corner, who cared if you only got five ounces of butter or two ounces of tea?

One evening in early December, when she was helping to pile sprouts and carrots and strong-smelling celery into her aunt's basket, she did ask Peg to take a bit more care. About not catching the flu.

'More care?' Peg pushed her glasses under her hat and stared. 'Now you tell me how you take care no' to catch the flu?'

'Well, you could wear a mask, or something.'

'That's a piece of nonsense, Lesley! Wearing a mask does no good at all, and neither does all that spraying the council's doing, or eating more porridge, or any of the other daft ideas folk've got. If you get it, you get it.' Peg endeavoured to look confident. 'Anyway, no' everybody dies, you ken.'

'Plenty do, though. Maybe you could keep out of crowds, eh? Just stay at home?'

'And I'm no' supposed to worry about you going into crowds, Lesley? You're in the train every day, you're working with folk at the hotel, you're more at risk than me!' Peg patted Lesley's hand as if she were a small girl again. 'Come on, now, you're looking that much better, you ken. Don't spoil it all by worrying about things you canna change.'

'Am I really looking better?'

'Aye, you're our bonnie Lesley come back to us. You've turned your dark cloud inside out, pet, and you're fine. You remember that.'

But Lesley, moving with Peg to see if there were any teacakes left at the baker's, wasn't sure yet if the dark clouds had silver linings. Ned and Adam weren't home from France, Joe's hip wasn't healed, Auntie Peg wasn't safe, nor was anyone. Loving people was the problem, and the fear of loss. If you'd once experienced loss, the fear of it was with you always.

'Och, I could do with putting ma feet up,' sighed Peg, as they made their way up the stair at Number Fifteen. Some of the vegetables they'd bought and a few groceries were for Carrie, and Peg had said she'd look in for a cup of tea before she took her own messages home. Lesley, sensitive as she was to Peg's welfare, felt instant guilt at letting her aunt carry any bags at all. Was she not puffing and blowing more than she should?

'Here, let me take the messages,' she ordered, and was trying to take Peg's shopping bags as well as her own, when a man's voice called from the top of the stair, 'No, let me.'

And a tall man in soldier's uniform leaped down the stair and took the bags from their hands. It was Adam.

Immediately, their spirits rose. To have one of the laddies back, to have Adam himself, so much the one to depend on, it made them feel for the first time since the Armistice that the war was well and truly over.

'Och, I canna believe you're really here!' cried Peg, kissing Adam's lean cheek, when they were all in Carrie's flat. 'And looking that well and all!'

He wasn't, in fact, looking well, thought Lesley, who found him thin and rather strained, with one shoulder now lower than the other. And when she too had reached up to

317

kiss him and met his eyes, she'd seen that same look that was in Joe's and all the eyes of other men who'd been to the front. Adam saw her, yes, as he saw his present surroundings, but he seemed to be seeing beyond, to another world civilians didn't know and never could. No doubt, when Christopher's memory had returned, he'd seen that world too, and the sight of it had driven him back. The thought made Lesley's hands on Adam's arms tighten, until he looked down at her in surprise, and then she blushed and let him go.

'You're here to stay, eh?' she whispered. 'You're no' going back?'

'Well, I'm no' exactly demobbed yet. They've sent me home to get ma shoulder re-set.' Adam looked across at Joe, who was leaning on his crutch, with a smile of fellow-feeling. 'You and me both, eh, Joe? How are you, then?'

'Grand,' Joe returned at once. 'Just got to get ma hip sorted out. And Carrie's well, and the wean.'

'Donald's in bed now,' Carrie said fondly. 'You'll see him tomorrow, eh?'

'Oh, wait till you do, Adam!' cried Peg. 'He's the bonniest laddie ever, the image of Joe!'

'I want to see him, I've been thinking of him.' Adam's eyes went from face to face. 'I've been thinking of you all.'

'And Ned?' asked Peg. 'When'll we see Ned?'

Ah, well, that of course, Adam didn't know. He would not be returning to France himself, and it was his guess that Ned would also be home soon. He'd brought letters, anyway, they were up the stair in his kitbag, he'd bring them down, soon as he'd unpacked.

'No hurry, no hurry,' said Peg. 'Your dad'll be waiting for you, anyway, Adam.'

'Aye,' Adam smiled. 'He's starting cooking already. Says I'm too thin, need feeding up, which is a piece of nonsense.'

'I'm no' so sure,' said Lesley. 'I bet Janie'll start cooking too, soon as she sees you.'

'Janie?' He laughed. 'That'll be the day. She'll say it's lucky I've had ma tea, when I go round to see her, if I know Janie.'

'Och, is it no' grand to have him back,' asked Peg, when Adam had gone up to his father's flat. 'It's done me good just to see him, I feel things are working out, after all. And soon it'll be our Ned's turn, eh? We'll be putting the flags out then.'

Putting the flags out now, was what Lesley felt like doing. Auntie Peg was right, Adam's coming home had given them all a boost, and Lesley was suddenly so relaxed, so much more confident for the future, she quite forgot her worries over Peg and the flu.

Chapter Sixty-Four

One evening in mid-December, Lesley was sitting alone in the living room, working on a pile of mending. It was late. Carrie, after visiting Joe who was in the Royal recovering from his hip operation, had already gone to bed, and wee Donald, of course, had long been asleep. Lesley, yawning over the sock she was darning, was thinking that she might turn in, too, for her day at the Louise had been as tiring as usual, when she heard a rapid knocking at the flat door.

Outside on the landing was Adam. In the glare of the gaslight, his face was a map of shadows, his grey eyes dark pools.

'Lesley! Thank God, it's you!' He put a dry hand on hers. 'I'm that sorry to bother you, but could you come up the stair, d'you think?'

'What's the matter, Adam? Are you no' well?'

'I'm all right, it's ma dad. Will you come up, then? Have a look at him?'

'Of course, I will!' She closed the door behind her and ran up the stair in front of him. 'But what's wrong?'

He shook his head, and at the door to his father's flat, caught at her hand again. 'I'm afraid, Lesley, I'm scared. I had to go to the hospital today, let them look at ma shoulder. You ken what's it like, I was away all day – when I got back, Dad was lying down. Said he had a sore throat.'

Adam shuddered. 'I didn't realise – Oh, God, Lesley – I never thought! But come in, come in!'

She followed him into the living room, which was orderly in the extreme, for Jock Kay kept his place as his wife had kept it, 'all shipshape and Bristol fashion', as he liked to say. 'Where is he?' she whispered, and Adam pointed ahead to his father's room.

'I put him to bed. He said he felt better, but then he started shivering. He was as hot as a furnace. I said I'd go for Dr Mason, but he didn't want me to leave him.'

They crept into the bedroom, where Jock lay in the double bed that had been his marriage bed. His breathing was loud and painful, punctuated by coughs, though he appeared to be asleep, but when she drew nearer and could see him more closely, Lesley felt herself grow cold. Jock's face was suffused with the violet-blue of cyanosis.

'Oh, Adam,' she whispered. 'Run for the doctor now. Hurry!'

'I don't understand,' he gasped. 'It wasn't like this when I left him! How's it happened? Lesley, what is it?'

'It means his heart's affected. Adam, for God's sake, go for the doctor! I'll stay with your dad.'

Adam turned and ran.

Lesley too ran, into the kitchen, to find a cloth which she soaked in cold water and put to Jock's burning brow, talking to him soothingly, though she was sure he could no longer hear her. She found more cloths and after loosening Jock's night shirt, sponged him down to try to lower his temperature. A fruitless effort, but she felt she had to do something, as the clock ticked away over Jock's bed and Jock's life trembled over the abyss.

The outer door banged and she heard footsteps on the stair. It was Adam, thundering in with the doctor. Not Dr Mason, but 'the lady doctor', as she was always called – Dr Buchanan, his practice partner, a sharp-faced young woman who stood no nonsense from those who thought she must be some sort of nurse, not really a doctor at all.

'How long has your father been like this?' she shot at Adam, as she bent over Jock to take his pulse.

'You mean that colour?'

'Heliotrope cyanosis, is what it is. How long?'

'No' long.' Adam's voice was hoarse, there was sweat on his brow and his throat. 'Half an hour?'

'Longer,' said Lesley, taking Adam's hand. 'A wee bit longer.'

'Well, as you probably realise, Mr Kay, your father has the influenza and I'm afraid it's already progressed to a serious stage.'

'But how can that be?' cried Adam. 'He was fine when I left him this morning. I canna believe it, I canna believe it could be so quick!'

'Sometimes happens that way.' Dr Buchanan snapped her bag shut. 'There's no point wasting more time here, I'm going to get your father into hospital. Please wait for the ambulance.' She glanced at Lesley. 'Well done, Mrs Kay, you did the right thing, trying to get the fever down.'

'I'm just a neighbour,' Lesley murmured. 'No' Mrs Kay.'

'My mistake.' The doctor made for the door. 'Keep on with the sponging, I'll see myself out.'

But Adam ran down the stair with her. At the door, he looked into her face, all his feelings showing in his own, and with brief kindness, she answered the question he was afraid to put.

'We'll do what we can, Mr Kay, but I have to advise you not to be too hopeful. I'm sorry.'

'I'll go with you, Adam,' Lesley said, looking up from his father, when he came slowly back, his head bent on his chest.

'It's good of you,' he said in a low voice. 'I'm grateful.'

'You wouldn't like me to run round for Janie?'

He shook his head. 'She's in Glasgow tonight. For some meeting. A friend's putting her up.'

'She'll be so sorry no' to be with you, Adam.'

'Aye.'

As Lesley continued to sponge Jock with cold water, Adam's eyes went to his father's face and never left it.

'I never thought he was so bad,' he whispered. 'It's my fault, eh? I should've gone for the doctor sooner.'

'It's no' your fault at all, Adam. Don't go blaming yourself, for God's sake!'

Fetching the doctor earlier would not have prevented the cyanosis, Lesley knew, and as soon as it appeared, there was not much hope, but she didn't like to say more.

'Your dad'll be in good hands,' she said quietly. 'They'll do all they can.'

He nodded and they did not speak again until the ambulance came.

At eight o'clock the following morning, Jock quietly died. After he'd spent some time alone with his father, Adam came for Lesley and took her in to see him. She touched his cheek and wept a little, for a hard life that was now over, for a good man now reunited with the wife he'd loved.

'I'll never forget you were with him on his last night,' Adam said quietly. 'He always had a soft spot for you, Lesley. Said you were like your ma. Very special.'

'I must tell Auntie Peg,' she sobbed.

'They've told me to go home for now, get some rest.' Adam smiled wryly. 'I don't feel I'll ever rest again. To think I went through the war and I'm still here, but ma dad's gone.'

They walked out together into the December morning that was still dark, Lesley wearing Adam's mother's shawl that he had found for her, she having no coat.

'I'll have to hurry,' she told him. 'Carrie'll have missed me by now, she'll be in a state.'

'Won't take long to get back.'

At the foot of the stair at Number Fifteen, Adam stopped and turned Lesley towards him.

'Just want to say thank you,' he murmured, then his

323

voice broke and his tears came. 'Oh, Lesley ...' He held her for a moment, before releasing her and running his hand across his eyes. 'Men aren't supposed to cry, eh?'

'You cry as much as you want, Adam. You should. You should cry for your dad. He was a good man.'

'Lesley, is that you?' called Carrie from the landing. 'Oh, my God, where've you been? I thought you'd been kidnapped!'

'Auntie Lesley kidnapped!' echoed Donald, hurtling down the stair towards them, and Lesley picked him up and kissed him.

'We've been to Leith Hospital, Carrie. There's bad news. Jock's died from the flu.'

Carrie, of course, couldn't get over the news, as she hurried about, making them tea, for she had insisted that Adam should come in and have some breakfast. And Lesley should ring up the Louise and say she couldn't go in that day. Why, she'd had no sleep! At the hospital all night!

'Oh, I'm going in,' said Lesley. 'But will you go round and tell Auntie Peg, Carrie?'

'And I'll go round and tell Janie,' Adam said heavily. 'I'm sorry, Carrie, I'll no' have any breakfast, if you don't mind.'

'You sit down, Adam. There it is. I've made it for you. Nice hot porridge, and there's a bit of bacon to follow.' Carrie's eyes filled with tears. 'Poor Jock'd no' want you to go without proper food, Adam.'

In the end, he made a good breakfast, though he said he felt bad about it, didn't seem right to be eating bacon with his dad dead. Afterwards, he left them, saying he would, after all, try to sleep for an hour or so, then he'd have to start on the arrangements. Lesley drank another cup of tea before putting on her hat and coat, ready for the train.

'Funny, isn't it?' she said slowly. 'I was all the time worrying about Auntie Peg, I never even thought about poor Jock.'

'That's life,' said Carrie. 'Never what you think.'

'The doctor said Jock might have had a heart condition anyway, that's why he went so quickly.'

'The flu's usually quick. Maybe that's a mercy.'

'Maybe.' Lesley suddenly reached out and held her sister's hand. 'Oh, Carrie, take care, eh? I feel I'm all on shifting sand, don't know what's safe, and what's not.'

'Anybody home?' came a voice from the door, and a stranger in army uniform stood looking in at them. At least, for a split second they thought he was a stranger, then saw that it was Ned.

'Ned! Ned!' they screamed and sprang to greet him. Ned home out of the blue for Christmas leave on this sad morning. Ned, looking thin as a rail, but well and just his old self, throwing down his kitbag, warming his fine musician's hands at the range.

'Anything to eat, then, girls? Do I smell bacon?'

Oh, it was a shame they had to tell him about Adam's father and see his joy turn to grief, but his first thoughts were for Adam, and they knew how much it would mean to Adam to have Ned back again. They were all neighbours, all friends, they went through things together.

'Thank God, I'm home,' said Ned, sitting down and drawing a wondering Donald to his knee. 'Now, I wonder, do I have some sweeties in ma pocket for a wee laddie, then?'

And as they watched young Donald's investigations, Ned's sisters held each other and shed a few more tears.

Chapter Sixty-Five

Christmas was quiet, because of the death of Jock, but Hogmanay was something the people of Number Fifteen felt they needed to celebrate. The first New Year since the war ended – och, they couldn't let that go by!

After they'd visited Joe, poor laddie, still in hospital, everyone gathered at Carrie's – family and neighbours and anyone who wanted to drop in for a drink and a slice of Peg's fruit cake. Ned, being dark-haired, was first foot and also played his fiddle again, all the old tunes they loved, though when it came to 'Auld Lang Syne', the memories were too much and some folk broke down.

Adam had gone by then. He'd only appeared briefly, looking around with his empty eyes, while Janie held his arm and kept watch uneasily. The only time Adam's gaze came to life was when it rested on Lesley, and she knew, as he knew, that there would always be something between them now. Some shared feeling that came from the long vigil the night Jock died, though as Lesley told Janie, she'd only done what any neighbour would have done.

'Aye, but it was good of you,' Janie murmured. 'I'll never forgive maself for no' being there, but I wasn't to know, was I? Trouble is, Adam is aye thinking I'm somewhere else and no' with him, but women have their lives to lead, as well as men.'

'That's true,' Lesley agreed.

'And if women like me didn't get on with things, we'd never have got the vote. Well, we haven't yet, seeing as they've only given it to women over thirty, which is ridiculous whichever way you look at it, but, still, it's a start, eh? Be sure you tell your Auntie Peg she's to vote the way she wants, Lesley, and no' what Sam says.'

Lesley looked across at her aunt, trenchantly giving Ned her views on whether or not Leith should go back to Edinburgh, and smiled.

'I don't think there's any danger of Auntie Peg no' voting the way she wants, Janie.'

'Aye, well some women canna realise that it's a secret ballot, eh?' Janie's eyes went to Adam, who was standing with his eyes cast down. 'Are you wanting away, Adam?'

'Aye. I'm no' in the mood for Hogmanay.'

'Should stay to see in 1919, though. Our first year of peace.'

'You stay, if you want.'

'No, no, I'll come with you. Say goodnight, then.'

As Adam made his farewells, Janie glanced at Lesley. 'He's very low,' she whispered. 'Canna blame him, eh? His dad's no' long gone.'

'It was good of him to come.'

'Yes, well, he'll feel better soon, 'specially when he gets his shoulder done. Gets a lot o' pain with that. Happy New Year, Lesley!'

Adam said nothing, but shook her hand, and when he and Janie had departed, the atmosphere eased a little and folk laughed and talked as Ned took up his fiddle and the clock moved on through the last hours of 1918.

Later, when they'd seen in the New Year and Ned was taking a break from playing, Lesley, observing him with a glass of lemonade in his hand, asked him if he was really all right now.

'Really all right?' he mimicked, laughing. 'You mean, do I no' have to have a drink? The answer is no, I don't have to have a drink, though I'd like one. Oh, God, yes. But I don't need one.' He drank his lemonade. 'That answer the question?'

'Heavens, what a lecture! I was only hoping you were happy about it, Ned.'

'Sorry, I'm still touchy.' He kissed her cheek. 'Yes, I'm happy. It's the best thing I ever did, giving up the drink, though don't tell Sam I said that, I'm no' keen to have him crowing over me.'

As Lesley smiled and was about to move away, he put his hand on her arm.

'Listen, what are you going to tell Paul?'

Her smile faded. 'I knew you'd ask me that.'

'Well, you've never said. And he is waiting for an answer.'

Paul Armitage, not yet demobbed, but due to be released soon, had sent his usual Christmas cards to Ned and Lesley, marking Ned's 'Please Forward', for of course he didn't know Ned was home, and including in Lesley's a letter.

Good news, he'd announced, about the Grand Forest! The patients had already left, it was soon to be handed back to the owners to be refurbished, and was expected to re-open in the spring. All the hotels in Glenmar were re-opening, no one could wait to bring the spa back to life again.

What had interested Ned was that Paul had been insistent that both he and Lesley should return, Ned to his trio, Lesley perhaps to something new. No need to be a waitress again, why not consider Reception, for instance? Paul had done preliminary checking and it seemed that Alison Gow had taken another job and would not be returning to her post. If Lesley would like to consider it, he could provide training, and though he knew there would be sad memories for her at Glenmar, things would be so different, he was confident she could be happy back in the Highlands. He awaited her reply, and was her very good friend, Paul Armitage.

'Well, there's a turn out for the book!' Ned had exclaimed, after reading the letter, but Lesley had been non-committal.

'You don't want to go back?' asked Ned.

'Do you?'

'Yes, why not? I liked it there, and so did Ella.'

'Ella wants to go back?' Lesley was surprised. 'You've written to her about this already?'

'Well, we were always told we'd get our jobs back after the war. I asked Ella what she thought, and she said she'd go back like a shot. She's had enough of London.' Catching the look in Lesley's eye, Ned shook his head. 'No, there's nothing between us. Don't start your matchmaking again. We're just good friends.'

'Ella told me you might go to see her when you got back.'

'Aye, when I'm demobbed, I might. But come on, Lesley, say what you think about going back.'

But Lesley had refused to be drawn.

For a time at Hogmanay, she was still refusing to discuss the matter, until she said suddenly, her lip trembling,

'The thing is, Ned, it's right what Paul says, I do have sad memories. I canna imagine being back at Glenmar without Christopher.'

Ned looked down at his hands. 'I know. I know how you feel. But life goes on, eh? And it'll no' look the same as when it was a hospital.'

'It'll look the same as it used to do. There'll be memories everywhere.'

'Might be a good idea to face 'em, then. You keep the lid on 'em, they're always there, you never really get over things.'

Lesley was silent, unsure how much of Ned's view she could accept.

'Come on,' he whispered. 'Come on back, with Ella and me! It'll be better than slaving on at the Louise. It was all you wanted at one time, to get away, and you could do something different this time. Rest your feet from waiting on! Think of it!'

'I'll see,' she murmured, and he sat back, pleased with his breakthrough, as Auntie Peg came up to ask if he was no' going to play for them again, before Sam began agitating to go home?

'And Lesley, pet, are you all right?' she asked, taking Lesley's arm. 'You look so far away!'

In the Highlands? thought Lesley. But she said nothing to Auntie Peg.

Chapter Sixty-Six

It was June before the Grand Forest was ready to open. Paul, now out of the army and on site in Glenmar with Mr Wilcox, sent Ned and Lesley regular reports. So many delays, so much frustration with builders and workmen, he couldn't describe his feelings, except his relief that everything was finally coming into place. And to give thanks for his luck in getting the staff he wanted.

New people, of course, but many from the old days that the MacKenzies would remember. Old Colum MacNee, and Miss Newall; the Murrays for the trio, and Veronica, in reception, who would have Lesley as her new assistant. Oh, yes, thank God, so many would be coming back, he couldn't be more grateful.

'So many coming back,' Lesley murmured. 'But no Nick Lithgow, or Bill Souter.'

'No Ivor Greig,' said Ned, his face taking on the closed expression of the ex-soldier looking back.

'No Moyra Gillan, either,' added Lesley. 'But she's married now, with a baby. You won't be seeing her, Ned.'

'Will be seeing Ella.'

'Saw her in London, too.'

'Aye.' Ned smiled. 'What a character her mother is, eh?'

Lesley knew his visit to Ella's home had gone well, but she no longer asked about his 'intentions' towards her friend, which were perhaps none of her business, anyway.

Just as long as Ella didn't get hurt. These days, Lesley was particularly anxious for folk not to get hurt.

Anxious for herself too, in that respect. Even though she had made the decision months before to go back to Glenmar, she still had sleepless nights, wondering if she'd done the right thing. Auntie Peg had made it plain she didn't think so.

'Och, you're asking for trouble, Lesley!' she'd cried, when the news was finally broken to her that both Ned and Lesley were away to the Highlands. 'Of all the silly girls! Did you never hear o' the burnt bairn that feared the fire? Once you're up there, where you met your laddie, it'll all come back to you, you mark ma words. I blame Ned, persuading you to go. He should have had more sense!'

'It is three years, Auntie Peg, since Christopher died. More than that since I lost him, to be honest.'

'Aye, and you're well over it here. But up in that hotel?' Peg shook her head. 'Och, it's your life, Lesley, I'll have to leave you to make your own mistakes.'

Shaken by her aunt's views, Lesley had wavered in her decision for a little while. Yet, the other side of the coin was that life for her at the present time appeared to be going nowhere.

Work at the Louise had become stale and dull. Now that her husband, Alex Mitchie, had returned from the war, Sally had left to become a housewife and prepare for her first baby, her sole topic of conversation when she called in from time to time. Even so, Lesley missed her. As for Alex himself, who had once been such good company, he now scarcely spoke and was, Lesley guessed, feeling guilt that he had returned and his brother George had not. No one else on the staff appealed to her, all she seemed to do was work hard and count the time to going home. But when she was at home, what did she do?

Very little. Visited Auntie Peg, helped Carrie. Not that Carrie needed help these days, and Lesley hadn't missed the briefest look of relief in her sister's eyes when she'd told her of the Highlands plan. She would have the flat to herself and Joe, of course, and you couldn't blame her for wanting that. She and Joe hadn't had much time together of late, and Joe could do with cheering up, seeing as his second hip operation hadn't helped and he was now permanently lame. At least he'd managed to get the job in the sorting office.

Of course, it was always pleasant to spend time with Auntie Peg, and now that the flu epidemic seemed to have passed, there was no more anxiety on that score, but Lesley couldn't spend her life with Auntie Peg, much as she loved her.

As she explained to Adam, when she met him once on the Shore, she felt herself ready again to make a move. 'Maybe it'll be the wrong one, but I think I should do it, that's the point.'

'Bonnie Lesley going over the Border again?' he asked without smiling. 'Seems to me we've been through this before.'

'You think I shouldn't go?'

He shrugged. 'No' for me to say.'

'I've the chance of a different job, you ken. Receptionist, no' waiting on.'

'Oh, well, then.'

'Are you feeling any better, Adam?' she asked, after a moment or two. 'How's your shoulder?'

'Fine, since the operation, thanks. Och, I've nothing to complain about.' He brought his gaze back from the prospect of ships in the harbour to look into her face. 'Sorry, I'm a misery these days. Canna seem to settle. Janie's always on at me to campaign for Leith's independence, and I do care about that, I don't want to see Leith go back to Edinburgh. But I leave it to Janie to do the work.' He gave a faint grin. 'Typical, eh?'

'It takes time, to get over things,' she said quietly.

'Aye. Well, don't forget to say goodbye when you go, eh?'

'As if I would!' she called after him, watching his tall figure disappearing towards the docks. Was there any truth, she wondered, in the rumours that he and Janie would soon marry, now that he was on his own? Men left alone were frequently spurred on to marry, for company and to be looked after, if nothing else, but it had always seemed to Lesley that Janie was the one who needed a spur to be married.

No doubt she was too busy at the moment, working to keep Leith's independent status, but she was fighting a losing battle there, everyone feared. Edinburgh was seeking to extend boundaries again and would almost certainly swallow up Leith, which in any case was finding it difficult to make ends meet.

When I come back from the Highlands, will I find maself in Edinburgh and not Leith? Lesley asked herself, and that evening asked the others what they thought.

'They can sign whatever papers they like,' Ned said robustly. 'I'll never belong to Edinburgh, I'm a Leither, and always will be!'

'When you're no' a Highlander,' Joe observed.

Ned and Lesley exchanged glances.

'We're just going to work in the Highlands,' Ned said, after a pause.

'You've got jobs here,' said Carrie. 'Lesley's at the Louise, you're at the Royal Albert.'

'No' the same.' Ned looked again at Lesley. 'But talking of jobs, we'd better get our notices in, eh, Lesley? We leave in two weeks' time.'

'Oh, no!' cried Carrie. 'Oh, Lesley! Well, I just hope you know what you're doing, eh?'

Oh, God, I hope I do, thought Lesley, taking out the pen and ink bottle from the dresser. 'Ned, have we any writing paper?'

Chapter Sixty-Seven

Journey's end. There it was, the Hotel Grand Forest, looking so much the same in the early evening sunshine, Lesley felt time had stood still and she was a young girl again, arriving for her new job, excited, brave-looking, inwardly scared. Now she sat next to Ned in the taxi carrying them from the station, stiff as a statue, her gloved hands together on her lap, her eyes fixed on the grand white turreted building ahead.

'You all right?' asked Ned, who was holding his violin case on his knee. He too was a little stiff, as though bracing himself for an ordeal, though the ordeal of course was not his. Maybe he shouldn't have made Lesley come back? As she slid her eyes away from the hotel to his face, she read the thoughts going through his mind.

'I'm a bit nervous,' she answered huskily.

'Looks good, though, eh? The hotel? They've painted it.'

'Everything looks lovely.'

That was true. The village was beautiful, loaded with greenery, trees in full leaf, rhododendrons still blooming, every house bright and welcoming, waiting for guests. If they turned their heads, they would see distant hills, empty at last of snow, but of course they looked straight ahead, eyes on the Grand Forest, as the taxi creaked up the drive and stopped at the portico.

'Round the back, please,' Ned told the driver. 'We're staff, no' guests.'

'I wass not thinking,' the driver answered, with a grin. 'Hotel only opens next week, am I right?'

'You're right.'

'And it will be a good thing, too, to have it open again, and all the hotels. Let us be getting back to normal after the war.'

'You in it?' asked Ned.

'From the beginning. Territorial.'

At once, Lesley was transported back to August 1914. A stiflingly hot day. Territorials marching down the hill towards the station, pipes and drums playing, mothers shedding tears. How many of those laddies came back? She didn't dare to ask. Besides, her thoughts had moved on. That had been the day Mrs Meredith left, with her companion and Christopher. Lesley could almost feel again her dress sticking to her in the heat, the straw of her hat biting into her brow, as she ran to say goodbye. Stop there, she told herself. Stop.

'Grounds are looking good,' observed Ned, as he paid off the driver at the rear of the hotel. 'Must've been some work going on here lately, eh?'

'Work?' The driver pocketed his fare and tip and grinned again. 'You have never seen the like. Everybody's been involved. Everybody's had a job, painting, building, gardening! Same all over Glenmar. The place hass come up like flowers after winter, you will see.' He touched his cap. 'Good luck to you.'

'Nice chap,' Ned murmured. He picked up their cases. 'Here we are, then, at the back door. I remember Bill joking about that. "We know our place!" he used to say. "It's the back door for us!"'

Bill. Nick, Ivor. Christopher. Ghosts. Lesley's heart was failing her, as her eyes met Ned's. Auntie Peg had been right. This was a mistake. She should never have come. Even Ned should not have come. Let new people staff the Hotel Grand Forest, folk who had no memories—

'Life goes on,' Ned said softly. 'Open the door, Lesley.'

And the first person they saw when they stepped inside the vestibule was Ishbel Ord, or, rather, Ishbel Lithgow, widow of Nick. No ghost, just the lanky young woman they remembered, with her flaxen hair twisted into a knot and no sign of her sorrow, except that she seemed mysteriously older. There were no lines on her face, no shadows beneath her eyes, yet she had changed.

I suppose most of us have, thought Lesley, who flung her arms round Ishbel's bony shoulders, and received a strong hug in return.

'Oh, Ishbel, it's so grand to see you! Ned, is it no' grand to see Ishbel?' Lesley drew back to study her again. 'We were so sorry, you ken, to hear about Nick.'

'Very sorry,' said Ned gently. And Lesley knew that memories would be flooding his mind, as he stood so close to the storeroom where Nick had put him that night he'd been drunk. What a friend he'd been! Getting Ned upstairs and into bed, trying to cover for him with Mr Armitage. Ned and Lesley had hardly been able to look him in the eye next morning.

'I didn't know you were coming back,' Lesley murmured quickly to Ishbel, to shut those images from her own mind. 'It must be hard for you.'

'I don't think so, it's where I met Nick. It's where I fell in love.' Ishbel's eyes moved away from Lesley's face. 'When Mr Armitage wrote to me, to offer me ma old job back, I wanted to come straight away. I wanted to be where Nick'd been.' She looked again at Lesley. 'Well, you've come back, eh? You understand?'

'I understand.'

They had to move on, pass through the rear parts of the hotel to the principal reception rooms, which were as grand as ever. No expense had been spared to return everything to such former glory. Gone were the hospital partitions, the green paint on the walls, the cheap furniture, the smell of antiseptic and stale cooking. Back in place were the splendid chandeliers that had been packed away, the fine chairs and tables, the landscape pictures in gilt frames. There was soft carpeting, and palms again in the Palm Court, the scent of flowers from the long, open windows, curtained as they'd always been, in expensive brocade folds.

'My God!' cried Ned. 'They must have spent a fortune, eh? All borrowed, I expect.'

'I told you it would all be the same,' said Lesley. 'They've put everything back just as it was.'

'They're hoping the guests'll be the same, too. At least, that they get as many.' Ned moved purposefully towards the reception desk. 'And here's Veronica. She's just the same, all right.'

It was true, the receptionist was as attractive as ever, her hair brightly copper, her green eyes shining, as the brother and sister came to her.

'Ned!' she shrieked. 'And Lesley, too! Oh, it's lovely to see you! How are you both? Are you exhausted? Want me to organise some tea?' She leaned across the desk. 'I'm really looking forward to working with you, Lesley, but I'd better let Mr Armitage know you're here. He's looking out for you.'

'Is Ella here yet?' asked Ned casually, and Veronica, instantly intrigued, told him Ella was upstairs. In the same room she and Lesley had shared in the old days, Ella had asked for it specially.

'Isn't it nice, being back again?' asked Veronica, then her eyes fell and she flushed a little. 'Sorry, Lesley. You must be – oh, you know what I want to say.'

'That's all right,' Lesley murmured, feeling a sudden weariness strike her, but her eyes were on the wedding ring on Veronica's left hand. 'Veronica, are you married? I didn't know. What's your new name, then?'

'Reynolds.' Veronica glanced carelessly down at her ring. 'Actually, I'm separated. He was a fellow I met down south when I was doing war work, a pilot in the Royal

Flying Corps.' She laughed. 'I was up in the clouds with him, I can tell you, but it didn't last. We're going to get a divorce.'

'Divorce?' echoed Lesley, glancing at Ned. This was something new.

'Folk have different ideas now, you know,' Veronica told them. 'We live in a different world. Watch out, here comes His Highness. You tell him you want a cup of tea, Lesley, you've been travelling all day.'

His Highness, as Veronica called Mr Armitage, was another who appeared not to have changed. It was four years since Lesley had seen him, when he'd looked tall and handsome in his uniform. Now, he was tall and handsome in his formal dark clothes. Rather pale, perhaps, but he'd always been pale, and his fine eyes held no hint of past suffering, unlike the eyes of Adam and so many who had returned from the front. As soon as he saw Lesley and Ned, he came to shake their hands with enthusiasm, pleased and perhaps surprised that they'd done what they said they'd do.

'Hallo! You came, then! I didn't know you'd arrived, I've been looking out for you. How was the journey?'

'They'd love a cup of tea!' called Veronica.

'Of course, of course. But I can't tell you how glad I am you made the decision to come back.' He was looking at them both, but addressing Lesley. 'I'm sure you've done the right thing, I'm sure you'll be happy. Tell me, what do you think of it? What do you think of the hotel?'

He seemed to Lesley to be unusually nervous and was for once showing his feelings. A lot of money had been spent on this refurbishment, a heavy load of responsibility must rest on his shoulders to make sure that the re-opening was a success. Mr Wilcox would be about somewhere, but everyone knew that the man who really ran the hotel was Paul Armitage. No wonder he was nervous. Yet in the old days you'd never have known. Perhaps the war had affected him, after all.

*

'I'm going to find ma room and Ella,' Lesley told Ned, when Paul had finally released them and they'd had a quick cup of tea in the reception office. 'What about you?'

'I'll bring your case up,' said Ned. 'I might as well see Ella, too.'

Chapter Sixty-Eight

'I knew you'd want this view again,' Ella said quietly. 'That's why I asked for the same room.'

Ned had left them and they were standing together at the window, as they had stood together years before, Lesley and Ella, old friends now, new companions then. Outside, the June evening light was fading at last, but they could still see the Square below, and the pump rooms, and, beyond, the line of smoke-blue hills.

'The view hasn't changed,' Lesley murmured. 'Nothing's changed. But it's no' the same to me.'

'I know what you mean. You look the same, though, Lesley.'

'And so do you, except that you've got thinner.'

'Aye. Lost weight when I had the flu.'

Lesley spun round. 'You didn't tell me you'd had the flu, Ella! Don't say it, you might have died!'

'Not me. I'm a tough old bird. Everyone had the flu round our way, wasn't it the same for you?'

'Quite a few folk died.' Lesley turned from the window, as a sudden memory of Adam's tears came to her. 'Men are no' supposed to cry,' he'd said. How sharp that memory was, over-riding for a moment all the memories so tightly woven into the Grand Forest. 'Thank God you came through it.'

'Ned's not put on any weight since I saw him last,' Ella

remarked, combing her hair and re-pinning it. 'He's all right, is he?'

'As far as anybody's all right these days.' Lesley looked at her trunk that had arrived earlier, and her small case that Ned had dumped on her bed. 'Canna face unpacking that stuff now. Shall we go down? Veronica said there'd be staff supper soon.'

'I just want to say, that I do admire you for coming back,' Ella said, her soft brown eyes serious. 'It must've taken some courage. I mean, to face the memories.'

'To be honest, I wasn't sure I'd done the right thing, until I saw Ishbel, but then I felt better. She's facing memories, too.'

Ella hesitated. 'As long as you can let them go.'

'You've been talking to Ned. Life goes on, is what he likes to tell me.'

'We just want you to be happy again, one day.'

'Well, of course I want to be happy! But one thing I've learned, you canna organise happiness for other people.'

Ella looked at her for a moment, reading her meaning. 'That's true,' she agreed, and put her arm in Lesley's. 'Let's go down then.'

The staff dining room was exactly the same as in the old days, except that it had been freshly painted, and Lesley thought that no one but herself would remember it filled with nurses, snatching hasty meals, until she saw Miss Newall looking at her and coolly nodding. Sadie would remember.

'Sadie, how are you?' she cried. 'How nice to see you!'

The housekeeper's pale eyes went over her, but she did not smile.

'I thought you said you would never come back here, Lesley? But then Mr Armitage asks you, and back you come.'

'He was asking everyone,' Lesley replied. 'We were all promised our jobs back.'

'Asked me,' put in Ishbel. 'Anyway, why should Lesley no' come back?'

'No reason at all, only I can't think why she'd want to!' snapped Sadie. 'I mean, I don't understand the ATTRACTION!'

As she moved away, with a rather scared-looking girl named Amelia, who was her new assistant, Lesley turned to Ella. 'Now, what's got into her? When I worked here for the nurses, she was as nice as pie. Now, seems I'm in disgrace again.'

Ella looked down at her plate. 'You had a ring on your finger before,' she said apologetically.

As Lesley flushed and lowered her eyes, Ishbel groaned.

'Don't say Miss Newall's still keen on Mr Armitage, is she? After all this time?'

'Sees Lesley as a rival again,' said Ned.

'That's crazy,' cried Lesley. 'I wish you wouldn't talk like that, Ned.'

'Canna help feeling sorry for her,' murmured Ella. 'I mean, she's never going to get anywhere, is she? What's the point of keeping on loving somebody who doesn't love you?'

Then her own colour rose, but she was spared from anyone's noticing by the arrival of the assistant chefs with massive steak and kidney pies and dishes of vegetables.

'I knew I had a reason for coming back here,' Ned said cheerfully to the group of waiters sitting near him. 'Damn' good food!'

'Aye, but they've no' got Mr Chater now, you ken,' Ishbel said. 'He didn't want to come back from London, and Mr Vass wouldn't leave the Caledonian, either, so there's a new head chef and a new head waiter. Aren't you lucky, Lesley, that'll no' bother you?'

'I liked Mr Vass,' Lesley replied. 'He was always very kind to me.'

The meal was over, and people were taking tea or coffee,

when Mr Wilcox suddenly appeared, accompanied by Paul Armitage. As most of the staff had now arrived for the start of the first post-war season, Mr Wilcox said he would like to say a few words.

'Does this not remind you of our last time here?' Ella asked Lesley in a low voice. 'When he came in to tell us we'd all have our jobs back one day? Can you believe that's nearly five years ago?'

Five long, hard years, thought Lesley. And we wondered then, who'd be back to take up their jobs?

She raised her eyes to look at Mr Wilcox, who had lost weight and appeared older. It was rumoured that he'd been involved in a zeppelin raid in London and was more edgy than ever, but as he'd always left the practical side of things to Mr Armitage, there'd be no change there. She supposed she'd better listen to what he had to say.

Welcoming new staff to the Hotel Grand Forest and welcoming pre-war staff back, Mr Wilcox was sure they all knew that the hotel had been the best in the spa, and would be again, and that they must all do their best to make the guests arriving next week as comfortable as possible. People had had four years of terrible war, they'd lost loved ones, seen their world change, with revolution in Russia, unrest and hardship throughout Europe.

What they wanted now was a return to pre-war order, a little luxury and helpful treatments, which the spa and its hotels, the Grand Forest in particular, would provide. He wished all the staff the best of luck and was confident he could rely on their excellent service. If any problems – Mr Wilcox cleared his throat – would they please see Mr Armitage, the assistant manager?

There was an uncertain round of applause as the two managers left, then members of staff began to drift away themselves.

'Nothing new, there,' remarked Ned, yawning. 'And I noticed they didn't ask for questions.'

'What questions would there be?' asked Ella.

'Well, about the future.'

'Pretty settled, ain't it?'

Ned shrugged and lit a cigarette. 'Remains to be seen.'

Lesley, who had no idea what she wanted in the future, yawned and said she was away to her bed. 'Me, too,' said Ella.

But on their way, Lesley couldn't help looking in again at the main dining room. There were no tables in place yet, but the dais was ready for Ned's trio, and she could picture the room as it had been before, as it would be again.

Here was where poor Nick had sung to her from *Florodora* – 'Tell me, pretty maiden, are there any more at home like you?' And there was the french door to the garden, where Christopher had stood, when she had sung the same tune herself. 'Tell me pretty maiden, are there any more at home like you? There are a few, kind sir, but simple girls and proper, too ...'

'That's where I'll be next week,' Ned murmured, looking at the dais. 'Start rehearsing tomorrow with Kirstie and Rob. Thank the Lord they're still around, eh?'

'Ned,' said Lesley. 'Don't play anything from *Florodora*, will you?'

'*Florodora*? Och, no!' He laughed. 'That's old stuff. Everybody'll have forgotten that by now.'

Chapter Sixty-Nine

A week to go, and it was not only the managers who were showing signs of nerves. Staff, some of them inexperienced, were naturally jittery about the re-opening of a great hotel after so many years, after such a terrible war. Mr Wilcox had said in his little speech that people were anxious to try again the luxury and treatments of Glenmar. Maybe he and the company who owned the Grand Forest were right. Maybe they were just hopeful. It was not knowing the truth of the matter that was causing the jitters.

'Time will tell,' Andrew Dunlop, of Accounts, said sagely. And, at least to begin with, bookings were good for all the hotels preparing to open for this first post-war season. The extensive advertising campaigns had paid off, the weather was fine, staff everywhere should just get on with their jobs and stop worrying. And if anyone was unsure of his or her duties at the Hotel Grand Forest, they'd better make certain they were sure by opening day.

Lesley, being instructed in reception duties by Veronica, was working hard to master them quickly and not let Mr Armitage down. She'd had no experience of this kind of work before, yet he had singled her out for it, certain, he'd told her, that she could do it and do it well. She had the looks and personality required for working with the public, and the intelligence to become efficient at the work she had to do. Now it was up to her.

'Don't worry about it,' Veronica told her kindly. 'Things may seem confusing to begin with, but they'll soon sort themselves out. It's just a question of keeping the records straight.'

'Sounds so easy,' sighed Lesley. 'But there's so many of them.'

The daily arrival list, the reservation chart, the room status board that showed which rooms were available, the alphabetical guest index, and of course the hotel register that had to be kept correctly, by law. Then there was the key and post rack and the information files, the telephone switchboard, the liaison with Accounts for presentation of bills, the keeping up with the duties of the porters and page-boys . . .

'And just knowing everything that people want to know,' Veronica added brightly. 'Local information, train timetables, what time is breakfast, where's the kirk, when is the pump room open, how to hire a car. I tell you, we're supposed to know it all.' She laughed. 'Of course, we do!'

'You mean, you do,' said Lesley.

'It'll all be second nature to you in no time.' Veronica lowered her voice a little. 'But a word of warning. Some of the chaps we get here are keen to try it on. You know what I mean. Perhaps you'd like to go out for a little drive after work, stop off for a nice little dinner, etcetera, etcetera. You just have to tell them where to get off right from the start. Politely, of course. I'm sure you've had the same sort of thing in the restaurants.'

'Happens sometimes,' Lesley agreed.

'Well, there are only a few of that sort, of course. Quite frankly, most of the old buffers who come up to take the waters won't give you any trouble at all!' Veronica laughed again. 'But that's really why I'm going to keep on wearing my ring, and if you've still got that nice engagement ring Sadie Newall told me about, I'd advise you to do the same.'

Lesley thought of the beautiful ring in her drawer in

Carrie's flat, along with the little gold brooch. 'I'll no' do that,' she said firmly.

'Oh, dear, I spoke out of turn.' Veronica's green eyes were full of contrition. 'I'm really sorry, Lesley, didn't mean to upset you.'

'That's all right. I'm over Christopher now, but I could never wear his ring.'

'Let's go and see Mr Dunlop,' said Veronica, taking Lesley's arm. 'Might as well get to know the people in Accounts. Pretty important folk, eh?'

When they could snatch a moment to talk to each other, Ella asked Lesley how things were going for her.

'No' so bad, as long as I'm with Veronica. But what I'll do when I'm left on ma own, I daren't think! How about you?'

Ella rolled her brown eyes.

'Ishbel was right when she said you were lucky not to have to worry about Mr Daniels, the new head waiter. Lesley, he's a terror! The boys are already calling him the Hun, though he's from Surrey, trained in London. Honest, he's got us on the hop before the guests have even arrived, heaven knows what he'll be like when they come.'

'Think I'd rather be in Reception, even with the telephone switchboard,' Lesley said, laughing. 'But I've met the new head chef and he seemed nice, anyway.'

'Mr Jacot?' Ella pursed her lips. 'Yes, he's nice enough now, but wait till the cooking really starts. I mean, he's French. He's temperamental.'

'I seem to remember that Mr Chater threw plates.'

'And my guess is that Mr Jacot will throw the kitchen stove, once he gets going.' Ella's brow cleared and she put her arm in Lesley's. 'Main thing is that we're back here together again, and Ned's back and all, and everything's going well. You're happy, eh, Lesley? Sort of?'

'Sort of,' Lesley agreed.

*

It had really turned out better than she'd feared, coming back. Of course, she still sensed Christopher's presence, she still remembered the heavenly days of being in love, running to meet him, kissing in the woods. She'd even gone to look again at the door of the room he'd had, not his hospital room, but where they'd made love that one time, and had stared at the number and the newly painted panels. Then Amelia Striven had come along to put in towels and had stared and blushed in her nervous way, and Lesley had run back to the stairs. Oh, yes, Christopher was here, and always would be, but the memories didn't hurt any more. She was just glad to have them, that was all.

Maybe it had been a help, that so much was going on in the hotel. So many people working purposefully away, preparing, smoothing, polishing, the beautiful machine that was the Grand Forest. So many people who were her friends, making the hotel feel like home again.

What a weathercock she was! She had quite swung round from the first day, when she'd thought Auntie Peg was right and she shouldn't have come. Now she'd settled down and Ned seemed really happy, practising with Rob and Kirstie again, never needing a drink, talking to Ella.

Talking to Ella ... Why didn't the silly laddie make it official? People were already saying that they were in love. But that was Ned for you. Cussed to the last.

On the day before the opening, Moyra looked in with her baby girl. Heavens, if only Lesley and Ella had had time to admire little Mhairi! But in a way, it calmed their nerves to talk to someone who was out of it all, but who knew what was involved.

'I have chosen a bad day,' said Moyra, smiling. 'Only Finlay was coming in with the van and I could not refuse. But I daren't try to see Miss Newall, she'll be up to her eyes, checking all the rooms a dozen times, eh? How's the new assistant housekeeper?'

'Terrified.' Ella laughed. 'Aren't you glad you're not here?'

'I'm not sure,' Moyra answered seriously. 'I'm very happy with Finlay, and it's so lovely to have Mhairi, but sometimes, you know, I miss the hotel.' She adjusted the baby's shawl, and said she must hurry, Finlay would be waiting for her in the Square.

Lesley went with her to the rear door, where they embraced around the baby, and Moyra touched Lesley's cheek.

'You look so much better, she murmured. 'Quite your old self. And Ned – how is he?'

'He's his old self, too. Apart from the drinking, thank God. Never touches a drop now, you ken.'

'Just out of interest, are they engaged? Ned and Ella?'

'No, they're not engaged.'

'I wish them every happiness,' Moyra said, all the same, and hurried away to her husband in the square.

'Nice to see her,' Ella commented. 'Fancy her saying she missed work, though.'

'Missed the hotel,' corrected Lesley. 'I think she still has plenty of work.'

'Got a husband and a baby, can't think what more she wants.'

Lesley smiled. 'Wants all of it, just like men.'

Chapter Seventy

The following day was THE DAY, or, as some of the young waiters were calling it, *Der Tag*. Everything was ready, from the bedrooms and bathrooms to the public rooms, the dining room, lounges, Palm Court, games rooms and two new bars, all in perfect order. Outside, the gardens had been weeded and watered, the lawns cut and rolled, the seats re-painted, and, as if on cue, the roses had come out and the sun shone high in the heavens. What a bit of luck, eh? The only things the staff couldn't control! Nerves or not, they couldn't help smiling.

'My word, Paul, the place couldn't look better!' Mr Wilcox exclaimed, for he, unusually, was haunting the entrance hall. 'Congratulations are certainly called for!'

'Thank you, but let's wait and see how the bookings go,' Paul answered, his eyes roving round at the florist's exquisite arrangements and the sunlight sparkling on the handsome chandeliers. The page-boys and old Colum were lined up at the glass doors, watching the clock, and Veronica, of course, resplendent in black, was at the reception desk, with Lesley, in dark blue, standing beside her, looking rather pale.

'Why, the bookings are good!' Mr Wilcox exclaimed. 'Don't depress me, Paul. Not today.'

'They're good, but we're not going to be full. As we used to be in June.'

'We've only just opened, we have to get back into our routine. Early days, you know.'

'That's true.' Paul gave a smile that was a little strained, the only sign of his apprehension. 'I'm sure it won't take us long to reach capacity bookings again.'

Excusing himself, he strolled over to Reception.

'Everything all right, Mrs Reynolds?' His dark eyes moved to Lesley. 'Not too nervous?'

'Oh, no!' cried Veronica, giving Paul a confident smile. 'But I've just been explaining to Miss MacKenzie here, that it can be a bit of a scramble when the guests come up from the station. I mean, they all want to register at once, and we have to keep them happy.'

'Which I'm sure you do,' said Paul. He too was now watching the clock. 'First guests are motoring over, aren't they? I should think they're about due.'

'They are, sir.' Veronica smiled again. 'Our first guests at the Hotel Grand Forest since 1914.'

Paul was silent, his eyes resting on Lesley. In both their minds were the years between.

The hands of the clock moved on and suddenly there was activity. Motors were arriving, guests beginning to appear in the entrance hall, Colum and the page-boys carrying in luggage. Mr Wilcox and Paul came forward, bowing, to greet the newcomers, while Lesley and Veronica worked fast at Reception, producing the register, handing out keys, joining in the managers' chorus—

'Welcome to the Hotel Grand Forest!'

There was talk and a little laughter, as guests gathered at the lifts or drifted to the Palm Court for morning coffee, some old hands exclaiming how nice it was to be back and how lovely everything was looking. And the pump room was open, just as before? Splendid! Why, it was all as it used to be, wasn't it? Who'd have thought there'd been a war?

*

Was it all as it used to be? Lesley, at the end of a long, exhausting day, stood looking in at the main dining room. Although not completely full, there seemed to be a good number of guests taking dinner, all beautifully dressed, of course, all apparently enjoying themselves, as Ned and the Murrays worked away at a selection from *Chu Chin Chow*. Surely, the scene was the same as any before the war?

Lesley's eyes went from face to face. She couldn't put her finger on it, yet felt a difference. Something in the atmosphere, perhaps? Some look of strain on a face in repose, some memory not to be confronted? It came to her, with poignant recognition, that most of the people here tonight would have lost someone in the war, and that what she was sensing was carefully concealed grief. Grief and uncertainty, where in the old days there'd been only serenity and wonderful confidence.

Oh, yes, it was confidence that had always marked out the rich. Even when things went wrong for them, they'd felt they could ride them out. But the war had hit them as hard as the poor. And these first post-war guests had not yet recovered.

It's too soon, thought Lesley. They shouldn't have tried to open the hotel so soon. Folk weren't ready. For a moment she felt a rise of panic. It was all going to fall like a house of cards, and all their work would have been for nothing …

Then she looked around the great room again and thought, maybe she was imagining things? Maybe the guests were as they first had seemed, quite happy, quite relaxed? After all, numbers were only slightly down, and everyone was saying it was 'early days'. She was probably just overtired and looking on the dark side—

'Lesley, where are you?' came Paul Armitage's voice, and she turned to find him next to her.

'Where am I?' She smiled uneasily. 'I'm here, I suppose.'

'You looked miles away, though. Is everything all right?'

'Oh, yes, I'm just a bit weary. Been a long day.'

'And you did very well,' he said warmly. 'Anyone would have thought you'd been in Reception for years.'

'Och, it's just like waiting on, really. You're giving folks what they want.'

'But you're glad you made the change?'

Her eyes followed the waiters, hurrying between tables, and lighted on Ella, red-faced with the heat, listening to some instruction from Mr Daniels, the Hun, who was waving his arms about and flinging back his shock of thick white hair. She smiled.

'Yes, I'm glad. I like it in Reception. And it's easier on the feet.'

He smiled and for a moment they stood watching the trio take their bow at the end of *Chu Chin Chow*, handsome Ned so much at ease, as he waved his hand towards Kirstie and Rob, that Lesley's heart swelled with pride. It was all his, what he had, none of it the result of drink, and he'd had the courage to fight his own battle and win. Her eyes went to find Ella again and saw that Mr Daniels had left her now and that she was standing, tray in hand, looking at Ned. And Ned had seen her, too, and was making her a special bow, that made her colour rise higher than ever.

'Think those two will make a go of it?' Paul murmured at her side, and once again Lesley marvelled at how he seemed to know everything.

'Goodnight, Mr Armitage,' she said softly.

'Goodnight, Miss MacKenzie,' he answered, making fun of their formality. 'At the end of a very successful day.'

'Hope they're all like this, then.'

He raised his eyebrows. 'I see no reason why they shouldn't be.'

She wondered if that were true.

Chapter Seventy-One

The hotel bookings did keep coming, however, and if there were not as many as in pre-war days, the numbers were still quite reasonable. Hotels elsewhere in the spa seemed to be managing well, too, and the pump rooms were doing good business, offering the same sort of treatments as before, to be followed by promenades in the Square, or rounds of golf or games of tennis. There was even a dance organised in the pavilion, and though there were few young people to attend, the older visitors turned out for it, dressed to the nines as usual, it was reported.

Seems I was worrying before I need, thought Lesley, although Veronica's brow was sometimes a little furrowed, as she studied the reservation chart and said they'd never had so many vacancies in the old days.

'As long as we're breaking even,' she murmured one morning, as she sorted the post.

'Oh, I'm sure we'd have heard if we weren't,' said Lesley.

'Too right. Mr Wilcox'd be running round in circles and His Highness would be giving a little frown.'

'Why do you call Mr Armitage His Highness?' Lesley asked, laughing. 'Does he seem so grand?'

'Always gives me the impression of thinking he is, that's all. I know he's very kind, just doesn't show it. Doesn't like to show his feelings at all.' Veronica gave Lesley a

quick glance. 'Sometimes, you pick 'em up, all the same
... Will you help me file the post? There's a letter for you,
by the way.'

The letter was from Auntie Peg, a frequent correspon-
dent, and as usual was addressed to both Ned and Lesley.
She just wanted to tell them, she wrote, that everyone was
well, Sam very busy, and Joe still managing all right at the
sorting office. Carrie had started talking about another
baby, but wee Donald was the sweetest laddie, anyway, and
if there never was another one, they'd be grateful for him.

There was news of Janie, who'd just got herself a new
job in Glasgow working for some magazine. Socialist, as
red as red, but not Communist, because even Janie
wouldn't want to be involved with the Communists after
what they'd done to the Russian Tsar. Shot in the cellar, all
the family, what a terrible thing. But Janie was coming
back at nights, to see to her ma, though she'd told Margie
and Shona to look out for her in the day. Now why should
they not, even if they were wed? Poor Hughie was gone,
and never did much anyway, but those girls were just round
the corner, it'd be no bother, but they left everything to
Janie, just as usual.

Peg and the family didn't see much of Adam, though Joe
said he'd told him that the port was nearly back to normal,
with just a few buildings now to be handed back by the
government and the navy. What a time it took, to get over
a war, eh!

Still a lot of talk about Leith going back to Edinburgh
and plenty of folk saying over their dead bodies and such
like, but seemingly there would be a vote and everybody
could say what they wanted. Sam said it all came down to
money, and that was nothing new.

Now, Ned and Lesley were to be sure and take care of
themselves up there in the Highlands, and try to put some
weight on, they both being as thin as skeletons. Beef tea
would do the trick, or failing that, milk stout, but of course
Ned couldn't take that. The letter was signed, with kind

356

regards from all, their loving Auntie Peg.

Dear Auntie Peg, on about beef tea again! Lesley could just imagine herself going down to Monsieur Jacot and asking for that. Maybe he'd throw the stove at her, as Ella said she was waiting for him to do. Anyway, Lesley didn't consider herself any skeleton. It was fashionable now to be slim, all the new styles were getting skinnier, and there was even talk of girls cutting their hair.

'Aye, you'll all look like a load o' laddies before you're done,' Ned had commented, but Ella, who was rapidly recovering her plumpness, said she couldn't see herself ever looking like a boy and Lesley said she would never cut her hair.

That would be just the kind of thing Janie would do, though, and be glad to say goodbye to hairpins. Probably Adam would be happy, whatever she did. Why didn't she marry him and put him out of his misery? Still all alone in his dad's old flat, and she working in Glasgow! But Lesley shook her head. Much as she might like to, there was nothing she could do to help Adam. She was only relieved that she seemed to have moved into calm waters herself. Long may she stay there!

Work at Reception really suited her and now that she had the routine at her fingertips, she found dealing with the public completely satisfying. Veronica was highly efficient, of course, but some of the older guests found her inclined to be a little too brisk and began to seek out Lesley for assistance, or maybe just to have a little chat from time to time.

'Such a sweet Scottish accent you have, my dear,' they would say. 'Now, that's Highland, isn't it?'

And Lesley would be reminded of Christopher, who had never been able to tell a Highland accent from a Leith one, either. But she would smile and explain where she came from, and was never surprised when they thought Leith part of Edinburgh. That might be true quite soon, anyway, depending on how the plebiscite went. No date for that had yet been fixed.

One August day, however, a tiny cloud appeared on the horizon, in the form of a little talk with one of Lesley's favourite old ladies, Mrs Chalmers. She was one of their pre-war visitors who had returned to them; small and frail, with a 'dowager's hump', but always well dressed and scented and wearing a variety of good jewellery. To begin with, in this new season, she had regularly attended the pump room to take the waters and allow herself to be lowered into peat with straps and hoisted out again, which were the treatments she remembered from the old days. Suddenly, on the day when the alarm bells began to ring, she told Lesley she would not be requiring any more appointments.

'Oh, Mrs Chalmers, but why?' cried Lesley, helping her into a seat near the reception desk. 'Is it too much for you going to the pump room? I could arrange a wheelchair—'

'No, no, dear, it's nothing like that. I'm no worse than I was.' Mrs Chalmers gave an apologetic smile. 'The thing is, I'm no better.'

'No better?'

'No. You see, during the war, when I couldn't have my treatments, I found that I was really just the same as when I came up here every summer.'

Lesley, her blue eyes fixed on Mrs Chalmers's face, swallowed hard and waited.

'I thought it odd,' Mrs Chalmers went on. 'But there it was. Anyway, when the war ended and I saw your advertisements in *The Times*, I decided that I really must make sure. I must come back and try again. I thought it only fair.'

'So you came back,' Lesley murmured.

'Yes, I came back and I had all my treatments, just as before. But it's been just the same as during the war. I don't feel any better.'

Lesley put her hand to her brow. 'The thing is, Mrs

Chalmers, the treatments do work for some people. They really do help. I mean, the spa wouldn't have kept going so long, would it, if no one had felt any improvement?'

'I suppose not.' Mrs Chalmers's expression was doubtful. 'On the other hand, my dear, it might be that if people always had the treatments, they wouldn't know until they stopped, whether they needed them or not.'

'I do think you should discuss this with the doctor,' Lesley said firmly. 'Would you like me to make an appointment?'

'I don't think so, dear. I'm quite happy being here, having a holiday. Shall we just leave it at that?'

'You will come back to us, though, won't you, Mrs Chalmers?' Lesley asked, handing the old lady her stick as she rose from her chair.

'Well, it is awfully nice here, I agree.' Mrs Chalmers leaning on her stick, looked round at the elegant entrance hall. 'But such a very long way from anywhere, you see. I think I might take my holidays a little nearer home. They say that Bournemouth is very nice and has a very good class of hotel.'

'Oh, my God,' exclaimed Veronica, when Lesley had recounted her talk with Mrs Chalmers. 'Is that what she said? She was just the same, with or without the treatments?'

'It was because of the war, you see. When she'd to do without them, she felt just the same.'

'But people do feel better, I know they do!'

'Yes, but there must always have been some folk they didn't help so much, and now they're finding that out.'

'Only Mrs Chalmers has said that so far.'

'I wonder how many others feel the same?' Lesley asked thoughtfully. 'I mean, why are we no' so fully booked as we were? Don't say it's early days, eh?'

'Well, it is early days!' Vernonica's green eyes were troubled. 'It's not a fair test, to check on numbers this year.

People might not be feeling ready to come back yet.'

'Mr Wilcox seemed to think they'd be desperate to come back. For their treatments.'

The two young women looked at each other, then Veronica lowered her eyes. 'We'll have to see how things go,' she said quietly. 'I mean, it would be silly to get worried, just because one old lady would rather go to Bournemouth than the Highlands.'

'It would,' agreed Lesley.

Chapter Seventy-Two

Yet it was from that day that a change seemed to come over the Grand Forest. Until then, there had been the feeling of rebirth about the place, a confidence that all would be as it had been before. After all, everything had been done to put the clock back, so to speak. Large sums of money had been spent to recreate the kind of hotel life pre-war visitors had wanted. Everyone was certain they wanted it still.

Hand in hand with hotel luxury, went the spa treatments. People came to Glenmar with a purpose – to enjoy a pleasant stay and to get better. Suddenly, rumours began to float that the treatments were of only slight efficacy. Cures had never been claimed, but obviously patients expected improvements. Now they were beginning to question whether there were improvements or not.

Neither Lesley nor Veronica had repeated Mrs Chalmers's views to anyone, yet somehow they had become known, perhaps because she had discussed them herself with her friends. Other guests began to wonder if they should cancel their treatments. Numbers began to decline at the pump rooms. One or two guests left early for shooting holidays elsewhere in Scotland. And the wonderfully secure Hotel Grand Forest appeared to tremble.

'I wouldn't be surprised if they closed the hotel for the winter,' said Ned, at staff supper one evening in

September. 'I've heard that quite a few hotels are shutting up shop in October.'

'They always did that,' Sadie Newall told him coldly. 'But the Grand Forest has never closed its doors. That's because it is a first-class hotel and first-class hotels are not seasonal.'

'Well, staff are,' Ned retorted. 'And I'm wondering who is going to get the boot.'

'Don't talk like that,' Ella said uneasily. 'We all worked through the winter before.'

'Not all of us,' said Ishbel. 'First year I worked here, I only did the summer. A lot o' folk expect that.'

'I don't,' said Ned. 'But any day now I'm expecting to be told the trio won't be needed till next spring. Have you seen old Wilcox lately? He looks like a wet weekend.'

'He's no' the only one,' put in one of the waiters. 'I wonder what the booking figures are? Have you noticed how they've all gone silent on them?'

'It's not for us to worry about the bookings,' Sadie snapped. 'Mr Wilcox and Mr Armitage will see that we're all right, whatever happens.'

Everyone's eyes went to her and one or two people laughed, at which she tossed her head in angry silence.

'You're saying they'll keep the hotel open for us, even if there are no guests?' asked Ishbel. 'Honestly, Sadie, do you think they're in business for their health, or what?'

'You should all get back to work and stop complaining!' Sadie cried, leaping to her feet. 'I think you're most disloyal and only thinking of yourselves.'

'And who are you thinking of?' Ishbel shouted after her, as Sadie hurried away, red spots burning in her cheeks.

'You shouldn't tease her like that,' Lesley murmured. 'You know this hotel is her life.'

'Och, she's an ostrich!' Ishbel answered with a grin. 'She should live in the real world.'

'Looks like we'll be back there soon,' observed Ned, rising and eyeing Lesley and Ella, who joined him on his way out of the dining room.

'What do you want?' asked Lesley. 'I can tell you want me to do something.'

'Couldn't you find out from Dunlop, or somebody, what the prospects are? We need to know the situation, to make our own plans.'

'What plans?' asked Ella nervously.

'I don't know yet.' Ned was looking at Lesley. 'You're well placed to find out what's going on, eh?'

'I don't know about that. It's usually Veronica who sees the Accounts staff.'

'Well, can't Veronica tell you what she finds out, then? Or, maybe Paul Armitage will drop a hint if you ask him nicely?'

'Paul doesn't talk to me specially.'

'Come on!' Ned grinned. 'Think we've no eyes? We've all seen him looming up at Reception when you're on duty. Everybody knows he's sweet on you.'

'Well, I haven't seen him lately,' Lesley said truthfully. 'And when I have, he's looked the same as Mr Wilcox.'

'Aye.' Ned continued to grin. 'Like a wet weekend.'

'The best thing to do, of course, would be to close for the winter,' Andrew Dunlop was saying in Mr Wilcox's office. 'Some hotels do.'

'Not the Grand Forest!' snapped Mr Wilcox. 'It's always been our claim that we can offer the spa's services all year round, and if the pump rooms are staying open, so should we.'

Andrew nodded. 'Very well, then, I think we can manage it. Bookings are disappointing, but they haven't dried up completely. I've been in touch with the company accountants and they believe we can carry a winter opening, provided we cut down as much as possible.'

'That would be acceptable,' Mr Wilcox said eagerly. 'We've always operated at a reduced level in the winter months.'

'How reduced?' asked Paul. 'I mean, how many staff are we going to have to lose?'

'Look at it from the point of view of how many we need,' said Andrew. 'The aim is to provide services for those who really have to keep their treatments going. They will obviously not require the whole of the hotel's resources.'

'As I say, we've always cut down,' said Mr Wilcox. 'This time, we can cut staff to the bone, cut heating in certain parts, reduce flower arrangements, axe the trio – oh, there are any numbers of ways we can reduce costs. Paul, would you work out some ideas for me? Then liaise with Andrew here, on figures ?'

'You're looking worried,' Andrew told Paul, as they left the manager's office. 'Not like you.'

'I don't like sacking good staff.'

'In view of the circumstances, none of 'em got permanent contracts for the re-opening, they won't be expecting to stay.'

'In the past, we've always kept a good number on throughout the winter.'

'Things have to be different this time. The aim is to keep going until next season rescues us.'

'You think it will?'

'Yes, I've every confidence.'

Paul allowed himself a brief smile. 'If an accountant says he has every confidence, I suppose I can relax?'

'Depends on the accountant,' Andrew told him with a laugh. 'Look, I've heard the rumours – that the spa's finished, no one wants to come so far and all of that, but I don't believe them. This place has as good a future as Bath or Harrogate or Cheltenham. We just need more time to recover from the war.'

Paul nodded. Until quite recently, these had been his own views. Now, he wasn't sure what to believe.

Downstairs, he found his steps taking him to Reception, where Lesley was on duty. Her eyes went instantly to his and he could read the questions in them. What's happening? To the hotel? To us? It wasn't the time to tell her, he had his report to prepare.

'Everything all right?' he asked, falling back on his familiar cliché.

'Oh yes.'

'Getting a bit autumnal out there, isn't it?' Not to say wintry, he added to himself.

'I like the autumn. The colours are beautiful.'

'In New England, you know, they make special trips to see the Fall, as they call it.'

'Folk could do that here.'

'We've still got the spa,' he murmured, turning away, because he could not answer her appeal.

For how long? was in both their minds.

Chapter Seventy-Three

The trio was to go, Ella was to go, Ishbel was to go, and half the dining-room staff, but not the head waiter, of course, and half the kitchen staff, but not the head chef. Sadie was to lose several of her housemaids, but not Amelia. Although Colum was allowed to keep his assistant driver for the motor bus, and Veronica kept Lesley, four page-boys had to go and the gardening staff was drastically reduced.

But these were just seasonal adjustments, no more than usual, Paul Armitage was at pains to insist. Anyone who wanted could apply for his or her job the following spring. As there could be no room for argument, he did not wait for comments when he made his announcement, but there were, as he would have guessed, plenty.

'Seasonal adjustments!' echoed the staff. 'No more than usual?'

Who was management trying to fool? The numbers leaving were far more than usual, and everyone knew the reasons for that. In fact, the 'adjustments', so called, were being repeated all over Glenmar, as the brilliant colours of autumn sparkled under an October sun. There was even talk of the pavilion closing for the winter, and the pump rooms laying off several assistants. There was nothing any of those given notice could do, except pack up and prepare to depart with a good grace. At the Grand Forest, Lesley, feeling very bad, organised their train tickets.

Still feeling bad, she gave whole-hearted sympathy to Ishbel, who was particularly unlucky to be leaving, when she had only come back because of Nick.

'Nae bother,' Ishbel replied. 'I guessed I'd be on ma way. I suppose I can think of Nick anywhere.' She shrugged. 'Maybe I'll apply for ma job back in the spring.'

'Always supposing the hotel's still here,' commented Ned.

'You think it won't be?'

'Just joking. 'Course it'll be here. Och, it's only what I expected, the order of the boot for the winter. It's no' the end of the world.'

'You'll find something in Edinburgh, I expect,' said Ella with a look of hopelessness. 'How about Kirstie and Rob?'

'They'll be all right, they're going back to teaching. But ma job at the Royal Albert's been taken.'

'There'll be other jobs for you.'

'And for you in London.'

'Suppose so.'

'Everyone's saying I'm so lucky to be staying on,' said Lesley. 'But I'm going to miss so many people. I only came because you made me, Ned, and you said Ella would be here.'

'Come to London with me,' Ella said impulsively. 'Why not?'

Lesley stared, taken aback. 'Go to London? Why, Ella – I never thought of such a thing!'

'Well, think of it now. Come on! Why not?'

'I – just – I canna see maself there, somehow.'

'I can,' said Ned.

'See me? Or, you?'

'Me, of course.' His eyes met Ella's that were suddenly very bright. 'Could your ma put me up, Ella?'

'You're thinking of finding something in London?'

'Worth a try, eh?'

'But you're a Scotsman, Ned!'

'Have you never noticed? London's full of Scotsmen. Ella, shall we go and talk about this?'

As though she were in a dream, Ella took Ned's hand and they moved away, leaving Ishbel and Lesley to stare wide-eyed after them.

'Is he going to propose?' asked Ishbel bluntly.

'I've no idea.' Lesley, stunned, was shaking her head. 'This is the first I've heard of any London idea.'

'Quite a character, eh, your brother? But if I was Ella I'd tell him what to do. He's had her on a string for far too long.'

'He doesn't mean to be heartless, he just doesn't think, you ken.'

'Well, they say there's always one that gives and one that takes. I do hope they'll be happy, though.'

'Hold on, they're no' engaged yet, you know!' cried Lesley.

But they were.

Everyone said it was the best bit of news they'd had in weeks. Ned and Ella engaged! Two of the most popular people on the staff, Ned so handsome and talented, Ella so warm-hearted and genuine, southerner or not! This called for a celebration, even if half the staff was leaving next day, and at supper that evening, Ned played Mendelssohn's wedding march and Paul sent down champagne, compliments of the hotel. This was much appreciated by everyone except Ned, who couldn't drink it, and Ella, who said she daren't, her head was going round fast enough as it was.

'Oh, I'm so happy!' she told Lesley. 'And to think how miserable I was this morning! It seemed so terrible, having to say goodbye to Ned, and here we are, engaged. I can't believe it!'

Lesley, hugging her, said, 'I've been waiting for this for a long time,' at which Ella laughed.

'Not as long as I have, dear!'

Even Mr Wilcox looked in, to drink the young couple's health and smoke a cigarette, before retiring to his office again, and Paul stayed rather longer.

'A bit of a shame, that this is a celebration and a farewell,' he murmured to Ned. 'I'm sorry we had to lose the trio, you know, but you'll come back, won't you?'

'Who knows? Depends what I find in the Big Smoke.'

'I have a feeling you'll do well there.' Paul sighed. 'Can't blame you, if you decide to stay. But you know my people live in London? We'll meet again, Ned.'

Next day, it was back to the station again, for more farewells, Lesley fighting tears, as she waved to Ishbel and others she was going to miss, and kissed Ella and Ned. They were going first to Leith, where they planned to surprise Auntie Peg and Carrie and stay for a few nights, then would move on to London, where, said Ella, her mother would be 'over the moon', she being so taken by Ned, and would probably organise a 'knees up' before they'd taken off their hats and coats!

'Then it'll be job hunting,' said Ned. 'Keep your fingers crossed. If all else fails, I can always go busking, eh? See how much I get in ma hat?'

'Busking,' Ella repeated affectionately. 'You'll be playing in a West End hotel, soon as they hear you!'

But Ned had spotted Paul, strolling down the platform to say goodbye to the staff he was losing, and leaned out of the carriage window to shake his hand and promise to look him up in London when he came down.

'Just you let me know when you come eh? You've got Ella's address?' Ned smiled and glanced at Lesley, standing a little away. 'And look after Lesley for me, eh?'

Paul, too, looked back at Lesley.

'Certainly, I'll look after her,' he said quietly. 'Don't worry.'

It was a relief when the train went out and Lesley could

walk back up the hill to the hotel, Paul at her side.

'I'm afraid you're going to miss Ned and Ella, Lesley. I'm sorry they had to go.'

'I think it's for the best. Spurred Ned on to propose.'

Paul laughed. 'Some fellows need that, I suppose.'

'Och, he just didn't want to take the plunge.'

'Maybe he wasn't sure of Ella's feelings.'

Lesley glanced at Paul's clear-cut profile and the firm set to his chin. Just for a moment, he reminded her of Adam. She couldn't imagine either of them not being sure of anything.

'I don't think he had to worry about Ella,' she told Paul. 'He probably didn't want to give up his freedom.'

'Freedom to be alone,' murmured Paul, as they walked round to the rear of the hotel. 'Is that worth so much?'

Lesley made no reply. At that moment, with the train carrying Ned and Ella south, she felt very much alone herself.

Chapter Seventy-Four

Although no economies had been made with the heating, the hotel began to take on a chill to Lesley, as the autumn faded into winter. Probably, it was just her imagination because there were so few people about and so little going on. It was true that guests had arrived from London and elsewhere, and they were taking appointments at the pump rooms, but there weren't enough of them to make even a winter season pay. Which meant that the hotel must be losing money and was just treading water until the spring, when it was to be hoped things would get back to normal. But how long would the present guests stay happy with their treatments and the hotel as it was?

Veronica and Lesley discussed the possibility of the Grand Forest's collapsing altogether, but Paul Armitage told them it wasn't going to happen. They were, as he put it, just 'weathering the storm'.

'And what happens if Mr Jacot resigns?' asked Veronica. 'There's talk he's getting tired of preparing meals for so few people. Mr Daniels feels the same, so I've heard.'

'Gossip,' snapped Paul. 'It's clear the waiters haven't enough to do.'

'Is the gossip not true, then?'

'Both the head chef and the head waiter are very well paid. We could have economised by replacing them, but the reputation of the hotel would have suffered. I think you'll find that they are happy to stay.'

'As long as the guests are,' Veronica murmured, as Paul stalked angrily away. 'Now, promise me, Lesley, that you're not going to slope off back to Leith, or something. I really couldn't stand being here without you.'

'I've thought of it,' Lesley admitted. 'But it wouldn't be fair. I took the job on, so I should stick it out.'

And what would she do at home, anyway? Go back to the Princess Louise, maybe? Or find another receptionist's job? Watch Janie neglecting Adam and feel annoyed? A slight flush rose to her cheek, as she asked herself why she had thought of Adam and Janie again. Adam was a strong enough character to take care of himself, he didn't need her sympathy over Janie. Whatever the situation between them, it must be one he'd accepted, and nothing to do with her.

'I do get a bit lonely,' she murmured to Veronica, who fixed her with her bright green gaze.

'Wouldn't care to make up a foursome some time?' she asked. 'I'm going out with a fellow from the golf club. Nothing serious, of course, I haven't got my divorce through yet and God knows when I will – but he could easily bring along a friend. Just for dinner, you know. Just a friendly outing.'

'Thanks very much,' Lesley said quickly. 'It's very kind of you, Veronica, but I think I'll say no. Hope you'll understand.'

'Of course, my dear. Just thought I'd ask. If you change your mind, let me know.'

'Oh, I will,' Lesley answered, thinking that she might be lonely, but not quite as lonely as that.

At least, Paul was always very friendly. He seemed to spare her more of his time than before, was always asking her if everything was all right, and when she asked if she might go home at Hogmanay, said he was sure they could find cover for Veronica's relief times. In fact, when she returned, Veronica told her he had done quite a few shifts at Reception himself, which was very accommodating of

372

him, but perhaps showed he wasn't as busy as he should have been.

It was a wonderful tonic for Lesley to be back in Leith again, talking of Ned's engagement with Auntie Peg and Carrie, hearing how much they liked Ella and of what they would wear for the wedding when it came. Then there was playing with wee Donald, who wasn't quite so small any more and hadn't yet any hope of a brother or sister, much to Carrie's disappointment. And seeing in the New Year with the usual party, where the main topic, apart from Ned's engagement, was the coming vote on Leith's future.

'They say we've come to the end of the road,' said Janie. 'But it's no' true, eh? All right, we canna expand, but why should Edinburgh expand? Tell me that. Why can we no' stay as we are?'

'I tell you, we canna afford to keep going,' Sam told her. 'We're too small, we need more cash.'

'For a new isolation hospital, they say,' said Peg. 'And we do need somewhere for folks to go. You ken that flu came back for a bit?'

Lesley shuddered. It was true that there had been another outbreak of flu, but it had not been so severe, thank God. She glanced at Adam, whose face was expressionless; grief for his father was battened down tight. But then the bells had rung out for the New Year and his look lightened. He and Janie kissed and embraced, and when Janie turned to hug Joe, Adam drew Lesley to him and kissed her on the lips.

'Happy New Year, Lesley! It's grand to see you back.'

'Happy New Year, Adam!'

She was thinking that it was the first time they'd ever kissed in quite that way, but of course it was only a Hogmanay greeting. Everyone was kissing and drinking toasts and saying they had no proper first foot, now that Ned was away. Where could they find a young man with dark hair?

'Too many blonds round here!' cried Janie. 'I'll be first foot maself!'

But there was no way they would let a woman cross the threshold first, and it all worked out well when Janie's sister, Shona, arrived with her husband, whose hair was black as a raven's wing.

'Did you come in first?' they all screamed, and he said, Aye, of course he had, and he'd brought his piece o' coal and fruit cake and all. Thank the Lord for that, they breathed. Now good luck was assured for 1920.

'Does anybody really believe all this?' asked Janie, but Adam shook his head at her.

'You don't ask questions like that on Hogmanay!' he told her.

But that was Janie, eh? Always asking questions. Lesley longed to ask Janie a question of her own. When was she going to marry Adam? Of course, that couldn't be asked at Hogmanay, or any other time.

Chapter Seventy-Five

One quiet afternoon in late January, she was alone in Reception, reading a letter from Ned. He had landed a job with a light orchestra in a fashionable London hotel, and couldn't be happier. Up till then, he'd only had casual work, but this contract meant that he and Ella would be fixing up to get wed in the spring. Did Lesley fancy being a bridesmaid again?

Oh, heavens, I'm far too old, thought Lesley, but her lips were curving into a smile at the idea, when she raised her eyes to find Paul watching her.

'Mr Armitage!' As she pushed Ned's letter out of sight, she felt herself blushing. Even now, though she knew him so much better than in the old days, he could have that effect on her.

'Mr Armitage?' he repeated. 'What's happened to Paul?'

'Well, we are at work.'

'There's no one around.' He smiled. 'So, you're an Edinburgh girl now, are you?'

'No, I'm still a Leither. I don't care if we're going back to Edinburgh, I'll never be anything else.'

'A strange result, wasn't it?'

Strange indeed, as more had voted against joining Edinburgh than in favour. Yet the amalgamation had gone through.

'Och, we never had a hope of staying independent,'

Lesley told him. 'And maybe we'll do better with Edinburgh, I don't know.'

'I really came to tell you I'd heard from Ned,' Paul said, after a pause. 'I expect you have, too?'

'Oh, yes, just today.' She kept her hand on the blotter over Ned's letter. 'Looks like there'll be a spring wedding.'

'Are you going to be bridesmaid? I remember when you were a bridesmaid before. Had to ask permission for the weekend.'

'That was a long time ago.'

'Seems even longer than it was.'

His eyes were still fixed intently on her face and she waited for his next question. Everything all right? She could have asked it herself.

'Would you care to go for a drive with me?' was what he actually said.

'A drive?' She started. 'With you?'

'I drive well, you'd be quite safe. And the weather's not too bad, at present.'

'But you haven't got a motor!'

'As a matter of fact, I have. I bought it second-hand at Glenmar garage. And petrol's not so hard to get now.'

She was blushing again, with pleasure this time. A drive! That was a novelty. She didn't know anyone with a motor.

'Where would we go?'

'I thought the Black Isle. Do you know it?'

'We cycled there once.' A shadow crossed her face, as she remembered Nick and Bill and the other young people who'd ridden off that day. All gone now, or scattered. 'That was years ago, too.'

'Of course, it isn't an island and it isn't black, which is about right for a local description, but it's interesting, isn't it? Not really like the Highlands.'

'I'd like to see it again. Thanks for asking me.'

'Could we meet on your afternoon off?' he asked quickly, seeming a little embarrassed that she'd said she'd go. 'Wednesday, isn't it?'

He knew it was Wednesday. She nodded.

'What time?'

He was about to answer when a familiar voice reached them as Sadie Newall, who had been passing through the hall, sharply changed course at the sight of Paul and brought herself up at the reception desk.

'Good afternoon, Mr Armitage! I just want to ask Miss MacKenzie for the new arrival figures for tomorrow.' She laughed, as her pale eyes went over Paul's face, then Lesley's. 'Must make up the correct number of beds, you know!'

'I gave you the figures this morning, Miss Newall,' Lesley told her.

'Did you? Are you sure? Oh, dear, Amelia must have put them somewhere.' She smiled. 'Never mind, I'll find them. Are you going back to your office Mr Armitage? I just want to check that the girls have replaced your curtains properly. After dry cleaning, you know.'

'I just have some information to give to Miss MacKenzie,' he said smoothly as he scribbled a note and passed it across the desk.

'Two o'clock on Wednesday at the Square,' she read, and raised her eyes.

'Thank you, Mr Armitage. I'll see to it.'

As he politely escorted the housekeeper from the entrance hall, Lesley smiled over his note. To meet at the Square meant that Sadie wouldn't see them together. Clearly, Paul knew how to avoid trouble. Or, maybe causing pain. Lesley herself couldn't help feeling guilty, that it was she who was going for a drive with him, when it would have meant so much to poor Sadie.

On the following Wednesday, a cold and blustery day, she made her way to the Square on the dot of two. She wore her warm coat and a pull-on hat, gloves and a bright blue scarf, and still felt her nose must look red. Was this a good idea? she asked herself. Did the new purchase have a top?

377

The motor was a rather smart red two-seater, with a dickey seat at the back, and yes, it did have a top. Paul, wearing a cap and a long tweed overcoat, was standing beside it waiting for her, and heaved a sigh of relief when she appeared.

'Thought you might have cried off,' he told her. 'It's colder today.'

'Always mild on the Black Isle,' she said bravely. 'Is that no' how it gets its name? Because it's no' white with snow in winter?'

'It's one theory,' he answered, as he settled her into the front seat and tucked a rug around her knees. 'Tell you what we'll do, we'll drive straight to Fortrose or Rosemarkie, maybe, and have a cup of tea. Right, you ready?'

As he started the motor with the starting handle, Lesley looked cautiously round the Square. But she couldn't see Sadie Newall, or anyone from the Grand Forest; in fact, there were very few people around at all. She began to feel a little unreal, as though she were in a play where she and Paul were the only characters. To be going out with him, just the two of them, it seemed so strange. She couldn't imagine how they'd get on together.

'Away we go!' he said cheerfully, taking his seat beside her as the engine sprang into life. 'Hope we don't break down! Or, do I? How would it be if we couldn't get back to the Grand Forest, Lesley?'

'You'd be in a state,' she said calmly. 'You know the hotel could never get on without you.'

'I do have other interests in my life,' he told her, as they left the Square for the main road out of Glenmar. 'I'll tell you about them some time.'

Chapter Seventy-Six

That drive to the Black Isle was the first of their outings together, and the beginning of a strange relationship. They were very careful, always meeting away from the hotel, never mentioning Sadie's name, but making sure that she never saw them together. If she had seen them, though, wondered Lesley, would she have believed that they were only friends? For that was what they seemed to be.

In all the times they were together, visiting old towns and ruined castles on the Black Isle promontory, walking on empty strands beside the wintry sea, driving down to Culloden, or Beauly Priory, Paul never gave any impression that he wanted to be anything more to Lesley than a friend. All this talk by other people that he was 'sweet on her' – why, she'd almost begun to believe it herself – and yet, here they were, alone every week, and he hadn't so much as held her hand. Perhaps he just wanted someone to talk to? For this strong, silent man was suddenly talking as she'd never heard him talk before.

He was an only child, he told her, but never lonely, for he'd been endlessly fascinated by the people who came to the little hotel his father managed off the Strand. His parents had wanted him to become a lawyer or a doctor, but hotel work was what he wanted, and to manage a great hotel his aim. Not in London or any city, but up here in the Highlands. This was the part of the world he loved.

Lesley had been curious about this love. How had he come to know the Highlands, anyway?

Through his uncle, the father of the cousin who was now in the music department at Edinburgh University. Uncle Grey was now dead, but it had been he who'd given his son and young Paul those wonderful holidays in Ross and Cromarty and Sutherland that had always remained in Paul's memory. Was it any wonder, that when he'd seen a post advertised in Glenmar he'd tried for it?

If it hadn't been for the war, he would surely have been manager somewhere by now, Lesley had suggested, and after a modest hesitation, he'd agreed.

Shouldn't he really be manager of the Grand Forest, she had persisted, but he wouldn't go into that. For the moment he had enough problems as assistant manager, without thinking about anything else.

So much talk about himself, but never any mention of relationships. A man of his age and looks must have had some love affairs? He never said.

The weather was changing, the days becoming lighter and a little warmer, as the winter moved into spring. Lesley, wearing jackets now and sometimes taking off her hat as they walked by the sea, was becoming restive with their curious arrangement. It wasn't that she wanted Paul to make love to her, she just felt she would like to know what was really in his mind. On a day in March, she almost asked him. At least, she asked him if he had ever been in love.

They'd returned from walking by a lonely loch some miles from Glenmar and were sitting together in the car, preparing to leave, when she'd suddenly looked into Paul's eyes and asked him that question.

'Have you ever been in love, Paul?'

He seemed stunned, his gaze falling before hers, his fingers fidgeting with the car keys.

'In love? Yes, of course. Often, as a boy.'

'What about when you grew up?'

'There was a girl who lived near us, a fair girl, very pretty. When I was about twenty, I fell for her very hard.'

'What happened?'

'She married a man with curly hair, who made her laugh.'

Lesley laughed herself. 'Paul, you've made that up.'

'No, I assure you, it's quite true. I had to go to the wedding. We were family friends. I can still remember the pain.'

She closed her hand over his and he stopped fiddling with the keys to sit very still. 'Poor Paul,' she whispered. 'There must have been someone after that, though?'

'No one.'

'You never met anyone you liked?'

'Until I met you.'

It was Lesley's turn to sit very still. She withdrew her hand from his.

'Did you never realise?' he asked quietly.

'Well – folk used to say—'

'They always do.' He took her hand back and held it firmly. 'What did they say, these folk? That I was in love with you?'

'Sweet on me,' she answered, trying to laugh. 'Sweet on me. I never believed them. No' really.'

'Sweet on you. You should have believed them, Lesley. It was true.'

'Why'd you never say?'

'I wanted to. In fact, I was getting up my courage to speak, when you met Christopher Meredith.' She was silent and he went on. 'I never believed he was right for you, I thought he would make you unhappy, all I wanted to do was warn you.'

'Well, you did warn me,' she said bitterly, and pulled her hand free from his. 'I seem to remember you telling me he'd never marry me. Then he gave me ma ring!'

'I was wrong about him, I admit it, but I was jealous.

You can understand, can't you? Afterwards, I came to see that he was sincere. I made myself live with that, because I thought there was no hope. Then, when Christopher was killed, I still thought there'd be no hope. I knew it would be a long time before you could consider another man.'

'But you wanted me to come here, be near you. Why was that, if it was all so hopeless?'

'For God's sake, Lesley, you've been in love! Of course I wanted you near me. And when I dared, I asked you to come out with me.' Paul ran his hand through his hair. 'I kept thinking I'd be able to tell, whether you wanted me or not, but you never made any sign, and I couldn't risk letting you know how I was feeling.' He cleared his throat. 'In case you turned me down.'

There was a long, long silence. He was waiting for her to speak and she didn't know what to say, what to think. She was like that girl in the story who'd opened a box and got more than she bargained for. Yet, she'd wanted to know the truth, and he'd given it to her. Now, she had to decide what to do with it.

'It's all a bit of a surprise,' she said at last. 'Because, I really didn't believe what people said. And then, we've been out so much, and you never gave me any hint. So, it's – well, it's a surprise, that's all.'

'A pleasant one?'

'Paul, I canna take it in. It's such a change, you see. It's all different.'

'I'm not asking you to say you love me, if you don't, but is there any hope? I mean, do you think you could love me one day? When it's not so much of a shock?'

She knew how much it must be costing him, proud as he was, to talk to her like this, to lay out all his feelings, risking at last being hurt. Impulsively, she leaned forward and kissed him on the mouth, at which he gave a great shudder, then swept her into his arms and kissed her back, over and over again, until they both lost breath and had to draw away. For a long moment, Paul gazed into her eyes, then he put hands round her face and held her still.

'Oh, God, Lesley,' he whispered. 'Oh, dear God!'

'We have to go back, Paul. It's getting late. I'm on duty this evening.'

'I know,' he said mechanically, and she laughed, because he was still the assistant manager, knowing everything.

'Come on,' she urged. 'It would be terrible to be late.'

'I don't know if I can drive, I don't know if I'm really here.'

'Well, I canna drive, Paul. How do we get home?'

They got home, of course, with Paul still floating in some world he never thought he'd find, and Lesley not sure where she was, or what she'd done, but very quickly discovering that she was in trouble. Up in her room, which was now hers alone, she found Sadie Newall waiting for her. She had let herself in with her pass key.

Chapter Seventy-Seven

Sadie's face was paper white, her eyes glittering, as she stared at Lesley, who had tossed her hat on to her bed and was slowly taking off her coat.

'Well, Miss MacKenzie!' Sadie cried breathlessly. 'Where have you been, then? Why don't you tell me? Go on, tell me!'

'Just what are you doing in ma room?' asked Lesley, aware that her lips were stiff and swollen from Paul's kisses, and afraid that Sadie would see. 'You have no right to come into ma room, even if you have a pass key.'

'Tell me where you've been!' Sadie cried again. 'Or, shall I tell you? You've been with Mr Armitage in his car, haven't you? You've been out driving, kissing and making love, haven't you? Kissing and making love!'

Any other day than this and I could've said no, thought Lesley. But, oh, God, what could she say now?

'I'm no' going to deny that I've been in Mr Armitage's car,' she answered levelly. 'Who told you?'

'Never mind who told me. You were seen. Seen getting into his car in the Square. And not for the first time, I suppose!' Tears were welling in Sadie's eyes, her voice was shaking with anger and hurt. 'How long have you been meeting him, then, and saying nothing about it? How long has he been taking you out and making love to you, sneaking out like a thief, or a - s - spy?' Sadie began suddenly to cry in earnest, sobbing into a handkerchief that soon became a small wet ball. 'How could he do it?' she wailed. 'Oh, God, how could he? When I've loved him for so long?'

'Sit down, Sadie,' said Lesley, taking her arm, making her sit on the bed. 'Please, sit down and try to understand. Mr Armitage never wanted to hurt you, honest, he didn't. He wasn't doing anything underhand, just trying no' to upset you, you see, that's all it was.'

'Oh, that's all, is it?' sobbed Sadie, rocking to and fro on Lesley's bed. 'He breaks my heart and he's not trying to upset me? I've loved him for years, worshipped him, and this is the way he treats me! Scorns me, takes out a silly young woman from Leith, never says a word, then I'm told by a waiter, who doesn't care a fig for my feelings. The shame of it! Oh, I've never been so humiliated!'

'Sadie, I'm really sorry you feel so bad, but it's no' Paul's fault, you must see that.'

'Paul? You call him Paul? In all the years I've known him, he's never asked me to call him by his first name! Because I don't count, do I? I have no rights, have I? I'm just somebody who's wasted half her life loving a man who doesn't want her.'

'Sadie, I'm going to get you some tea,' Lesley said with a desperate attempt at normality. 'You just rest there till you feel better.'

'Feel better? That's a laugh. When am I going to feel better?' But Sadie did lie back, collapsing against Lesley's pillow, as though she no longer had the strength to sit up. 'I'm going to resign, you know!' she called, as Lesley reached the door. 'That's what I'm going to do. I'm not going to stay on here to be treated in this way. He'll see that he can't humiliate me and expect me to stay on, I'm going to resign and let him find another housekeeper as good as me if he can.'

'All right, Sadie, all right. I'll just get the tea.'

When she came back with a tray of tea, Lesley found

Sadie lying back with her eyes closed. She looked exhausted, might even be falling asleep, and Lesley, already late for duty, tiptoed away.

Veronica, due to go for her break, cast a knowing look over Lesley's flushed face and hair that needed attention.

'Well, better late than never, eh? Had a nice drive?'

'Drive?' Lesley's colour deepened. It seemed that Sadie wasn't the only one the waiter, whoever he was, had told about herself and Paul. 'Who's been talking?' she asked with resignation.

'Albert MacGregor.' Veronica shook her head. 'I'm afraid it's all over the hotel, Lesley, about you and Paul Armitage. I always did wonder why he was never available on Wednesday afternoons.'

'We've a perfect right to go for a drive together. Why all the fuss?'

'Because you kept it secret. Much better to shout everything from the house tops, then nobody gives a damn.'

'You'd better go for your tea,' Lesley said shortly.

It was a relief to be alone for a few minutes, to try to calm her nerves, slow down her fast-beating heart. Fortunately, if there were no arrivals due, this was a quiet time, when guests liked to rest before dressing for dinner, and if the telephone did not ring, Lesley thought she might just be able to manage. But Sadie's onslaught had upset her more than she'd thought. Her hands were still shaking, her head still spinning, when Paul came to stand beside her and put his hand on her shoulder.

'Oh, Paul!'

'It's all right, it's all right.'

'Have you heard about Miss Newall? She was in ma room when I got back.'

'I know. Mr Daniels told me she'd been telling everyone she was going to speak to you. "Have it out with you", was the phrase she used, I think. Lesley, I'm so sorry.'

'It's no' your fault. I told her that. She was going on and

on about you, and crying and wailing, and I told her it was no' your fault. But, she's so unhappy, Paul, I don't know what we can do.'

'There's nothing we can do,' he answered heavily. 'I wish there were. But where is she now?'

'Still in ma room, as far as I know. I made her some tea and left her to rest. If she can rest, that is.'

'I'll have to speak to her tomorrow, though God knows what I can say.'

'She said she was going to resign.'

'That might be the best thing.' Paul drew up Veronica's chair and sat down. 'But this business with Miss Newall isn't the only thing I wanted to see you about.' He ran his hand over his brow. 'And it's more trouble, I'm afraid.'

'Why, what else is wrong?'

'We've had some bad news about the spring bookings. I've just been talking to Mr Wilcox and Andrew Dunlop.'

'The numbers are down?'

'They're practically non-existent. By this time of year in the old days, we'd always had a firm block of reservations for the spring season. People who'd come back year after year, plus new ones. This year's different.'

'Folk aren't coming back?'

'No, and new people aren't coming, either.'

'Maybe it's still too early?'

'I don't think so. Nor does Andrew Dunlop. Nor does head office.' Paul's face was dark as his eyes went round the empty entrance hall. 'We're all afraid that the writing is on the wall. Mr Dunlop has made discreet inquiries with the other hotels here. It appears, they're in the same boat.'

'No one wants to come to the spa,' Lesley said quietly.

'Not enough.'

'What will happen?'

'We're not sure, yet.' Paul hesitated. 'The thing is, I'm worried about Mr Wilcox. He's not been really well since that time he was caught in a zeppelin raid. I don't know that he's up to coping with this latest worry.'

'Couldn't you take charge?'

Paul shrugged. 'It's not for me to say. I'll do what I can.' He glanced at his watch and stood up. 'In fact, I think I'll go up and see him now, try to get him to relax a bit.'

'It's all like a nightmare,' Lesley said slowly.

'A nightmare,' he agreed, but he put his hand over hers. 'Except for you.'

As two old ladies suddenly appeared from the lift and began to make a slow progress towards the Palm Court, Paul looked up, smiled and bowed, and took his hand away from Lesley's.

'Try not to worry too much,' he said in a low voice. 'And leave Miss Newall to me.'

'What if she's still in ma room when I go back?'

'Tell her, I'll see her in the morning.'

'Paul, do you realise that Albert MacGregor has told everyone in the hotel that he saw us together this afternoon?'

'What of it?' asked Paul. 'It's a relief, that people know. In fact, I'm glad.'

Their eyes met and she knew he was waiting for her to say she felt the same.

'I'm glad they know, too,' she said at last. 'Anyway, what does it matter now?'

Chapter Seventy-Eight

As Sadie Newall made her way to her own room, working out in satisfying detail what she would say in her letter of resignation, Mr Wilcox was lying on his bed in his handsome bedroom on the third floor. He was wearing a dressing gown over his pyjamas and smoking a cigarette, as his eyes travelled over the sheets of figures the accountant had left with him. When someone knocked at his door, he threw the figures aside and called, 'Come in!'

'I hope I'm not disturbing you, Mr Wilcox?' asked Paul, somewhat surprised to see the manager already ready for bed. 'I went up to your office, but was told you were in your room.'

'I felt pretty weary, Paul, thought I'd have an early night.'

'Don't blame you.' At the manager's invitation, Paul pulled up a chair. 'I just wanted to have a word about Andrew's news.'

'Depressing, Paul. Too depressing. I mean, what can be done?' Mr Wilcox drew on his cigarette, then stubbed it out and set about lighting another. 'It's not just us, is it? It's the whole bloody spa.' He gave a tremulous grin. 'It's goodnight, Glenmar, eh? Finished. Kaput.'

'I wouldn't altogether say that.'

'Changing times, I'm afraid. People want different

things. They don't want to do just what they did before the war, that's the point.'

'We thought they would,' said Paul, watching the smoke from the manager's cigarette rise and circle. 'Our mistake, perhaps.'

'When I think of the way we've worked, the money that's been spent, I could cut my throat.' Mr Wilcox coughed and waved a hand around his room. 'Look at the decor, the refurbishing, the furniture! We fitted the chef out with a completely new kitchen, we replaced, we cleaned, had everything repainted and polished, spent a mint, far more than we got from the government—'

'I know, I know. We've just got to decide what to do.'

'Provided the company allows us to decide.' The manager shook his head. 'They won't, Paul. They'll write us off. Close down the hotel and send us packing. All right for you, you'll find something else, but I'm too tired, I'm too ill. And I've got a wife to support, and boys at school. What am I going to do?'

'I've been thinking,' Paul said, leaning forward. 'You're absolutely right that things are changing. Maybe the spa should change, too. If people don't want the baths and the treatments, maybe they'd like to come for the place itself? It's beautiful, it's different. Maybe we should concentrate on that aspect, and just forget the waters?'

'You're talking about tourism?' The manager's mouth twisted. 'Char-a-bancs? Buses? I'd rather die, than see this place full of trippers, Paul. I'm surprised you can even think of it. The Hotel Grand Forest taking char-a-banc folk?'

'I think it would be worth putting up to the company,' Paul replied. 'As an alternative to closure. We could advertise nationally, but concentrate on Scotland. We could put Glenmar on the map.'

'I'm not going to discuss it.' Mr Wilcox lay back against his pillows. 'At least, not now. See me in the morning, eh, Paul?'

Paul stood up. 'Very well, we'll talk in the morning. You'll feel better when you've had a good night's sleep.'

'Perhaps.'

'Would you like me to get you anything? A drink, perhaps?'

'No, thanks. I'll just have one last cigarette. Always find a smoke calms the nerves, you know.'

'I'm sure.' Paul hesitated a moment. 'Well, if there's nothing else, Mr Wilcox, I'll say goodnight.'

'Goodnight, Paul.'

Alone again, the manager took off his dressing gown and lay back against his pillows, smoking and thinking. His eyes moved to the photograph of his wife by his bed. If only Mildred had come up with him . . . Of course, she couldn't, she had to stay down south to see to the boys. Anyway, she wasn't fond of the Highlands. Far too cut off from everything, she always said. But if she had come with him, he might not have felt so depressed.

It was late now, and a wind had risen, rattling the window frames, wailing down the chimney. March going out like a lion, he thought, but there were no other sounds. His grand hotel had settled down for the night, and he'd better settle down, too. Tomorrow, he must have his wits about him, to argue with Paul about his crazy plan. Charas in Glenmar, indeed! Chara folk at the Hotel Grand Forest!

How tired he was! He felt himself drifting, longing for the sleep Paul had said would make him feel better – his assistant manager had been right about that, at least. Yes, in the morning, he would feel better, and things would look better, too, they always did. As he smiled confidently, Mr Wilcox's eyes finally closed.

Chapter Seventy-Nine

Lesley was dreaming. All about Paul and Miss Newall. They were making so much noise, shouting and crying, and Sadie was suddenly ringing a bell. Ringing and ringing, ringing and ringing—

Suddenly, Lesley sat bolt upright in her bed. There was a bell ringing. It was the fire bell. And in her nostrils was the pungent smell of smoke.

'Oh, my God!' she screamed and sprang out of bed, forcing her bare feet into her shoes, hauling on her winter coat, running to her door.

Fire. Every hotel worker's nightmare. Fire. The Grand Forest was on fire.

The corridor was full of smoke. Two young men she could just make out as waiters were running down it, making for the west staircase.

'Don't take the lift!' they shouted, and after a moment during which she stood like a statue, Lesley ran back for a scarf that she tied round her face, then went running down the corridor herself, straight into the arms of Paul, who was coming towards her. He was wearing a collarless shirt and trousers with braces and was carrying a torch and a file, which she knew from fire drill would contain the list of names of every person present in the hotel that night.

'Oh, Lesley!' He held her tight, but only for a second. 'Take those stairs now, don't use the lift, go straight to the assembly point and give your name to Andrew Dunlop. Then help with the stirrup pumps, all right?'

'But where are you going?' she shrieked. 'You're no' staying here?'

'I'm checking the rooms, I'll be down as soon as I can. But the fire's spreading and the wind's fanning the flames. Lesley, go, NOW!'

'I'm coming with you, if it's safe for you, it's safe for me!'

'Go back, go back!' he cried, holding a cloth to his nose and mouth, but she ran with him, opening doors, and calling names. The lights had now failed, but by the aid of Paul's torch they could see that every room was empty except the last, which was nearest to the east staircase. That was Sadie Newall's room, as Lesley knew, and Sadie was still there, coughing and spluttering from smoke, unable to speak.

'Oh, my God!' cried Paul. 'Lesley, give a hand!'

They wrapped her in her dressing gown, then Paul, covering her face with a damp towel snatched from her washbasin, picked her up and ran with her, followed by Lesley with his torch and file, back into the corridor.

'Are the east stairs all right?' cried Lesley, pointing to the closed door, but Paul shook his head.

'On fire, don't open the door. We should be able to use the west stairs, if not, there's the fire escape, but that won't be so easy.'

'No' carrying Sadie!' she gasped.

'Come on, back the way we came, and hurry, hurry!'

Sadie was moaning as they sped along the corridor and down the stairs, running round and down, round and down, till Lesley's head was spinning and Paul's breath was coming in tortured gasps, as he bore his burden. And then they were in the entrance hall that was still intact, though pitch dark and full of noise from burning timbers crashing elsewhere, and Lesley was wrenching open the front doors to let them run out into the blessedly fresh night air.

393

As someone lifted Sadie from them and wrapped her in a blanket, Paul and Lesley took long agonised gulps of air, then turned to look at the hotel, now illuminated in the night sky with hideous light. Neither could speak as they clung together, watching the flames engulfing the upper storeys, the wild March wind fanning them and sending sparks shooting upwards like some macabre fireworks show.

'That's where we were,' whispered Paul. 'That's the top floor. Oh, my God, we just made it!' He turned to Lesley. 'Quick, run to your assembly point, I have to make sure that all floors have been checked.'

'Where's Mr Wilcox?' asked Lesley, but Paul shook his head and hurried away.

Now, Lesley could see that people were everywhere, hotel staff manning chains with buckets of water from the hydrants, guests in coats and furs, huddling together, or wandering aimlessly across the laws.

'Has anyone called the fire brigade?' voices were crying, over the noise of the fire bell that was still echoing round the grounds. 'What about the ambulance? I need to go to hospital, I can't breathe. What are we going to do? I have my jewel case, but where is my money? What am I going to do for money? I left my bag. I should go back for my bag . . .'

Paul seemed to be everywhere, talking with the head waiter, calming down the guests, while Mr Jacot was coughing, Colum groaning, and Andrew Dunlop calmly ticking off more names at the assembly point.

'Where's Veronica?' asked Lesley. 'I haven't seen Veronica!'

'Mrs Reynolds is safe, she'll be somewhere about,' Mr Dunlop told her. 'In fact, everyone is accounted for, except Mr Wilcox.'

'Mr Wilcox?' Lesley turned to look up at what had been the third storey of the hotel. 'He's up there? Oh, no!'

'He may have got out, he may be somewhere around.'

But no one had seen Mr Wilcox.

Fire engines came from the nearest market town and even from Inverness. Ambulances came from the cottage hospital. Local hotels and guest houses offered beds, local people helped with the fire-fighting. Everyone did everything they could, but by daybreak it was plain that only the ground floor rooms of the Grand Forest would survive and that even they would be severely damaged. Nevertheless, things could have been worse, as the fire crews and police pointed out. Although there had been some injuries and many people were suffering from smoke inhalation, it looked as if there might be only one fatality.

As more and more people were now leaving the site, Paul went to look for Lesley. He found her with Sadie Newall, who was about to leave by ambulance for the cottage hospital.

'Sadie!' said Paul, bending over her. 'How are you?'

Her eyes flickered, perhaps at his use of her first name, but she turned away her head and did not reply.

'Her lungs'll be red raw,' one of the ambulance crew told him. 'She'll not be wanting to talk for a while, I am telling you.'

'Sadie, I'll come to see you,' Lesley whispered, but the ambulance man was already closing the doors, and she stepped back to stand beside Paul.

'You saved Sadie's life, you know,' she said quietly, as the ambulance moved off. 'I wonder if she realises that.'

'She'd probably have got out, anyway.' He put his hand to his reddened eyes. 'God, what a night this has been!'

'It's no' over yet.'

'For you, it is. I want you to go and get some rest. Have you found a place to stay?'

'We're going to the Rose Down Guest House, Veronica and me. I stayed there once before, during the war.'

'That's good, that's good.' Again, he rubbed his eyes.

'It's occurred to me, I'm going to have to organise some clothes for people, they've nothing but what they stand up in. Andrew's already got through to somebody in London, they're authorising advance payments. Then there'll be one of the senior company men travelling up with the insurance assessors as soon as possible.'

'So much to do, I wish I could help.'

His gaze was sombre. 'The worst thing is, Mrs Wilcox will have to be told about her husband. He hasn't been found yet.'

'He'll be dead, no doubt about it,' Andrew Dunlop declared. 'When the heat dies down and they can get to his room, he'll be there. My guess is, he never left his bed.'

It was almost dawn. Andrew and Paul were watching the firemen still at work on the stricken hotel building, playing their hoses on the ruined roof and the once lovely rooms now open to the air. From time to time, tiles and timber crashed down into rubble that had been carpeted floors, sending dust flying, and Paul and Andrew would cough and look away.

'If we'd only discovered the fire earlier,' Paul groaned, wiping his dry mouth with a blackened handkerchief. 'If there'd only been someone closer.'

But the manager's suite at the end of the third floor had been isolated from hotel guests. The nearest, Colonel Fenn, one of the pre-war faithfuls, was half a corridor away. By the time he smelled smoke, most of that corridor was already alight; he'd only just had time to raise the alarm and get neighbouring guests out and down the west stairs before it was fully ablaze. No one had had a hope in hell of entering the manager's room.

Of course, it was just possible that Mr Wilcox had got out before the fire took hold, but then he would have raised the alarm himself and he had not. They could only fear the worst.

'I reckon he died from the smoke,' Andrew said now, as he and Paul exchanged glances. What he meant, as Paul knew, was that he hoped the manager had died that way. It was a possibility; at least, he had not been seen at his window, trying to jump from the third floor. But of course the post-mortem would establish the cause of death.

'You think the fire was started by a cigarette, don't you?' Andrew asked quietly. 'Happens all the time in hotels. People smoke in bed, fall asleep and set the bedclothes on fire.'

'Could have been that.' Paul's look was wary. 'Or, faulty wiring, maybe. We'll have to leave explanations to the experts.'

'I agree, there's no point in going into it now.' Andrew touched Paul's arm. 'Come on, let's get to the Mount Hotel and take them up on their offer of beds.'

'I'm wondering if I could have done something,' Paul murmured, not moving.

'Such as what?'

'Well, checked on Mr Wilcox. He wasn't well, you know. He never really recovered from that zeppelin incident.'

'Paul, it wasn't your responsibility to check on him. Don't start thinking on those lines, or you'll drive yourself crazy. I say we leave now, we can't do any more tonight.'

'You're right,' Paul agreed after a moment. He sighed heavily. 'I'll speak to the fire officers. Tell them where we are.'

'You'll feel better when you've had a bath and some sleep,' Andrew told him, as they moved away. 'And breakfast, of course.'

'It's going to be a long time before I feel better,' said Paul.

Chapter Eighty

Mr Wilcox's body was found later that morning, still in the twisted wreckage of his bed, as Andrew had predicted. It seemed the final blow to the misery caused by the fire, and all thoughts went to his poor wife and boys. Arrangements were being made for Mrs Wilcox to come to Glenmar, as she apparently wanted to do, and Paul would be on hand, as he was for everything at that time.

Everyone admired his energy and efficiency in the next day or two, as he rushed around in a borrowed suit, talking to the police and the fiscal, fire chiefs, insurance assessors and company representatives, discussing insurance claims, and how best to make funds available for those who'd lost everything. Why, he'd even arranged for a selection of clothes to be brought over from Inverness and displayed in the pavilion, so that hotel staff and guests could find something to wear.

'And that'll be nice,' said Veronica, who like Lesley, was wearing clothes borrowed from Moyra. 'It was sweet of Moyra to lend me this dress, but seeing as she's thin and I'm not, it just about fits where it touches.'

In spite of their shock and misery over the tragedy of the hotel fire, all the women quite enjoyed turning over the clothes, trying things on, asking how they looked. It made them feel life was getting back to normal, whereas the young men didn't care and simply grabbed the first suit that came to hand. The aim for them all was to be able to travel home, for that was where they were headed, guests, too. The staff would have to begin looking for other jobs, the guests would rest and recover and dine out on their experiences. No one wanted to stay in Glenmar.

Lesley, too, would have liked to go home, but she wasn't sure what she should do. Paul, on his lightning visits to see her at the guest house, seemed to take it for granted that she would be staying on, yet they'd had no private conversation since the fire. What did he want from her now? Again she wasn't sure. When Veronica said she was going home to Perth, and surely Lesley was going home to Leith, she really didn't know what to say.

'You're coming with me to take a last look at the hotel?' Veronica asked on the morning of her departure, but Lesley would only wait for her at the end of the drive. She said goodbye to Monsieur Jacot there, and the fiery Mr Daniels, both of whom still looked deeply shaken, while other hotel workers were brushing tears from their eyes as they left for the station. Even Veronica was crying, and holding a handkerchief to her nose to block out the acrid smell of smoke that still hung everywhere.

'You're right not to go up,' she told Lesley. 'I wish I hadn't. It looks worse by daylight.'

'Do you think they'll demolish it?' asked Lesley. 'The ground floor's no' too bad.'

'Oh, I don't think they'll try to save any of it, and won't rebuild, either. There's no point. This spa is finished, anyway.'

Lesley was silent. The words pierced her heart, but she believed them to be true.

'End of an era, eh?' Veronica was murmuring. 'Now, we all have to start again. I expect Mr Armitage'll get something good, manager of some big London hotel, probably.'

'He'd like to stay in the Highlands.'

'Did he tell you that?' Veronica smiled. 'I think he'd like to stay wherever you are, Lesley.'

'I don't know,' said Lesley. 'After what's happened, I don't know what he wants. I don't even know where I'll be.'

'Wherever it is, keep in touch, then.' Veronica threw her arms round Lesley and hugged her. 'Now, I'd better go for my train. Don't think I look too bad in this two-piece, do you?'

'You look lovely, you always do. But do you mind if I don't see you off? I thought I'd get the bus to the cottage hospital this afternoon and say goodbye to Sadie Newall.' Lesley hesitated. 'In case I do go back to Leith.'

'You're going to say goodbye to Sadie?' Veronica stared. 'What a very forgiving girl you are, then. If she'd treated me, the way she's treated you, I'd say goodbye, all right – and good riddance to bad rubbish!'

'I feel sorry for her. I know what it's like to lose somebody.'

'The point is, she never had Mr A in the first place.'

'That's even worse,' said Lesley.

Miss Newall was recovering well, a nurse informed her when she arrived at the little hospital, but she still found talking painful and visits must be kept short. Lesley said she quite understood, she'd really only come to say goodbye.

'Aye,' said the nurse. 'There's been plenty of hotel folk coming in to say goodbye to these poor smoke victims. You're all away home, then?'

'That's right. I expect I'll be leaving soon.'

'Well, the best of luck, dear. Miss Newall's in the end bed.'

Lesley, smiling at other patients she recognised, tiptoed up to Sadie's bed and produced her bunch of daffodils.

'Don't try to talk,' she whispered. 'I just came in to see how you were.'

Sadie's eyes widened. 'Lesley?' she croaked. 'Oh, Lesley – I don't know what to say to you—'

'You're no' supposed to be saying anything.'

Sadie, propped against her pillows, shook her head.

'I feel – so ashamed.'

'Listen, there's no need for that!'

'I was so foolish. Crazy. I – don't know what got into me.'

'Sadie, don't say any more.'

'And Mr Armitage rescued me. Yes, I've been told.' A flush rose to Sadie's pale cheek. 'To think – he'd do that!'

Lesley was looking round, in case the nurse told her to leave. 'I've brought you a few flowers, Sadie. I'll find a vase, and then I think I'd better go.'

'Just want you to know – when I get better – I'm going back to Peebles. I won't bother Mr Armitage again.' Sadie raised herself in bed and began to cough. 'Will you – tell him that?'

'I did ask you not to let her talk,' the nurse said reproachfully, as she held Sadie during the paroxysm. 'Perhaps you'd better make a quick goodbye now. Never mind the flowers, I'll deal with them.'

Lesley, apologising, touched Sadie's hand, smiled and waved, and got herself out, breathing a sigh of relief. Poor Sadie, then! But maybe, away from Paul, she would find a new life, find someone else to love, who would love her, too. At least, that last little scene had cancelled out the other, when Sadie had screamed at her with such awful bitterness. At least, Paul would feel better when she told him. She knew she would be seeing him the following evening.

Chapter Eighty-One

Mrs MacRobie, of the Rose Down Guest House, very obviously approved of Mr Armitage as a visitor for Miss MacKenzie. Puir lassie, eh? Losing her young man in the war? Mrs MacRobie had not asked about the 'friend' in the hospital, but Lesley had told her of Christopher's death. Now, after the disaster of the fire, it seemed only right that a nice gentleman like Mr Armitage should come calling on Miss MacKenzie to cheer her up, even if he never stayed long. He was clearly a very busy man, but he wasn't going to let a pretty girl like her escape him – you could see it in his eye.

On that evening when Miss MacKenzie had said she was expecting him, he came about six o'clock. Mrs MacRobie would have liked to offer him something, tea or coffee, or even a dram – of her own, of course, she wasn't licensed – but Lesley was ready in her coat and new hat, and he said they were going for a walk. To get some fresh air, clear his head.

'Aye, you look as if you've been doing too much,' Mrs MacRobie told him. 'Now, if you are wanting my advice, take it easy, Mr Armitage. The world can wait.'

He smiled at that, as he replaced his own new hat on his dark head. 'I wish that were true, Mrs MacRobie, but thanks for the advice, anyway.'

'I won't be late,' Lesley said, as she and Paul left the

guest house. 'Mr Armitage will have to be back at his hotel quite soon.'

'You're right, I do have to be back at the Mount,' said Paul, as they walked towards the Square. The March evening, though still light, was chill, with a stiff breeze, not the best time for them to be walking together, but the only time Paul had. 'Mrs Wilcox has arrived, Andrew and I are seeing her for dinner, then we'll discuss the – arrangements for her husband.'

'Oh, the poor soul!' cried Lesley. 'How is she, then?'

'Devastated, but brave. So far, she hasn't asked to see him.' He shook his head. 'I hope she won't.'

'Will the funeral be down south?'

'That's what she's planning, but I don't know when the body will be released to her. We haven't had the results of the post-mortem yet, and then there'll be the fiscal's fatal accident inquiry.' Paul sighed. 'Wherever I look, there are problems. My only break is the time I spend with you.'

They stood for a moment, looking at the darkened windows of the two pump rooms which had closed for the evening. How long before they closed altogether? Paul took Lesley's arm in his.

'Let's walk on, Lesley.'

But she was afraid. They seemed to be making for the hotel, the dark silhouette of which still overshadowed the Square. Here was the entrance to the drive, churned by the firemen's vehicles, filled with rubble, and Paul was drawing her on, up the well-known way, he was making her look again at the Grand Forest.

'I don't want to see it, Paul, I canna bear it, it's too sad. Let's go back, please!'

'No, I think we should see it. I think we should be able to look at it and see what it might become.'

'You want to see another hotel here? Paul, that's crazy!'

'I don't know, I'm just thinking. Wondering.'

'It wouldn't be possible.'

Lesley shuddered, gazing up at the wreck of the once beautiful place that had been so much a part of her life. Her eyes went over the empty windows, that used to glitter so in the sunshine, the gaping rooms and blackened walls, the sagging remains of the roof that looked likely to descend at any moment.

There were warning signs, put up by the police, at the old entrance doors, where the guests had arrived. Lesley, shivering in the evening breeze, could still picture Veronica at the desk beyond the doors, her coppery hair immaculate, her polished welcome ready. 'Good afternoon, sir, good afternoon, madam. Welcome to the Hotel Grand Forest.'

But, KEEP OUT! the signs read. DANGER!

Soon, it would all have to come down. Everything that she remembered would be buried. Those young people of the past – and she was one – would descend to dust. All those she had worked with and known, and Christopher, whom she had loved. All of them, as they once were, would be gone for ever.

That's nonsense, she told herself. You don't need a place to have memories, the memories are in your head. And she was still alive, and so were the others, except for the men killed in the war. But their past selves were dead, along with Bill and Nick, Ivor and Christopher. Just as the hotel where they had lived and worked was dead, demolished or not.

'Please let's go,' she said to Paul. 'This is no place to be.'

'It's where I learned to love you.'

And where she too had learned to love.

'Have you thought about me?' he asked quietly.

'Yes, of course!'

'Seems a long time ago, doesn't it, since we were together, in my car?'

'A lifetime,' she answered with feeling.

'Yet, the thought of it is always in my mind. Whatever I'm doing, it's there. You're there.' Paul turned her towards him. 'Have you come to any decision yet?'

'Decision?'

'About me. I asked you, if there was any hope. You remember, don't you?' He laughed shortly. 'It's not really a lifetime ago.'

'But so much has happened, Paul, it's all been so terrible. I've no' been able to think straight.'

'I know, I know.' He held her close.

'And I wasn't even sure, what you wanted. After the fire, I mean. With everything being upside down—'

'You weren't sure of what I wanted? Why, Lesley, you knew what I wanted! What I want now! I want to marry you. Isn't that what we're talking about?'

Marriage? She felt a little light-headed. Marriage, he was offering? Well, of course. But everything had been so vague to her, she hadn't been able to believe that the two of them, herself and Mr Armitage, could even be talking about love, never mind marriage. She'd heard his words, she'd felt his kisses, she'd even kissed him herself, yet when she tried to hold on to all of that, the reality of it seemed to be slipping away.

'Lesley, can't you say something?' he asked, holding her by the shoulders, looking into her eyes.

'I'm sorry, Paul. I'm no' trying to upset you. It's just – like I said in the car – it's all been such a surprise. I still canna take it in. Maybe it's worse now, because of what's happened.' Her eyes went bleakly to the ruin of the hotel. 'I think I'm just too shocked, to make a decision.'

'Too shocked,' he repeated, letting her go. 'Well, it's understandable. Maybe I should have waited, until you felt better. Yes, that's right. I should have waited.'

'And if I go home, I can sort things out,' Lesley said quickly. 'I do need to go home, Paul. They'll be wanting to see me. I sent them a telegram, so they know I'm all right, but I know they'll want to see me, anyway.'

'Yes, I agree. You should go home.' He turned away, to look down the drive. 'When would you go, then?'

'Well, tomorrow.'

'Tomorrow?'

'I think it'd be best.'

'All right.' He straightened his shoulders. 'You go home tomorrow and have a good rest. And in the meantime, I can keep on hoping?' He gave another short laugh. 'You haven't written me off?'

'No, Paul, I haven't written you off.'

'So, when do we meet again?'

She shook her head. 'I don't know. It's difficult.'

'I'll have to come and see you. When I can.'

'You'll let me know?'

'Of course.'

They exchanged long steady looks, then one long kiss.

'Now, I'll take you back,' said Paul. 'Time's getting on, I have to be at my hotel, for dinner with Mrs Wilcox.'

The following day, Lesley departed for Leith. She had asked Paul not to come to the station, and he did not, so there was no one to wave her goodbye. Only the ghosts.

Part Five

Chapter Eighty-Two

'Is that you, pet?' Peg cried, flinging her arms round Lesley in Carrie's living room. 'Is it really you back? Och, we've been that worried, Ned and all, I canna tell you!'

'I did send a wire,' said Lesley, hugging her aunt hard. 'I knew you'd be in a state.'

'State?' echoed Carrie. 'When we saw the picture of the fire in the paper, we nearly died! Well, we thought you had, or might have.'

'Auntie Lesley's no' dead!' cried wee Donald, joining in the hugging. 'Auntie Lesley's here!'

'Thank God,' said Joe. 'We were all for coming up, you ken. Aye, we'd nearly packed our bags, when Peg got the telegram.'

'And that was bad enough,' said Sam. 'Peg was too scared to open it at first – got me to do it!' He also embraced Lesley. 'Och, the relief, when it wasn't what we thought.'

'Well, I'm all right, as you can see,' said Lesley. 'In fact, only one person died, and that was poor Mr Wilcox, the manager, though a lot of folk had breathing problems. Oh, but let's no' talk about it! I'm just so happy to be home.'

But, of course, they wanted to hear all the details. How the fire had spread very quickly before anyone knew, and how folk had had to escape wearing only nightwear, although Lesley had been able to grab her coat and shoes. How the assistant manager had been wonderful and got them all clothes to wear and provided a little money to tide them over. Of course, there would eventually be insurance payouts, but Lord knew when any of them would get those!

'And how did the fire start?' asked Joe. 'It said in the paper that it might have been a cigarette.'

'No one knows for sure,' Lesley told him. 'But there's going to be an inquiry.'

'Would you credit it?' asked Peg. 'A cigarette? And that whole lovely building gone!'

'Once stuff's set alight, a fire can spread very quick,' said Sam. 'If it got a good hold before the alarm went, and there were wooden floors and stairs, it can just go whoosh, you ken!' He waved his hands and said again, 'Whoosh!'

Everyone was silent, for a moment, picturing the flames, then Peg said Lesley must be dying for her tea, they'd better get on.

'And if you want to borrow any clothes, Lesley, you can see what I've got,' offered Carrie.

'I'd be very grateful, Carrie, thanks. I've a few old things here and this one outfit I got after the fire. But if I've got to find a new job, I'd better get smartened up for interviews.'

'Will you no' just go back to the Louise?' asked Peg.

'I fancy being a receptionist again. I enjoyed being on the desk at the Grand Forest.'

But as she said the old name, unexpected tears sprang to Lesley's eyes, and when she bent her head, trying to smile, saying she was sorry, Peg put her arm round her, and everyone said, 'Quick, get the girl a cup of tea, she's out on her feet!'

They were almost ready to sit down to Carrie's fish pie, when there was a knock on the door and Adam came in. Joe had sent Donald up the stair to tell him to come down for his tea, to welcome Lesley home, and here he was, looking happier than he'd looked in months, Carrie said afterwards.

As soon as he saw Lesley, he went across and hugged her so hard, he almost lifted her off her feet.

'Och, am I glad to see you!' he cried. 'We all feared the worst, you ken, the whole street was scared you'd been caught in the fire. But you're safe, and looking grand!'

'You're looking well yourself,' said Lesley, getting her breath back. 'How's Janie? Is she around?'

'No' here,' he answered carefully. 'In Glasgow. But she'll be pleased to know you're back.'

'Sit yourself down, Adam,' called Carrie. 'Everything's on the table. Donald, d'you want to sit next to Auntie Lesley?'

'Aye, I want to sit next to Auntie Lesley. I want to hear about the fire, I want to hear all about the fire!'

'We've heard quite enough about the fire,' Joe told him. 'The main thing is that Auntie Lesley's safe.'

'That's the main thing,' agreed Adam.

'Feel we should have had something to drink,' Carrie murmured. 'No offence, Sam.'

'Aye, champagne!' said Joe, with a grin.

'Well, we might be having that pretty soon, eh?' Peg put in. 'There's Ned's wedding, don't forget. I shouldn't be surprised if he could get champagne cheap from that hotel o' his.'

'It's only going to be a registry office wedding near Ella's place,' said Carrie, handing plates. 'He told us it'd be nothing grand.'

'Still have a good do afterwards,' Joe remarked, but Lesley was looking stricken.

'I'd forgotten all about Ned's wedding! When is it?'

'End of April,' Carrie told her. 'You'll have to get an outfit.'

'Well, at least I'm no' a bridesmaid,' sighed Lesley.

At the end of the meal, when they were having tea, Sam took out his cigars, but only Joe accepted one. Adam said he'd given up smoking.

'Like to keep maself fit,' he said with a grin.

'Why, a good cigar'll do you no harm!' Sam exclaimed. 'And all the ladies like the smell, eh?'

'If you get to be an MP, you'd look good smoking a

cigar,' Carrie told Adam with a laugh, but Lesley was looking surprised.

'What's this about being an MP, Adam?'

'Och, it's no' definite, but the union wants me to stand for one of the Leith seats at the next election.' He looked down in some embarrassment. 'Our fellow's retiring, but I'm no' even sure to be selected.'

''Course you are!' cried Joe. 'And it's a safe seat, and all. You'll walk it, I'm telling you!'

'Well, it'll be some time before the next election, so I don't see maself being an MP for a while, even if I do get selected.'

'You'd make a wonderful MP, Adam,' Lesley said quietly. 'Though I always thought it'd be Janie who'd go into politics.'

'She has other interests,' said Adam.

Alone in her little room, Lesley took out Christopher's photograph and studied it for some time. It was foolish, perhaps, to expect that what she felt for Paul could ever be the same as the love she'd felt for Christopher. That had been a wild, exciting love, a young person's love, something romantic, whereas her feelings for Paul would obviously be calmer and more mature. It didn't mean that she couldn't be happy with him. She was sure she would be very happy, she would have the sort of life she wanted. And how happy she could make him! That was the other thing to think about.

But as she replaced Christopher's photograph next to his ring and the brooch he had given her, she knew that she wanted to experience again that sweet joy she'd once known. Would it never come again? Well, not with Paul.

Yet, he was such a fine, good man. Not only Sadie would think she was crazy, to throw away love like his; most women would be ready to search the world for someone like Paul.

So? She hadn't thrown his love away – at least, not yet.

I'll ask Auntie Peg's advice, she decided. Auntie Peg would know what to do.

Chapter Eighty-Three

The following morning, Lesley took Peg and Carrie for coffee in Logie's, Edinburgh's grandest shop.

'My treat,' she told them, as they sat with round eyes, gazing not so much at the silver-plated coffee pots and exquisite little cakes, but the elegant clientele of the restaurant.

'Will you look at thae clothes?' asked Peg. 'And pearls on their jumpers! Think they're real?'

'Bound to be, if they match these prices,' said Carrie, studying the menu. 'How can you afford this, Lesley?'

'Och, I can manage. It's time you two had something nice.'

'And when you've come through what you've come through, you need something nice, and all,' remarked Peg. 'Or, is that why you're spending your money? Maybe money doesn't mean so much any more, eh?'

'After I nearly didn't need it?' asked Lesley. 'I think you do have a different attitude to things, if you've been at risk. It's like the way the men felt, who came back from the war.'

They were silent, looking out at the bustle of traffic in Princes Street, but then the waitress brought their coffee and the cake stand, and they gave themselves up to the pleasure of making their selection.

'Och, this is so grand!' cried Carrie, finishing her chocolate

413

confection. 'I just wish I could stay, but I've to get back for Donald's dinner, you ken. I'll no' want him missing me.'

'He's doing so well at school,' Peg told Lesley, as Carrie left them. 'Just started, but he's taken to it like a duck takes to water. He'll be a credit to Joe and Carrie, mark ma words. It's a great shame they've no' had another bairn yet, but you canna have one to order, eh?'

'Plenty of time yet,' said Lesley, pouring more coffee. 'You wouldn't rather have had tea, would you, Auntie Peg?'

'Och, I would, then, but coffee's the thing here, eh? Put plenty milk in, please.' She added sugar and stirred her coffee, then fixed Lesley with a solemn eye. 'Now, then, Lesley, what was it you wanted to talk to me about?'

'Oh, Auntie Peg, how do you do it?' Lesley burst into laughter. 'Anybody'd think I was a pane of glass, the way you see through me!'

'Just tell me what's wrong.'

'There's nothing wrong. Only, you remember the assistant manager I told you about, Mr Armitage? The one who helped us all after the fire?'

'And the one who was kind to Ned? Yes, I remember him.'

'Well, he's asked me to marry him.'

Peg set down her cup. 'Oh, yes?' She did not add congratulations, seeing from the look on Lesley's face, that now was not the time for them. 'What did you tell him, then?'

'I told him I'd think about it.'

'He sounds like a fine man, Lesley. One who'll do well?'

'Oh, yes, he'll do well. I'm sure he'll be manager next.'

'So you'd have a nice life with him.'

'I would, but I'm no' just thinking o' being comfortably off, and all that. He's kind and sincere, and he really loves me. All along, he's looked out for me. I know he always would.'

'But you've only told him you'll think about it. Is that because he's no' Christopher?'

Lesley looked down at her coffee. 'I suppose it is.'

Peg reached across the table and touched Lesley's hand. 'I know how you feel,' she whispered. 'Same thing happened to me, after I lost ma laddie. I never settled for anyone who wasn't like him till I took Sam, and I was a lot older then.'

'Did you ever regret no' taking someone before?'

'Well, I might have had bairns of ma own, there's that. But I wasn't ready for somebody else, and I think you are, Lesley. I think you're ready for a new love.'

'I think I am too,' Lesley said in a low voice. 'But I don't know if it's Paul. It could be. I don't know.'

Peg looked at her for a long time. 'I canna tell you what to do, pet.'

'I thought maybe you'd advise me.'

'In the end, folk have to make their own decisions.'

Looking round, Lesley caught the waitress's eye for the bill. 'You're right,' she murmured, looking back at Peg. 'Shall we go, then?'

'Folk have to make their own decisions', Auntie Peg had said. Sounded so easy, but Lesley felt herself tossed on a hostile sea, struggling from one rock to another, as she tried to make up her mind what to do. Settle for Paul? Arrive in safe harbour? Or, stay in the waves, taking what came?

At least she had a breathing space, for the days went by and he did not give her warning of his coming. He must be very busy, but then so had she things to do. Read the job advertisements, for instance, and go clothes shopping, with what money she had left. In spite of splashing out at Logie's for Auntie Peg and Carrie she really had very little and there was her wardrobe to replenish, and an outfit to find for Ned's wedding. Her pale blue coat and skirt would have been just the thing, but of course they'd gone in the fire. Still made her feel a little sick, to think of the flames curling round her clothes, and her pretty hats, although she

415

always ended up rebuking herself. She was all right, wasn't she? Think of poor Mr Wilcox!

She had returned from a shopping expedition to the Bridges, where she had finally found a wedding outfit she could afford, when the outer door banged and there were steps on the stairs.

'Somebody for us?' asked Carrie. 'Put your head out, eh, Lesley, and see.'

'Anybody home?' came Ned's voice.

'It's Ned!' cried Lesley.

'No' just me,' he said cheerfully. 'Guess who I met at the station?'

'Hallo, Lesley,' Paul Armitage murmured from the top of the stairs. 'I hope it's all right to arrive without warning.'

Chapter Eighty-Four

The sisters were, as they told Peg later, completely taken aback. 'Caught on the hop,' as Carrie put it. But how could they have expected to see Ned from London, or Mr Armitage from the Highlands? And there were Donald's toys all over the sofa, and a pile of ironing on the table, nothing but plain biscuits in the tin, no' a bit of cake or shortbread or anything.

'I was just going to run out to the shop for a few things, you ken,' Carrie moaned. 'And then there they were, both in their dark suits, and Ned with his case. Well, no' that I was worrying about Ned, I mean, he can take us as he finds us, but Mr Armitage, he's a stranger, and that grand and all. Used to thae big hotels and everything the best, and probably thinks I always have ma ironing piled up like a mountain, and nothing to eat in the house!'

While Carrie, pink and flustered, ran around tidying up and Donald began tearing paper from the box of soldiers Ned had brought, Lesley, still in her hat, tried to appear calm and welcoming.

'What a lovely surprise!' she cried, drawing Paul into the flat. 'But weren't you going to tell me you were coming?'

'I'm sorry, I didn't have time,' he answered, keeping his eyes on her face and clearly quite oblivious of Carrie's tidying efforts. 'An opportunity came to get away and I

417

took it. I'll be staying at my cousin's and haven't told him, either.'

'And I just came to check that you were in one piece,' Ned told Lesley, putting his arms around her and kissing her cheek. 'How are you, then?'

'I'm fine, Ned.' Lesley hugged him hard. 'But fancy you coming all this way to see me! I canna believe it!'

'Well, Ella wanted to come too, but she's in the middle of this wedding caper, so I came to see you for maself. Thank God you're safe, eh?' Ned looked at Paul and smiled. 'And you and all, Paul. What a thing to happen to the old Grand Forest, then! Canna get it out of ma mind.'

'So, you've come all the way from the Highlands, Mr Armitage?' Carrie asked, as she shakily poured the tea. 'Would you like a biscuit? I'm really sorry I've no cake.'

'That's quite all right,' Paul answered, taking his tea. 'I won't have a biscuit, thanks.' He was sitting on the sofa, now cleared of Donald's things, and still looking at Lesley.

'Actually, I'm here on a visit to my cousin,' he went on. 'Thought I'd take a short break.'

'Oh, yes? That'll be nice. I'm sure you need it, after all you've been through.' Carrie turned to Ned. 'And Ned, what a surprise to see you! Why didn't you let us know you were coming? I could've got something in.'

'Och, I'll no' be staying long. Just had to see Lesley, you ken, and have a rest from wedding talk. Did you know I'd fixed the date, Paul?'

'You told me it would be soon.'

'End of the month, in London. Hope you want to come, I'm sending you an invitation.'

'Of course I want to come, Ned! I'm staying at the Mount – don't know if you remember it.'

'Aye, nice place, eh? No' quite up to the Grand Forest, though.'

'Was anything up to the Grand Forest?' Paul asked with a smile.

'And now it's gone.' Ned, somewhat subdued, drank his tea. 'They had the inquiry yet?'

'It's been arranged for next week.'

'The newspapers are saying the cause was probably a cigarette. That right?'

'Could be. I can't say.'

Ned grinned. 'Same old Paul. Cautious.'

'You're wrong, Ned. I've changed in many ways.'

'Paul,' cried Lesley. 'Would you like me to show you Leith?'

Eyes shining with relief and gratitude, he leaped to his feet, but he didn't forget to thank Carrie for the tea and to say he was so glad to have met her, Donald too, and would Donald like half-a-crown?

'He'll be your friend for life,' said Lesley, as she hurried Paul down the stair, while Carrie, still blushing, cried her thanks and wee Donald, trying to follow, was restrained by Ned.

'See you at the wedding!' Ned called after Paul, setting Donald on his shoulders.

'I'll be there!' answered Paul, but then his eyes were on Lesley again.

'Thank God, we're on our own,' he said fervently.

'What did you think of our tenement, then?' she asked, straightening her hat, as they met the bustle of the Kirkgate.

'Very nice.'

'Same as every other tenement to you, I suppose?'

'Why, no, I'd say it was better.'

'You've seen a lot of tenements, have you?'

'Can we stop talking about tenements and talk about us?' Paul was skirting round the stalls of fruit and vegetables lining the pavement, apologising as he and shoppers collided, picking up a ball and handing it back to a small complaining boy. 'I don't think this is the place, is it? I mean, to talk?'

'We could go to the Shore, look at the harbour. Though it's no' much quieter than this.'

'What about the famous Links?'

She hesitated. For some reason, she couldn't seem to see herself with Paul on the Links, where she'd always walked with folk from Leith.

'I think we'll just go to the Shore,' she said at last.

'I don't care where we go, as long as we're together,' he told her, as they made their way through the streets full of motors, vans, horses and carts, people jostling them at every step. He took her arm in his. 'You know, in all my visits to my relatives here, I never did get to see Leith. Where's this Shore, then?'

Chapter Eighty-Five

'This is it, the heart of Leith,' she told him, as they sat on a wooden seat and looked out at the boats and yachts on the water. 'At least, that's what it used to be. After the docks came, it was never so important, of course.'

'It's fascinating.' Paul's voice was a little strained. 'I wish I could take it in, but I can't think of anything but you. It's been so long, Lesley ... I don't know how I've got through the days.'

'You'll have been busy,' she answered, looking around as people passed. Thank God, no one seemed interested in herself or Paul.

'Think that helps? Nothing helps.' He was looking at her expectantly, but when she said no more, did not press her, only took her hand and sat gazing over the water.

'What have you been doing?' she asked at last.

'Well, there are some new plans around now for Glenmar, and for our hotel. I've been involved. Very much so.'

'Whose plans?'

'Mine, originally. I actually told Mr Wilcox about them the night of the fire.' Paul looked down at Lesley's hand in his. 'He wasn't in favour, but I found out later that other Glenmar managers were thinking along the same lines. Tourism is the thing, Lesley.'

'Tourism?'

'We want to attract a different clientele, people motoring, people who take char-a-banc holidays. They don't want the spa treatments any more, they don't want to spend weeks at a time visiting. That means offering a different service. Less grand, more modern, everything streamlined. And that's the way the Grand Forest is going to go.'

'It's really going to be rebuilt?'

'Oh, yes, completely. I've been in talks with the company and what we have in mind is something smaller and more economical to run. Still top quality, though. The advantage will be that there won't be the same risks.'

'So, what'll happen to the spa, then?'

'I'm afraid it's had its day. We live in changing times. We have to change with them.'

'This new hotel – would you be manager?'

'Certainly. I'm part of the plan. What do you think of it?'

Lesley looked across the harbour and shook her head. 'I don't know, Paul. I canna imagine Glenmar without the pump rooms and the big hotels. It wouldn't be Glenmar.'

'It would be better. Not just for the rich any more, but ordinary people who've never been able to enjoy the Highlands before.'

'Ordinary people with motors?'

'Ordinary people in buses and char-a-bancs. Why shouldn't they go travelling, too?'

She heaved a long sigh. 'Well, if it's what you want, I hope it's successful. You'll make a wonderful manager, anyway.'

'With you as my wife,' he said softly.

She couldn't escape him now. This was the moment he'd been building up to, ever since he came. Still, she played for a little time.

'You wouldn't need me. What could I do?'

'You'd work with me. You'd enjoy it, Lesley. It would be a challenge, it would be exciting. Think about it.

Working together, to make a new Glenmar!' He made her look at him. 'Wouldn't that appeal? I mean, what are you going to do here in Leith? Be a waitress again? Do reception work?'

She was silent, and he leaned forward.

'Lesley, I've waited so long. Can't you give me your answer now? Think what I'm offering. I know I'm not Christopher Meredith, but I love you just as much, just as sincerely. And if you don't love me now, the way you loved him, it will come, I promise you.'

'I don't love you now,' she admitted. 'No' the way I think I should.'

'But I'm saying it will come, Lesley! Many marriages begin this way, and they last, because people are clear-eyed, they know what to expect.' He was holding her hand between both of his, and breathing fast, his eyes never leaving her face. 'I would never expect too much, and I would give you time. All the time you needed. I can be patient, as you know.'

'Yes, you're a patient man.' Lesley suddenly stood up. 'I think everything you say is true. I could have a wonderful life with you, but would it be fair? You should have somebody running to you, no' holding back, like me.'

Paul stood with her. 'Lesley, you're the one I want. That's all that matters. You'll learn to love me, we'll learn together to be happy. If you'll just accept me.'

After a long, long silence, she said quietly,

'I will. I will marry you, Paul.'

To see the look of joy that replaced the anxiety in his eyes made her feel glad. It was wonderful, to make someone look like that. All the same, she asked if they could keep their engagement a secret for the time being. It could be an understanding, perhaps, just for a while.

'Why?' he cried. 'Why, Lesley? I want to tell everybody I meet!'

'Just till I get used to it, Paul.'

She cut his doubts short by kissing him in full view of

423

everyone walking along the Shore, after which he didn't argue.

They were slowly making their way back towards the Kirkgate, Lesley's arm in Paul's, when they met Adam Kay.

'Why, Lesley!' he cried, and took off his cap, his grey eyes going immediately to Paul. 'Nice to see you, eh?'

'Adam!' Hastily dropping her arm from Paul's, Lesley made the introductions, explaining that Mr Armitage had come down from the Highlands to visit his cousin in Edinburgh.

'Hope you didn't take any harm from the fire, Mr Armitage? We were all a state about it here, thinking of Lesley.'

'It was pretty bad at the time,' Paul answered gravely. 'But, no, I wasn't hurt, thanks. In fact, most of us were lucky.'

'Ned's home for a day or two,' said Lesley. 'You'll look in, won't you, Adam?'

'Aye,' he grinned. 'Always keen to see Ned. We were at school together, Mr Armitage, then both got sent to Gallipoli. Finished up in France.'

'You were lucky to get out of Gallipoli. What a débâcle! I was in France myself.'

The two men exchanged polite smiles, then Adam replaced his cap and said he'd better be getting on.

'Nice to meet you, Mr Armitage.'

'And you, Mr Kay.'

As soon as Adam had left them, striding off in his characteristic way, Paul turned to Lesley.

'You say that young man's from your tenement?'

'Yes, he took on the flat after his father died.'

'So, you've known him a long time?'

'Years. You heard him say he was at school with Ned.'

'You seem very fond of him.'

'Adam? We're all fond of Adam. He's part of the family.'

424

'He's not, though, is he? Part of the family?'

Lesley's eyes widened. 'Paul, what are you trying to say?

'I'm saying he's in love with you.'

'What?' She laughed. 'That's nonsense. A piece o' nonsense.'

'Is it?'

'Of course it is!'

But something wild was racing through her blood, just for a few heady moments before the world steadied. 'Adam's engaged, Paul, Or, as good as.'

'As good as?'

'Well, he has an understanding with a girl who was his childhood sweetheart.'

'But hasn't married her yet.'

'I think Janie's the one who'll say when they get married.'

'Are you sure?'

'Paul, what's the matter with you?' Lesley asked gently. 'You're seeing something that isn't there.'

'Am I?' He ran his hand over his face. 'Well, perhaps you're right. I'm just jealous, I suppose.'

'You've no need to be jealous of Adam. I told you, he's spoken for.'

'Let's forget him, then, let's think about celebrating. Where would you like to go for dinner tonight?'

'Tonight?'

'It's my only night. I have to go back tomorrow.' He held her close. 'Where will it be?'

'Anywhere except the Princess Louise,' said Lesley.

Back at Number Fifteen, she braced herself for interrogation.

'Well?' asked Carrie, bright-eyed, as Lesley took off her hat and coat.

'Well, what?'

'When are you seeing Mr Armitage again? What a lovely

425

man! You never told me he was so handsome!'

'We're having dinner tonight.'

Carrie and Ned exchanged glances.

'Then he has to go back to the spa tomorrow.'

'Auntie Lesley! Auntie Lesley!' cried Donald, hurling himself against her. 'It's no' fair! That man gave me half-a-crown and Mammie won't let me spend it!'

'It's for your money box, Donald,' Carrie said sternly. 'Canna spend half-a-crown!'

'I wish he'd given me a ha'penny, I could ha' spent that!'

'Poor Donald.' Lesley looked in her purse for a ha'-penny. And poor Paul, trying so hard . . .

'So, Mr Armitage is going away tomorrow,' Carrie murmured. 'Then what?'

Lesley shrugged. 'I'll be seeing him at Ned's wedding.' She glanced at her brother. 'Fancy you inviting him, Ned!'

'Why not?' asked Ned, smiling. 'He's practically family.'

Lesley, hurrying away to look for something to wear that evening, knew he expected a reply, but made none. Nor did she allow herself to dwell on Paul's remark about Adam. That road was closed to her.

Chapter Eighty-Six

The day before Ned's wedding, they all went together by train to London – Peg and Sam, Carrie and Joe, Lesley and Adam, and Donald, though Janie Scott had sent her apologies, she couldn't make it. Sam said it was daylight robbery, what they had to pay for the tickets, and then they'd have to pay for the boarding house as well, seeing as Ella's mother couldn't put them all up, and he supposed he'd have to give Roddie a bit extra, because he'd been left in charge. Now, if only Ned had got married in Leith, it could all have been avoided!

'Come on, Sam,' said Peg. 'You ken fine, weddings are at the bride's place. Now, why should Ella come all the way up north to get married, just because you don't want to pay for the train tickets?'

'Aye, well as long as he's happy.' Sam shook his white head. 'Marrying a southerner, wouldn't suit everybody.'

'Ella's a lovely girl, and Ned's going to be working in London, anyway. Stop your moaning, and have a sandwich.'

True to form, Peg had brought a massive picnic for the journey, which Donald was investigating before they'd even left Waverley. No need for them to go to the buffet and pay exorbitant prices, though Lesley and Carrie said they'd have liked to go to the restaurant car and have a proper meal and bottle of wine, all served at little tables with white cloths – at which Sam almost had a heart attack, until they said they were only joking.

Still, the journey was a long one; they wished they could have broken it up somehow. As they couldn't afford the restaurant car, they walked up and down the corridor, ate more of Peg's picnic, even slept, though Lesley didn't feel much like sleeping, and nor, it seemed, did Adam. At one stage, they found themselves together, leaning on a brass rail at the corridor window, looking out at flying scenery. English fields now, and English sheep hurrying from the sound of the train, cattle under trees, for the sun was high. As she glanced at Adam's strong profile, Paul's words about him came again into Lesley's mind.

'He's in love with you.'

Adam? In love with her? Whatever had possessed Paul to come out with something like that? He'd taken the words back, of course, admitted he was just jealous. And he didn't know about Janie. As Adam felt Lesley's gaze on him and turned to look down at her with those keen-sighted grey eyes of his, she felt her colour rise. Thank God he wasn't a mind reader.

'A shame Janie's no' with us,' she said hastily.

'Aye. Couldn't get away.' Adam kept his eyes on her. 'But Mr Armitage is coming, eh?'

'How – how did you hear that?'

'Och, Carrie said.'

'Well, he was very good to Ned, you ken, when he worked at the hotel. Ned was keen to invite him.'

'Seems a nice chap.'

'He is.'

'Very efficient, I should think. Very professional.'

'Oh, yes.' Lesley studied the landscape. 'Why so interested, Adam?'

'I was thinking more he was interested in you. To come all the way from the Highlands.'

'He was visiting his cousin!'

'He was visiting you.' Adam too was now studying the

428

landscape. 'Does he want to marry you, Lesley?'

Her colour deepened, rose now from her throat to her brow. 'He's asked me,' she admitted, and waited, but Adam did not press her to tell him what her answer had been. Perhaps he thought he already knew.

'He'd be the one to give you the kind of life you want,' he said, after a pause.

'How do you know what kind of life I want?'

His eyes returned to her face. 'Weren't you bonnie Lesley? Away over the Border? Or, up to the Highlands? You always wanted something different, didn't you?'

'You'll be leading a different kind of life yourself, if you get into parliament.'

'Still have the same ideas, same sort of aims.'

'Like Janie, I suppose?' she asked sharply.

He shrugged and took out his watch. 'Shall we go back and sit down? See if your Auntie Peg's got anything left in that basket of hers?'

Her thoughts churning, Lesley followed him back to the compartment, where he ate a last ham sandwich and lay with his head against the dusty upholstery, as if he were asleep. But though his eyes were closed, Lesley had the impression that he was still no more ready for sleep than she.

Chapter Eighty-Seven

From the moment they arrived at Ella's home, it was party time. Rooms had been booked at a local boarding house for everyone except Lesley, who was to stay with Ella, but nobody was going round there until Mrs Bailey's fish supper had been eaten, and Ned had played his repertoire of Scottish tunes. The neighbours joined in the sing-song with such gusto, Sam said, well, maybe southerners weren't so bad, after all.

'You'll no' be fiddling at your own wedding tomorrow, Ned?' Joe shouted, to which Ned replied, 'Want to bet?'

And Ella cried, 'No takers!' while her mother, in her element at entertaining such a crowd, kept coming round with more tea, or beer, plates of jam tarts and apple pies.

Peg kept saying that Ned really shouldn't be in the bride's house the night before the wedding, he'd better get along to the boarding house, but Ned only said, Och, who cared, he'd be going soon enough. Though if Peg really wanted him to depart, he might go to the pub with Joe and Adam and watch them take a drink, which was the best he could do for a stag night, seeing as he was permanently on the wagon. Why, even Sam could join them for a lemonade, but Sam said he suddenly felt ready to put his head on the pillow, he and Peg were going to the boarding house with Carrie and Donald. After that, the party began to thin out.

*

When everyone had gone, Ella sent her mother to bed, then she and Lesley washed up and tidied the little kitchen, hung the tea towels up to dry and sat down for a cup of cocoa. Ella, having heard all about the fire and poor Mr Wilcox, the plans for a new Grand Forest and a new Glenmar, kept looking at Lesley, as though there were things she knew she hadn't been told.

'Are you thinking about Christopher?' she asked at last. 'Has being here brought it all back?'

'Yes, I've been remembering him. How we went to Richmond, and he gave me ma ring.'

'I remember. You showed it to Mum and me.' Ella's brown eyes were soft with sympathy. 'So, what about Mr Armitage, then?'

'I suppose Ned's been talking, has he?'

'Well, he's been guessing. Look, I don't want to pry, dear, but I think Mr Armitage'd be right for you. I know he's not Christopher, but he's a fine man. You could be happy with him.'

'Might as well admit it, Ella, we're engaged.'

'Lesley!'

'You're the first to know, apart from Paul's parents. I'm going to meet them tomorrow. We'll probably announce the engagement after that.' Lesley smiled. 'Canna keep it a secret for ever.'

'But why is it a secret now?'

'Och, you know how it is – just couldn't face everybody making such a fuss.'

'Most people like that, don't they? Remember that time Mr Armitage sent down champagne when Ned and me got engaged? I was thrilled!'

'You call him Mr Armitage, Ella. That's how you think of him?'

'Well, I suppose so.'

'The thing is, that's how I think of him, too.'

Ella laughed. 'What, when you're going to be married? That'll change! Anyway, you call him Paul.'

'I do. But somehow, he's still Mr Armitage.' Lesley rose and put the cocoa cups in the sink. 'Listen, why are we talking about me? It's you who's getting married tomorrow!'

'And I'm in such a state, Lesley. Never thought I'd be so nervous!'

'Girls are supposed to be nervous, aren't they?'

Ella blushed. 'Well, to tell you the truth, Ned and me have jumped the gun, the way folk do – or, some folk do – specially when he's been staying here, you see. But it's the ceremony I'm worrying about. Having to stand up and make vows at that registrar's, I'm sure I'll never get through.'

'You'll be fine.' Lesley took her arm. 'But maybe you should get your beauty sleep now. Shall we go up?'

'I don't feel I'll be able to sleep a wink, Lesley. Do you really want to go to bed now? Or, would you like to see me dress for tomorrow?'

'I'll see your dress!' cried Lesley. 'Who needs sleep?'

Chapter Eighty-Eight

In the event, it was Ella who sailed through the marriage ceremony as coolly as though she got married every day of her life, while Ned sweated and shook and rubbed his finger round his collar as he made his responses. But the ordeal was soon over and he was able to sigh with relief and kiss his bride, as the witnesses signed the register, and then it was out into the afternoon sunshine and away to the wedding breakfast.

'Heavens, Ned, what a crowd!' cried Lesley, as she arrived at the café where the reception was to be held. 'Who are all these people?'

'Well, for a start, Mrs Bailey seems to be related to half the East End and they're all here, and then the orchestra lads have got the afternoon free, and Ella and me seem to have made a lot of friends, and couldn't leave anybody out. So it's all sort of snowballed.' Ned grinned. 'But don't worry, we've all chipped in to pay the bill, even Auntie Peg, so you just enjoy yourself, eh? Where's Paul?'

There he was, looking perfectly turned out, with a white carnation in his buttonhole, and his eyes ranging through the guests, looking for her.

'Paul! Over here!' she cried, and he was swiftly at her side.

'Thank God, I couldn't see you! Thought you hadn't come!'

'As though I'd miss Ned's wedding!' She took his arm. 'Come and get a drink, then.'

'How lovely you look,' he murmured, as they moved through the crowd. 'Is that new?'

She looked down at her pale lemon dress that had a straight skirt and a belted waist and smiled. 'Everything I have is new, if you remember.'

'Apart from you and the bridal pair, I scarcely know a soul here,' Paul murmured, as they took their drinks, but Lesley was already leading him over to meet Peg and Sam, who were talking to Joe.

'Auntie Peg – Sam – this is Mr Armitage,' she said with a slight tremor in her voice. 'Paul, I should say. Paul, I want you to meet ma aunt and uncle, Mr and Mrs MacNab, and Carrie's husband, Joe. You met Carrie at the flat.'

'And wee Donald,' Joe said with a grin, as they all shook hands. 'He's no' forgotten that half-crown you gave him!'

'Half-a-crown!' exclaimed Sam.

'So, this is Paul,' Peg was saying quietly. 'I want to thank you for all the kindness you showed our Ned and Lesley, Paul. We're very grateful.'

Paul, flushing slightly, bowed. 'I don't think I can take any credit,' he murmured. 'But I'm very glad to be able to meet you at last, Mrs MacNab. And Mr MacNab.'

'Och, I'm just the husband,' said Sam.

'You must call me Peg,' said Peg, knocking Sam with her elbow. 'Did I hear that your folks stay in London, Paul? They'll be relieved to see you, eh? After that fire!'

'They have been worried,' he agreed. 'And I'm seeing them again tomorrow. With Lesley.'

'With Lesley?' Peg, Sam and Joe turned their eyes on Lesley, whose face was scarlet. 'Fancy. Well, that'll be nice, eh?'

It was on the tip of Lesley's tongue to say at that point, 'Auntie Peg, we're engaged. Congratulate us!'

But the words didn't come, and she took Paul's arm and moved away, saying they were being called in to the meal.

'Why didn't you tell her?' Paul asked. 'Why didn't you tell your aunt about us?'

'Oh, I will be telling her, but this isn't the place.'

'It doesn't seem right to be telling my parents, and not her. She means so much to you, doesn't she?'

'I said I would be telling her, Paul, don't worry about it.'

His eyes flashed a little, but he made no answer, and they took their places at the top table where Ella and Ned were now so completely relaxed and happy in their starring roles, folk were saying it made the tears come to their eyes to look at them.

'Och, what a bonnie couple!' murmured Lesley, and Carrie, sitting next to her, said archly, 'That'll be you and Paul, eh?'

At which Paul laughed, and said that of all the descriptions in the world, 'bonnie' was the one that least fitted him.

'But Lesley's always been called bonnie Lesley,' Carrie told him. 'From the Rabbie Burns poem, you ken.'

But Paul didn't know the Burns poem.

'"Oh, saw ye bonnie Lesley, As she gaed o'er the Border?"' Joe quoted. 'It just suits Lesley.'

'"Bonnie Lesley,"' repeated Paul. 'I'd say it would.'

'Oh, please,' groaned Lesley, looking away. And met the grey eyes of Adam Kay, watching her from a distance. She saw that he was looking very smart in the dark suit he called his 'negotiating suit', the one he wore to meet the bosses, and was smiling faintly. She smiled back, but Paul had caught her look and followed it.

'So there's someone I know,' he murmured. 'Mr Kay. Is his fiancée with him?'

'She couldn't get away,' said Lesley.

The meal, confounding Carrie's fears that it might be pig's

trotters and jellied eels, which she was sure was all East End folk ever ate, was conventional ham, with trimmings, followed by a selection of puddings. What a relief!

'Mrs Bailey, you've done us proud, that was grand,' she called down the table.

'Lovely,' said Lesley.

'Excellent,' said Paul.

'Now, we've just got to have the speeches,' muttered Sam, as Mrs Bailey blushed and reached across to clutch at Ella's hand.

But Ned's speech was witty, and Joe's was short. It was soon time for the toasts, and then for dancing in the adjoining hall.

'Where's ma fiddle?' asked Ned, but it was only a joke. A three-piece band had been hired, and first on the floor was Ned himself, leading Ella, radiant in her cream pleated wedding dress, to dance the opening waltz, after which there was tremendous applause and everyone else took the floor.

Lesley, of course, danced with Paul, and tried to remember how long it had been since they'd danced together. Christmas, 1913, she decided, then turned her thoughts away, because that seemed so very long ago, and so many terrible things had happened since that they could never have foreseen. Glancing around, she saw Peg pushing Sam on to the floor, and Ned dancing with Mrs Bailey, Ella with someone unknown and Adam, yes, there was Adam, dancing with Carrie, because of course Joe couldn't dance any more.

For some time, as she circled the floor with Paul, she kept seeing Adam and Carrie, Adam looking at her over Carrie's shoulder, she looking at him over Paul's. Adam's gaze was serious; no more faint smiles, it seemed. No doubt her look was the same; she didn't try to smile, anyway. When the music stopped, Paul asked her if he might dance with her again, or should he ask Carrie? He'd been so sorry, he added, to see that Joe was permanently disabled, yet he seemed so cheerful.

436

'Joe's always cheerful,' said Lesley. 'But, I'm sure Carrie would love to dance with you, Paul.'

'I'll ask her, then, and come straight back to you!'

She smiled, and waited.

'May I?' asked Adam, and she went into his arms.

They had danced before, often, but never like this. From the moment that they moved away together to the music of a modern waltz, something electric seemed to pass between them. It was as though their minds knew they were only dancing, but their bodies felt they were meeting, in no friendly way, but as lovers. While other couples chatted easily, they were silent, their faces pale and still unsmiling, their eyes alight.

Then Adam did speak. 'Lesley, when I asked you yesterday if Mr Armitage wanted to marry you, you said he'd asked you.'

'That's true.'

'But you didn't say what you'd told him.'

'No.'

'Are you going to marry him?'

'People are looking at us, Adam. Perhaps we should sit out.'

'They aren't looking at us. Why should we sit out?'

She could scarcely stand the strain, and as they danced past Paul and Carrie, saw Paul's eyes on them, dark and intense. How must they seem to him? To everyone? She was certain people were watching, could tell what she was feeling, yet when she looked around again, saw that no one was watching, no one could tell. Except Paul. She dropped her hand from Adam's shoulder and stood still.

'I think I will sit out,' she whispered. 'Don't come with me.'

Before he could make a move to follow her, she ran from the floor and out of the hall into a corridor. There was a ladies' cloakroom somewhere and she hurried from door to door until she found it, praying to God that it might be

437

empty. Luck was with her, it was, and she could splash cold water on her face and stand looking at herself in the mirror, or at least, stand looking at the stranger there. So pale, that girl was! Even her eyes seemed to have lost their colour. She was like a ghost, a ghost of bonnie Lesley.

'What's happened?' she cried, in her head. 'What's the matter with you?'

And the ghost answered, 'I canna marry Paul.'

Time passed, perhaps only a little time, but it seemed eternity. A young woman Lesley didn't know came in, said 'Hallo! Lovely wedding, ain't it?' and slammed into one of the cubicles.

'Lovely,' murmured Lesley and put on some of the new lipstick she had only just dared to buy and hadn't before dared to use. Now the ghost was wearing lipstick! She slipped out, and made for the exit door, where she breathed fresh air for several long moments. Then she returned to the hall, sliding in as though she could make herself invisible, but it was all to no avail. Paul was waiting for her.

Chapter Eighty-Nine

She had never seen him look so stern, never seen his eyes so cold, and it came to her that always in the past, whenever he had looked at her, it had been with the indulgence of love. But now his hurt had masked his love, and she could no longer count on his indulgence.

'Are you ill?' he asked, close to her face, so that the dancers behind him shouldn't hear.

She shook her head, not looking at the dancers, not looking anywhere in case she should see Adam.

'We'll have to talk, Lesley.'

'Yes.'

'But not here. Not at your brother's wedding, for God's sake!'

'They'll be leaving soon. They've a taxi coming, to take them to the station.'

'For their honeymoon journey.' Paul's mouth twisted. 'We'll have to see them off, then. Perhaps you'd better dance with me again. It would look better.'

Lesley never knew how she got through the next hour or so, until Ella's going away. She danced with Paul twice and Ned once, and then sat out to talk to Joe. Paul scarcely spoke, Ned never stopped talking, Joe was his usual uncomplaining self. She did not see Adam.

At long last, there was a rush to the doors of the hall as

Ned and Ella, changed into their travelling clothes, ran out, laughing, to the waiting taxi. Everyone pelted them with rice and confetti, and the driver frowned, as someone tied a can to the back of his car.

'Oi!' he called from his window. 'That's enough o' that, mate! I charge extra for tin cans!'

'What's a tin can between friends?' cried Ned. 'I'll pay!'

'Where are they going?' people were whispering.

'It's a secret,' someone said.

'It's Eastbourne!' said someone else.

'No, it's Brighton!'

Wherever it was, Ned and Ella were on their way, waving from the back of the taxi until it had turned the corner, when Mrs Bailey burst into tears and said everybody must come back to her place and carry on the party. She didn't want to be on her own, now that Ella had gone.

'I'll get some beer in,' said Joe. 'Where's Adam?'

But Adam was kissing Mrs Bailey goodbye and saying he had to pick up his bag and get to the station. He'd decided to catch the night train to Edinburgh.

'Why, Adam, it's Sunday tomorrow, you needn't go back now!' cried Peg. 'We said we'd make a weekend of it.'

He only said he'd things to do and waved his hand, sliding his eyes to Lesley once and to Paul not at all. Then he was away, striding fast, head held high.

'Is he all right?' asked Peg. 'He looks under the weather, eh?'

'It's all this drink folk take at weddings,' said Sam. 'Never does any good.'

'Better make your excuses,' Paul told Lesley, as people began to move away with Mrs Bailey. 'Say you'll be along later.'

And Lesley, avoiding Peg's sharp eye, gave Ella's mother a hug and said it had been a lovely wedding, she hoped Mrs Bailey wouldn't mind if she and Paul just went for a walk, to clear their heads?

'Of course I won't mind, dear! I know you want a bit o'

time with your young man. You come back when you're ready, we'll still be there!'

'Where shall we go?' Lesley asked Paul, when they were alone.

'Well, I don't care to wander round Hackney. I'll get a taxi, we can go to the West End.'

Though they had no appetite, they went to a little restaurant Paul knew, where he ordered omelettes and white wine.

'It's the only place we can be alone,' he told Lesley. 'I can't take you to a pub, it's too late to be sitting on park benches, we must just try to eat. I could certainly do with a drink, anyway.'

Their table was in an alcove, away from other diners. Once the waiter had served their omelettes and poured their wine, they were free to talk, and Paul looked at Lesley. He seemed a little less stern, a little less cold.

'Tell me what is going on,' he said quietly.

She looked down at the great golden omelette on her plate.

'I'm sorry, Paul. I feel so bad, but I have to say it. I canna marry you. I never should've said I would. That was wrong, that was so wrong—'

Her eyes filled with tears, so that the omelette seemed to float before her, yet was as large as ever and she knew she would never eat it.

'It's Adam Kay, isn't it?' asked Paul. He drank some wine. 'I knew as soon as I saw you together that day in Leith, I knew there was something between you.'

'There was never anything between us!'

'Then you must both be blind.' As Lesley stared at him, he said again, 'Blind! Not to see what was there to see, on each other's faces!'

'Adam's never been more than a friend, Paul—'

'A friend?' Paul laughed. 'That was a friend you were dancing with this afternoon? Look at me, Lesley, and tell me that that was the way you dance with a friend! You won't do it, will you? Because it wouldn't be true.'

Paul began to eat his omelette, then threw down his fork. 'Oh, God, it tastes like ashes!'

'Paul, I'm so sorry! I'm so sorry, for what I've done. I'll never forgive maself, never!'

Their eyes locked, then Paul gave a long sigh, as the anger that had helped him began to fade. Ahead of him was the pain of loss, made the worse because he'd thought he had escaped it.

'Don't blame yourself,' he said dully. 'I know you didn't love me, you never said you did. But I went ahead, I made you agree to marry me. That was where I was wrong, you see.'

'I agreed maself,' said Lesley. 'You couldn't have made me, Paul.'

'I kept on, though, didn't I? But I'd waited so long. Watched and waited. Then we began taking those drives, and you seemed happy with me. I thought there was a chance for us. We went through the fire together – it seemed an omen.' He smiled painfully. 'Like *The Magic Flute*. Trial by fire for the hero and heroine. And after that, there were the plans for the new hotel. I knew you'd be interested, knew it would be your sort of life. And when you said you'd marry me, I thought I'd been right all along, to make you realise love could come.'

He poured himself more wine. 'Then we met Adam Kay.'

'Don't say any more,' Lesley whispered. 'Please, don't say any more.'

'Won't you have some of this wine?'

She shook her head. 'I think I'd like to go now, Paul.'

'Know who I'm thinking of?' he asked, not listening. 'Sadie Newall. Always so tiresome to me. Why'd I never try to be more sympathetic?'

He leaned forward. 'And this girl of Adam Kay's – it's going to be heartbreak for her, too, I suppose? When you marry him?'

'I'm no' marrying him! What happened – that was just something I canna understand. It didn't mean anything.' Lesley stood up. 'Please, let's go, Paul.'

'Didn't mean anything? It meant everything.'

'Is there anything wrong with the omelettes, sir?' asked a waiter, appearing at their table. 'If so, would you care to order something else?'

'There was nothing wrong with the omelettes,' said Paul bleakly. 'We just weren't hungry. May I have the bill, please?'

Outside in the summer darkness of the London street, Paul said he would find a taxi.

'You needn't take me back,' Lesley said in a low voice. 'I can take the taxi.'

'Of course I'll take you back.' He put up his hand as a taxi appeared. 'It's the last thing I can do for you.'

At Mrs Bailey's house, he paid off the taxi and they stood together, watching its tail lights disappear.

'I thought you'd keep it,' Lesley said.

'No, I wanted to say goodbye.' Paul put his hands on her shoulders and turned her to him. 'This is goodbye, isn't it? You realise I'll have to tell my parents you won't be coming tomorrow?'

'I'm sorry, Paul.' Lesley suddenly leaned against him. 'Oh, I feel so terrible!'

'I told you not to blame yourself.'

'I needn't have done it, I needn't have said we could be married!'

'I'd still have been unhappy, if you'd said no.'

But she'd taken away what she'd given, that was why she blamed herself, why she carried the guilt, and neither of them put that into words.

'You will find someone—' she was beginning, but he put his hand over her lips.

'Don't tell me that, or that you still care for me, because I don't want to know. Maybe I will find someone. I can't imagine it now.'

'I do want you to be happy!' she cried. 'You canna stop me saying that!'

443

'When I feel better, I might want the same for you.'

They exchanged one last kiss that was hard and meaningless, then Paul stepped back and Lesley went to Mrs Bailey's door.

'Aren't you going to say goodbye?' he called, but she couldn't speak. After a few moments, she heard his footsteps echoing down the street and knew he had left her. It seemed strange to her to think that she would never see him again.

Chapter Ninety

There was a note waiting for Lesley when she returned from London. It was from Adam. 'Tell me when I can see you', he had written.

She didn't answer it. She didn't want to see Adam. She didn't dare.

In any case, she felt so sick with herself, she could have crawled away like an animal and hidden somewhere, but of course she couldn't do that. She needed money, apart from anything else, and when the Royal Albert Hotel offered her a job as receptionist, she was glad to take it. Ned had once played in their trio, since abandoned, and it helped, taking up the new post and meeting new people, to know that Ned had once been there.

Everyone in the family had been very understanding about the ending of her engagement that had never been announced. Peg said Lesley had done the right thing, no doubt about it, Paul was a lovely man, but no' for her. Sam said it was a shame, because he'd have been a good provider, but if Lesley didn't want him, she didn't want him, and it was better to find out sooner than later. Carrie had sighed and looked disappointed, but she too had agreed, better no' to make a mistake, eh? Though why Mr Armitage should have been considered a mistake was not something she could understand. As for Joe, Ned and Ella, they said it was Lesley's decision, not for them to interfere, and if Ned and Ella felt disappointed too, they didn't let on. To her relief, no one mentioned Adam, but why should they? She kept carefully out of his way.

Travelling to work on the train every day, she sometimes felt the years had fallen away and it was 1913 again, but of course it wasn't. The war had changed so much, taken away not just lives, but all the old confidence and security. People talked of a better world, they hoped for it, they tried to put their faith in the League of Nations that had just been formed, but the real faith they'd once had in the future – that would never return.

Lesley, looking up from her paper one morning, saw a familiar face smiling down on her. It was the cheerful young man who'd travelled on the train in the old days. She hadn't seen him in years, but recognised him immediately and thanked God he'd survived, for she could tell he'd experienced the war. Cheerful or not, he had the look of an ex-soldier.

'Well, well, if it isn't Miss Blue-Eyes!' he cried. 'How very nice to see you! Mind if I squash in next to you?'

'Miss Blue-eyes?' she repeated with a smile.

'That's what I used to call you, never did know your name.'

'Lesley MacKenzie.' She put out her hand and he shook it.

'Johnnie Rowan. I can't believe you're back on the train and looking just the same.'

'You look the same, too.'

'Not quite.' He raised his left hand and she saw that it was gloved and strangely stiff. 'Lost this, in France.'

'Oh, I'm sorry!'

'It's all right, wasn't my right hand, I was lucky.'

'So, you're back in the same job?'

'That's right. And married, too. Got a little girl. How about you?'

'No, I'm not married.'

His eyes were sympathetic. She knew he was thinking she'd lost someone in the war, but she said nothing.

'Didn't you go to the Highlands?' he asked.

'I did, but now I'm back.'

'To stay?'

'I think so.' She smiled. 'I'm a Leither, after all.'

'Leithers are Edinburgh folk now.'

'Never!' she cried, and they laughed.

As the train pulled into the city station, he rose and tipped his hat. 'So nice to see you again, Miss MacKenzie.'

'And you, Mr Rowan.'

She did feel the better for having seen him. He had not come through the war unscathed, and she wasn't just thinking of his hand, but he was home, he was married, he had a little girl. It was good to remember that for some folk there had been happy endings. But Paul still filled her mind.

Some weeks after their parting, she was amazed and fearful to receive a letter from him. It had grieved her so much to think he might hate her. No one in her life had ever hated her, for even Sadie Newall's hostility had not been personal, she would have felt the same for any rival. But Paul's feelings would be very personal, and she had hurt his pride as well as his heart. Sometimes, she could imagine his hatred, flowing down to her from the Highlands, which was why she had almost been too afraid to open his letter.

But it was friendly, it was kind. He must have guessed what she'd been thinking and had taken the trouble to re-assure her. He didn't hate her. Now he'd had time to consider, he understood that she'd been thinking of himself when she'd agreed to marry him, she hadn't wanted to hurt him. That had made him feel happier.

He went on to tell her about plans for the new hotel, and said he and the company architects would be supervising rebuilding, as soon as the dear old Grand Forest was demolished. He was going to feel pretty bad when it went, but of course had to think of the future.

It had been established that Mr Wilcox had died from the effects of smoke, but the results of the official inquiry into the causes of the fire had been inconclusive. That had been a relief for Mrs Wilcox. Paul had seen her at the memorial service arranged in London for her husband. She was still bearing up very well, and the two boys were splendid young fellows.

'Please don't worry about me,' Paul closed. 'I haven't much time for anything but work these days, which suits me very well. You'll remember that I said when I felt better, I'd wish you happiness? Better or not, I do want you to be happy. I won't send you my love, though it's there, only my good wishes. I am, yours sincerely, Paul.'

When she had finished reading the letter, Lesley shed some silent tears. As everyone said, Paul was a fine man. She wished she could have loved him as he deserved, but folk weren't given a choice where loving was concerned. It wasn't possible to love to order.

Thank God, he didn't hate her, though. Now she might be able to stop hating herself.

Chapter Ninety-One

One Sunday afternoon, when she didn't have to go to work at the Royal Albert, Lesley put a blue ribbon round her straw hat and said if Carrie didn't mind, she'd go out for a breath of fresh air.

'You and your fresh air!' cried Carrie affectionately. 'Now, why would I mind you going out?'

'Well, you've Auntie Peg and Sam coming for their tea and I could give a hand.'

'Aye, but remember how Auntie Peg never wanted us under her feet when she was baking? I'm the same.' Carrie smiled. 'Even to the flour on the floor! Will you look at it?'

'I'll sweep it up for you.'

'Whisht! Away you go! Wi' Joe and Donald at the park and you on the Links, I can get on.'

'Who says I'm going to the Links?'

'Why, you always do, eh?'

Always did, maybe. It was a long time since Lesley had walked out in Leith on a Sunday. A long time since they'd all walked together – herself and Carrie, Adam, Janie, and Joe. Now Joe limped painfully to the park with Donald, but no farther. Carrie was always busy. Ned, away. Somewhere, there would be Janie, but they never saw her. And Adam? Lesley's thoughts dwelled on, then veered away from Adam.

'I'm away,' she told Carrie. 'I'll no' be long.'

'Take your time, I can manage.' Carrie, already poppy red from the heat of the range, watched as Lesley, slender in a pale blue dress, put on her hat at the mirror by the door. 'No cornflowers now?'

'This is a different hat, Carrie.'

'So it is. I was forgetting the fire.'

Now that, I'm never likely to do, thought Lesley, running down the stair.

The afternoon was pleasantly warm, though the sunshine filtering through the few clouds was weak, which perhaps was just as well. Certain parts of Leith did not look their best in strong sunlight.

Lesley did not go immediately to the Links, but slowly made her way to Junction Bridge, where she looked down at the murky waters of the Water of Leith. No change there. Still the same debris and filth from the ships and industrial workings. Surely, some day, the water would run clear and sparkling again, as it had run long ago? What would it take to achieve that? More will than she could imagine. More money, probably, than could ever be spared.

Adam came into her mind again and this time stayed. They had stood here together on the day of Auntie Peg's wedding, and looked down at this water and thought the same things. How long ago that seemed! She'd been due to return to the Highlands, where the rivers were unclouded and pure. He was soon to be away, fighting in the worst war the world had ever seen.

Adam . . . It was almost as though he was there again beside her. She even turned her head, thinking to see him, but of course she was alone. After a moment or two, she set off for the Links.

Ghosts joined her there. All their young selves, running ahead, she could see them as clearly as though they'd really been there. Then she shook her head and laughed at herself

450

and began to walk across the grass, appreciating the space again, the air that seemed fresher than in the streets, the pale sky that seemed higher. Leithers were out in force, playing with their children, exercising their dogs, or sitting on benches, enjoying their Sunday afternoon. Lesley's eyes went over them, but did not see the one she was looking for. He wasn't there, why should he be? She just felt, he might have been.

On she walked, and stopped. He was sitting on a bench in the distance, his back towards her, his cap awry on his fair head. Waiting, though not knowing it, for her. Just as she, not knowing he would be there, had watched out for him.

'Adam?' she murmured, going to him and facing him.

'Lesley!' He leaped to his feet.

The two of them, meeting in mysterious rendezvous, stood gazing into each other's eyes.

'Lesley, is it you?' Adam asked, pulling off his cap, smiling at his own absurdity.

'It's either me, or ma ghost.'

'Oh, God, Lesley, where've you been hiding?' He drew her to sit beside him on the bench. 'Why'd you no' let me see you? You never even answered the note I left you.'

'I'm sorry, Adam. I should've answered it, but it didn't seem right. I mean, to see you.'

'Why? Why shouldn't it be right?' He held her hands. 'Carrie told me about Paul Armitage, so why shouldn't you see me?'

Lesley looked away, watching a boy chase another across the grass. 'Partly because I felt so bad about Paul.'

'You'd no reason to feel bad. These things happen. You found out you didn't love him enough to marry him. You had to tell him, eh?'

'I never should've said I would marry him. I knew, deep down, it wasn't right. But I went ahead. I made him happy, then I took it all away.' Lesley's voice trembled. 'It was terrible, Adam, it was a terrible thing to do.'

451

'I know he must've taken it hard, but it's like I say, these things happen. You canna blame yourself for ever.' He hesitated. 'You said "partly", eh? What's the rest of it?'

She looked bravely into his grey eyes. 'Janie.'

It was his turn to look away, then he stood up, pulling her to her feet. 'Let's walk, Lesley. And I'll tell you about Janie.'

Chapter Ninety-Two

For some time they walked, arm in arm, step for step, without speaking, Lesley outwardly calm, inwardly so strung up, she felt ready to snap, Adam searching for a way to begin.

'You know Janie and me were childhood sweethearts?' he asked at last.

'Everybody knows that, Adam.'

'Well, when we grew up, I suppose we thought we should be the same.'

'You were, weren't you?'

'Aye, seemed to be. Though I'd got ma own way of thinking and Janie had hers.'

'There are plenty of couples like that,' Lesley commented.

'I daresay. Only, we weren't a couple. We meant to be, we meant to get wed. Never seemed to get round to it.'

'Janie was very upset when you went to the war, Adam.'

He nodded. 'She didn't approve of it, didn't think I should go, but I went anyway. When I came back, I'd changed, and so had she.' Adam gave a long sigh. 'Truth is, we'd grown away from each other. I knew that was true, because it didn't hurt, when I lost her.'

'You lost her?'

'Aye, long before she went to Glasgow. Long before she found someone else.'

Lesley halted, dropping her arm from his. 'Someone else? Janie's found someone else?'

'She has.' Adam seemed embarrassed. 'A fellow who works with her in Glasgow. And this time, she's really in love. This time, she says, it's the real thing.'

'As though you weren't!' cried Lesley. 'Why, she's kept you on a string for years!'

'Och, I've told you how it was. Thing is, before she found him, I'd found someone else anyway.'

'Who?' asked Lesley fearfully.

He bent his head to look into her face. 'You ken fine who, Lesley.'

'You never told me.'

'How could I? You were still in love with Christopher, even after he was dead.'

'Christopher had given me up before he died,' Lesley said in a low voice. 'It wasn't his fault, but he didn't want to marry me.'

Adam's eyes searched her face for a long moment, then he raised his strong chin.

'Lesley, he was a brave man. The sort of officer we all admired. Look at the way he died, saving one of his men! So, don't think I'm criticising him. But, I want to tell you this. No matter what'd happened to me, I'd never have given you up. Never in a thousand years.'

Lesley was silent, keeping her head down so that he shouldn't see the tears in her eyes. But he took her gently into his arms, disregarding the interested stares of a few children playing at a distance, and held her until she had command again.

'Old wounds,' he whispered, letting her go. 'I'm sorry, I shouldn't have said anything.'

'All healed,' she answered, and they walked on.

'I wish I'd known about Janie,' she said after a pause. 'You might have told me, Adam.'

'I wanted to tell you. Then I met you in Leith with your Mr Armitage.'

'Oh.'

'Imagine how I felt, eh? At the same time, I thought I might still have a chance. Know why?'

'Tell me.'

'It was when you saw me coming. You had your arm in his and you took it away. I thought, Lesley's no' in love with that fellow, or she'd be hanging on to him, the way sweethearts do.'

Lesley flushed, remembering. 'That was quick of you, Adam.'

'Lovers are quick,' he said quietly.

She looked at him with anguished eyes. 'No' me. I couldn't see beyond Janie. I never knew how you felt.'

'When we danced together, I let you see.' He hesitated. 'I took a risk, you ken. Maybe you didn't care for Paul, but did you care for me? I wasn't sure.'

'For a long time, I wasn't sure maself.'

'You were remembering Christopher. I understood that.'

'After he died, I thought I'd never love again,' Lesley said slowly. 'But as the years went by, I realised I might. I realised it wouldn't be disloyal. He'd still be special to me, I'd never forget him, but – it was true what Auntie Peg once said.'

She took off her hat and for a moment rested her bright head against Adam's shoulder, then stood back and looked into his face.

'You know what she said, Adam?'

'What did she say?'

'She said I was ready for a new love.'

'A new love,' he repeated quietly. 'But I'm no' so new.'

'No.' Lesley kissed him. 'Because I think I've loved you for a long time without knowing it.'

'It was the same for me. Until that night you helped me with ma dad. Then I knew how I felt. Oh, God, yes.'

'Adam! Since then?'

'Aye.' He shook his head. 'We've wasted a lot of time, Lesley. But we needn't waste any more.'

To the delight of the children who had followed them,

they kissed long and passionately, until Lesley finally pulled herself away and put on her hat, as Adam threw some coins to make the children scatter.

'See how money's always more interesting than anything else?' he asked with a laugh, as they turned for home. 'Did I tell you I'd been selected for parliamentary candidate?'

'No! Adam, that's grand!'

'First step on a long road. You going to help me?'

'Addressing envelopes?'

'I mean, to work for change. You want to help me change things for the people here? The ordinary folk? They shouldn't have to live the way they do.' He shook his head. 'But, you've only to look at what's happened to the Water of Leith to know what we're up against. We canna even keep the river clean!'

'Adam, I'll do anything I can,' Lesley told him quickly. 'I'm a Leither, you ken, in spite of all ma wanderings.' She gently ran her fingers down his face. 'In spite of thinking I wanted things I didn't want at all.'

'Bonnie Lesley,' he said fondly. 'Remember the other bit in that poem? "To see her is to love her, And love but her for ever ..."?'

'I remember being teased about it.'

'But I'm no' teasing.'

She knew he wasn't. She knew he was as serious as she, on this, the threshold of their life together. They kissed again, and finally, slowly, made their way back from the Links, walking hand in hand.

'Here comes Lesley,' called Joe, from the living room window that overlooked the street. 'And Adam's with her.'

'That's good,' answered Carrie, warming the teapot from the kettle. 'He can come in and have his tea. Give him a shout, Joe.'

'What, from up here?'

'No! When he leaves Lesley at the door, o' course!'

456

'Doesn't look to me as though he will leave Lesley,' said Joe. 'They're holding hands.'

'What's that?' asked Peg, as Carrie set down the teapot. 'Holding hands? Where?'

'I told you, in the street,' Joe answered laughing. 'See for yourself.'

Peg and Sam, Joe and Carrie, and even young Donald, crowded to the window, to look down on Lesley and Adam quietly coming up the Kirkgate, and, yes, holding hands. Lesley's head was bent, they could only see her hat, but the look on Adam's face was such that the watchers at the window drew back in blank surprise.

'Well,' breathed Peg. 'What does that mean, then?'

'It means I was right all along,' cried Carrie. 'Did I no' always say Adam was sweet on Lesley?'

'Aye, but there's Janie,' said Joe.

'Now when did we last see Janie?' asked Peg. 'I've known for a long time there was something wrong there.'

'She's found someone else,' Carrie declared. 'I'll bet you any money.'

'No betting,' said Sam. 'But I'd say you were right. She's found a fellow in Glasgow.'

'We don't know that,' Joe murmured. 'We don't know anything.'

'That's true,' Carrie agreed. 'But Lesley and Adam are holding hands.'

'I'd be so happy, if it meant anything,' Peg said, sighing. 'Poor young folk, eh? Been through so much?'

'Matchmaking again,' groaned Sam. 'Why do women always want to marry everybody off? Carrie, are we ready for tea?'

'Joe, go and see if they're coming,' said Carrie, picking up the teapot again. 'Lesley and Adam.'

'They're coming,' called Joe from the door. 'Don't say anything, eh?'

'Who's going to say anything?' asked Peg. 'We'll leave that to them.'

But when Lesley and Adam came in together and stood for a moment, looking round at the raised, expectant faces, it seemed there would be no need at all to put anything into words.